CHOKEPOINT

A US NAVY SPECIAL AGENT MIRA ELLIS THRILLER

DECEPTION POINT
BOOK 4

CANDACE IRVING

PROLOGUE

He should've killed himself when he'd had the chance. A bullet to the brain, a makeshift noose about his neck—hell, even standing hip-deep in water and smashing his fist into a light socket. Anything would have been preferable to this. Definitely quicker.

His left leg was broken. At least, he was pretty sure. He'd lost count of the number of times that goddamned iron pipe had slammed into his shins, but he was fairly certain he'd felt the bone crack a minute ago.

Or was that an hour?

How long had he been dangling from his wrists inside this sweltering box?

Days? Weeks?

Months?

He no longer knew. All he knew was pain. He welcomed it. It gave him something to concentrate on in place of their incessant questions.

One of the bastards was at his ear again, the man's foul breath spilling over the right side of his face. If only the fucker would whale that pipe into his stomach instead of his kidneys for a change. He just might be able to puke on him. He settled for second best. Gathering the saliva he'd hoarded, he turned his head and spewed it into that yammering mouth.

Too bad his eyes were swollen shut. What he'd give to see the turd's expression.

He felt it instead as another rib went the way of his shin. He inhaled sharply, then wished to heaven he hadn't.

Breathe!

Can't. Goddamn it, he'd lost a lung. No, wait—it was there. Merely collapsed, the air knocked halfway to Mecca.

The haji was in his face again. Taunting. "Save yourself, *kafir.* No one else will. Surely not Allah."

It was true. He had no illusions. They'd been shattered long before his leg and his ribs. Nor would God—this asshole's or anyone else's—deign to help. When push came to shove, the good Lord couldn't be bothered to save his own son.

No, it was up to him. And her.

Time.

It was all he had left to offer. To her and his country. He'd be damned if he'd held on this long, only to blow it now.

"This is the last time I ask, kafir. *Where is she?*"

He found another ounce of spit and used it.

A strangled groan ripped free as the pipe crashed into his collar bone. Unlike his lung, this dent wasn't popping back out. He dropped his chin to his chest, sucking in stale air and his own bloody spittle as he fought the plea clawing up his throat.

He was dimly aware of the scrape of metal on metal in the blistering existence that followed.

Perhaps the bastard was right and there was a God, because somehow, he found the strength to open his left eye. Just a crack. The haji on his far left was bending over a heavy-duty, deep-cycle battery, attaching a pair of jumper cables. The ends had been stripped down to bare, taunting wire. The man crammed his meaty fists into rubber gloves, then retrieved the cables and snapped the raw ends together.

Twelve chilling volts sparked and spitted to life. More than enough to stop a human heart. They wouldn't even have to douse him in seawater for max effect.

He was drenched in sweat and blood.

"Last chance, kafir."

"Go to hell."

The wires closed in. A split second later, his entire body convulsed—broken bones and all—as white-hot lightning ripped through his groin. And then his body went slack, twisting in the nonexistent wind...until the wires returned.

Again and again.

Somehow, the secrets he'd locked deep within escaped his splintered brain and invaded his tongue. He was pleading with them now. Shamelessly.

Another jolt, and the truth finally tumbled free.

That's when he knew it was over.

He never saw the haji move, only smelled the blessed absence of that putrid breath beneath the stench of his own burning flesh.

Then he heard the order. *"Aqtalhi."*

Kill him.

It was done. The most important mission of his life—and he'd failed.

1

Her reprieve came early. Thirty-one hours and eighteen minutes—and not a second too soon.

Air ripped through Mira's lungs as she vaulted down from her aerobic climber to follow the shrill of her phone out of the bedroom of her Washington, DC, sublet. The phone trilled again as she raced past the galley kitchen and into an equally cramped living room. Adrenaline surged, supplanting desperately courted, exercise-induced endorphins as she reached the coffee table and caught sight of her caller ID.

Ramsey. A case.

For a moment, guilt battled with her own desperate, selfish need.

Need won.

Mira dragged in a steadying breath as she grabbed the phone. "Who died?"

"And hello to you, too, Special Agent Ellis. If I'm not mistaken, the clocks have ticked past midnight along the entire Eastern Seaboard. Odd time to work out...especially since you're supposed to be on vacation."

Vacation her ass. Try eight days of mind-numbingly slow, guilt-riddled leave. And the man who'd "suggested" she take it was on the other end of her line.

"Blame the neighbor's cat. He's still spending his nights trying to seduce the stone planter outside my window."

"This the cat that got run over last month?"

Crap.

Silence more pregnant than the five remaining felines infesting the alley filled the line.

"Still having trouble nodding off, eh?"

"Nope."

Nodding off wasn't the issue. It was the inevitable waking up shortly thereafter that had her clinging to the outer edges of sanity—despite the shrink session that this man had also convinced her to attend. Not only had the session not helped, all the lengthy discussion had done was burn into her brain the very image—and guilt—that she'd give just about everything to excise.

Mira stared at the bottle of scotch that'd taken up residence on the coffee table following her return from the shrink's office. At least the glass beside the bottle was empty—and clean.

Now.

"You want to talk about it?"

She flushed, and not because of the offer. It was his tone.

The raw compassion infusing the line didn't belong to William H. Ramsey, Special Agent in Charge of the US Naval Criminal Investigative Service's Washington Field Office. Hell, it hadn't even come from the NCIS agent who'd walked out of a senate committee briefing almost two weeks earlier to beat feet to Creighton Middle School upon learning that she'd discharged her service weapon into a depraved piece of shit bent on concealing his true nature behind a chest full of medals, his sixteen-year career as a Navy corpsman and a twelve-year-old boy.

No, the sympathy still oozing through her phone line had come from Bill, the closest thing to an uncle that she was lucky enough to have.

Somehow, that made it worse.

Mira turned her back on the half-empty bottle of scotch and checked the clock above the fireplace. Ramsey and her instincts were right. It was a quarter past midnight. Worse, though she'd been working out for nearly an hour, she wasn't breathing hard anymore. Amazing what a colossal case of remorse could do for the body.

At least on the outside.

Mira concentrated on the disembodied Arabic accent of a stewardess running through preflight checks as it spilled out of the phone and into her right ear. It beat focusing on those strangely silent, soul-stripping sobs that had been haunting her since she'd taken that shot with her service weapon—along with those huge brown eyes and the utter devastation that had been within.

Devastation that *she'd* caused.

And when she added on the old acidic shit that had been dug up as a result and publicly sprayed into her face via the local news...

"Hon—"

"You want to tell me why you're calling from a runway halfway around the globe, or am I supposed to guess?"

The silence returned—even with that droning stewardess— and this time it was terse. *Uncle* Bill had left. Special Agent in Charge William Ramsey had taken his place, and he was not happy that she'd cut him off.

Mira clamped down on her phone, waiting for the reprimand she deserved.

Ramsey sighed instead. "There's been a murder. Commander Theresa Corrigan. She was a Navy JAG. I'm told Corrigan was a recent transfer to the Pentagon, dealt with espionage cases mostly."

Mira sifted through her memory. "Never heard of her."

Not surprising. She snagged a rumpled, but clean hand towel from the laundry basket she'd left beside the couch the night before. She might've been investigating the scourge of the Fleet for six years now, but there were over nine hundred lawyers hard-lined to the Judge Advocate General's office—and not only were those JAG lawyers scattered around the globe, but they also specialized in everything from Military Justice and National Security to Civil Litigation and Maritime Law.

Even during her initial tour with NCIS at the San Diego Field Office, she'd tended to focus on the former, investigating violent crimes almost exclusively. For good reason. She appeared to have a knack for solving them.

Who knew?

Mira mopped the perspiration from her face and hooked the hand towel over her shoulder. "What do we have?"

"Not much. It's not even our case. Yet. The commander's body was found earlier this evening—in her bed. Her townhouse is a couple of blocks northeast of Dupont Circle. As you can imagine, there are...issues."

She'd just bet there were. And every one involved jurisdiction.

Dupont Circle was located within spitting distance of the White House and a good three miles from the closest naval facility, the Washington Navy Yard. Not only did jurisdiction for the commander's murder not automatically fall within NCIS' purview, it fell squarely within the DC Metropolitan Police Department's. Nor was MPD's current chief known for passing off cases, especially when the victim was high-profile. A category for which a Navy JAG who worked terror cases definitely qualified.

The disembodied voice of the flight attendant saturated the line once more, asking passengers to turn off their phones. Mira ignored the request along with Ramsey as she headed out of her living room. "We could flash the national security card."

"We may have to. But, so far, we don't have cause. And if MPD finds out we pulled a fast one, it'll piss off their chief in a major way. I'd like to avoid that if possible."

So would she. Cops had long memories.

Mira reached her bedroom and culled one of the suits from her closet. The plane's engines cut in and began to whine as she turned to toss the dark-blue jacket and slacks onto her bed. "Who caught the case?"

"Detective Dahl."

"*Jerry* Dahl?"

"The one and only."

Mira grinned. She might not know why Jerry had abandoned his plan to join San Diego's finest after he'd retired from NCIS, but she knew exactly why Ramsey had phoned her tonight—despite Ramsey's directive that she ease her way back onto the case roster upon her return to the Field Office come Monday morning.

She and Jerry had history. The kind that made a cop grateful. Indebted even.

"You still out of town?"

She snagged an ivory blouse from the opposite end of the closet and added it to the growing pile of clothes on the bed. "I never left. The realtor called before I could hit the road. He had a potential buyer who wanted to fly in to see the place. Some captain with orders to teach at the Academy. I decided to stay here."

She'd told herself it was because there might be additional showings.

The real reason lay in those brown eyes and the silent sobs that had been dogging her every moment these past thirteen days—sleeping and waking. Imagine how much more gut-wrenching they'd have been if she'd spent the past seven incarcerated in the family mausoleum in Annapolis as planned, sifting through what was left of her and her brother's childhood memories stored up in the attic so they could finally unload the place?

"Did you get an offer on the house?"

"No. The guy changed his mind during the showing and asked to rent." And this time around, she was determined to sell. Even if she could reach her brother to discuss it, she knew Nate would agree. That said, the abode she was most interested in at the moment did not come with a prized sailboat slip within view of the US Naval Academy. "You got an address for the murdered JAG?"

"Yeah. I just texted it." The whine of the plane's engines increased in pitch as her boss' phone pinged. "Damn. I gotta go. Keep me posted."

"Will do."

Mira hung up, already forming her coming strategy as she tossed her phone onto the bed before heading for the bathroom to turn on the shower.

By the time Ramsey's plane touched down in DC, she *would* be working the Corrigan investigation. If she had to abuse her past with Jerry Dahl to get herself waved through the door, so be it. She simply could not take another night, let alone another week with nothing but Caleb McCabe's dark, devastated eyes filling her head.

Not if she wanted to stay sane.

THE BLUE AND RED, strobe-lit circus was in full swing when she arrived.

Mira eased her black Chevy Blazer in behind the dozen-odd MPD cop cars, crime scene vans and unmarked SUVs clogging the townhouse-lined street. She was willing to bet her own federal credentials that at least one of those Explorers was registered to a colleague from the J. Edgar Hoover building across town. Confirmation came in the approaching clean-shaven, twenty-something Boy Scout sporting a red pinstriped tie and higher-end version of her JC Penney's navy-blue special.

Definitely FBI.

Judging from the *no joy* stamped along the Feebee's jaw as he tossed his shiny, stainless-steel crime scene kit onto the rear seat of the nearest Explorer before climbing into the front to fire it up, Jerry had already won at least one pissing contest tonight. Fortunately, she'd long since discovered that the Scouts were only partially right. Sometimes it was prudent to come prepared...and sometimes not.

Or at least, to not look like it.

Mira retrieved the bare necessities from her own battered crime kit, secreting the protective booties, latex gloves and a few other crucial items she unearthed within her trouser pockets as she bailed out of the Blazer and into the unusually chilly late March night.

Suppressing a shiver, she headed for the blood-red brick facade of the JAG's Victorian townhouse, making it to the crime scene tape before an MPD uniformed patrol stopped her.

"Excuse me, ma'am. I—"

She flashed her credentials. "Special Agent Mira Ellis, NCIS. I'm here to see Detective—"

"Mir!"

Jerry's stocky, rough-and-ready Irish form bounded through the townhouse's gaping door and down its trio of stone steps. Mira was still tucking her credentials home as Jerry elbowed the uniform aside so he could reach over the wrought-iron gate to haul her into his generous warmth for a soul-balming hug.

"Damned good to see you. Though, given the customer upstairs, I can't say I'm surprised." Jerry eased back, patting the side of her face as if he had forty years on her instead of twenty —and she let him. "You look great, Mir."

She laughed. "You look gray."

His grin deepened, splitting into the lines bracketing his lips. The same lines that stress had begun to carve in during the fiasco that had heralded the twilight of Jerry's own career with NCIS. "I see those manners and that mouth haven't improved."

"Not a chance."

The uniform cleared his throat.

Jerry spared the kid a glance as he swung the gate wide and waved her in. "She's with me, Mandello." Jerry hooked his beefy right arm about her shoulders and gave her another squeeze as they headed up the stone steps. "I'd heard you'd made it back to town. Meant to holler sooner, but MPD put me on the homicide roster the same day I swore in, and it's been a nonstop shitstorm since. Then the news broke about that goddamned pedo chief— along with the garbage his widow's been spewing into the ear of every reporter in town this past week." Jerry shifted his callused palm to the back of her neck and gently nudged her into the townhouse's narrow, empty foyer, his voice dropping low as they came to a halt midway in. "I left a message for you at the Field Office."

Mira focused on the closed door of the ground-floor condo, unable to deal with that all-too-seductive compassion face to face and from this man any more than she had over the phone with Ramsey. "I took some time off."

Not that it had helped.

"That's what Aisley told me. Figured I'd wait 'til you got back in the saddle before I reached out again." He gave Mira's arm a final squeeze, then dropped his hand. "How you holding up?"

"You know me."

His clipped nod was tempered by nearly three years of working together across abutted desks on the opposite side of the country...and a few stark confessions on both their parts as Jerry's mentorship had drawn to a close. "They suggest you see someone?"

"Yup."

"Go. It helped me."

She blinked.

"Yeah, I know. Back then, I'd have sworn that the only way you'd get me on a shrink's couch was if you marched me into the room at gunpoint and cuffed me to it. But things change. I changed. Blame it on Shelli. I never told you, but things weren't all that great between us before that Kelter witch accused me of blackmailing her for sex while her husband was on duty. And when it got out that Shelli and I had started dating before the ink was dry on the divorce papers with *her* asshole of a sailor? Let's just say it got a lot worse before it got better."

That surprised and infuriated her. "I could've sworn Shelli believed you."

"She did. It was everyone else who didn't—except you. Shell and I had other issues, ones there weren't easy solutions to. That witch's lies just made it all worse. And I don't have to tell you that exoneration counts for piss in this profession. Suspicion lingers—even after your electronic sleuthing blew the Internal Affairs investigation out of the water. Hell, it got so bad that I seriously considered bailing on eighteen years and a pending pension and heading off to parts unknown."

It was her turn to squeeze Jerry's shoulder. "I wish I'd known."

But she had. At the time, she'd simply respected Jerry's unspoken wish to *leave it alone*. The life-weary detective pulling a set of protective crime scene booties from the pocket of his own JC Penney's special had known it too. Just as Jerry had known that she'd received the same tainted kiss from her so-called colleagues and friends at the beginning of the end of her painfully short-lived career as a naval officer.

One false accusation and her Officer Candidate School graduation and three grueling months at the Fleet's nuclear power school in Goose Creek had been flushed down the tubes—though, unlike Jerry's, her charges hadn't been leveled maliciously.

Not entirely, anyway.

Not that it had mattered. Nor had her own subsequent exoneration. She'd still gotten those sidelong looks from her former fellow sailors. The whispers.

Worse, the three a.m., self-doubting *what-ifs* egged on by an increasingly empty bottle of booze.

Unlike Jerry, she had bailed.

Three years before Jerry's rude awakening in San Diego, she'd turned her back on the Fleet and applied to work for its watchdog agency, NCIS. But for her own fucked-up first career, she wouldn't have been able to salvage Jerry's.

The irony hadn't been lost on either of them at the time.

Guilt cut in over her willingness to abuse his old pain to snag a case...no matter how desperately she needed the distraction.

The guilt deepened as Jerry offered her the booties and an exculpatory shrug. "You needed to focus on yourself, not me. You deserved that slot in Yokosuka. You'd worked your ass off; I didn't want to see you blow it by looking back."

He was right. If she'd known he needed her, she'd have

stayed in San Diego. Though she should've taken the time to check back in on him now and then.

Mira swallowed her regret. "So what happened?"

How had he gone from *shrinks are evil incarnate* to the poster cop for therapy?

"Shelli. It got to the point where I'd come home and dump everything on her. She finally had it. Said I had to see someone —with or without her—*or else.* Chicken shit that I am, I chose without. Damned if it didn't help. I still go now and then, to touch base and vent. We're both happier, and things have never been better between us."

"I can tell. You look fantastic."

Jerry grinned as he ran a hand over the silver that had firmly overtaken the ruddy thatch at his temples. "Despite the frost?"

"Absolutely. Makes you look distinguished." That couldn't hurt in this town.

"Plus, it scares off the pups. You should've seen the one the FBI sent to try and steal this gig."

"I did. He had his tail between his legs as he crawled into his SUV."

"*Good.* Gloves?"

"Thanks."

Jerry pulled a pair from his jacket, his gaze narrowing suspiciously midway to handing them over. "You have your own, don't you?"

"In my pocket. Booties, too."

"I'll be damned. At least you had the brains to leave your kit in the car."

She smiled. "I did learn from the best."

Presumption was more than a pet peeve with Jerry. It was a cardinal sin.

He tossed the gloves to her anyway and turned to the stairs

that presumably led up to the JAG's third-floor condo. "Put 'em on. I left your partner in the commander's study."

Partner? Since when?

"The Field Office sent another agent?" Irritation surged as Jerry nodded. Why hadn't Ramsey mentioned it? "Who?"

"Guy named Sam Riyad."

She shook her head. "Don't know him."

"Me neither. But I've been retired for two years. He's FCI, by the way, and new to town."

That explained it. Still, "You left him in *your* crime scene unattended?" She didn't know whether to be stunned or impressed. As Foreign Counterintelligence, Sam Riyad was all but guaranteed to be a far cry from an experienced detective. Closer to a full-fledged spook. A category that fell somewhere below shrink in Jerry's book.

Or had.

Jerry shrugged. "Wasn't my first choice. Someone busted the combination locks on the JAG's filing cabinet and safe. Dumped the contents everywhere. Appears to be casework mostly, but more than a few sheets are marked CUI/NOFORN. If there's higher sensitive or outright classified material lying around—much less missing—I don't want to know. Someone's gonna be navigating shit's creek before this is over as it is, and it ain't gonna be me."

A sage pronouncement if there ever was one. Controlled unclassified information that carried a no-foreign-nationals prohibition was bad enough. But if there were papers stamped higher in that condo, she definitely wanted to know. Unlike Jerry, she still answered to the brass at NCIS, so she had no choice but to grab an oar along with her fellow mystery agent and start paddling.

Not to mention, given Ramsey's revelation that the victim upstairs had worked mostly espionage, FCI's attendance would be expected eventually.

Mira was about to follow Jerry up the stairs when the MPD uniform poked his head into the foyer.

"The medical examiner's here, Detective."

"*Damn.* Okay, on my way."

Mira waited for the uniform to leave. "You want me to loiter outside 'til he's done?"

Jerry shook his head. "If you were gonna screw me over, you'd have done it long before now. Might as well stay for the main attraction. I'll work it out with my boss later."

"I appreciate it."

"So get your butt up there before I change my mind. She's in the bedroom at the end of the hall."

"Thanks." Mira was halfway to the second floor by the time Jerry headed out into the night.

Another uniformed cop stood guard at the third floor, just outside the JAG's open door.

She donned the protective booties Jerry had given her and produced her credentials. "Special Agent Ellis, NCIS. I'm with Detective Dahl. He's briefing the ME."

Mira added her name and stats to the crime scene roster and entered the condo's surprisingly chilly foyer. She swore it was colder in here than it was out front. Worse, an unmistakable odor tainted the breeze that drifted down the hall.

Had someone opened a few windows to combat that smell?

Or had the killer left them open?

Glancing into what was clearly the JAG's study, she caught sight of a set of oddly scarred, dusky fingers reaching for a sheet of paper on the desk with nothing but a folded over Kleenex between them and the evidence they were about to snag.

"What the hell are you doing?"

Fingers and tissue firmly clamped about the sheet, the man turned. A split second into her glimpse of the dark, distinctive features above that neatly cropped, mosque-ready mustache and beard, the surname Jerry had offered made sense: Saudi.

Irritation tossed another log onto the fire of her ire.

The source appeared impervious to both as he reached inside his suit jacket with his completely buck-naked hand, so he could flash his badge. "Special Agent Sam Riyad, NCIS. I'm assist—"

"Wrong. What you're doing is blowing this for us." If Jerry spotted that TV-detective, Kleenex stunt, he'd go ballistic—as Jerry should.

"Us?"

She flashed her own credentials for the third time that night. "Mira Ellis; I work out of the Field Office. Where are your gloves?"

"In my car. But this will suffice—"

"No, it won't." One look at the sheet of paper that had made it into Riyad's tissue-shielded fingers and the plethora of cross-contaminating fibers they were most likely leaving behind, and Jerry would toss them out on their collective asses.

Former colleagues, old friends and classified hot potato or not.

Riyad's cheeks flushed as he appeared to accept that he had indeed committed the most basic of procedural violations.

Mira ignored the man's embarrassment in favor of her surging panic as she caught the faint thump of boots climbing the stairs. Any second now and the ME would be passing this room—and Jerry would be with him.

Talk about shit's creek.

She tugged the spare gloves from her trouser pocket and tossed them to her de facto partner. "*Hurry.*"

She'd deal with the fallout of extraneous prints and fibers with Jerry later.

The thumps reached the third-floor landing and came to a

halt outside the condo door as her fellow agent blew precious seconds working the first of his "size-large" hands into her "size-small" gloves. The thumps resumed.

"Turn *around*."

The boots reached the study door as Riyad complied, then continued on. Jerry's loafers did not.

"Everything okay?"

Mira caught the soft snap of a successfully sheathed second glove as she pivoted to the doorway. "Yup."

Jerry nodded. "Let's get in there then. The ME's ready to do his thing. Name's Simon Kent—and by the way, he's got a bit of a complex. Prefers to work in silence, even at crime scenes. Talking's okay—just not with him. At least, not until he's finished."

Curiosity piqued, Mira abandoned Riyad to the study and joined Jerry in heading down the hall. They passed a meticulously pristine galley kitchen and followed the increasingly sickening stench of days-old death into a bedroom that was anything but.

"*Jesus.*"

Jerry cracked his gallows grin. "Ah, Mir. Didn't realize you'd found religion."

She shook her head. "I haven't."

Another few rooms like this, and she never would.

At first glance, the JAG's private sanctuary looked a lot like the floor of a *halal* slaughterhouse at the close of *Eid al-Adha*. Dark rust, almost black vestiges of the victim's blood were everywhere, staining damned near everything. The gauzy sheers bunched at the corners of the iron four-poster were splattered with it, as were the pale peach walls beyond. Hell, even the mint-green area rug was covered in smeared swathes and the distinct arcs of dried arterial spurts. Dozens of tented, yellow crime scene numbers were scattered about the room as well, some nestled in amid the blood, others marking remaining evidence of interest.

But that wasn't what drew her attention.

It was the body.

The victim was naked and tied spread-eagle atop a rumpled, once-white satin coverlet. It was a good thing they knew the JAG's name, because battered, bruised and painfully bloated forms did not make for easy ID's. But that wasn't the worst of it. The poor woman had been violated in at least two orifices. In the mouth—and lower. A filthy gag spilled from now blackened lips, while the bulk of the wine bottle that'd once complemented the shattered goblet on the floor was visible between the woman's legs.

Despite the amount of blood outside the body, the sheer extent of those bruises confirmed that the JAG had been alive for damned near all of it.

Mira turned to Jerry as the eerily mute ME leaned over the body to insert a thermometer into the JAG's liver. "Whoever did this wanted something. Badly." She had no idea what, but she'd also lay odds that the bastard also had a serious issue with women in general or this woman in particular.

Given that the woman was a lawyer, Mira's instincts were leaning toward the latter.

Jerry nodded.

"But judging from the contusions—" She pointed toward the JAG's legs. "Not to mention the depth of that bottle, I don't think he got it."

Another nod.

Mira caught sight of an antiqued photo frame on the night-stand. An intriguing square of blood-splattered paper lay folded up beside it. But as she stepped forward to get a better look, the photo shanghaied her attention. The paper's mysteries on hold, she took another step. Like almost everything else in the room, the glass covering the photo was marred with splotches of dried blood. She could make out the outline of a man and a woman beneath the splotches, striking the standard female-hand-in-male-crooked-arm pose snapped at the beginning of countless formal military functions. Both the man and the woman in this picture were wearing Navy Service Dress Blues.

Something about the visible portion of the woman's deeply dimpled chin teased at the recesses of Mira's brain.

She arched a brow toward Jerry. "May I?"

"Go ahead. Initial photos are done."

She eased the frame from the nightstand, flipping it so she could unlatch the prongs on the reverse as the ME cut the scarf securing the victim's right hand to the bed. Mira slid the photo free, her stomach bottoming out as the couple came into view.

Oh, shit.

"What's wrong?"

Mira held up the photo, drawing Jerry's attention to the impressive diamond and white-gold wedding band on the woman's left ring finger as the ME cut the second scarf from their victim's wrist. The JAG's swollen fingers came into view as the ME drew her arm down from the headboard.

The rings matched.

Disappointment bit in as Mira realized she'd lied to Ramsey on the phone earlier, albeit unwittingly. Not that it would matter. Nor would Riyad's procedural gaff. She'd lost this case all on her own and not because of what she'd done right here and now—but because of what she hadn't done...seven years ago.

"Mir?"

"She got married."

"Who?" Jerry jerked his chin toward the victim. "Commander Corrigan?"

Mira nodded.

"That a problem?"

And then some. "You remember the lying witch who damned near killed your first career?"

"Yeah?"

Mira stared at the obscenely mutilated body on the bed. "This is the woman that obliterated mine."

2

Jerry's low whistle filled the room as he hunkered down to get a better view of the face of the corpse. "*Fuck me.*"

Mira frowned. "I think that's my line."

Nausea that had nothing to do with the view roiled in as she studied the strands of blood-encrusted hair, searching in vain for the silky tangle of vibrant auburn curls that were forever seared into her memory. The woman's deceptively sweet peaches-and-cream complexion had long since fled as well. But as Mira skimmed the bruised and mottled flesh left behind, she succeeded in picking out enough of the delicate features captured in that photo and her own ancient memories to form a positive ID.

It was her. Lieutenant Tess Linden—aka Commander Theresa Corrigan, following two promotions and at least one wedding. The mutilated body belonged to the same JAG who'd once ripped through the fabric of Mira's life, relentlessly severing every thread until there was nothing left to hold it—and her—together. Her promising career as a Navy nuclear surface warfare officer, her circle of so-called friends, her easy-going, trusting relationship with her brother. Hell, even Mira's own once-pending marriage to a fellow sailor. This woman had had a hand in destroying them all.

Jerry's palm cupped her left shoulder. "You okay?"

The twin, dangerously seductive demons of anger and regret slithered back into their respective holes as she nodded. "Absolutely."

Admittedly, there'd been more than a few moments through the intervening years when she'd entertained fantasies of various ills befalling the mutilated woman still arranged spread eagle on this bed, but nothing like this. Mira took in those clouded, sightless eyes. The rag stuffed inside blackened lips. That goddamned bottle.

The plethora of flies and other insects eagerly jockeying for position in and around all three.

Nope, not even close.

She pulled in her breath, ignoring the putrid stench of the past and the present as she faced Jerry. "You want me to leave?"

"Shit, no. If anything, your insight may help."

His instant certainty and steadfast support soothed her nerves, not to mention the insidious surge of self-doubt. Had anyone else offered it, she'd have embraced it with no qualms. But this was a friend talking, her old NCIS mentor. Not some simple MPD colleague. "You sure, Jerry? Your chain is bound to scream conflict of interest."

So would hers. But, by then, the case would be at least half *theirs*.

Mission accomplished.

Instead of agreeing, he turned to the bed. "What do you remember about her?"

"Other than that she was determined to obliterate my personal and professional lives? Not much. I'm surprised she made time for anything outside work, much less men. The Lieutenant Linden I remember was determined to forge her mark on

JAG, and she didn't care how many sailors she annihilated in the process. She knew that, based on the timeline, the odds of my sneaking into the instructor bay and stealing that laptop were slim to none. But the moment she discovered that my dad had bailed on his family and his country to set up shop in Al Jubail with some shiftless Saudi, I was toast. She taunted as much. I don't know who was more livid when that laptop reappeared—without my prints or DNA anywhere near it—the instructor who'd left it out...or *her*. She was convinced I was her ticket to admiral. At least she made commander."

Mira met the ME's damning stare over the corpse. Unlike Jerry, the doc appeared affronted by her summation.

Too bad. She was simply relaying the facts.

If Corrigan had wanted a kinder eulogy, she shouldn't have dogged Mira and her equally unfortunate former classmate as rudely and ruthlessly as she had.

Hell, the woman had damned near destroyed *two* careers that day.

Unlike Frank, Mira had taken the JAG's stiff apology and the official, grudging offer of reinstatement she'd brought with her, and had told her where to shove them. She'd officially resigned her Navy commission, and then accepted Ramsey's invitation to apply to the Navy's civilian watchdog agency, NCIS, determined to not only succeed but also spend her alternative career ensuring that at least one pillar of the Fleet's judicial system had its base planted firmly upon the time-honored principle of innocent until *proven* guilty.

The ME ceded the silent stare-off, shifting his attention to the thermometer he'd inserted upon arrival. Mira watched as he removed and read the instrument, before she turned to slip the photo of the JAG and her husband back into its frame.

She set the photo on the nightstand, a fresh wave of goose-flesh rippling beneath her suit as Jerry joined her.

"It's *freezing* in here."

He nodded. "Looks as though whoever did this turned on the A/C and jammed it down to fifty-five. It's just over that now."

Odd. It was as if the JAG's killer had wanted his vile work preserved.

But why? To send a message?

If so, the bastard had left one hell of a statement behind—though damned if she could decipher it. Given the severity and placement of those bruises, Commander Corrigan had definitely been tortured prior to her death. And not by some random, twisted fuck who'd spotted the JAG on the street. But there was more to the torture. There was a palpable level of rage present that suggested...revenge.

The kind that was personal.

Jerry tipped his head toward the body. "You feel it too, don't you? The hate."

"Yeah." She pointed to the folded square of paper that had initially attracted her attention. "May I?"

Another nod.

Though gloved, Mira took care to open the paper by its corners. A printed flight itinerary lay within. The JAG appeared to have purchased a round trip ticket to San Antonio on the second of March. According to the times listed, Corrigan's outgoing flight should've left Dulles International roughly eight days ago, the evening of the nineteenth.

That explained the level of decomposition, despite the icy temperature.

But not the rest.

Yes, the commander would've needed to take leave for the trip and, since the return flight had landed this past Friday afternoon—a mere thirty-four hours earlier—Corrigan was most likely not scheduled to return to her office until roughly the same time as Mira, at 0700 Monday morning. But surely someone had known where the JAG was headed—and why. Had even anticipated her arrival. Surely, he or she would've reported Corrigan missing, or at least contacted her office at some point.

And who'd found the body, anyway?

The husband?

Mira doubled-checked the triple gold stripes encircling the left cuff of the man's Service Dress Blues in the photo, along with the visible portion of cropped blond hair and almost boyish features. She hadn't spotted that face down on the street on her way in.

"Where's *Captain* Corrigan? At your station?" *He* should've noticed his wife was missing. Unless that trip to San Antonio hadn't included the husband.

Had the two been estranged?

According to the itinerary, Theresa Corrigan had purchased a single ticket.

Jerry shook his head. "The Corrigans are geographical bachelors. She's stationed across town at the Pentagon; her husband's the commanding officer on a submarine."

"Homeport?"

"Kings Bay."

One mystery solved. Not only was Kings Bay located in Georgia, the base was home to half the Navy's ballistic missile subs. Boomers had two things over attack submarines—a bit more wiggle room and the unique concept of crew rotation. The Fleet's boomers were assigned two complete contingents, from the commanding officer all the way down to lowly Seaman Schmuckatelly at the bottom of the roster. But for a handful of days necessary for crew turnover and refit, the dual-manning strategy allowed boomers to deploy for three and a half months at a pop—continuously.

"Blue or Gold crew?"

"Blue."

"Let me guess, Blue's underway and currently incommunicado."

"Right the first time. According to Agent Riyad, your guys are drafting a message to send to the sub as we speak. But since only a handful of personnel know a boomer's precise location, who knows how long it'll take the captain to arrive."

That explained the husband's absence. It also explained Agent Riyad's early presence—and so much more.

Her boss hadn't left her in the dark. Special Agent in Charge or not, Bill Ramsey had been shut out right along with her, at least until those in the upper echelon had a chance to get their proverbial ducks in a row. A viciously murdered JAG who worked espionage was one thing. A viciously murdered JAG married to the commanding officer of an Ohio-class submarine on active, classified patrol was another. Particularly in light of the boomer's mission: nuclear deterrence via its stash of ever-ready Trident II ballistic missiles.

The latter scenario raised several chilling specters. All were cloaked in terrorism.

Enter Riyad and his Foreign Counterintelligence credentials. The man might know squat about crime scene procedure, but as an FCI agent, Sam Riyad was far better equipped to deal with the contents of that ransacked office than she was, *especially* if those contents ended up tainting the submarine's commander.

Mira turned to the bedroom door, startled to find the agent in question, not where she'd left him in the office, but marking time just inside the room. Like the ME, Riyad appeared to embrace the concept of silence.

Fine with her.

So long as he kept those damned gloves on.

Mira swung back to the bed, shifting her position so the ME could pass. Though still mute, the doc's features spoke volumes as he paled noticeably upon reaching out to encase the JAG's swollen left hand, wrist and the still-knotted scarf in a preservation bag in an attempt to protect any potential evidence that might be clinging to it.

The requisite, leakproof body bag would be on its way up the stairs along with a gurney any moment now.

Was that why the doc preferred quiet? The better to contain his own threatening nausea?

Mira left that particular mystery untouched and focused on another. "How did MPD get the call?"

"Corrigan's paralegal let herself in—a woman by the name of Bertha Rodriguez." Jerry swept his hand toward the files and papers littering the floor at the foot of the bed. Unlike nearly everything else in the room, they were devoid of dried blood. "Rodriguez had been tasked with dropping off those so the commander could get a leg up before Monday morning. The paralegal tossed the paperwork upon spotting the body and beat feet to the landing, where she paused long enough to dial nine-one-one. I imagine she'll regret that instinct by morning—if she doesn't already."

Undoubtedly. Like the JAG, the paralegal either wore the uniform or was government service and employed by the Fleet. Either way, she should've known enough to alert the NCIS Field Office instead. At the very least, Rodriguez should have phoned her own office. A call to either the NCIS or JAG duty officer would've allowed the Navy to plant its flag in this room first. An event that took on critical significance in a town where everything—including the assignment of corpses—was political.

Though given the state of the room and of this particular corpse, Mira couldn't blame the paralegal. Hopefully, Rodriguez hadn't known Corrigan well, let alone been friends with the commander.

Not that that bit of distancing would help with the nightmares that were bound to set in.

Lord knew, it wouldn't be helping Mira. She suspected that Caleb McCabe was about to garner some competition.

Whether she wanted it or not.

Jerry sighed as the ME moved around the bed to bag the JAG's right hand. "I've got uniforms canvassing the neighborhood in hopes that someone'll recall something noteworthy in or around this building since the commander signed out on leave."

"Any leads yet?"

"Not a one. I'm not holding my breath either. Given the amount of time it took the bastard to do this and the fact that he was able to keep the commander relatively quiet through it all, I doubt he was dumb enough to leave witnesses, much less prints."

She was forced to agree. As the ME grasped the JAG's body, clearly intent on turning it, Mira started for the opposite side of the bed, then stopped. By the time she reached the ME's side, the man would be finished.

Despite Jerry's advice, she risked speech. "See anything unusual?"

A sharp Bostonian accent clipped across the bed as the ME shook his head. "Just additional contusions along the ribs, special attention to the area in and around the kidneys. It's as if he'd set out to pulverize them."

Mira ignored Jerry's curse, stepping closer as the ME eased the body into its original, supine position, her attention captured by a small speck of metallic yellow now glinting up from the edge of the gag still shoved in the JAG's mouth. Before she could alert the ME to the sight, the distinctive rhythmic clip of a rolling gurney echoed in from the condo's hall, and the doc departed the room to greet it.

Mira shifted to the right, and the glint intensified. "Jerry, there's something trapped in that gag."

"What?"

"No idea...yet." She reached into her suit. Her former mentor's brows shot up as she withdrew her trusty tweezers.

"Christ, Mir. Got fingerprint and DNA kits in there too?"

She returned his smirk. "I might."

Jerry followed her up to the body as she bought the tweezer's tips within an inch of the gag.

"May I?"

"Hell, you brought the barbecue tongs; you get the honor. But be quick. If the ME catches us, I'm blaming you."

Mira swallowed a snort as she used the tweezers to nudge the gag aside. Her snort morphed to a curse as the object the ME had accidentally dislodged when he'd shifted the body slid partway out of the JAG's mouth.

Curiosity propelled her closer.

Jerry joined her. "What the—" He pointed at the two-inch-long section of gold. "Is that what I think it is?"

Mira nodded. "Water wings."

"What?" *Riyad.* She'd forgotten the man had joined them at the back of the room. From the way Jerry had stiffened, so had he.

Jerry edged into Mira's side, his body heat radiating through the fabric of his suit and hers to temper the condo's surrounding chill. Riyad took the hint, squeezing a surprisingly dense, muscular frame for a taller Saudi into the remaining narrow space beside the bed as well.

Jerry shifted his head so she could meet her fellow agent's stare.

"It's a warfare insignia pin. Sailors don them after they qualify in their branch. Aviators have wings; submariners wear dolphins. This one's gold, meaning its owner was an officer. The edge of the ship's bow you see cutting through the waves also means the insignia belonged to someone certified to drive surface ships."

Instead of nodding, Riyad frowned. "I know what it *is*, Agent Ellis. I was expressing surprise at your finding one inside the woman's mouth."

Mira caught sight of Jerry's rising brow as the surrounding temp plummeted once more—though this shift had nothing to do with the condo's over-active air conditioning.

She ignored Jerry's surprise and Riyad's ire.

So she'd mistakenly assumed the agent was a rookie, fresh from his NCIS Basic Course and obligatory six-month, follow-on stint with criminal investigations. Why not? The man hadn't even known enough to don gloves within the outer crime scene.

Mira glanced at the water wings, then Jerry.

Her old partner nodded, no more in favor of waiting for the ME's return than she was.

Using the tips of the tweezers, Mira gave the edge of the gag a second, slightly stronger nudge. A bubble of the decomp gas that the ME had disturbed earlier did the rest, sliding the warfare insignia pin all the way out of the JAG's mouth and into Mira's waiting latexed palm with a nauseating plop.

Definitely water wings.

She turned the pin over and spotted the engraving on the reverse.

Shock ricocheted in as she straightened, threatening to knock her all the way down to her knees. If she hadn't reached out to grab the edge of the bed with her free hand, she'd have hit the floor less than six inches from the sorry remains of the very woman who'd mercilessly shredded her life all those years ago.

Not only did she know the victim on her latest case...there was an outstanding chance she knew the man who'd killed her, too.

3

Mira suppressed a bone-weary yawn as she leaned against the wall of the deserted corridor to await her catch-up session with Jerry and the subsequent autopsy they were scheduled to attend at eight a.m. Retrieving her phone, she straightened and shifted sideways, sinking into the closest metal chair opposite the suite's door to study the official Navy commissioning photo she'd downloaded hours earlier.

The Incredible Mr. Limpet.

Limpy for short.

She'd have felt guilty for even recalling the nickname Farid "Frank" Nasser had been saddled with on a chilly Newport night seven years ago, but for the fact that she'd spent most of last night and this morning in a deserted NCIS Field Office across town, scouring Limpy's less than impressive service record at Jerry's request.

Upshot?

Murderer or not, Frank didn't appear to have changed in the intervening years—much less grown into his potential. Not even remotely.

In the initial officer fitness review that had been filed shortly after he'd been assigned to his first ship, Ensign Nasser had been labeled "adequate." In the second, his performance had been deemed "acceptable." A year later, Lieutenant Junior Grade Nasser's professional skills had improved slightly with "meets expectations," only to backslide following Frank's promotion to full lieutenant when the dual, career-throttling albatrosses of "acceptable decision making" and "competent watchstanding" had been slung about his still-scrawny neck. Nothing like being damned with faint praise—or less.

Especially in the Type-A-personality dominated Fleet.

And if the officer so "praised" was a nuke, scrabbling for advancement to lieutenant commander? Said officer would most likely be passed over for promotion and advised to not let the watertight door smack him in the ass on his way out.

As Frank had been.

In his defense, the then fellow recent Boston University graduate with whom Mira had attended Officer Candidate School hadn't been all bad. In fact, Frank Nasser possessed one of the sharpest brains she'd encountered to date. Unfortunately —brilliant or not—Frank had been at best awkward and stiff in every other area of his life, particularly those that required social skills. During their shared thirteen weeks of OCS and nearly twelve more at the Navy's Nuclear Power School, she'd rarely seen Frank interface with anyone voluntarily. And when he'd been forced into it?

Well, the results had been even less pretty.

Limpy.

Not only had the nickname stuck, but as much as she was loath to admit it, the moniker had been spot on.

But did that mean the man who'd earned it was capable of the carnage she'd seen tonight?

Despite the presence of those water wings, her gut still voted no.

Granted, Frank Nasser had once had reason to outright hate Commander Corrigan. More so than Mira. She might've been manning the duty desk the night that classified laptop had disappeared, but Frank had been the roving patrol.

And there was *his* family. If possible, Corrigan had salivated over the "questionable" quality of Frank's DNA more than Mira's. While her father had ditched the States in favor of setting up shop in Saudi Arabia, Frank was ethnically Arab...a fact that had caused Corrigan's pure, *Daughters of the American Revolution* blood to curl.

Limpy's grandfather had been a naturalized American from Oman, of all places.

Seven years ago, with the country's post-9/11, chase-down-the-terrorists-where-they-live mindset fully engaged—and the bombing of the *USS Cole* next door in Yemen still embedded deep within every sailor's psyche—snagging Frank's Omani ethnicity and impressive Arabic skills for the Fleet had been a coup. At least according to the recruiter she and Frank had met during the career fair they'd attended prior to graduation from Boston University.

Not so Corrigan.

At the final joint meeting the JAG had subjected them to, Corrigan had let slip an Arab slur so filthy that Mira had nearly lodged a formal complaint. But what would've been the point? She'd already been all but booted from the Navy.

In the end, Mira had simply added the JAG's simmering prejudice to Corrigan's overt suspicion regarding her father's permanent address in Al Jubail and had firmly rejected the Fleet's official *mea culpa* and offer of full reinstatement.

Frank had not.

For all his professional shortcomings and social flaws, Limpy had been a staunch idealist, at least back then.

Frank hadn't just believed that the laptop would turn up during the entirety of the eleven-day search that had followed; once it had, the man had swallowed their CO's flowers-and-rainbow assurances that the Navy would forget all about the snafu that had nearly incarcerated them within the walls of Leavenworth.

But it hadn't turned out that way, had it? At least not for Frank Nasser. Because while that *unfortunate incident* had indeed been expunged from the official personnel record Mira had accessed via her laptop at the Field Office, unofficially nearly every sailor Frank had served with since had known exactly what had happened back at nuke school...and had wondered if there hadn't been a whiff of truth to it.

The evidence was embedded within those lackluster fitness reports.

In the end, Corrigan had succeeded in her vow to drive them both out of the Fleet. Frank had simply hung on a few years longer.

Hell, given the timeline established by the JAG's outgoing flight to San Antonio, Corrigan had probably been able to turn on the news the day before she died to hear that all the old, rancid mud that Corrigan herself had nurtured years ago had been scooped back up and flung Mira's way in attempt to destroy her second career.

Ramsey and the rest of the brass at the Field Office had been stunned when the story had broken about her supposed involvement in that not-quite-missing, *classified* laptop. Mira hadn't been. After all, most folks had a handful or two of sludge sloshing through the bilges of their past...whether they were willing to admit it or not.

Chief Umber's wife had simply been devastated and humiliated enough that she'd hired someone with the right connections to dig into Mira's past and dredge up hers.

Mira had told the shrink the truth. Given that she was the one who'd been forced to shoot Umber the week before, she couldn't resent the chief's widow for attempting to smear her name. Nor had she been offended over the accusation that she'd joined NCIS so she could trash stellar Navy careers out of revenge for the implosion of her own.

No, it was those devastated eyes of Caleb's that she couldn't get past...and the fact that they were currently closed.

Caleb had been the true victim—and hero—in all this. Whether the kid would ever be able to accept that, or not.

Mira clicked out of the commissioning photo she'd saved of Frank and pocketed her phone. Perhaps the agency shrink was right. Maybe she should reach out to—

"Well, now, there's a sight I never thought I'd behold again. Special Agent Ellis, patiently marking time outside an autopsy suite, waiting for my lazy old ass to show."

Mira checked her watch, smiling as she rose from her metal chair and turned to take in Jerry's lumbering approach.

Yeah, she'd blown yet another chunk of her life waiting for the man, but she refused to rub it in. The creases in that crumpled suit and face looked as exhausted as she felt, and Jerry was holding *two* Styrofoam coffee cups, both of which were steaming.

He extended one of the cups as he reached her side. "Sorry. I hit up both machines, but the cream and sugar options were offline across the board."

"S'okay. I'm desperate." The oversized caramel latte she'd grabbed at a drive-thru on her way to the Field Office had been left forgotten beside her printer, its contents congealing as she'd gotten sucked deeper into her electronic research and the few, but mostly productive, calls she'd managed to make. Mira took a healthy sip from Jerry's bare-bones, but heart-felt offering, suppressing a grimace at its bitterness as she tipped her head toward the door opposite them.

It was still closed.

"Besides, legally you're not late. The pathologist hasn't even poked his head out yet."

"Probably still wrapping up the x-rays and getting set up. We're just lucky the advanced state of decay got us bumped up in the schedule. Pretty sure they just want this one out of the way before it gets any riper." Jerry shifted the remaining Styrofoam cup to his right hand and took a swig. "You catch a nap?"

"Didn't even try."

Why? Though the office had a duty cot she could've crawled into, she'd have ended up spending every moment inside it trying to evade the same nightmare that had been plaguing her in her bed at home these last nine days.

Her old mentor chased his second swig with a sigh. "Yeah, me neither. I got hung up on a call with my boss. That's why I'm late."

Shit. "He changed his mind, didn't he?"

Jerry waved her off with his cup as he turned to brace himself against the wall of the corridor beside her. "Nah. The big guy's happy to let you tag along until this is solved, as a resource if nothing else. What about your end? Ramsey get back to you?"

"No." Which was weird.

She'd not only left a detailed voicemail regarding her ancient, if lurid connections to both Commander Corrigan and Frank Nasser before she'd departed the condo, but she'd also followed up her unanswered call with half a dozen texts to keep Ramsey updated as she'd pushed through the past decade of Frank's life—not a single text of which had been acknowledged. Which meant one thing, of course, and it wasn't good.

Whatever fire Ramsey had been ordered to fly overseas to extinguish this weekend was still actively raging.

"Ramsey say where he was, and/or when he's due back stateside?"

"Nope." Her only hint had come via that stewardess' accent: Arabic.

As clues went, it was seriously vague.

Jerry took another sip from his cup and shrugged. "I wouldn't sweat it. If someone on your team screams conflict of interest later today, we'll deal with it then. As far as MPD and I are concerned, you raised your hand. That's all you can do."

True. Not to mention that in his last orders to her, Ramsey had stated that NCIS wanted this case, and badly.

Well, here the agency was. If the upper brass needed a different incarnation bearing the badge, all Ramsey had to do was respond.

"So, you get anything from Nasser's files?"

Mira downed another mouthful of the bitter brew. "Nothing case-breaking. Frank's sea tours were less than spectacular. No major screwups, but not a single evaluating officer during his career thought he walked on water either. Exact words were 'acceptable decision making' followed by 'competent watch-standing.'"

"*Ouch.*"

"I know, right?"

"Does that wimp-ass assessment track with what you knew of the man back then?"

"Yes and no. Frank was awkward in groups, but he did okay one-on-one. He was also scary smart. I didn't know him well before that laptop went missing, but the night he and I dined with the Navy recruiter after our business fair at Boston University, he impressed the heck out of me. His take on the state of the Fleet and what improvements were needed was spot on. And don't get me started on his chemistry brain. The man's a flat-out savant there. That's why the Navy wanted him. Well, that and his Arabic skills. Anyway, Frank wrapped up his surface career as an assistant liaison for the Rim of the Pacific exercises. He must've impressed someone in the Japanese fleet, though. Because while Frank was over there, working through the coming logistics, he scored an interview with the head honcho at the power plant at Ishida."

"Ishida? That's a nuclear-powered electric facility, isn't it?"

"Uh-huh." And not a surprising shift career-wise. Frank had been a US Navy nuclear engineer. Though the prestige quotient wasn't as high, a private sector job with Ishida would've come with more money and better sleep.

Go, Frank.

"Anyway, Ishida made him an offer. Frank resigned his commission roughly a year ago and moved to Japan. I haven't come across any recent flight manifests in his name into or out of the States, but neither have I been able to definitively place him at work in Ishida on the nineteenth—yet. I'm waiting to hear from his supervisor. By the way, I downplayed my initial call over there as a standard NCIS 'just following up' query regarding someone else in our Fleet who Frank once served with."

"Excellent."

Mira nodded. She figured he'd approve.

She and Jerry had been in agreement before she'd even left the condo. Given the files and CUI/NOFORN-stamped papers that had been blown across every surface in Corrigan's office, they needed to proceed carefully.

Not to mention that if Chief Umber's widow had managed to dredge up the old nuke school dirt that connected her and Frank to the JAG, Corrigan's killer could've done the same—and possibly decided to set Frank up to throw suspicion off himself.

Or at least to delay the narrowing in on him.

"What about Corrigan? You get any more on the commander or her husband? Something that will help us navigate our way through this mess?" Jerry swallowed the dregs of his coffee and held out his free hand.

Mira blinked down at her cup, surprised to see an exposed bottom. She was so tired, she'd downed the contents without realizing it.

She passed the Styrofoam to Jerry so he could stack her cup inside his, waiting until he'd balanced both at the edge of the chair beside them before she continued. "I do know why Corrigan bought the ticket to San Antonio. She had a sister who was pregnant and scheduled to give birth via Cesarean on the twenty-second—which the sister did. But Corrigan never showed. According to the agent I sent to perform the death notification, Corrigan phoned her sister on the nineteenth, about the time she should've been leaving for the airport. Corrigan said something critical had come up at work and she might be out of touch for a while. She promised to reschedule and call her sister back with the updated trip details, but she never did."

"That would explain why there was no missing person's report phoned in by the sister to the folks at the JAG office, let alone mine."

"Yep." And with the husband's submarine operating deep beneath the waves for the past two months...somewhere... there'd been no one else phoning Corrigan and wondering why she wasn't picking up. "I'm still waiting on the dump from Corrigan's phone, but I suspect the data will bear out the sister's story. I also called Corrigan's number myself a couple of hours ago; it goes straight to voicemail. Since your team couldn't find her phone in the condo, I'm guessing it was taken and destroyed by whoever killed her."

"Agreed—but *damn*. I hope to hell the pathologist finds something with the body. Other than one hell of a fucked-up crime scene, we've got squat."

As much as she hated to admit it, he was right. "What about—"

Her phone vibrated, redirecting her attention and jacking up her hopes as she reached for it. *Please* let it be Frank's supervisor at Ishida.

It wasn't.

Nor did she need caller ID to know who was behind that number.

She rejected the call, then took the time to open her phone app so she could block the number and prevent it from interrupting her again—ever.

She shoved her phone back into her trouser pocket with more force than she'd intended.

"Mir? What's wrong?"

"Nothing." *Everything.* And, damn it, she didn't need it all pummeling through her brain. Least of all this morning. Not with a pending autopsy for what was already shaping up to be a particularly consuming case that, for some reason, still appeared to be half hers.

"Bullshit. I know that look. Who was that?" Jerry sucked in his breath and scowled. "*Christ.* Was that your old man?"

Nope. Though dear ol' Dad had deigned to reach out to her recently. The morning after the shooting, in fact. She'd hung up on that bastard, too. She'd even deleted the voicemail that had followed—without listening to it.

"Mir?"

She met that familiar stubborn stare and sighed. "No, it wasn't my dad." Nor had the call been case-related. Not this case, anyway. "That was Josiah Briggs." *Again.* "He hounds victims professionally, their friends and families too, on behalf of the

DC Dispatch."

Sunday morning had barely begun and the paper's leading leech had already commenced his daily harassment of her.

Joy.

"This about that accusation Umber's wife made about you looking to get even for what happened to you and Nasser back at nuke school?"

"Yeah." But Briggs wouldn't be stopping there. From the half-dozen previous voicemails the reporter had left, he wanted it all. Her sobbingly emotional take on what it had been like to make that *perfect* head shot when her own admittedly *barely makes the grade* qualifications suggested she shouldn't have made it at all, to her private thoughts on the not-so-hero chief corpsman who turned out to be a coward and a pedophile. And, of course, Briggs wanted her to serve up every salacious detail on what it had been like to work a case where the victim was so ashamed that he'd denied *being* a victim.

Even after his abuser was dead.

Nothing sold papers like pain, did it?

If it bleeds, it leads. Chief Umber might not be bleeding anymore, but his wife was. Emotionally, anyway—just as Caleb McCabe would be again.

But first, the boy would have to wake up.

Until that happened, the best thing she could do for everyone, including NCIS, was to keep her mouth shut. About everything. Only then would this nightmare fade from the news. And only then could Caleb begin to heal.

If that was even possible at this point.

"The kid still denying the abuse?"

"Not...exactly."

Jerry's brow rose over that cryptic comment, but then he nodded. "Well, that's good, I guess. At least it's not still your word against the dead war hero's rep and his widow's blind outrage and diarrhea of the mouth."

Mira shook her head. That part had been negated at least. "They found Umber's stash a week ago Thursday. Photos and video. All boys, all sickeningly young. They were stored on a memory card in a burner phone that the chief kept locked up in a private post office box." Ironically, the widow's brother had come across a monthly debit for the mailbox while he'd been sorting through his grieving sister's bills. He decided to stop by the storefront the following day to close the box so that the reoccurring charge would cease. The man had been so horrified by what he'd found on the phone—password protected by his sister's birthdate, no less—he'd walked it straight into NCIS and turned it over to the duty agent without even telling his sister.

A lot of good the discovery had done.

For Caleb, least of all.

The majority of the videos on that phone had been of him, age eight to his current twelve, being coerced into doing all sorts of vile things...and having that same filth done to him—over and over again.

And that night, when Caleb had been told of the discovery of the phone and had realized that his own father had seen several of the videos on it?

"The boy broke into the family medicine chest, found the fresh bottle of oxycodone a Bethesda doc had prescribed for phantom pain following his dad's old leg amputation and swallowed every blessed pill."

"*Fuck*."

Yeah.

"I am so sorry; I didn't know."

He wouldn't have. Out of respect for Caleb and his father, outside her, Ramsey, key NCIS personnel and, of course, the boy's medical team, no one had been told.

And if Briggs and the *Dispatch* found out?

"Is he going to be—"

"Okay?" She shook her head. "I have no idea." Just the million-odd prayers she wanted to believe would help—but didn't.

How could she?

She'd begun this morning with yet another hopeful call to the nurses' station outside the boy's intensive care unit at Bethesda, only to receive the same soul-shredding assessment: *I'm so sorry, Agent Ellis. There's been no change.*

For nine damned days now.

Mira folded her arms, rubbing her palms up and down the sleeves of her tired suit in an effort to stave off the chill that had closed in on her as she slumped back against the corridor's wall. It didn't help. "Caleb's still in a coma."

And *if* the boy came out of it?

Well, then he'd be forced to deal with the surfacing of that phone all over again, along with the "proof" that Umber's widow had so vocally been demanding.

Not that Talia Umber had accepted it once it had surfaced. While Caleb had been in the ambulance on his way to the ER to get his stomach pumped, Talia had been putting the final piece of her charming revenge against Mira into motion. Aware that her husband's survivor's pay and benefits were about to evaporate along with his reputation, Talia had struck back at NCIS, the Navy and Mira in one fell swoop.

Talia had phoned Josiah Briggs personally to reveal the dirt her private eye had uncovered about that old classified, *not missing after all* laptop.

As for Briggs and his "opportunity" for Mira to offer a rebuttal in print?

The leech could rot in hell with Umber.

And *herself.*

"Hey," Jerry's fingers gently hooked the bottom of her chin as he stepped in front of her, forcing her to look up. Worry swirled through that soothing brown. "You okay?"

God forgive her, she gave the man the same lie he'd given her all those years ago in San Diego when his own sanity had been hanging by a thread, along with his eighteen-year career and, apparently, his already shaky marriage. "I'm fine."

"It was a good shoot, Mir. A damned good shoot."

"I know."

He squeezed her chin. "Good. Because that bastard deserved it. Umber messed up that kid's life three times over. First, by abusing him, then by jamming that scalpel into his neck. And finally, by leaving the boy to deal with the fallout from his own twisted shit. No, Caleb's life won't ever be the same, but he will *have* a life. Because of you."

She nodded. Because that's what the agency shrink had said. Ramsey, too.

She might've been able to believe it, too...were it not for those huge eyes that she just could not get out of her head. The utter devastation that *she'd* caused.

Umber had been a truly despicable monster. But she was the one who'd turned a lazy, late-afternoon, middle-school classroom into an active crime scene.

Shivers set in as the cold inside her deepened.

"Mir?" Jerry's fingers shifted to catch a drop of the shame that had escaped to trickle down her left cheek. "Hey, it's okay. Come here."

She closed her eyes as he gathered her close. Savored his rock-steady warmth as it gradually spread into her.

Maybe that's what did it. Having this man to lean on.

An old friend, yes, but one who'd once been trapped right where she was—and had somehow found the strength and the means to claw his way out.

She sucked up the rest of the tears and sighed, stepping back a bit as she forced herself to face the truth head-on for the first time in nearly thirteen days. To voice it aloud. "I screwed up, Jerry. I *never* should have gone into that classroom to confront Umber. Caleb would've been better off without me."

"Oh, hon. That's just not true, and you know it. What did Nate say?"

She managed a desolate shrug.

"Shit." A frown bit in, deepening the creases around Jerry's mouth as his stare narrowed in comprehension. "Your brother's undercover again, isn't he? Leaving you to push through this on your own." Jerry shook his head as he reached up to soothe her cheek. "Well, you're *not* alone on this. You've got me back in your life; Shelli, too. She said as much when she called earlier. And I'm betting Ramsey's never left, so—"

Someone cleared a throat. Loudly.

Not Jerry.

And that decidedly insolent sound hadn't come from her either.

Her old partner's hand fell away as they turned in unison to confront the FCI agent they'd both met in Corrigan's blood-drenched condo hours earlier.

Sam Riyad.

Open suspicion tinged the agent's stare, darkening it as Riyad closed the remaining distance to the autopsy suite—and them. "I'm not interrupting a...private moment, am I?" Judgment settled in, confirming the FCI agent's sordid assessment.

Asshole.

Jerry's icy snort answered for the both of them. "Just old partners catching up. You know how it is, Agent. If not, you will—if you're lucky."

Touché, Jerry. Especially when the surrounding air was still frosted with the comeback the detective had wanted to offer, but

—for the sake of professionalism and their presence outside an autopsy suite that, from the sound of the rattling instruments and muffled voices within, was now occupied—hadn't.

She and Jerry had never stepped over the line, on the job or off.

Not now and not back then.

Not that *any* aspect of their relationship should concern the man who'd taken it upon himself to butt in so very rudely.

Riyad reached the trio of chairs that hugged this side of the corridor and bent down to retrieve the empty coffee cups. He studied the stacked Styrofoam for a moment, as though he had something to add regarding their supposed intimacy too. But then he shrugged and stepped around the chairs to toss the cups into the waiting bin.

Mira spotted the swift, sidelong quirk to Jerry's bushy brows, the last three years falling away as she caught the silent query embedded within.

Did you invite him?

The micro-shake of her head telegraphed her answer.

Curious.

If neither of them had phoned Sam Riyad, why was he here? When she'd left the condo six hours earlier, the FCI agent had been holed up back inside the JAG's home office, sifting through the papers still strewn from one end to the other, as was his job. Albeit, during that pass, Riyad had been wearing gloves.

So, who'd told the agent when and where this morning's activity would be going down? He didn't intend to actually view the autopsy, did he?

But he must. Why else show?

Either way, unless Riyad had found something in those papers that changed the course of the case, he'd made yet another procedural error. This one in not phoning the homicide detective who owned this case to ask permission to view the postmortem, or at the very least, to politely suggest that he should be here.

Had Riyad found something in those papers then? Something that bore a heftier classification than CUI/NOFORN?

Better yet, had he come across something that could explain the utterly obscene carnage in that condo...if that was even possible?

Before Mira could ask, a male voice within the suite increased in volume. A split second later, the door opened.

A stocky Hispanic diener waved them inside.

Ivan Zanchetta, a tall, distinguishedly graying forensic pathologist she'd worked with on a case shortly after her arrival in DC, stood at the opposite end of the room, just past the head of the slanted, stainless-steel autopsy table. Zanchetta's nod encompassed all three newcomers to the suite as he continued to offer up his opening monologue toward the grille of the microphone suspended from above, detailing the results of his external examination of the body and a description of the specimens that had already been collected for toxicology.

She, Jerry and Riyad waited as the diener paused beside a rolling table to retrieve a trio of protective masks. The diener passed a mask to Jerry, and another to her as she and her once-again, if temporary partner headed up the right side of Theresa Corrigan's still naked, but now thoroughly cleaned body.

Riyad received his mask where he'd chosen to remain, at the commander's feet.

The ubiquitous squat blue jar appeared next, and that was handed off to Riyad first. Her fellow NCIS agent stared down at the jar for several awkward moments, as if he couldn't quite figure what he was supposed to do with it.

The diener tapped the lid. "It's Vicks." He shifted his finger, sliding the tip across his upper lip, just beneath his nose. "Slather it here, and it'll help combat the odor."

For despite the chill in the room, there was an *odor*. Not surprising since a brutalized body that had lain on a bed and decayed for nine days tended to carry one. And in this case, it was particularly nauseating.

Riyad waved off the jar.

Mira did the same. Experience had taught her that inhaling Vicks for several hours would lead to a jackhammer of a headache that even the emergency ibuprofen packet in her wallet wouldn't be able to quell. And *that* was a distraction she could ill afford while actively working a case. She'd rather deal with that stench.

Jerry waved the jar off too, because—bless him—he knew if he sported the salve this close to her, the jackhammer would still find its way inside her skull.

"Thanks."

He shrugged as they stepped up in unison to the raised lip of the table, instinctively closing off their nasal passages from within as they studied the darkened, abused and bloated flesh that had once belonged to Theresa Corrigan.

The pathologist wrapped up his initial comments and stepped closer as well to reexamine the split in the flesh riding the crest of the woman's right cheek before reaching out to manipulate the zygomatic beneath.

Mira already knew from Dr. Zanchetta's recorded monologue that the bone had been shattered. The facial damage dovetailed in with the smear of dried blood that she and Jerry had noted roughly five and a half feet up the wall from the floorboard just inside the door to Corrigan's bedroom. That smear and the damage to the bone, along with the lack of tool marks in and around the locks at the condo's front door—when added to the phone call the JAG's sister had received in San Antonio— suggested the rest.

Corrigan had entered the condo after work to pack. But her

killer had been waiting for her in the bedroom, where he'd already unfolded and gleaned the details of that flight itinerary, as Mira had. Once he'd slammed the commander's face into the wall, Corrigan would've been motivated to make the call to her sister and offer up a convincing recitation of the excuse the killer had demanded.

But was that killer Frank?

Mira took in the contusions that covered the woman's chest. To create those, Corrigan would have to have been punched in both breasts repeatedly, *while* she'd been alive. Without the bedcovers bunched against her torso and hips, it was clear the kidneys had sustained a vicious beating too. The gaping slice at the front and sides of the neck accounted for the arterial spurting at the scene. And there was the damage to the wrists and above the ankles from where Corrigan had been bound to those iron bedposts, not to mention the marks from the gag that'd been in her mouth. Finally, the bruising between the woman's inner thighs—and higher—from that damned bottle.

Was Frank Nasser capable of this much hate?

Mira returned her attention to the right hand inches from her.

There was something odd about the fingers. They appeared more swollen than even this horrific bloating would've allowed for—or should.

She glanced up to see if Jerry had noticed, only to catch sight of Riyad's intense focus out of the corner of her eye. Strangely, that murky stare of his was leveled not on the body, but on her. For a split second she could've sworn that the level of anger she'd been attempting to align within Frank was simmering inside the agent just off her right.

It was mixed with disgust too—and directed at *her.*

But...that was insane. It had to be.

The stark lighting in here had to be affecting her eyes. That, and she was exhausted. Her all-nighter at the Field Office had come on the heels of twelve previous nights of stunted sleep. She hadn't logged a decent stint since she'd confronted Umber.

That's all this was.

Mira turned her head to her left. But as she attempted to shake off the sensation that she was being watched, she realized that Jerry was looking past her—to Riyad.

Her old partner's attention shifted, zeroed in on her.

And she *knew*.

It wasn't the stark light. Or her exhaustion. Jerry had seen Riyad staring her. That anger and disgust she'd spotted within the agent's glare had been real.

But why? What the devil had she done to offend him?

Usurped a slot in an investigation he'd thought was his?

But that was insane too. Riyad's expertise lay in counterintelligence.

Oh, shit. The files and papers. The ones that had been yanked out of the breached safe in the condo's office and scattered about the room. Had Corrigan kept her old notes regarding the accusation of the not-missing laptop? Had the JAG added to them over the years? If so, what the hell had Corrigan written about Frank?

About *her*?

"Mir?" There was a wealth of warning in that truncated version of her name. Along with a pointed assessment, and an even more pointed question from Jerry to her. First Riyad's asinine comment out in the corridor. And now this?

What the hell was going on?

Mira shook her head, telegraphing a message of her own. *Later*. This was not the time for them to get into it. Much less to press into Riyad.

Jerry nodded—and let it go.

She, however, was forced to clench her fingers to control the anger still simmering within. The motion reminded her of where she was; of what she'd noted earlier. Corrigan's fingers. They were definitely more swollen than they should be.

It was almost as if—

"Yes. They were dislocated."

Mira glanced up to find the pathologist's attention settled on her. "*All* of them?"

Zanchetta nodded solemnly, before tipping his head toward the pair of x-rays still hanging in the glowing light box on his left. "As you can see, each digit was dislocated at the base of its metacarpal, then returned to its normal, anatomical alignment."

"What?" *Riyad.*

Mira glanced past the woman's legs to find the agent's stare finally fixated on the body on the table, and not her. And in place of the anger and disgust?

A fierce glint she couldn't quite decipher.

It seared straight up the body and into the pathologist. "You're saying *all ten* of the woman's fingers were dislocated at the knuckle and then wrenched back into place?"

Zanchetta nodded. "Yes."

With that confirmation, the FCI agent clipped a nod of his own, then abruptly turned on his heel—and strode out of the suite. Just like that. No explanation, let alone an *excuse me* or a muttered *goodbye*. Riyad didn't even bother closing the door behind him.

The diener was forced to do that.

What the hell?

She turned to Jerry. But he'd already shrugged off the bizarre departure and refocused his attention on those hands. From the terse pinch to his frown, Mira not only knew why, but she knew also what the detective was thinking.

Because she was thinking it too.

The lack of tool marks and other forensic evidence that the

killer *should* have left behind at the scene, but hadn't? The lowering of the temperature inside the condo, most likely to screw with the determination of the time of death? The coerced phone call to Corrigan's sister, which provided just enough of an explanation to keep the sister from calling Corrigan back—or informing others? The repeated blows to the JAG's kidneys and breasts? The gag that had muffled her screams?

And now this? The deliberate, double whammy of excruciating pain that would've come as each joint had been snapped out of place and then ruthlessly shoved back in...as questions were undoubtedly asked and quite possibly answered?

"He's a pro."

Jerry nodded. "Yep."

But what the hell had the bastard wanted?

Because her boss had been right about one thing during that call he'd made to assign her this case. For the past several years, Corrigan had been stationed at the Pentagon, working anti-terror almost exclusively. Had the JAG's killer been after classi-fied and/or compromising information from one of her cases? If so, given the carnage in that condo—not to mention the anger and frustration revealed by the savage insertion of that wine bottle—Mira didn't think the bastard had gotten it.

And the surface warfare insignia that had been shoved down the woman's throat? Had those water wings been planted to throw off the investigation, after all?

Or had Frank simply been in the room, a cold-blooded spec-tator enjoying his sick, belated revenge?

"I'm guessing your night's research into your old classmate suggests that this—" Jerry waved his hand over those abused fingers. "—isn't in Nasser's wheelhouse."

Despite the water wings, her brain and her gut agreed with him.

Before Mira could share the assessment, her phone vibrated.

Excusing herself, she stepped back from the table, noting the international numerical prefix for Japan as she checked her caller ID.

Ishida.

She excused herself again, this time as she headed across the room, half expecting to find Riyad growling into his phone just outside.

But the corridor was empty.

She closed the door and accepted the call. "Special Agent Ellis, how may I help you?"

"Agent Ellis, this is Carl Bremmer. I work at Ishida." The crisp, decidedly American twang continued, "You called this afternoon asking about Frank Nasser?"

"I did." Though the query had taken place during the night —for her in DC. "I apologize for taking up your time, Mr. Bremmer, but I'm tying up a loose thread on something. Is Mr. Nasser available? If so, may I speak to him? Afterward, I'd like to speak to his supervisor if possible, so I can verify something."

Namely, Frank's story.

"I'm sorry, I'm afraid Frank's not in the plant today. But I am his direct supervisor. Is there something I can help you with?"

Damn. She'd really wanted to start with Frank; give the man a chance to lie. To see if he would.

At least she'd gotten his supervisor on the line.

Mira turned to pace down the hall, then stopped short. Given the timeline they'd been able to establish, Corrigan had been murdered during the evening of the nineteenth. But Japan was thirteen hours ahead of Washington, DC, so, "Sir, can you tell me if Frank Nasser was at work on March the twentieth?"

"He was not."

Oh, boy. Were her research and her gut wrong?

It wouldn't be the first time, would it?

She headed up the corridor, coming to a halt beside the

chairs. "Mr. Bremmer, do you know if Mr. Nasser was in Japan at all that day?"

"I can't say for certain, but I don't believe so. Frank took emergency leave that entire week. Something to do with a break-in at his grandfather's house in the States. The old guy was in intensive care for several days. I don't recall the hospital or the city. Sorry."

Well, shit. Professional torture session or not, she definitely needed to question Frank—in detail, and in person.

Barring that, "Sir, do you have Mr. Nasser's home address in Japan?" She could have a fellow NCIS agent from Yokosuka knocking on his door within the hour.

"Well, now. I do. But it won't do you much good, Agent. Frank's not in Japan at the moment. He flew straight from the States to France. He's visiting a facility in Marcoule with another member of my team. I can give you Frank's number, but it may be a few days before he's able to return your call, possibly longer."

Frank would be out of touch for several days or more? To the extent that he couldn't even take a phone call?

What was Bremmer not saying?

Unfortunately, given that the *facility* Bremmer had mentioned was located in Marcoule, she was better off not pressing her curiosity. Not over the phone. Instead, she asked Bremmer to text her Frank's number, then thanked him for his assistance.

The door to the autopsy suite opened as she hung up.

Jerry joined her in the corridor, closing the door behind him. "What's going on?"

She shook her head. "I'm not sure."

Yet.

She recapped her conversation with Bremmer, nodding at Jerry's low whistle as she reached the part about Marcoule.

His brows shot up. "Marcoule...the nuclear facility?"

She nodded slowly. Carefully. Although neither she nor Jerry would ever be savants like Frank, they were both more than capable of adding up all the seemingly disparate facts they'd spent most of last night and this morning gleaning.

A murdered JAG who worked anti-terror cases for the Pentagon, who was also married to the commanding officer of a nuclear-powered *and* nuclear-capable, Ohio-class submarine? A less-than-stellar-performing, former Navy nuke who—though he'd been part of the surface-ship side of the Fleet—was now employed by a Japanese nuclear-powered electric plant? The fact that that same former nuke's old water wings had been shoved down the JAG's throat? Water wings that could've easily been stolen by whoever had broken into his grandfather's home back in the States?

And now, that former nuke's presence at a French nuclear site that any terrorist worth his IED-construction skills would be champing to slip inside...quite possibly to gain access to the radioactive material that was stored within?

"Jerry, I think I need to fly to France."

His answering nod was swift, and even more decisive. "Let your chain of command know, and *go*."

4

C reighton Middle School, Washington, DC,
    Two weeks earlier...
        Mira caught the attention of the civics teacher,
who stepped into the conversation she and three of his fellow
instructors had been sharing in the teachers' lounge. "Did you
say that Chief Umber hosts the after-school biology club on
Mondays now? So he's here today?"

The heavily freckled man nodded. "He had to switch the
timing, something to do with his schedule at Bethesda, I think.
But the chief still finishes at four. Traffic."

Mira nudged the cuff of her suit jacket aside as the teachers
began to collectively argue over just how long it took to get from
Creighton Middle School to the northwest side of the capital
and Chief Umber's second shift position at the Walter Reed
National Military Medical Center at this hour of the day.

Not that the answer mattered to Mira. The hands of her
watch revealed twenty-two minutes after four. She'd missed
Umber completely, though not by much.

Probably for the best. This was a fact-finding mission.

As much as her instincts pointed to it becoming more, she

was determined to remain patient and impartial. In any NCIS investigation, there tended to be at least one military career at stake. A career that could be shredded, and so very easily, if the agent wasn't careful. She knew better that most just how swiftly the shredding could occur.

And most of the time?

Well, there was no stitching it back together.

As for this investigation, if the accusations within the anonymous letter that had been addressed to her and mailed to the Field Office were true, the shredding would be more vicious than most.

All the better to tread slowly and meticulously, especially in this lounge, with this savvy bunch.

The civics teacher tilted his mass of freckles to the side. "You were just here on Friday. Couldn't you have asked us about the chief then?"

In short, no.

While she had given her toned-down, "a day in the life of an agent" presentation to the sixth-to-eighth graders in this very school three days ago, the letter that contained the accusations against Ronald Umber hadn't shown up until this morning. The choice of words by the author had pegged him as a young, possibly still prepubescent male.

And since the auditorium she'd spoken in last Friday had been brimming with two hundred plus eleven-to-fifteen-year-olds, half of whom were male, she'd decided it was prudent to return here first.

She couldn't offer the truth though, so she smiled. Lied. "You know how it is. One hand never knows what the other's doing, especially when both are welded to the anvil of bureaucracy. My boss tapped me to give your presentation last week. Another agent was asked to verify a write-up we received this morning." She pushed forth a light shrug, just enough to enhance her lingering smile. "I was stopping by to drop off the agency brochures I promised to your librarian anyway, so I offered to vet the write-up, too."

"The chief has been nominated for another commendation, then?"

Mira held fast to her smile, allowing the assumption within the fifty-something English teacher's query to hold as she met the woman's stare. Despite the distinct glow of admiration within the blue, Mira couldn't quite manage an accompanying nod. During the cursory research she'd done to tailor her canned "day in the life" presentation to this specific school, she'd discovered that a good portion of the students who attended were sons and daughters of active-duty military personnel. A number of Creighton's staff also had service connections. More than most, those kids and staff members understood what simply being tapped for a Navy Cross meant, let alone receiving it.

As Chief Umber had already done.

According the medal's write-up, then Petty Officer First Class Ronald Umber had been serving as an independent duty corpsman with a Marine platoon in Iraq four years earlier when, while pinned down by enemy fire, he'd transferred more than a pint of his own blood via a direct, arm-to-arm transfusion to a Marine with minutes to live—while Umber and other Marines were actively taking and returning that fire.

Though First Sergeant Malcolm McCabe had eventually lost his right leg, Umber's actions on the battlefield had saved McCabe's life, along with the lives of three additional Marines that day.

But had that act of heroism over there, and the meritorious medal that had resulted from it, provided the chief the necessary moral cover to conceal a viper's nest of nauseating crimes back in the States, right here in the nation's capital?

According to the anonymous letter she'd received, *yes*.

And when Mira had phoned the school and discovered that not only did Umber volunteer at Creighton, but the chief also mentored several boys through the school's biology club...one of whom appeared to be the son of the same first sergeant whose life Umber had saved?

That's when her hackles had gone up—and when she'd headed here.

Mira turned toward the door to the lounge as a short, thickly muscled man strode in. The physical education teacher, Tim Modrcin, if she remembered correctly.

The PE teacher nodded to her, returning the round of greetings from his co-workers as he headed for the refrigerator at the far end of the room. The civics teacher split off, briefing Modrcin on the purported reason for her follow-up visit as the man opened the fridge. But instead of reaching inside, Modrcin turned back to her.

"You're here about the chief? He's still here. I just saw him. You'd better hurry though. The kids and I finished batting practice. We pass the biology room on the way in. Umber and his assistant are wrapping things up as we speak."

"Umber has an assistant?"

Modrcin nodded. "A sixth-grader. Caleb McCabe. He always stays behind to help. I think today was Frog Dissection Day, so there's bound to be a mess."

Shit. Not only was Chief Umber on the premises, he had a twelve-year-old boy within in his reach? The same boy whom she suspected had written that note?

And the two were alone?

"*Where?*"

"Excuse me?" The coach's confusion was mirrored by the other teachers in the lounge. Probably because of her tone.

She hadn't been able to keep the panic entirely suppressed.

Mira forced herself to calm down. Even managed to push forth another polite smile. "Where is the biology room? Since he's here, I'd like to speak to the chief too."

Speak, hell. If the accusations she'd read were true, she might not be able to resist the temptation to nail the bastard to the nearest wall and use *him* for batting practice.

Her latest smile might not have been as smooth as Mira had hoped, because the English teacher turned to pull the door open.

"I'll show you."

Given the clipped pace the older woman set as they exited the lounge to pass the dormant lunch room before turning down an equally desolate hall, Mira's suspicions increased. It was a challenge to keep up.

But she did.

The teacher led them through a second turn and stopped short. A gently labored breath escaped the woman's tightened lips as she pointed to a dark wooden door several feet further down the hall and just shy of the exit that most likely opened onto the school's sports yard.

"That's the biology room."

Mira stepped forward, peering through the rectangle of glass embedded above the knob to assess the layout inside. Fifteen black lab tables were arranged in a platoon formation of three tables across and four rows deep. A denim-and-blue sweater-clad adult male of roughly five feet six and a lanky, dark-haired young boy closer to four feet even, wearing the school's ubiquitous white Oxford and tie, stood facing each other in the first row, behind the centermost table. A pair of stainless-steel trays crowded its surface. Though she could only make out the right side of that head of cropped, sandy curls and ascetic features, she recognized them from the photo she'd pulled at the Field Office.

Chief Hospital Corpsman Ronald Umber.

As for Caleb McCabe, she could see him perfectly. Caleb's dark brown stare was fused to the chief's face—and there was a glimmer of tears within.

For a split second, she wasn't sure what bothered her most.

Those tears, or the chief's hand.

Umber's left palm was cupped to the boy's rigid shoulder, trapping Caleb in place as a chillingly adult thumb stroked across a portion of hidden collarbone before moving up the exposed flesh of that vulnerable, twelve-year-old neck.

The stunted swallow that clogged the boy's throat screamed *no*.

Everything else bellowed *inappropriate*—especially within Mira.

This would not happen again. Not on her watch.

She directed a murmur toward the woman behind her as she reached for the knob. "Ma'am, it would be better if you remained here."

Easing the door open, Mira stifled a curse as the English teacher ignored the suggestion and followed her into the room.

But at least the woman had hung back by the door.

Caleb met Mira's stare as she stepped closer to the desks.

The boy flinched.

Umber yanked his hand away and whirled around. "Who—"

"Special Agent Mira Ellis, NCIS." She reached inside her suit jacket with her left hand to retrieve her credentials, calmly flipping the leather bifold open as it surfaced. "I dropped by the office a few minutes ago to vet an item on a security clearance for a former student. Heard there was a sailor in here, so I came by to say *hey*."

She could feel the teacher stiffen behind her.

Unfortunately, her contradiction to the attaboy assumption that she'd let stand in the lounge was necessary. Not only would a Navy chief know damned well that special agents didn't vet routine military commendations and medals, she needed the man to remain calm. Because *this* Navy chief was also the child rapist she sought.

If the panic that had sparked in Umber's eyes upon hearing her title hadn't convinced her, the recognition and terror now wracking his victim did.

Not to mention the guilt.

Twelve years old or not, Caleb knew exactly who she was and why she was here—because he'd asked for her.

Mira closed her credentials, willing the terror, remorse and shame that were still pulsing through those huge brown orbs to ease as she pocketed the badge's bifold. If Umber swung back to the kid and realized that NCIS was on to him—

Too late.

The chief shoved his right hand into the tray of instruments on the desk. A split second later, Mira shoved hers inside her jacket, this time to grab the butt of the SIG Sauer P239 that was tucked into the shoulder holster within.

But by the time the persuasive end of her 10mm pistol had surfaced, Umber had wrenched Caleb's slight body around and squarely in front of his...and a gleaming, stainless-steel scalpel from that tray was now pressing into the side of the boy's throat, directly over his carotid.

A near-silent whimper escaped those trembling lips as she leveled the SIG's sights directly between the eyes of bastard above and behind them.

The chief responded by pressing the scalpel deeper.

A scarlet line of tiny droplets beaded up, connecting together as they coated the scalpel's razor edge, drawing another strangely subdued sob from the boy.

"Chief Umber, you don't want to do this."

Hell, *she* didn't want him to do this. For a number of reasons.

Not the least of which had to do with the fact that she was *not* a marksman. She was damned lucky to simply pass her weapons qualification every quarter—and she knew it.

Yes, she'd take the shot if she had to. But there was a very real chance that she might not hit that magic T-box between the chief's eyes, even from this distance.

Not cleanly enough to save the trembling boy who was still staring at her. Those huge damp eyes of his *begging* her to save him.

"Chief?"

The scalpel pressed deeper as the man scowled at her, causing the line of beads to double up and swell. "Lady, you don't know what I want."

Oh, but she did. She'd read that letter. She knew the exact level of filth that this cowardly piece of shit desired.

And now, that same stinking ball of dung was using the innocent child he'd been visiting all that filth upon for four goddamned years as his living shield.

Some hero.

But as much as Umber truly was a monster, he was also trained to use that zealously honed blade.

One slash in the right spot, and the boy would be dead within seconds.

With the level of panic that had to be closing in and suffocating any remaining logic in the chief's mind, Umber might even believe that without Caleb alive to testify at his court-martial, describing in detail what had been done to him and what he'd been forced to do, the extent of his depravity would remain hidden.

Or he might just slit the boy's throat out of revenge.

If there was any logic left in that twisted brain, Umber had to know that both his illustrious naval career and phony beard of a marriage were over.

Nor could she rule out the snap decision of suicide by agent.

Mira could hear the English teacher behind her, sobbing quietly as she tried to keep it together. She prayed the woman had the sense to remain silent—and inside the room. Hell, even approaching the door might tip the chief over the edge.

But the door swished open. The panic in Umber's gaze evaporated.

Deadly determination replaced it.

Shit.

Umber had made his choice. The proof came as the scalpel sliced deep, causing scarlet to spurt over the back edge of the blade and down the side of boy's throat.

She took the shot.

Relief and disbelief seared in as the chief's body fell away from Caleb, only to surge into shock as someone grabbed onto her shoulders and shook firmly.

What the hell was going on?

Who—

Mira came up swinging, her fists slamming into camouflaged fabric stretched over twice the depth of muscle that Umber had honed during his stint with the Marines.

Confusion pummeled through her brain, along with a surrounding rumble so heavy and persistent that it was vibrating through every bone in her body as she fell back against a metal seat.

The classroom disintegrated, leaving a cavernous steel belly in its place.

Airplane.

She wasn't back at the Creighton Middle School in DC; she was in the air, aboard the US Air Force C-17 Globemaster she'd caught at Joint Base Andrews.

And the brawny British SAS captain she'd chatted with off

and on for several hours before she'd apparently succumbed to exhaustion?

Well, he was looking at her as though he was afraid she might need to be committed. Medically. "Agent Ellis, it's me, Kipp Styles. Are you okay?"

"Yeah. Sorry." She shook her head as she attempted to purge the vestiges of her confrontation with Umber and that shot she'd taken, not to mention those stricken eyes that were once again haunting her brain.

It all still felt so damned real.

The knowledge that went with it made it that much worse. Carotid arteries ran barely an inch and a half below the surface of the skin of an adult neck. She didn't know how deep Caleb's left carotid ran, only that the ER doctor who'd stitched the boy's throat back together had said that mere millimeters deeper, and it would've been severed.

His official assessment? If she'd waited so much as a split second later to take that shot, Caleb McCabe would've followed Umber into death within five to fifteen.

The doc had probably phoned to pass that tidbit along because he'd thought it would help her deal with it all—and it had. Until the rest had come to pass.

The surfacing of the chief's burner phone and those foul videos and photos on it.

That damned bottle of oxycodone.

She sucked up the ache and the guilt that came hand in hand with *that* memory and nodded to the British captain. "Thanks for waking me. And, again, my sincere apologies. I didn't mean to strike you."

The man shook his head, his grin wide and forgiving. "Not a problem. I've had a few rotten dreams myself."

Dreams. Right.

Only that hadn't been a dream, had it? That had been a

memory. The same excruciating memory she'd been reliving for two weeks now.

Had she really believed it would fade simply because she was working a new case?

"Anyway, you asked me to let you know when we hit the coast. According to the crew chief, we crossed over it a few minutes ago. We should be landing shortly."

"Thank you, Captain. I appreciate the update."

Mira watched the SAS officer's trek across the belly of the bird. Once there, he sank into the flip-down seat beside the plane's only other passenger. She had no idea the nature of the business that Captain Styles and Major Hunt had had at the Pentagon, much less why it had been so important for an SAS squadron commander and his second in command to confer on site and in uniform, but she was grateful.

Those two Brits were the reason this American C-17 had filed a flight plan to RAF Lakenheath.

While this hop wouldn't get her as far as she needed to go, the Globemaster had been slotted to take off from Andrews less than two hours after her conversation with Jerry, making it well worth the detour she'd made to the Field Office to grab her go-bag. With the Royal Air Force base located firmly on British soil and leased out to the US Air Force, she'd been able to request a second, shorter hop from Lakenheath and over the channel to Orange-Caritat in France minutes before the C-17 had gone wheels up.

Heck, the next pilot could drop her off at the French airbase of his choice. She could always rent a car to Marcoule.

As for Jerry, her once-again, if temporary partner was back in their country's capital, dogging the case from that end and looking into the story of Frank's grandfather and the supposed break-in at the man's house that led to his hospitalization. She also knew from working across a pair of abutted desks for nearly three years in San Diego that Jerry would be taking the time to poke into Sam Riyad as well.

Because something was off with *that* man.

Not even those FCI credentials could explain, much less excuse Riyad's behavior in that autopsy suite. She still had no idea who'd told the agent about the postmortem, much less which link in NCIS' lengthy chain of command had ordered him to the condo in the first place. But if it had been Ramsey, surely he'd have mentioned it?

Speaking of which—

Mira fished her phone from her trouser pocket. She cleared the low power warning, then tapped into her text messages. The C-17 had been in the air for over seven hours and there were still none from her boss. No missed calls, either. Surely the voicemail she'd left Ramsey about Corrigan's dislocated knuckles, along with the other evidence that suggested the JAG had been murdered by a pro, would've rated a response? Not to mention the information she'd added regarding where she was currently headed—and why.

Then again, Ramsey was her boss. And the paperwork for her to make this flight had been approved—so he was definitely up to date. Unfortunately, he was also mired so deep in his own current tasking that he hadn't even had time to send a *got it* text.

What the devil was Ramsey dealing with?

Hopefully, they'd connect before she reached Marcoule.

Mira rubbed the vestiges of her nap from her eyes. Noting the local time at the top of her phone's screen, she pushed up the left sleeve of her suit to expose the watch her brother had gifted for her birthday years ago, then spun the hands around until they settled on 0037. If her hop was waiting for her as requested, she just might be able to catch another nap—in a bed, this time—and still be able to greet Frank Nasser at Marcoule's main security gate when he arrived in the morning to accomplish...whatever the man had been sent to France to accomplish.

Her watch reset, Mira tapped into the first of the texts she'd missed from Jerry.

She could feel the C-17 dropping in altitude as she scanned what little evidence the pathologist had been able to glean during the remainder of the autopsy. Other than the fact that the stomach contents matched a meal of egg foo young that Corrigan had consumed over lunch on the nineteenth of March, there wasn't much. With any luck, the toxicology report would offer more when it came back. Though Mira doubted it.

From the scowling emoji he'd added, so did Jerry.

Tapping into the detective's subsequent missed text, however, did reveal—and suggest—more than the internal portion of the JAG's autopsy had.

The document her old NCIS mentor had tracked down and attached was a police report from Nashua, New Hampshire. Frank hadn't been lying about the reason for his request for emergency leave. The write-up Jerry had forwarded detailed the break-in to Abdul Nasser's modest brick home on the eleventh of March. According to the report, Abdul heard a noise in the middle of the night and had come downstairs to check it out with a shotgun in his hands. There, Abdul had discovered two men upending his living room. He'd raised the weapon and ordered them to stop.

Instead, the two advanced.

Within seconds, Abdul's shotgun was in the hands of the closer perpetrator, who then proceeded to beat the shit out of the old guy with the stock of his own gun.

It had taken three days of treatment in Nashua's intensive care for Abdul to regain consciousness. By then, the thugs who'd assaulted him were long gone. Though Mira doubted that Abdul regaining his wits sooner would've changed anything.

Both assailants had been wearing balaclavas.

And from the way the entire house had been systematically searched, before and after the old man's beatdown? The assessment in the police report was clear.

Pros.

Jerry's final text contained the most intriguing information yet. Jerry had called Nashua around the time that Mira had nodded off on the plane and had spoken at length with Abdul Nasser. The old man had been so very proud that Frank had sought and received a commission in Abdul's adopted country's Navy. He'd been prouder still when his grandson had stayed in, despite what had happened at nuke school, and had gone on to complete his surface warfare qualifications so he could pin on those gold water wings. But with Frank thoroughly disillusioned by the time he'd resigned that same commission—to the point that he'd talked of tossing his warfare insignia into the trash— Abdul had requested it.

Abdul had planned to return the insignia once his grandson had had a chance to cool off and reflect on the years of service he'd given to their country.

Alas, upon returning home from the hospital, Abdul realized that the water wings had been stolen along with his deceased wife's jewelry.

She and Jerry were in agreement. Yes, Frank's history with the JAG made him the perfect patsy. And learning that his insignia had been stolen should've gone a long way to exonerating him. But with the man now working for Ishida and in the middle of a hush-hush visit to the nuclear site at Marcoule, they were forced to wonder.

Was there more to Frank's part in this than a savvy setup?

That wine bottle said *yes*. Corrigan might've been tortured by someone well versed in man's most heinous art. But the insertion of that bottle had been personal.

So how did it all connect?

Locating Frank and talking to him was the first step to figuring it out. That conversation would involve detailed answers, too—his. Because if Frank clammed up, in light of where he worked, not to mention his current location, his civilian nuclear career would end up just like his military one had. Dead in the water.

Mira retrieved the ends of her seatbelt and clicked the metal together as the Globemaster commenced its final shedding of altitude.

Within minutes the plane's wheels had embraced British cement.

Several more, and the C-17 had taxied off the runway and come to a halt. The engines cut out as the rear ramp began to lower.

Mira released her safety belt. Hefting her leather suit bag and smaller canvas duffle, she followed the two SAS officers out the aft end of the plane.

There wasn't a star in sight as they reached the edge of the tarmac. The moon was AWOL too, smothered out by a thick blanket of clouds that were threatening to open up and release a heavier dose of the steady drizzle that had soaked the waiting British—not American—airman who appeared to be her welcoming committee.

No, the camouflaged sergeant wasn't waiting for her.

At least, not completely.

The man's ebony hand came up, silently requesting that she mark time where she stood, while he and the two other passengers from their flight moved far enough away to conduct a private, but palpably intense conversation.

Bemused, Mira watched as the SAS squadron commander retrieved his phone and initiated not one, but two equally subdued, yet tense calls. Major Hunt hung up from the second, clipped a nod to his second in command and immediately took off down the tarmac with the sergeant in tow, leaving Captain Styles to return to her.

"What's wrong?"

Because something had gone to shit.

It was in that slow swipe of fingertips making a pass across the captain's forehead, just shy of the bottom of his sand beret. "Your intent in flying to Lakenheath was to catch a second flight to Marcoule so that you could question one of your country's former naval officers about a murder—a Frank Nasser?"

Oh, boy. While she and Styles had chatted at length during the first half of the flight, she hadn't shared that information with the captain. Not a single piece. Even as she wondered who'd relayed it to him now, and why, she knew the *why* was the more significant question. Almost as significant as the tense of the verb Styles had used.

Was.

"Yes, that was my intention, Captain. And I'm asking again. What's wrong?"

"Nasser's not in Marcoule."

She held her tongue. Because there was more to come.

It was in that second, slow swipe.

She could feel the SAS officer weighing what he wanted to tell her against what he'd been ordered to relay. "Until a few days ago, Nasser was in Cherbourg. He's now aboard a ship in the Atlantic, one soon to turn south to travel down the northwest coast of Africa before swinging up and around the capes and the bulk of Southeast Asia to head for Japan."

Cherbourg? And that particular voyage?

She released the strap on her duffle to cross her fingers. Hard. "Which ship?"

"The *Pacific Tern*."

The duffle slid off her shoulder and smacked onto the tarmac.

Styles nodded. "The *Tern* was originally scheduled to depart Cherbourg this coming Saturday, but Greenpeace had arranged a protest. Since an unusually large number of ships were to be present in the flotilla, Clearwater Transport felt it prudent for the *Tern* and her escort ship, the *Kittiwake*, to get underway as soon as they were able."

Clearwater Transport?

There was a word missing in there. A rather heavy-hitting descriptor. The full name of the company that owned and operated the *Pacific Tern* and her purpose-built sister ship, the *Pacific Kittiwake*, was Clearwater *Nuclear* Transport.

An important fleshing out, since that single word was the reason she and Captain Styles were having this conversation.

And why Major Hunt had made those calls.

Clearwater and its dedicated class of nuclear transport ships were also hardlined to the UK. And, given what must've been relayed to the company—and higher—Clearwater wouldn't care that Frank was an American citizen currently employed by Japan. The company wanted Frank's suddenly very questionable ass off that ship and away from the radioactive cargo the *Tern* was undoubtedly carrying.

"You're taking a helicopter out to get him, aren't you?"

The wide grin Styles had given her after she'd woken up on the C-17 returned. "Would you like to accompany us, Agent Ellis?"

Now there was a no-brainer.

"When do we leave?"

The grin deepened as the captain reached down to hook her duffle off the tarmac and sling it over his camouflaged shoulder. She had her answer.

Now.

SHE NO LONGER KNEW WHERE she was.

Mira turned to peer out of the oversized ballistic window embedded within the helicopter door to the left of her seat.

Heck, she couldn't even be certain about the time. It was still dark out, but the battery on her phone had given up the ghost in the middle of the unsent, heads-up text she'd been typing to Jerry as she and the SAS captain had followed the same path down the tarmac that his commander had taken. As for the watch her brother had gifted her? As lovely as its minimalistic face and luddite hands were, it was as old-fashioned as Nate's taste in women—and just as emblematic. It didn't light up.

Mira did know that the thundering British Wildcat she and Captain Styles had climbed aboard had already stopped to refuel at Bordeaux-Mérignac in France, then again in Lisbon, Portugal, putting their total time in the air at well over four hours.

But that was it. Whether there would be a third pit stop on this leg of their rotary-winged journey remained to be seen.

Since they were flying over open ocean now, that wasn't likely.

As for the purpose of their impromptu, joint mission?

From what Styles had been able to relay before the helicopter's blades had spun up enough to make lengthy conversation impossible, Clearwater would be happy to welcome her aboard the *Tern*—so long as she took Frank Nasser with her when she left. Though she still had no idea who'd informed the company's upper tier of Corrigan's murder, she did know that by the time they'd learned of it, she and that C-17 had departed Andrews.

Discovering that two SAS officers well-versed in executing dicey missions were aboard her flight had been a boon, at least to Clearwater. They'd simply asked that the men be re-tasked to accompany her.

Since the *Tern* was a British ship, Styles and Hunt would be responsible for actually ejecting Frank from the vessel—by force, if necessary.

Mira was in agreement with the overall tasking though, and its timing.

Better to remove Frank now, days into what was scheduled to be an eight-to-nine-week voyage to Japan due to the *Tern's* and the *Kittiwake's* slow speeds, than to wait. Why give the situation time to fester?

Especially since the longer this murder investigation dragged out, the less certain Mira was becoming about Frank and his oblique involvement in it. There were too many damned coincidences. And they were multiplying.

That said, everything appeared normal with the *Tern's* and the *Kittiwake's* current voyage to deliver a shipment of reprocessed plutonium and uranium in the form of mixed-oxide fuel assemblies bound from Cherbourg to Ishida's nuclear reactor in Japan.

According to Captain Styles, ship-to-shore communications were online as well. In fact, one of those calls that Major Hunt had made on the tarmac at Lakenheath had connected with the satellite phone of the senior nuclear constable stationed aboard the vessel actually carrying the MOX assemblies—the *Tern*.

Since the constable was in charge of the two dozen men responsible for the vessel's security, he ought to know if something was amiss with Frank—or anyone else currently aboard the ship.

Styles had assured her that the entire class of purpose-built container ships was unmatched in safety too. Not only had the engines, propellors and rudders been doubled up during their construction phases, the *Tern's* and the *Kittiwake's* automatic voyage monitoring systems had been transmitting each ship's exact position, speed and heading to the report center in the UK since they'd left Cherbourg. Styles had gone on to extol the fact that the massive casks that had been designed to contain those MOX nuclear assemblies were bolted to the ship's structure.

Finally, there was the Royal Navy submarine that would've been tasked with shadowing the sister ships from Cherbourg all the way to Japan.

Despite those measures, Mira was on edge—because those two SAS officers taking up two of the three passenger seats across the compact belly of this rumbling Wildcat were on edge. While she hadn't been around many soldiers in the SAS, she had dealt with her fair share of US Navy SEALs and Army Special Forces. These two British special forces soldiers were of the same ilk. And yet, both those SAS jaws were clenched.

The cause? Again, she had no clue.

Shortly after they'd taken off following their refueling at Lisbon, an intense discussion had sparked between the SAS officers and the Wildcat's pilot and co-pilot over the comm link all four men shared. Following that discussion, those SAS jaws had been locked down. Unfortunately, while she had been handed a pair of rabbit ears at Lakenheath to dull the constant thumping of the helicopter's blades, she was not privy to the military party-line inside this bird.

Nor could she whine about the exclusion.

This wasn't her Navy.

Mira turned to check the window to her left. The sky was just beginning to lighten. She could make out the barest hint of red glistening along the distant, curved rim of the Atlantic Ocean. She stared at the faint glow, allowing the rhythm of those powerful blades above to combine with two solid weeks of inadequate shut-eye to seduce her down to the edge of sleep.

She hovered there, debating the wisdom of sinking all the

way into the abyss when something—someone—tapped her left knee.

Styles.

The man leaned back into his seat and pointed toward the cockpit behind her.

Following the captain's silent directive, she twisted around to her right to look through the cutout between the pilot and copilot.

There, in the distant dark. The faint glow of running lights.

The *Tern*?

Styles nodded as she twisted back. Three raised fingers followed.

Definitely the *Tern* then. And in three minutes, they'd be touching down on one of those massive, cargo-hold hatch covers on her deck.

Mira twisted once more, this time catching the hint of a second set of running lights well ahead of the *Pacific Tern* and offset from the *Tern's* port side. Since nuclear transport ships traveled in pairs, another set of lights that close would have to belong to the *Pacific Kittiwake*.

Except...there was a third vessel visible now.

Since this one didn't have any lights configured, the vessel was more shadow than solid form. The unexpected vessel was also significantly smaller than the *Tern* and directly abeam of the MOX transport ship's starboard side.

Dangerously so.

Had there been a collision?

Adrenaline folded into dread as the thundering helicopter closed in on the *Tern*. They were just off her stern now. The white paint of the container ship's superstructure stood out against the dark blue of her lower hull and the inkier hue of the ocean below. But that smaller vessel abeam of the *Tern* wasn't one vessel, but two.

Both smaller ships also appeared to be painted mostly white. No, not ships; those were offshore fishing boats.

Neither boat appeared to have suffered a collision with the *Tern*. In fact, both were definitely, deliberately, steaming alongside her.

Pirates?

Mira swung back to the center of the helo to find herself the odd one out of yet another terse, four-way tense discussion over the helicopter's comm headsets.

She could feel the Wildcat climbing in altitude as they swooped up over the top of the *Tern*'s superstructure to get an unobstructed view of the transport ship's main weather deck and the offshore fishing boats, as well.

Styles shouted and pointed forward.

Mira swung around. This part of the world's still slumbering sky filled the cockpit's windows. And in the middle—the telling trail of ragged, fiery smoke.

Missile.

It was headed straight for them.

A split second later, the helicopter banked sharply to the left —and the world exploded.

5

The world was on fire.

No, *she* was fire. Her legs, her abdomen. The left side of her chest. The lower half of that same arm. Nearly every part of her body hurt. Even her neck was killing her.

A moan escaped as Mira tried to move...and failed.

Her eyes refused to open. And her *head*.

What the hell had happened?

The past twenty-four hours pulsed in. Frank Nasser. The *Pacific Tern*. Those twin, offshore fishing boats. That ragged trail of smoke—and the surface-to-air missile that had created it. The helicopter's evasive maneuver. The crash.

The Wildcat must've slammed into the deck.

Oh, God—the pilots, the SAS officers; she couldn't hear them. Just the hiss and spit of dying electronics, and the distant sound of waves pummeling into the hull of the ship, causing it— and her stomach—to pitch and yaw. Ruthlessly.

"*C-captain S-styles?*"

Nothing.

She sucked in an agonizing breath and tried again. "*Major Hunt?*"

Her only answer was a bitter, March-Atlantic wind so strong the salt riding it stung at her face.

Confused, Mira forced her eyes open. She was blind on her left. What remaining night vision her right eye offered up was blurred almost to the point of uselessness.

And the world. Either it was spinning, or she was.

She tried to focus and nearly threw up. Probing her fingers along her forehead, the tips met the distinctive squish of open flesh at her left temple.

Head wound.

That would account for the throbbing in her skull. Her shitty vision. Her initial, sluggish thoughts. She could feel her concentration returning, though.

Strengthening.

Thank God.

Her right eye was cooperating now—mostly. Though despite her revived night vision, all she could make out was that shadowy sky. Where the hell were the men?

She couldn't even find the aft section of the helo.

It took a moment to realize why. For her battered brain to accept what she *wasn't* seeing. Denial spun into desperation as she forced her head to the right, squinting at the glinting shreds of steel and sparking electronics—and the shadowy, white rail of the ship beyond. It was true. The SAS officers had been seated across from her up in the sky. They were missing now—because the entire back half of the helo was *missing.*

That missile must've ripped the Wildcat in two.

Except...that didn't make sense.

There were no open flames, no stench of burning rubber or leaking fuel piggybacking on the salt in that biting wind. Nor could her right eye make out scorch marks on those massive shreds of metal where the Wildcat had split. Had the helo slammed into the top of the *Tern*'s superstructure, then? Its skin cracking open at the edge of the uppermost deck like an egg on the lip of an iron skillet?

Was that why she was lying on her back and staring *up* at the sky while she was still strapped in her seat?

The pilots. She'd been back-to-back with the men in the air; that meant they were beneath her now, facing the *Tern*'s viciously rolling and pitching deck. But she couldn't hear either man. Nor could she see or hear anyone else.

Someone had fired that missile. So where was he? Still on one of those boats with the rest of those bastards? Was that why no one had moved in to cull through the wreckage and slit any surviving throats?

Because that should have happened. Those fishing boats hadn't ferried a ragtag bunch of pirates from their den on the northwest coast of Africa. That patient lying in wait before the firing of the surface-to-air missile proved it.

Terrorists. They must not have boarded the ship yet. That meant there was time to turn this catastrophe around.

Mira forced her head to the right, then left, assessing the situation as best as she could. There was a massive wall of white to her left, mere feet from the Wildcat's wreckage. Add a plus to her paltry column. If those bastards had made it aboard the *Tern*, she must be hidden from them. That, or they'd assumed everyone in the bird was dead. Lord knew, she felt like it. Every muscle and bone in her body hurt.

It didn't matter. *She* didn't matter. Only the ship did.

She had to get out of here; find Styles and his commander. *Protect the ship.*

That cargo.

Her right hand found the latch to her safety harness. She got it unclipped, but couldn't move her left forearm. Using her right, she twisted out of the harness and then the seat—only to have that bitch called gravity kick her again as she fell through the bird's missing door. A strangled scream escaped as she smashed onto the shifting deck.

Christ. Her entire left arm was now as useless as her blind eye.

Pushing up with her right, she came face to face with the unmistakable glassy stare and broken neck of the copilot. The pilot was dead too, impaled by what appeared to be an iron spindle from the ship's upper railing. They *had* slammed into the *Tern*'s superstructure, then, as they'd careened down.

Was the tail section still up there?

She prayed so. Because the SAS officers just might be alive.

Mind over body, damn it. It was the only way to get through this.

Move!

Her good hand connected with the cold skin of the ship's superstructure. She managed to claw her way to her knees. But her body wrenched back control, smacking her down to the deck. She nearly passed out from the agony in her ribs as she vomited up the acid churning through her stomach along with the remnants of the coffee Styles had handed her in Lisbon, until there was nothing left but froth.

What the hell?

Yes, the deck was rocking and rolling beneath her palms like a rollercoaster ride straight through the gates of Hell, but she never got seasick, no matter how violent the ocean became.

It must be the head wound.

Keep driving on. There was no other option. A few years ago, she'd read the after-action review from a SEAL mission in Iraq. The senior chief who'd led it had been ambushed in a compound in the Anbar Province by terrorists. He'd taken twenty-seven rounds to his body, plus shrapnel from a grenade

—and he'd still managed to take out the terrorists and clear the compound. And then he'd *walked out* under his own power and climbed aboard the helicopter that had been waiting to exfiltrate him and his men.

If the senior chief could do that, she could sure as hell stand and drag her sorry ass up to the top of this damned vessel and find Styles and Hunt.

She'd claw her way there if she had to.

Nausea battered in again as her hand found the ship's skin once more.

She managed to wobble all the way up to the soles of her dress shoes. She gave thanks for the layer of rubber at the base. It gave her a bit more traction against the brutal motion of the ship.

Her head-swirling scan of the forward section of the main weather deck revealed—nothing. No tail from the helo and not a sole member of the container vessel's crew. Definitely no terrorists. She couldn't even locate one of those two dozen elite nuclear security constables that Styles had touted.

Where the hell was everyone?

Inside the ship? Fighting for control of the vessel—and its radioactive cargo?

Fuck.

The helo's comms were probably as dead as the bird beside her. Nor could she risk stumbling around in the open to verify that. But if she could get to the bridge, she might be able to hit a single emergency switch and shoot off an automated SOS.

Though, God willing, the call for help had already been sent.

Except if it had, wouldn't the Royal Navy submarine that should be trailing the transport ships have moved in to investigate by now?

The sub, too, appeared to be missing.

A dogged scan of the superstructure brought the shadowy

seams of a watertight door into focus just past the nose of the helo. That door led to tenuous safety—or certain death. Either way, she was headed though it.

And then, *up.*

It wasn't until Mira took her first steps that she realized her legs really were on fire, or had been. The fabric from the lower half of her right trouser leg had been singed away, leaving blistered flesh behind. And the left? While still technically there, a good portion of the navy blue had melted into the skin beneath. She could feel it tugging and tearing free along with layers of weeping skin as she reached the watertight door that led into the ship. When her fingers closed around the handle before she'd even *thought* to ensure that her SIG Sauer was still in its holster, she knew she was more rattled than she'd feared. Hell, she hadn't even searched the cockpit and pilots for additional weapons and ammunition.

She now knew why. The excruciating thunder in her head? Her sketchy balance and lop-sided vision? Not to mention the nausea that wouldn't leave, despite that savage purge of her stomach. They all added up to one thing.

Concussion.

But at least she'd drawn her weapon, and both she and her 10mm pistol had made it through the door and into the interior of the ship. Though the well-lit state of the latter gave her pause. The sun hadn't risen yet.

Shouldn't the ship still be dimmed inside?

Either way, she was grateful for the light. The lines and angles of the bulkheads within the passageway were still wavering, but she could see well enough to spot several doors to her right. The farthest one appeared to be cracked open.

She inched her way along the passageway, cursing the waves that were pounding the hull of the ship. Her battered human body and uneven gait were lurching more than enough on their own. Her final approach was neither silent nor stealthy.

Worse, as she reached her goal—that slightly cracked door —she lost her balance, whacking her good shoulder into the side of the passageway.

As the door swung open with the motion of the ship, she realized her thud hadn't mattered. She'd also found most of the constables and crew. There were close to three dozen men and several women in the compartment.

Every last one was dead.

Some of the bodies had fallen onto the shifting deck. Others were still splayed over chairs and the meeting tables that had been arranged in a U. Squinting brought the face of the closest man into focus long enough for Mira to see what appeared to be a stain of neon green beneath the man's nostrils and dripping down from the lower end of his mouth.

Had the crew been gassed?

Doubtful. While agonizing, the shallow breaths she'd been managing since she'd regained consciousness out on the weather deck appeared to be unaffected. Besides, if these men and women had been poisoned via a toxin in the air, it was likely too late for her. It was definitely too late for the ship.

The *Tern* had already been taken.

But where were the terrorists who'd taken it?

She couldn't hear anyone moving through this passageway or the one above. Just that steady rhythmic creaking of sheet metal, piping and other manmade materials.

Back out on the *Tern*'s weather deck, all four of the massive cargo-hold hatch covers had appeared to be in place. But those transport casks beneath the covers?

The ones that contained Ishida's radioactive mixed-oxide assemblies?

According to Styles, those casks weighed in excess of a

hundred tons apiece. That was a lot of weight to sling around. Impossible for human hands and arms.

It would take a crane.

Were the terrorists holed up on the bridge then? Threatening the captain and his surviving crew while they waited for a larger vessel to arrive on station? One displacing a hell of a lot more weight than those offshore fishing boats put together and sporting an onboard crane with the capacity to pluck the reinforced MOX transport monsters right out of the bowels of the ship? If so, where was that crane?

When was it due?

And how had the terrorists managed to contain news of the ship's takedown for as long as they had? Was the captain being held at gunpoint, forced into maintaining a series of *everything's fine* reports akin to the one his senior constable had given Major Hunt back at Lakenheath? Or had there been a hint of this fiasco already budding following the Wildcat's second pitstop at Lisbon? Had it surfaced during that terse conversation she hadn't been privy to on the helicopter's private comm link?

It didn't matter. Not to her.

Only her mission did: *pushing on—and up.*

Closing the door on the horror in the compartment and in her heart, she kept moving. She had to find a ladder. If the tail section of the helo had landed on top of the superstructure gently enough that Captain Styles and Major Hunt were alive, the men would be making their way down, most likely to the bridge too. Once all three of them linked up, they'd need to work out a plan to take back the ship.

Hell, those men were battle-tested SAS.

If they were alive, they already had a plan.

She was more than motivated to toss her sole working arm and hinky partial vision into the mix. But to do that, she'd have to locate a ladder.

There.

Success seared in, momentarily overtaking the agony in her left ribs as she stumbled drunkenly toward the bottom step. The ache returned with a vengeance as she climbed, then turned to confront three additional ladders. By the time she'd cleared the top of the highest one—and located the bridge on the *Tern*'s uppermost deck—the full-blown whimpering that escaped her lips was louder than her constant wheezing. But there was no one around to hear it.

It didn't make sense.

Nor did the lack of live bodies inside the bridge.

As for the deceased, she could make out seven here. Like the victims in the conference room below, these crewmen were splayed on the deck near her feet and slumped over the chart table, as well as the long monitoring console that bisected the length of the bridge. Unlike the victims below, these had been shot. Every blessed one.

And with an icy proficiency that put the placement of the round she'd sent into Chief Umber two weeks earlier to shame.

Pros.

But if those pros were missing from this compartment too, who the hell was driving the ship? Maintaining the *Tern*'s course and speed? Auto functions could only do so much, and only for so long. And they sure as hell couldn't report back to the UK via a give-and-take conversation that all was in the clear.

The reporting center. If she could access the ship's communications, she could make the call that would instantly convert that reporting center into Clearwater's emergency command and disaster center. And that would mobilize an armed team and get it to the ship.

Hopefully before that ocean-going crane arrived and the radioactive fuel in those MOX assemblies departed.

Spotting what appeared to be the *Tern*'s comm station amid

the shadows, she took a lurching step toward it, only to halt as something caught at the periphery of her sole functioning eye—on the outside of the ship.

Motion.

She was sixty, seventy feet above the waterline.

Instead of holstering her SIG, she raised the weapon as she inched closer to the window embedded within the weather door to her right. There was someone on the *Tern*'s starboard bridge wing. Make that, two someones.

And they appeared to be fighting.

SIG front and center, she crept down the working side of the bridge's central console as best she could, noting the active radar picture and a slew of other shipboard systems and status monitors that all appeared chillingly up to date and churning out an array of data regarding the vessel's current, captain-less voyage. As Mira passed the sightless gaze of a crewman hanging over a shorter console behind the main one, she spotted the blur of gold-striped epaulets belonging to a much more senior uniform through the window in the weather door.

If that was the captain, he was alive.

But not for long. The back of the man's torso was bent over the top of the bridge wing's safety rail—with a dark-haired male in jeans and a long-sleeved, chambray shirt crowding his front, physically encouraging him to make the rest of what would likely be a deadly drop into writhing open ocean, unless he was able to get his flailing body to assume the abandon-ship position before it broke the surface of the water. Because at this height? The waves below would be as soft as a slab of concrete.

And that other male, the one in chambray?

Frank Nasser.

A moment ago, she might've wondered if Frank possessed the skills and stomach to torture Commander Corrigan back in that DC condo. But here? Now? Not only had *Limpy* hardened his spine, he'd made the physical and emotional jump to cold-blooded murder—willingly. Frank's fingers were wrapped around the captain's throat. From the purple tint flooding the balding man's face and scalp, her old classmate had no intention of letting go.

Her left arm useless, Mira juggled her SIG in her right as she pulled the weather door in far enough to stumble through the opening. Weapon back in hand and sighted in, she stepped up beside the men.

"Frank!"

His face jerked toward her, those familiar brown eyes and darker lashes of his blown wide with shock. "*Mira*? How the hell—"

"Let him go. Now. Or I'll shoot."

"I *can't*."

"Goddamn it, Frank. I'm NCIS. I put a round though some shithole's skull two weeks ago; don't force me to do it again. Because I will." Whether she'd be able to make this shot with one haphazard eye and an admittedly jittery grip remained to be seen.

She lurched closer to better guarantee her preferred outcome.

Her new proximity and determination must've convinced the man. Frank scowled as he released his hands from the captain's neck, then shoved him clear of the safety rail.

There were four lines of gold braid stitched onto both those epaulets. Definitely the captain. No name tag, though, and now wasn't the time for social niceties.

She tipped her head in the direction of the weather door.

The older man moved toward the handle, but instead of opening the door and retreating onto the bridge, he remained outside, watching them.

Why?

Didn't he have an emergency call to make? Or had he already managed to trip a hidden alarm? For that matter, why the hell didn't the guy appear at least mildly livid that his ship had been boarded? That those fuel assemblies he'd been tasked with protecting and transporting from Cherbourg to Japan— while still currently cradled safely within the *Tern*'s cargo hold —were very much at risk of being stolen?

"Fuck." *Frank*.

She leveled the full, if wavering power of her right eye on the former US Navy nuke she was about to arrest for the attempted theft of said nuclear material, not to mention treason. Though the captain's demeanor was giving her considerable concern, at this precise moment her old classmate was the more dangerous of the two.

Frank shook his head, the fury he'd vented toward the man beside that door tamped down, at least for now. Bemusement had replaced it. "You were on that helo."

Well, she sure as hell hadn't swum here.

Nor was she in the mood for twenty questions. Not until those murderous, non-limpy hands of his were securely cuffed —and *she* was initiating the queries.

Unfortunately, she had one working arm, and it was currently aiming her SIG. Worse, she'd just realized that the weight she should be feeling from the set of handcuffs she kept looped over her trouser belt was missing, because the cuffs were missing. They must've gotten caught on her safety harness as she'd fallen out of the Wildcat.

What now?

Shit, her brain really had taken a beating—her wallet: she kept a spare zip cuff within. And she could feel the weight of *that* wedged in her left rear pocket.

She was about to ask the captain to retrieve her wallet for her, then the cuff, when she caught a flash of bright white light as it bounced off the port side of the closer of the fishing boats maneuvering off the *Tern*'s starboard beam.

No. Not a flash—a glow. A round, very steady glow. It was shining out from *inside* the skin of the *Tern*...and below the weather deck.

There were no portholes that low.

Even if the cargo hold was lit up like the deck of a Saudi prince's party boat the moment it crossed into international waters, there should be no giant, round spotlight shining out into the world. Nor was it even possible.

Not unless—

Oh, *Jesus*. The bastards who'd shot down the Wildcat and had taken this ship? They didn't need a larger vessel with a crane to come alongside and unload her cargo.

Those mixed-oxide fuel assemblies bound for Ishida?

They'd already stolen them.

The bastards had managed to cut a hole through the *Tern*'s reinforced, double hull. They had to have used an industrial plasma torch. It was the only thing powerful enough to cut through the steel skin of the ship and able to do it quickly.

And if they could figure out how to rig one of those while hanging off the side of a vessel that was not only rocking and rolling through the night but also getting battered by some of the ugliest waves on the planet? Whoever had accomplished that could damned sure find someone brilliant enough to convert the plutonium locked inside the ceramic pellets in those fuel assemblies back into the core of a nuclear bomb.

And one of those brilliant folks who just happened to know how to undertake that conversion? He was standing a mere two feet away from her.

Frank Nasser.

From the mix of shame and resignation that flashed into those dark eyes of his, he knew she'd figured it out.

"Christ, Frank. How *could* you?"

The shame deepened.

She ignored it. "Captain? There's a wallet in my right rear pocket. Inside that, a flex cuff. Would you get the cuff for me?"

She didn't have to explain the why of her request; the dead weight of her left arm had done it for her. She heard the man move forward. But instead of feeling the wallet slide from her pocket, the captain's palms slammed into her upper back, sending her entire body flying into Frank's. Like some twisted game of hot potato, Frank spun her around and sent her flying again, this time into the ship's safety rail.

Agony seared in as her already cracked ribs struck metal, dumping what little air she'd been hoarding from her lungs and blinding her with pain as well. She was dimly aware of one of the men reaching around to her chest to jerk at something —hard.

The emergency lanyard.

Until that moment, she hadn't realized that she was still wearing the inflatable life preserver Styles had passed her with those rabbit ears back at Lakenheath.

The yoked balloon inside blew up over her shoulders and around the back of her neck. A split second later, she was being knocked into the rail again.

This time she went flying over the top.

Sweet Jesus!

She could hear the wind shrieking against her ears as the momentum sent her screaming down past that sixty, seventy odd feet of the *Tern*'s superstructure and freeboard. For some reason, her seven-year-old training from OCS on how to abandon ship instinctively locked in. She tucked in her chin as best as she could and pulled her right arm across her chest to secure her left as she simultaneously clamped one straightened leg over the other.

She needn't have bothered with the latter.

From the agony shearing through her lower right leg, at least one of the bones within had snapped as she breached the surface of the water.

She fought the spike of pain, the freezing, furious waves and her own increasingly useless body as she tried to suck in enough oxygen to re-inflate the left lung that had been knocked offline when she'd hit the ship's rail.

That didn't work either.

This was it, then. She'd survived a helicopter crash that she was now all but certain had killed Captain Styles and Major Hunt along with both pilots, only to drown like a blind, battered rat, alone in the middle of her least favorite ocean.

If she was lucky, she'd freeze first.

Surely, the less painful way to go.

The cold had already made her right arm as deadened as her left. With one barely functioning lung, there was nothing to do but wait for the inevitable.

Even if someone aboard one of those boats had seen her death dive, no one would want to save her. Besides, she couldn't hear the *Tern*'s engines anymore. She'd been officially abandoned to Poseidon's whims—and that writhing, trident-wielding bastard was about as forgiving as that stolid bitch, gravity.

Dizziness crashed in with the next wave.

Regret came with it.

Jerry.

She wished there was some way to leave her old mentor a message—about the case, and about the two of them and what was mere minutes from happening. Yeah, Bill Ramsey and her brother loved her. There were other friends who'd miss her, too.

But Jerry?

He was going to carry the weight of this for the rest of his days. All she could do now was pray he'd be able to push through his guilt and his grief long enough to use that tenacious brain of his to solve this puzzle in time to locate those stolen radioactive assemblies before Frank could complete the conversion. If not, thousands upon thousands of innocent people would be dying—and soon.

Just like her.

6

S he could see the light.

That's when she knew she was dead.

She should probably care, but she didn't. Because the pain was gone. She welcomed the numbing lethargy that had replaced it.

But the rest...it was all so confusing.

Even if she'd wanted to walk toward that light, she couldn't. She couldn't move at all. And the light itself? She'd never died before, but she'd swear it was all wrong.

It was too white. Too bright. Too harsh.

And what was up with her throat?

There was something jammed all the way down it. Whatever it was, shouldn't she be unable to breathe with her windpipe blocked?

But she was breathing.

She could hear the air pulling in, then pushing out, over and over again, along with the muted sound of something that mimicked the rhythm of a beating heart.

And...voices?

There seemed to be several, both male and female. Offering

up incomprehensible murmurs that she couldn't quite grasp, but they were there.

Maybe this was what the afterlife was really like. After all, the warm, gentle abyss that kept beckoning to her had come with a light.

But the light was blinding now, and way too close.

She closed her mind against it.

And drifted back into the comfort of the dark.

7

"Agent Ellis? Mira? Can you hear me?"

That disembodied voice. The deep one with a crushed-velvet lilt. She'd heard it before, more than once, mixed in with those other murmurs.

Not only had the voice returned, but the light had come back with it. Blinding like it had before, and still far too close.

But it was quick this time. Flashing in and out of one eye a few times, then the other.

The soothing dark followed.

"Agent Ellis, this is Colonel Hartwig speaking. You're at Walter Reed in the ICU, and I'm your physician. If you can hear me, please open those beautiful blue eyes of yours."

He'd asked that before, and just like that. She'd even managed to fulfill the request once or twice, but she'd been unable to keep them open.

She redoubled her efforts and felt her lashes flutter, then lift. Success!

Not only had her eyes opened, they stayed that way. Focused. Both of them.

She could see the doctor's eyes too, the inky spikes of his lashes. They were close, and as dark as his voice.

"Outstanding." A warm smile curved the man's lips as he backed up a bit, pocketing what appeared to be a penlight. "Welcome back to the world, Agent Ellis. Again. You've been fading in and out for a while, but I think you're ready to stay with us now."

He was right. The first few times she'd woken, she'd been more out of it than in, and so overwhelmingly confused. But this time felt different.

She felt different.

She felt...alive.

How was that even possible? Hadn't she been destined to become fish food?

She opened her mouth to ask, but couldn't. Panic set in as she realized why. There was something in her throat. With that realization came the sensation of needing to gag and choke. She moved her head from side to side, letting her frantic stare beg for her.

Get it out—please!

"Just a moment. Close your eyes, Agent, and try to relax while I take care of that pesky tube for you. It'll be easier."

Desperate to regain control over the rhythm of her own breathing, she forced herself to comply.

She felt the tube sliding free and coughed.

Her ribs. They were tender, with an odd, almost pinched sensation pricking in. But the excruciating pain was gone.

Thank God.

The doctor reached out to tug a rolling, stainless-steel tray closer. He deposited the breathing tube on the tray and retrieved a plastic cup before turning back.

"There, now. Better, yes?"

Mira took several more breaths, deepening them and sighing with relief when she realized she could. "*Mmm.*"

Much.

"Excellent." Hartwig lifted the cup to her lips, dampening them with chips of ice from inside. "I'll be honest; you're lucky to be with us, Agent. I understand you took an Olympic-worthy dive off a very tall ship—following an earlier, rather hard landing in a helicopter."

Images flashed through her brain. Most of them corresponded to the doctor's claims. But there were other images too. A man. No...two men. One of them was an officer wearing some sort of uniform. But not a Navy one.

Why was that?

She waited patiently for the doctor to lift the cup of ice again and dampen her lips, then wobbled out a nod. "W-what... happened...to me?"

Why wasn't she fish food?

That warm grin reappeared. "You were rescued, of course. Five weeks ago. Plucked from the sea by the crew of a passing Spanish warship. Well, from what I understand, they weren't merely passing. Your ship had gained their attention for some reason and they changed course to investigate. One of their lookouts saw you fall from the ship and alerted his captain. How fortuitous was that? You'll have to speak to your boss about the rest of the particulars when he returns for his next visit, or even your partners, Detective Dahl and Agent Riyad. They've all taken to camping out here on and off, as well. But what I can tell you is that, along with the crew of that passing ship, the temperature of the water that day saved your life. It lowered yours enough to preserve your heart, lung and brain function. Frankly, that you're here with me now, as coherent as you are and speaking to me, is a miracle. It bodes very well for your recovery."

She didn't feel coherent. She felt fogged. Exhausted.

So very, *very*, exhausted.

She lifted her right hand to rub her temple, hoping that the stimulation would help keep her eyes open, only to notice the tangle of tubing and leads connected to it and the arm beneath. She lowered her hand and raised her left instead.

A cast?

She forced herself to focus on the doctor's nod, the words that followed. "In addition to your ribs, you suffered two other fractures. The scaphoid in your left wrist and the fibula in your right leg were realigned upon your arrival. Fortunately, your breaks were clean, and they're healing well. Both casts should come off this week. As for your other injuries—you underwent surgery to reattach your left retina. We'll have a specialist evaluate your vision soon. But that, too, appears to have healed well. Your left shoulder was dislocated and you suffered numerous bruises, as well as lacerations to your left temple and abdomen, possibly from flying debris during the crash. The edges of those wounds were fairly clean, and they too have healed nicely. As did your shoulder and the burns on your legs. Finally, and most importantly, you suffered a serious concussion; I assume during the crash. It was most likely exacerbated by your fall from the ship and those minutes in the ocean before the Spanish helicopter reached you."

Wow. That was...a lot.

Her reaction to the assessment must've made it to her face, because this nod was slower and even more serious. "I see you understand why my entire staff and I are thrilled to have you doing so well." He reached out to tap a switch on one of the many monitors beside her bed and adjusted another, then returned his attention to her.

"Now, Agent Ellis. Do you have any questions for me?"

A million. But she couldn't seem get them organized, much

less nudged out onto her tongue. She was completely wrung out, and growing strangely lightheaded.

From simply lying here, listening to him...and breathing on her own.

She tried to focus, to fight the fluttering in her lashes.

Her lashes won—the one question that had made it to the fore of her brain now pulsing through her entire body as she drifted into sleep.

What the hell had happened to that stolen radioactive fuel?

8

Two more weeks had passed and Mira still didn't have an answer to that profoundly pressing question. Equally frustrating, the one man who could even provide her with an update into the search for those missing mixed-oxide fuel assemblies was out of the country and stubbornly incommunicado.

Again.

Though Bill Ramsey had been by her bedside when she'd next woken in the ICU, and had been to visit several times since, he'd soon left. Ramsey had been gone for over a week this time. Like before, she had no idea where he'd gone, much less what was keeping him there. She could only hope her boss' efforts were leading him and every other agent in NCIS straight to Frank Nasser—and the *Tern*'s stolen cargo.

Until Ramsey surfaced, all she could do was follow Colonel Hartwig's list of mind-numbingly repetitive instructions to the letter.

The doc was right: getting her brain and body to where they'd been before that Wildcat had crashed was her ticket out of this hospital.

It was also the only way she'd make it back to the Field Office.

Unfortunately, though daunting, the physical therapy regime that Hartwig and his staff had set did not fill every minute of her day.

During Hartwig's rounds this morning, she'd not only told the doc the truth, she'd snarled it at him. She was going stir crazy.

She hadn't even had Jerry's visits to break up the last few days. A US senate staffer appeared to have murdered his on-again, off-again lover and Jerry had caught the high-profile case. The assignment made sense. Not only was Jerry the best detective out there, he could keep his mouth shut. And he absolutely detested the limelight. A win-win as far as his current publicity-battered, leak-prone department was concerned.

Nor did she begrudge Jerry the all-consuming absorption of a new investigation. It wasn't as though he was still working their last, joint one.

Sam Riyad's final act following his trio of silent, scowling visits to her ICU room after she'd woken had been to get Jerry and his civilian department officially kicked off the Corrigan murder. Though, granted, pulling the case from MPD had been prudent, since what had happened in the condo was clearly connected to the *Pacific Tern*'s takedown.

Imagine what Josiah Briggs and the *DC Dispatch* would do if someone within the Metropolitan Police passed *that* information to him.

And, yes, she'd appreciated Agent Riyad's clipped, confirming nod when she'd mentioned her suspicions regarding the timing of the Spanish warship's rescue during the FCI agent's final, morose visit to her ICU room. Though even without that terse nod of his, she'd known precisely how the *Tern* had garnered the *SPS Juan Carlos I*'s attention: that surface-to-air missile. Its fiery trail had lit up the sky as it screamed toward them.

The same SAM that had caused the Wildcat to crash had saved her life.

The irony of it.

Mira finished her dinner and shoved the rolling hospital table away from the side of her bed. Hopefully, those mostly empty dishes and the nap she'd taken earlier would have her nurse pasting two gold stars on her recovery chart.

Though if Hartwig didn't sign her out of Walter Reed soon, she just might sign herself out. Jerry might be off the case, but she wasn't. Not—

"Hey, kiddo."

Ramsey.

She jerked her head toward the door, relief burning through the past week's frustration in one fell swoop. Her boss was leaning against the jamb, those sinewy, pullover-clad arms of his folded across his chest. He'd worn the same thin, forest green sweater a week and a half ago when he'd finally succumbed to her questions about the helo crash and admitted that, while the tail section had landed above the *Tern*'s superstructure, there'd been nothing she could've done to assist the SAS officers had she made it that far. According to their British counterpart, a section of rotor had broken free during the collision, glancing off the deck and back inside the bird, decapitating Captain Styles and Major Hunt. The men had been found still strapped in their seats.

She'd told Ramsey the truth. From the moment she'd realized that the helo's entire tail was missing, she'd suspected Styles and Hunt were dead.

But she'd hoped.

The possibility that the men were trapped and requiring her

assistance was what had gotten her out of her own section of the wreckage and moving.

The confirmation that two soldiers with whom she'd spent so many hours had died so horrifically was just one of the many reasons she hadn't needed time alone with her thoughts this past week, despite what Hartwig maintained.

The ache eased a bit as Ramsey flashed that blinding smile of his, the one that lit up his dark, leathery, so-very-welcomed features from within.

He straightened off the jamb and turned to seal the door shut, affording them the coming necessary privacy—even in a military hospital—as he sauntered all the way into the room to stand beside the bed. "I heard you shouted all of Walter Reed down this morning. Something about you being ready to get the hell out of here?"

"I am."

"Well, let's let Colonel Hartwig be the judge of that, shall we?"

Shit. "He voted *hell, no*, didn't he?"

"Nope. More like, *let's wait and see how tomorrow's test results look*. And I agree." Ramsey tapped the skin beneath the three-inch, bright-red scar she'd seen cutting across her left temple when she'd looked in the mirror these past two weeks. "You should, too."

She nodded. Mostly because that serious glint that had flashed through those unusual amber eyes of his had added the rest: she *had* to.

Mira sank back against the pillows as Ramsey hooked his denim-clad right hip over the edge of the bed and sat.

"I see your casts are gone."

"Yep." They'd come off after Hartwig had let her swap her stepdown unit bed for this one. Her vision was holding its own too, mostly. But for a defiantly fuzzy column along her far right periphery and the annoying lightheadedness that plagued her when she stood too fast, she was fine. Heck, even Hartwig believed that given time, there was an excellent chance those issues would right themselves, too.

Though she refused to be greedy.

"You look good, kiddo."

"I feel good." To be honest, all of last week and into this one had been a different story. Most of the time she'd been so profoundly tired that, even after more than a full night's sleep, she'd manage one or two repetitions of one of the exercises on the list her physical therapist had drawn up and she'd be desperate for a nap.

And when she'd given in and surrendered to her exhaustion?

The dreams that spun through her brain had been far from restful. Worse, Ramsey's and Jerry's visits had gotten mixed up in her head, along with conversations from friends scattered around the globe. The resulting vivid and at times psychedelic nightmares had lingered long after she'd woken. Especially those involving her friend Regan Chase and Sam Riyad, as well as her parents and brother, heck even an ex-boyfriend or two. The conversations she'd had with her brother in particular had felt so real that, more often than not, she'd woken looking for the smartphone Ramsey had brought to the ICU to replace the one Poseidon had accepted as a sacrifice in her stead. She'd been so certain she'd find a waiting voicemail or two from Nate.

But there'd been none.

Her dad had missed the boat, hadn't he? If there had been one from *him* these past two weeks, she might've actually listened to it. Fortunately, her father had gotten the message when she'd picked up the phone the morning after she'd shot Chief Umber, only to realize who was on the other end. Stunned that he hadn't even asked how she was doing, let alone mentioned Nate, she'd hung up on the man and deleted his subsequent voicemail. Her father hadn't bothered her since.

As for the vivid dreams, Hartwig assured her they were normal. But that hadn't helped. Not after she'd started incorporating visions of Captain Styles and Major Hunt into those nightmares, alive...and dead. She didn't even want to think about the recurring dream she'd woken from this morning. That one had featured a certain, precious twelve-year-old boy who was still lost to the world, trapped inside his own coma in this very hospital.

While she was out of hers and doing fine.

It wasn't fair.

"Mira?"

She shook off the guilt. Focused on those striking amber eyes of Ramsey's.

It was easy. They were just so damned glad to see her, whole and healthy. "I'm fine. I was thinking about something. Someone."

"Nate?"

And Caleb. Though there was no way she was admitting to the latter. It was going to be hard enough to get her boss to sign off on her return to duty before the week was out. "Yeah." But since he'd brought up Nate, "Were you able to get ahold of him?"

She suspected not. If her brother had known she was in coma, he wouldn't have left messages, he'd have been here.

"I'm sorry, kiddo. I tried. Nate's under deep this time. You know MARSOC. They won't tell anyone what he's doing, much less where he's doing it—until it's over."

True—if they'd cop to it then. The Marine Special Operations Command did like its secrets. She not only understood why, she also whole-heartedly supported the stance. Loose lips did more than sink ships; they got sailors and Marines killed.

And when that Marine was her brother?

If Nate was capitalizing on his partial ethnicity, plus his Marine Raider expertise and connections, to get in with another member of Abu Sayyaf or their ilk in the Philippines or elsewhere, she didn't want anyone's lips flapping until he was back in the States, safe.

She was about to remind Ramsey of exactly that when his right hand came up, those dark mocha fingertips and lighter palm skimming the tight silvery curls cropped a quarter of an inch from his scalp. There was something in the way Ramsey's fingers paused at the forefront of his afro, just long enough to flex, that gave *her* pause.

And there was another glint inside that amber glow of his. One she swore he was trying to conceal. The way he averted his stare to seemingly study the clock across the hospital room might've fooled any other agent in their Field Office.

But not her.

She'd spent more time with this man growing up than she had with her own father. Even before dear old Dad had abandoned them. And when Ramsey shifted back to her, and he caught sight of the scar he'd touched at her temple earlier—and she saw the new glint that slipped into his eyes?

Oh, God. "It's connected, isn't it? Nate's current, critical mission—and what happened on that ship. What went missing."

Who had taken it.

"Maybe." Those fingertips made another skating pass over his silvery curls. Another sigh followed. This one was heavier and rife with all the prayers Ramsey liked to send upward, whether he'd been able to make it to church that week or not. "Lord, we hope so."

"But you're not sure."

Those fingers finally came down. He shook his head.

Then they had to leave Nate in play, no matter what. Meanwhile, she'd be doing everything she could to support that same mission—from her end.

She pushed the blanket off her scarred lower legs. Bare toes hit the tiled floor as she stood. Once the irritating wave of light-headedness had passed, she began pacing. It was the only way to deal with the anxiety churning through her gut.

The thought of her brother out there alone and with backup too far away to do any good as he cozied up to yet another group of ruthless zealots who more often than not were ready, willing and eager to turn suicidal at the donning of a rigged vest...

It just got to her.

It always had.

Three passes in, Mira stopped in front of the hospital room's narrow window and spun around. "Okay. What about the rest? The suggestions I sent this morning?"

More importantly, the questions she'd included.

She knew Ramsey had gotten her email. Just as she knew he'd wanted her to start sharing her thoughts on what had happened on the *Tern* and everything else, once she'd had a chance to figure out where her battered brain had been hiding them.

Why else had he brought her that phone while she was still in the ICU? And promptly told her she had a fresh set of NCIS credentials and a SIG waiting for her at the Field Office to replace the ones resting on the bottom of the Atlantic.

"*Well?*"

Instead of offending the man, her impatience earned her a grin that reached all the way up into the amber. "Hartwig's right. You have made it back to us in one piece."

"You've been checking in with my doc."

"Damned straight, I have. All of them. Your physical thera-pist, too. I'm not ashamed to admit it. From what I hear you're the current poster patient for traumatic brain injury *and* coma recovery."

Yeah, well, Colonel Hartwig might believe she owed the fact that she'd escaped the crash and subsequent swan dive with her marbles banged up, but otherwise intact, to the Atlantic's chilly temperature off the southern tip of Portugal that day. She knew better. Her so-called miraculous recovery had been forged by an iron-clad motivation fueled by two words.

Frank Nasser.

"Have you found him?"

"Nasser? No." Her boss studied her face for several long moments, and then he nodded. "I didn't need this morning's update from Hartwig to know you've got all those brain cells slotted into place; I could tell when I read your email. So, let's start at the beginning and go through it all one more time. Get us both up to date. You said you noticed something off after the helo refueling in Lisbon. And later—when you realized the ship had been taken—you wondered if that mystery conversation between the pilots and SAS officers was related somehow."

"And?"

"It was."

"How?" She leaned back against the window, the slick chill of the glass invading the fleecy top to the pajama short set Jerry's wife had dropped off after Mira had whined about the insistent itch in the healed burns on her shins—and how clinging fabric irritated them even more.

"You know about their sub tasking?"

"The one the Royal Navy assigned to shadow the *Tern* and the *Kittiwake* for the length of the voyage to Japan? Yes. What happened to it?"

Obviously, something had.

"We're still not sure. All we know is that right around the

time that your Wildcat was being refueled, the sub went dead in the water. Mechanical failure—or so the Brits are saying."

Yeah, with a nuclear submarine involved, anything from a mainspace fire to a mutiny involving all hands could've occurred and DIW due to "mechanical failure" would still be all the explanation they were going to get. Not that their own Navy would've offered anything more had the positions been reversed.

But it also explained why Styles, Hunt and the pilots had kept her out of the discussion.

That said, given that the sub had gone dead in the water roughly two hours prior to the Wildcat reaching the *Tern*? And when she added on that those mixed-oxide assemblies had already been removed from the cargo hold by the time the helo had arrived?

"Whatever killed that submarine was deliberate." And there was an excellent chance that whoever had initiated the incident that knocked the sub out of the game was part of the group responsible for the *Tern*'s takedown.

"I agree. As for the Brits—they're not saying."

Again, no shocker there. There were some things a country shared with its closest allies...and there were somethings a country just didn't.

That would never change.

But if the British sub had been off station for at least two hours, why hadn't Clearwater Transport's reporting center in the UK shifted into emergency mode?

But she knew.

"The captain." The man's behavior out on that starboard bridge wing had been odd, to say the least.

Ramsey nodded. "Your instincts were on the money there too. The *Tern*'s captain was nursing a serious grudge against this country. They found a letter in Captain Whitby's stateroom. Whitby had a son who served in the Royal Marines. He was killed a few years back in Afghanistan. Fratricide. Speculation was that the shooter was the by-blow of one of their leading politicians by an old mistress—so everything was swept under the rug."

"That would screw with anyone's head."

And stoke their fury.

Ramsey nodded. "Yep. From the letter Whitby left, it did. Unfortunately, that note didn't explain how he got mixed up with the plot to steal those assemblies, much less provide us with a goddamned hint as to where to start looking for them."

Shit. But still, although Whitby making a series of *all's well* calls back home during the takedown would've kept things calm in the reporting center until the last possible moment, that didn't explain—

"The *Kittiwake*'s captain?" Ramsey nodded.

"Yup." Evidently, she wasn't the only one who could read expressions between them. Ramsey could use hers to suss out her thoughts, too. "I know the *Kittiwake* was several thousand yards ahead and to port of the *Tern* when the Wildcat arrived on station." And, granted, the radar signature of those low, offshore boats could've been masked by the unruly wave action that night. "But surely someone aboard the *Kittiwake* noticed something off about the *Tern*." They had to have had human lookouts.

"Someone did. But Captain Elgin brushed it off."

Good God. "What was Elgin's excuse?"

"He didn't give one. And he can't. Elgin's dead. He ate his gun in his stateroom while the *Kittiwake* was reversing course to return to Cherbourg."

"*What*? Why?"

Ramsey crossed his arms as he leaned back against the side of the hospital bed. "At the time, no one could figure it out. All we knew was that Elgin had just heard that Whitby's body had been found out on that bridge wing, shot in the head. He finished plotting the course change and ordered it up, then headed for his stateroom to do the deed. A week later, it became clear why. It seems that shortly before the ships departed Cherbourg, Elgin's entire family left for the ancestral home in Wales for a vacation. His wife, young child, both sets of parents and a remaining grandmother. The Welsh police found them all—dead. There were forensic signs that they'd been held hostage before the *Tern's* takedown, and that proof of life might have been transmitted to Elgin shortly before the ships got underway from Cherbourg and the day or so after to force him to do their bidding. But right around the takedown, that ended. They found the bodies laid out in one of the bedrooms. They'd all been poisoned—including the three-year-old girl."

Oh, *Jesus.*

That did explain Elgin's suicide—to a point. If Elgin had been told or even suspected that his fellow captain was part of what was about to go down, and had then learned that Whitby had been coldly executed after the fact anyway? Elgin had known then that his entire family was already dead, or they were about to be. Sure, Elgin could've waited for confirmation. But in the end, Mira suspected that the man preferred to die without knowing for certain, clinging to that tiny flicker of hope.

Unfortunately, the bastards behind this had extinguished that too.

They'd poisoned a kid barely out of diapers, for Christ's sake.

Poison. The neon green she'd seen beneath the nose of one of the constables from the *Pacific Tern's* conference room flashed in.

"Do we know what substance killed them?"

Ramsey shook his head. "Just that it's manmade. And while it does match the chemical makeup of what killed the crew members on the *Tern*, they're still trying to figure out what went into it and how it works. I am sorry; I should've said all this sooner, but I didn't want to tell you while you were still on the mend."

"It's okay. I get it." She probably hadn't needed that added image in her head while her brain was still spinning out those psychedelic dreams.

She welcomed it now. It helped fuel her motivation.

She curled her fingers beneath the sill of the window and straightened a bit to take the chill off her back. "What about Frank's place?"

"The apartment in Japan? Our office in Yokosuka linked up with a Japanese team and went through every room with a microscope, including the toilet. Another team combed through the bedroom and house Nasser stayed in when he visited his grandfather in Nashua, plus a storage unit Frank Nasser had rented out in the same city before he made the move to Japan. We couldn't find a blessed thing in any one of the spots to connect the guy to the plot to steal those assemblies."

"Do we know how many they got?"

Ramsey knew exactly what she was asking.

The last time they'd spoken, he hadn't been able to give her an answer to that other most profoundly pressing of questions —because the Japanese and the French had yet to provide an answer to Ramsey. At least, not an official one.

Why? Because that answer would reveal precisely how much plutonium and uranium could be converted from the ceramic pellets contained in the rods of those mixed-oxide assemblies— and harvested for use in a nuclear bomb.

Unfortunately, she didn't possess Frank's brilliance. She understood the basics of the conversion process, and that was it.

But she did share Frank's terminal curiosity.

The new phone Ramsey had given her had come in handy this past week. When she hadn't been passing out with exhaustion following her latest session down in physical therapy or tied up elsewhere in the hospital, undergoing the endless tests and procedures that Hartwig seemed to take morbid delight in subjecting her to, she'd done some intensive googling.

Various open-source articles and studies had revealed several pertinent facts regarding those MOX assemblies...and every one had been chilling.

From what she'd read, each assembly for a pressure water nuclear reactor contained more than thirty kilograms of plutonium. Thirty kilograms was enough to create three nuclear bombs—at least. For while the bomb that had exploded over Hiroshima had consisted entirely of highly enriched uranium, the one that had been dropped on Nagasaki contained plutonium. Just over six kilograms' worth.

And those six kilograms?

They'd been responsible for twenty-two thousand deaths on that first day and another seventeen thousand in the months that followed, at a minimum.

How many would *she* ultimately be responsible for, if she couldn't track down Frank and his murderous cohorts in time?

"Sir?"

The concentration in those amber eyes shifted inward. Yeah, Ramsey had gotten that official answer. He just didn't want to voice it aloud.

She understood that.

Doing so made this all that much more real, didn't it?

He finally sank down on to the edge of the bed and sighed. "There were a dozen assemblies in the cask they managed to open. The centermost four were taken."

She jerked up from the windowsill, only to lean back against the glass until her lightheadedness had cleared.

Four assemblies?

Holy shit. If those terrorists had committed themselves to

the more technical and showier, big bang route, the agency was looking at tracking down *twelve* nuclear warheads.

And if the terrorists' intentions lay along the less technical? If they'd decided to simply add that radioactive shit to conventional explosives and detonate a series of dirty bombs around the globe?

Lord only knew how many of those the bastards would be able to create.

"And there's been no alerts since we last spoke?" No spikes in the radiation detectors at any of the world's major ports, military or commercial? No cities either? No third world countries—hell, even second or first—who've been testing munitions they shouldn't have access to, based on the radiation signatures of those tests?

Ramsey shook his head. "Nope. Nothing."

In *seven weeks*?

That was more than enough time for Frank and whoever was assisting him to convert the fuel in those assemblies back to their more dangerous single-element components. Especially if the lab Frank was using had been set up beforehand. Which, given the pre-planning and organization these assholes had displayed up to now, it had.

Which meant one truly horrific thing.

Those bastards were lying in wait, just as they had with that surface-to-air missile. They had a coordinated, multi-part plan for those bombs they were making.

And it was huge.

She carefully pushed off from the sill of the window, then crossed the room to the side of the bed. She didn't stop until all she could see were those unusual eyes.

Until all they could see were hers.

Only then did she make her case. "Boss, you have to find Colonel Hartwig. Get him to sign off on my release and my return to duty tonight. I need to be back at the office so I can work this. I know Frank. Yes, it's been a while. But I understand that man better than anyone else you have on the payroll. I will find him. And when I do—"

"—*You* won't be headed anywhere, Agent Ellis. Not officially. Certainly not to the Field Office and definitely not chasing off after your old buddy, Nasser."

She and Ramsey stiffened in unison. A split second later, her boss spun around. With Ramsey's broad shoulders and torso this close to her, he was blocking her view of the entire door to the hospital room. She couldn't see who'd interrupted them.

But she knew that voice. *Sam Riyad.*

Anger filled her.

Ramsey vented his first. "Where the fuck do you get off—"

"You know where. The decision's been made, and it's final." With that, the FCI agent stepped deeper into the room, coming to a halt just past the foot of the bed to face off with her and her boss as the latter turned to stand beside her.

What decision?

And *who* had made it?

Not that it mattered. It couldn't. Because this did not make sense. Riyad might be foreign counterintelligence, but Ramsey was a senior NCIS agent with two decades of experience under his belt *and* he was in charge of the capital's Field Office.

Riyad should be kowtowing to him.

But he wasn't.

Stranger still, Ramsey was not pushing that chain of command, let alone reaching out—verbally or physically—to knock that seething knot of arrogance right back out of the room. The same Ramsey who hadn't hesitated to smack down a four star admiral for cause. She'd watched it happen.

But it wasn't happening now, which meant this jerk did have the authority.

Was that bizarre turnabout the source of those undercurrents? The ones she could feel simmering between the men, despite the fact that Riyad was looking at her.

That darker, filthier scowl shifted to Ramsey. "You can leave now."

Her boss' mouth opened as he stalked forward, then closed as his phone rang. Fury all but vibrating off him, Ramsey stepped away to yank his phone from his trouser pocket. "*Shit.*" His ire downshifted to an equally palpable frustration as her boss ignored Riyad completely and turned to her. "I've gotta take this."

"I'll be fine."

Duty warred with the concern still radiating off Ramsey's entire frame.

She reached out, squeezing his forearm as she tipped her chin toward the judgment now encompassing the both of them. "Go. I can handle him."

Ramsey shot her an apologetic nod as his phone continued to trill, then crossed the room, closing the door behind him as he left.

The FCI agent's arms were folded across his chest as Mira turned back, much like Ramsey's had been upon his arrival. But the sinew that lay beneath the black Henley on this man was substantially thicker and locked rigidly into place. As was that scowl.

"Handle me? No—" A sharp scoff escaped. "—you can't."

Wrong.

That narrowly evaded surface-to-air missile? Surviving the crash that followed? An involuntary, seventy-foot swan dive into freezing, open ocean?

She met that scoff and raised him a nod. "Yeah, I can."

The judgment hardened. Turned blacker than that Henley, and the matching cargo pants and polished but scarred leather jump boots beneath. That stare might've cowed an entire harem back in the old Wahhabi, locked-in-their-fundamentalist-ways country that its owner had been born in, but it didn't even dent her resolve.

Bring it, Asshole.

Because she would. "You may have been able to kick Jerry Dahl to the curb, but I'm still on this case." She hadn't woken from that coma, and then worked her brain and her butt off for two damned weeks in this place to get sidelined now.

"Is your mind still fogged, woman? Or did you not hear me earlier? Not only are you off this case, you will not be returning to NCIS—in any capacity—anytime soon. If *ever.*"

Woman?

It wasn't even that fact that he'd used that word. It was the sneer that had tainted it.

She forced herself to let it go. Because the opening salvo this jerk had fired at Ramsey upon his arrival had finally swung back around to ricochet through her. *The decision's been made.* One question answered.

Now for the second. "On whose authority?"

"Mine."

That, she was willing to push—and was about to, when another one of those earlier comments pummeled in: *...chasing off after your old buddy, Nasser.*

"Buddy?" He'd not only gotten her pulled from this case but was also bent on killing her career because of that ancient, not-missing laptop?

One more reason to detest reporters. "I presume I owe your opening crack regarding my supposed personal relationship with Frank Nasser to that nauseating article Josiah Briggs wrote for the *DC Dispatch.*" She shot *this* bastard a sneer of her own. "You're FCI, Agent Riyad. You want to know what really happened back in nuclear power school? Check the damned files. Ten days after that laptop disappeared, it turned up, locked in a safe. Where it had been the *entire* time. The lieutenant who owned the laptop screwed up. *He* violated procedure. Not me, and not Frank. Lieutenant Bowles left it on his desk after working late one night. Ensign Harker had also been working late and spotted it. Not wanting to get Bowles in trouble, Harker secured it in his safe. But then his wife called. She'd gone into labor three months early. Harker signed out on emergency leave for the delivery of his two preemie girls and their eventual funerals."

Once she'd found that out, she couldn't even blame Harker for not keeping up with the allegations and the shitstorm of finger-pointing that had been going on back at the nuke school. "I parted ways with Frank and the Navy the same week the truth came to light. And contrary to that *Dispatch* article, I have not been nursing a grudge all these years."

At the time, she'd have sworn Frank hadn't either.

But from the state of Corrigan's body and the blood in that condo, not to mention those stolen MOX assemblies, it looked as though she'd blown that assessment.

Riyad stalked closer. "And what about your partner in crime?"

"I just told you. There was *no* crime. So how could Frank have been my partner?"

Jesus, what was it with this man?

She spun around and stalked back to the window, just to put some space between them. Unfortunately, Riyad had moved deeper into the room as well. He was looming near the middle now, next to the chair beside the rumpled bed.

"But you admit, you and Nasser were close. Correct?"

"Until that day—not at all. But later?" During the whole laptop fiasco? She shrugged. "Sure."

Nor was she ashamed of the connection and confessions

she'd once shared with Frank. At the time, no one else had understood what they'd been going through. The initial belief that the accusations were a huge mistake; the confusion and horror when a leading petty officer had come forward and signed a sworn statement claiming that he'd seen them searching the drawers in Bowles' desk; and finally, the fury when —after Harker returned from his babies' funerals and produced the laptop—the petty officer admitted that Corrigan had intimated that the Navy needed a witness, and that if a statement could be submitted into evidence, the case would be closed quickly, quietly, and with the least amount of fallout for the nuclear power school.

So, yes, for two whole weeks at NPS, friendship had blossomed.

Until her boyfriend had stuck his antiquated, meathead views into it. Given whom she'd been dating then, it hadn't made sense. She swore he'd been jealous of Frank—his brain, even his ethnicity. Definitely that Frank had been born stateside.

"Agent Ellis?"

"What do you want from me? To spell it out? Fine. *Yes*, Frank and I became close. So what? We also lost contact after I got out of the Fleet."

But perhaps if they hadn't—

Stop. Frank's actions were on him. She hadn't even needed Ramsey to make that clear during one of his earlier visits. Though it had helped.

Apparently her answers hadn't helped with Riyad, let alone eased his ugly suspicions about her. The man continued to glare, albeit silently. She could almost feel him turning some twisted thought over and around in that dark, thick head of his. What, she had no idea. Nor did she care.

But her anger had cooled enough for her to realize what she

was wearing. The pajama shorts that Jerry's wife had given her to help ease the itching of her scars.

Mira managed not to stiffen as that irritating stare slid lower until it settled on her naked thighs and pair of freshly battered and healing shins.

Creep.

She hoped he liked what he saw—because she didn't.

Hell, she now had scars from cuts and burns in places that she hadn't known could get injured. Nor had she felt their corresponding wounds after the crash. The pain and confused thoughts of her concussion and her overwhelming need to get to the bridge had overridden her awareness of everything else.

Well, she was aware now.

She stalked closer to the man still staring at her legs. Upon reaching the chair beside him, she snatched up the matching ivory fleece robe Shelli had also gifted her and shoved her arms through the sleeves, blessing Jerry's wife all over again.

Mira secured the robe's belt and whipped around to face her uninvited guest. "Got your floor-show fix for the night? If so, *outstanding*. You can leave now, too."

But he didn't. He and that scowl just stood there.

Silent.

"I said, *go*."

"Why didn't you tell me you were leaving the country to fly to France?"

She shook her head, more bemused by that question than the agent's inexplicable, but apparently accurate belief that he could control who worked this investigation. "Why would I have done that?"

Especially seven weeks ago, without that bizarre standoff with Ramsey still fresh in her head?

"Because we were both working the murder."

"No. *I* was working the murder. A murder I was told to grab during a call from my boss. *You* were simply there, fingering the JAG's titillating briefs."

His brow sharpened at the double entendre.

She let it stand. He'd been the one staring at her damaged legs when even she wasn't comfortable looking at the ugly swaths of healed burns yet.

"You know what I meant."

She shook her head. "Actually, I don't. I told you: as far as I knew, you weren't working the murder itself. Period. I'm not in the habit of sharing case details with anyone on the outside of an investigation, let alone one that involves a homicide. So there was no reason for me to keep you informed about anything. Certainly not what I had discovered during the course of the investigation, nor my then current suspicions regarding who had done what—and hence, what tips and leads I intended to pursue—and definitely not where I planned on going next, mentally *or* geographically."

"Then what's your excuse for not informing anyone in your chain of command that you were climbing aboard that Wildcat and heading out to the *Pacific Tern*? You didn't even inform Detective Dahl. I know, because I asked him."

What the hell?

"The decision to go to the *Tern* was last minute—and I was damned glad to get the offer of a lift. For your information, I was in the middle of texting Jerry the details when my phone went dead. If you don't believe me, feel free to take a *very* deep dive to the bottom of the Atlantic to verify that typed, but ultimately unsent, text."

And feel free to stay down there.

She hadn't added that last aloud, but from the way the agent's scorching glower had narrowed, not to mention the tension and barely suppressed rage in those clenched, oddly scarred fingers of his, she was fairly certain he'd caught it anyway.

She was about to pull her stare from those fingers, when something clicked deep inside her brain.

Frank.

Seven weeks ago, on the bridge of the *Pacific Tern*, he'd been livid, too—with the *Tern*'s captain. And yet, upon spotting her, Frank had simply been...stunned.

And embarrassed.

The first emotion was understandable. After all, she had shown up at sea in the middle of a hijacking. But the latter?

That embarrassment was...fascinating. The more she thought about it, it was also flat-out revealing.

Adrenaline surged in. She had the missing piece to those stolen assemblies. It had been right there in her battered brain this entire time. And if she was lucky, she might also know where she could collect it—*him*—eventually.

"Agent Ellis?"

Mira purged the adrenaline as she forced herself to refocus on the here and now, on that molten glower and the man still attempting to incinerate her with it.

"Yes?"

"*That's* your excuse for masking your movements? A dead battery?"

Masking? Just what did he suspect her of?

Surely, he didn't—

Holy Moses on the Mountain. Riyad *did*.

Her past with Frank. The fact that they'd once gotten along and had even been—if briefly—friends. The score that it appeared Frank had finally, brutally settled with Commander Corrigan. The implication that she, too, dreamed of settling that same score with the JAG, possibly in the same horrific manner.

Questioning her investigatory methods and intentions during the course of the case. And now this—suggesting that she'd deliberately tried to conceal her presence aboard that flight to the *Tern*.

"You actually think I'm involved, don't you? In the theft of those assemblies?"

She expected him to deny it. Even prayed he would.

But he didn't. He simply shrugged. "That remains to be seen. But you are communicating with a known terrorist sympathizer."

What?

She stalked forward, ignoring the pinch in her neck as she glared up at that jump-boot enhanced, six feet plus of pure insolence. "Buddy, I don't give a shit what you think of me—professionally or personally. But if you're calling me a traitor, you'd better cough up some hard, fucking proof, and you'd better do it right now."

The insolence didn't shift. But his right hand did. It slipped inside the hip pocket of his cargo pants. A small square of yellow paper surfaced between his fingers.

Riyad held it up.

She snatched the paper from his hand. A sticky note? Unfolding the square, she skimmed the series of digits that were scrawled out in black ink.

A phone number.

But not just any number. She'd seen this one before.

That 966 country code? The two-digit city prefix and seven additional digits that followed? This was the unknown number that had shown up on her phone the morning after she'd been forced to shoot Chief Umber. And the man whose voice she'd heard on the other end of the line when she'd picked up?

Her own father.

The darkness roared in. It wasn't mild and manageable like the bouts of lightheadedness that had been dogging her since she'd come out of her coma. It was blistering and nausea-inducing, and so all-consumingly fierce that it sucked her straight into the center of a dizzying vortex.

She fought it. Just as she fought that filthy, blackened stare.

She lost to both.

9

Mira stowed the last of her toiletries into the oversized brown leather tote that Jerry and his wife had stopped by her sublet to retrieve the previous evening, along with the gray Boston University sweatshirt and jeans she'd donned before she'd started breakfast. Tucking the short set Shelli had given her on top, Mira shifted the leather bag to the foot of her made bed.

Three days.

That's what Riyad and his accusation had cost her and the mission to track down Frank and those stolen mixed-oxide assemblies—and the plutonium and uranium that'd most likely already been culled from within. Three additional days trapped in this hospital while Colonel Hartwig reran every exam and test he'd already subjected her to since she'd woken from that coma, and then some.

Why?

Because she'd fainted.

Hartwig believed that her blackout had been related to the concussion she'd suffered during the crash and he'd worried that he'd missed something.

He hadn't. But it wasn't as though she could explain the shock she'd sustained to the doctor, let alone the filthy charge behind it.

That blackout, plus the last three days wasted to repeated tests that had only confirmed that she was past ready to go home? Those were on Riyad. Worse, Hartwig had admitted he'd been about to release her—and sign off on her fitness for duty— until she'd fainted. Yet another reason to despise the FCI agent: the fact that she *had* fainted.

Something she'd never done before in her life.

Given Riyad's icy attitude from the moment he'd walked into her room, she would've expected the man to have left her lying on the floor, in a puddle of her own drool, as he'd stepped over her to leave.

But he hadn't.

According to the nurse who'd been with her when she'd woken, Riyad had hit the call button and refused to let up on it until he'd received confirmation that someone was on their way. He must've placed her on the bed, since she'd been splayed out on it when her nurse, Captain Swanson, had entered. But if Riyad thought she'd be grateful, he had another think coming. Nor did she care that he'd freely admitted to the nurse that her faint was his fault; that he'd revealed information he should've waited to share.

That's when Swanson had kicked him out.

Mira wished the nurse hadn't.

The FCI agent hadn't been back since—meaning she still had no earthly idea what proof that asshole thought he had. Let alone been able to argue her way back onto the critical search for Frank.

She couldn't even ask Bill Ramsey to get to the bottom of this.

Once again, her boss' number was going to voicemail.

Though Ramsey had shot off a text this time, letting her know that the situation behind the call he'd taken as he'd left her room would have him out of touch for a few days, possibly a week. He'd inform her as to when he was back in DC, and when he did return, they needed to talk.

About what?

That slur Riyad had leveled against a man who she'd admittedly thought very little of for most of her life, and for so many excellent, if personal reasons?

If so, she was more than ready to listen. Because despite those reasons, Riyad's allegation did not make sense. Benjamin Barclay Ellis, IV, might've been a spineless son, the husband from hell, and an absentee father, not to mention a man wholly incapable of accepting responsibility for the choices he'd made in his life, let alone the fallout from them—but a traitor? That was *not* one of her father's failings.

Nor did she have time to waste on Agent Riyad's delusions. She should've been back on the job more than seventy-two hours ago, hunting for Frank and the deadly radioactive material from those damned assemblies.

Fortunately, she was about to resume that hunt—officially or not.

She already had a plan. One that she'd be able to put into play just over twenty-four hours from now. She'd done her due diligence, had even managed to place a key phone call in between all those asinine, unnecessary tests. All she had to do now was get out this hospital and get herself to Annapolis so she could initiate it.

FCI or not, Sam Riyad was an idiot. She *did* know Frank. Well enough to know who Frank would trust if he couldn't go to his grandfather for help.

God help Riyad if he got in her way again.

Mira forced herself to draw a steadying breath as she

turned to pace across the hospital room. Even with her lingering issues with lightheadedness upon standing, she'd passed her final neurological test. Hartwig had already conducted his morning rounds and given her the good news. As soon as the floor nurse arrived to hand over the signed paperwork, she was out of here.

But not the hospital. At least, not quite yet.

There was one more stop she needed to make before she called a Lyft and headed home to pack for Annapolis. One more room to visit.

This particular room belonged to a certain twelve-year-old boy she hadn't been able to scrape up the courage to face during a single one of these past seventeen days at Walter Reed that she'd been conscious for, despite the fact that his room had been down the hall from her initial digs in the same intensive care unit.

She could sit here and wait for the nurse to show with that official release, or she could head back to the ICU and end this seductive cowardice.

Damn it, just do it.

She owed it to the boy, even if Caleb wouldn't be aware of her presence.

Mira sucked up the guilt and marched across the room, leaving the brown leather tote at the foot of the bed as she closed the door behind her.

There, she paused, half-hoping one of the lieutenants at the nurses' station would notice her and shoo her back into the room.

Both were busy juggling charts and phones.

Resigned, Mira turned away from the station and made her way through the maze of echoing, early-Thursday-morning corridors and several sets of stairs as quickly as she could, before her flagging nerve got the better of her. All too soon, she was back amid the seriously subdued halls of the ICU within Walter Reed's south complex.

Several of the nurses smiled and nodded as she passed. Even if she hadn't recognized their faces from her own stay here, she'd have been able to match the names on those uniforms to the voices that had been offering up that endless string of *I'm so sorry, Agent Ellis; there's been no change* during the daily calls she'd resumed after she'd been transferred out of the ICU following her own coma.

Upon reaching the door marked Caleb McCabe, Mira paused, shoring up her courage as she braced herself for what she'd find on the other side.

There was still no change in the boy's status. She didn't need yesterday's call to this same floor to know that. Nor had the knowledge come from the sad smile of the nurse she'd just greeted. It was threaded through her gut.

Panic twisted in with it, knotting up her nerves as she forced herself to push the door open. God as her witness, she'd rather crawl into another helo destined to slam into the deck of another ship at sea than find Caleb lying in an ICU bed, his woefully slender body trapped amid a deceptively peaceful sleep that was anything but.

Because her gut was right.

But it was also so very wrong—because the sight and sounds that greeted her were so much worse than she'd feared.

The low lights, the steady beeps and the whispering whoosh of the various machines and monitors that were crowded in around the head of the bed. The subtle, but distinctive tang of hospital-grade antiseptics that hung in the air. It hadn't been this stark and depressing down the hall in the room she'd been in. It couldn't have been.

Could it?

The hell with that doomed helo; if Caleb would just flutter

those gorgeous lashes of his, she swore she'd lift the boy out of this bed and crawl in to take his place.

But those lashes didn't lift.

And that soft, unrelenting whoosh continued to fill the room as oxygen was pushed in, and then out, of those woefully young lungs.

Damn it! It wasn't fair. That should be her in that coma, not—

His eyes.

Beneath those pale, delicate lids, the boy's eyes were *moving.*

Mira closed in on the right side of the bed and reached over the safety rail to slip her fingers around his. "Caleb? Are you awake?"

Strong, but slightly uneven-sounding footsteps moved into the room from off her right, coming to a halt at the bedrail beside her. "It's normal. The eyes, they can move around quite a bit. Or so the nurses tell me. But, no, he's not awake."

She knew without turning to whom those footsteps and that low, rasping voice belonged. Ironically, she'd never actually met the man, not officially. But they had seen each other at a distance just over two months ago at the Field Office...twice.

First Sergeant Malcolm McCabe, US Marine Corps.

She withdrew her hand from those slender fingers and turned to face the father of the boy who her actions had put in this bed. "Hello. I'm—"

"I know who you are."

Of course he did. The first sergeant had been as aware of her on those two occasions as she'd been of him. Malcolm McCabe had also been viciously opposed to meeting her—quite vocally, at the Field Office and in newsprint. And now she was intruding on his privacy and his pain.

Worse, the Marine had Caleb's younger brother with him.

Bobby McCabe moved deep into the room, to the reclinable

chair in the corner. He had a small Lego kit with him. The seven-year-old version of Caleb glanced up at her, then his father, before turning to dump the Lego bricks and specialty pieces from the box out onto the vinyl cushion, so he could sort through them.

"I'm sorry, First Sergeant. I had no right to barge in here and—"

"*Yes*, you do." McCabe reached up to rub his fingers along his tanned scalp. "Though after the quote I gave that bastard with the *Dispatch*, I'm surprised you took the time. I'm also grateful." The Marine lowered his fingers to trail the calluses marring the tips along the painfully smooth and unblemished skin of the lifeless hand that she'd released. "My son needs all the prayers he can get." McCabe drew his hand back and turned to face her; those dark, soulful eyes he'd gifted Caleb and his brother while the boys had been in their mother's womb stared down at her. "I apologize for what I said to Josiah Briggs. I was an asshole and an idiot. This was *not* your fault."

"It's okay."

"No, it's not—"

She pressed her fingers into that powerful, globe-and-anchor tattooed forearm. "*It is*. I mean it."

The first sergeant had been a raw, grieving father at the time. The vitriol and slurs that Josiah Briggs had gleefully quoted and printed hadn't truly been meant for her. She'd known that then. No man who could raise a child as sweet and brave as Caleb would have said what Malcolm McCabe had, unless he'd been locked in the throes of shock.

The Marine nodded. "You're a better person than me, Agent Ellis. Smarter, too. You figured it out and believed my boy when he hadn't even signed his name to that letter."

Silence settled in between them with that admission, punctuated by the soft, constant whooshing and steady beeps that marked Caleb's vitals so that his nurses could ensure that those vitals remained constant and steady.

Mira had no idea what to say to the boy's father. She sure as hell wasn't about to admit to McCabe that his son's letter hadn't been the first testimony of abuse that she'd had to follow up on during the course of her job...nor would it be the last.

Even the military had monsters.

After all, the Fleet was simply a microcosm of society. Yes, the vast majority of recruiters actively screened for would-be traitors and the truly sadistic beasts who hid among men. But somehow, a few always slipped through.

It was up to her and her fellow NCIS agents to track those traitors and beasts down—preferably before they left their foul marks on the innocent.

The first sergeant's gaze drifted down to the gentle, placid face of someone who Mira hadn't even known had needed protection...until it was too late.

McCabe's rasping voice threaded within that steady whooshing in a deliberate attempt to keep his younger son's innocence intact. "The night you shot Umber, I asked Caleb point blank if that bastard had so much as seen his willy, let alone touched it. He denied it. I wanted so damned badly to believe him. And when they searched that fucker's house and *didn't* find anything, I stuck my head in the sand." The Marine reached down and tapped the top of what she knew was a prosthetic right leg. "Just like I'd been doing since I left the other half of this in Iraq. I'm ashamed to say that it was easy. There was so much *shit* going on. So much I couldn't fix. I just...tuned out."

Mira nodded. She knew about the other *shit* too.

Caleb's mother had been diagnosed with leukemia shortly after his father had lost his leg. Within months, the first sergeant's wife and his boys' mother was dead.

Mira suspected that was when the grooming had begun.

Chief Umber had used the boy's loneliness and grief against him. To weaken him. And when Umber had felt he'd "courted" the boy long enough—that's when the rapes and the rest of that sick bastard's abuse would've commenced.

Her fury and disgust must've shown, because the first sergeant nodded. "Yeah. That's how the fucker got in. He was corpsman. So knowledgeable, so *helpful*. And it didn't hurt that he'd saved my life over there. But none of that matters. And it sure as shit doesn't absolve me. Because I was not paying attention, and I damned well should've been."

The first sergeant pressed his fingertips to the inner corners of his eyes to keep the glistening that had begun from welling up further and spilling over.

He blinked several times, then straightened to his full height. "Well, I'm paying attention now—and I have no intention of stopping. Ever. I just wish Caleb would open his eyes so I can tell him that...and *beg* his forgiveness."

McCabe turned, his damp stare drifting over the younger boy still kneeling at the chair in the corner, quietly making headway with that car he was building.

The first sergeant's voice threaded between the masking sounds of the monitors once more. "The Navy called that twisted fuck a hero. Hell, the Corps called me one, too. They were wrong about Umber, and they were wrong about me." He sighed, finally losing the battle with those tears as he swung back to the son lying on the bed. "Caleb's the real hero."

That he was, and Mira knew why.

The bigger picture had snapped into focus the moment she'd realized that First Sergeant McCabe had *two* sons, five years apart. The letter Caleb had sent to her suggested that his abuse had been occurring for several years.

And that was a problem...for the chief.

Caleb was on the verge of aging out of Umber's sick, preferential-victim range—and Caleb had known that.

Just as he'd known that his brother was next.

That's why Caleb had sent the letter. Not to save himself. To save Bobby.

Less than an hour ago, Colonel Hartwig had pronounced her tough. She wasn't half as tough as the kid trapped in this bed. The one who'd been willing to sacrifice his heart, his body and his very soul to keep his little brother's unblemished.

Mira started to bend down, then paused to glance at Caleb's father.

The first sergeant nodded.

Dipping her head the rest of the way, she brushed those chocolate curls from the boy's right temple with her fingers as she whispered into his ear. "Hey, Caleb. It's Agent Ellis. Mira. I just stopped by to visit and tell you that you can get through this. You can wake up now. You're safe. Your dad and your brother, and so many people love you. We're all waiting to see those amazing eyes of yours again. So please open them. *Please.*"

She wasn't sure what she'd expected. That he'd squeeze her hand? Do as she'd begged and actually lift those thick, curling lashes?

Because he didn't.

She hoped to hell Caleb and his father could forgive her, because she couldn't take another moment of that godawful, relentless whooshing.

Her eyes began to burn and her fingers trembled. She might've even swayed slightly as she straightened. But that was okay. She wouldn't have minded passing out right then and there from the intense emotion of it all.

Because unlike Riyad, *this kid* was worth fainting for.

Bobby McCabe had finished building his Lego car; he'd rushed up to the side of the bed to describe it to his older brother in bubbling, tongue-tripping detail.

And she was in the way.

She stepped back so the younger boy could get right up beside his brother's seemingly serene face, then turned to their father. "I should go."

The first sergeant offered up a smile held captive by the stark reality of this bed and this room. All those damned monitors. "I know you've been calling the nurses' station every morning for an update—before and after you were down the hall, stuck in a bed yourself. It's okay. You can call the room direct if you want. I'll answer."

Because he'd still be here.

The burning in her eyes returned with a vengeance.

Mira nodded. It was all she could manage.

Caleb's brother had fallen silent. He was watching her curiously now, and she didn't want to scare Bobby any more than he already had been.

She raised a hand to gently brush this boy's curls too, then headed for the door.

One foot in front of the other, damn it.

She could do this.

The mantra got her past the nurses' station and all the way to the lounge. She took one look at the rough and ready form standing beside an end chair, and lost it.

By the time Jerry had dropped the leather tote she'd left on the bed in her hospital room, Mira was sobbing into his chest.

Her old mentor's arms came up, wrapping around her and pulling her closer as he squeezed tight. She stayed there for some time, finally venting the pain, the fear and the grief—and, yeah, even the guilt—that had been eating away at her confidence since she'd woken up two and a half weeks earlier in a room down the hall from where they were standing.

Eventually, her sobs turned to sniffles, then hiccups.

Jerry loosened his arms as she straightened enough to use

the sleeve of her sweatshirt to soak up the tears that were still dripping down her cheeks.

A final hiccup escaped as she stepped back. "How did you know where I was?"

That earned her a scoff that was bruised with more than a hint of righteous offense. "Hey, I'm a detective, remember?"

Yeah. He was.

His right hand came up to swipe at the tears she'd missed. "You didn't think I was going to let you make your own way home today, did you?"

If she had thought that, she shouldn't have. Because here Jerry was.

Which was even more curious.

She was fairly certain Shelli had mentioned last night that Jerry would be on call to catch cases for his department today, but Mira didn't push it.

Instead, she grabbed the gift of a true friend with both hands as she filled her lungs with a long, cleansing breath. She let it all out with a shudder.

"Thank you."

"You're welcome. But it gets even better." Jerry reached inside the jacket of his navy-blue suit and withdrew several folded up sheets of paper. "I've got your *get out of jail* paperwork right here, signed by Warden Hartwig himself. You ready to escape?"

Oh, Lord, yes.

And riding with Jerry? It beat the hell out of crawling into the back seat of a stranger's car.

Though the ride home would've been much longer if Jerry hadn't badged his way onto Joint Andrews Airbase nearly two months ago. Because that was where she'd left her Chevy Blazer parked, shortly before she'd climbed aboard that C-17 bound for RAF Lakenheath. She was still in the ICU when Shelli had sent Jerry for coffee and relayed the tale.

As Mira had feared, her old partner had been racked with guilt over the helo crash and her involuntary dive into the drink. His mood had sunk so low that Shelli had finally suggested that Jerry get a spare key made for Mira's SUV, so that when he located the Blazer, he could park it in front of her sublet for her. Because, of course, Mira would be recovering. When she did, she'd need her wheels.

And, granted, the mission had given Jerry a proactive task to focus on at the time, to keep him sane while they waited for her to wake up.

Smart woman. Mira had told Shelli so, too.

Mira had known for years that Jerry was lucky to have Shelli in his life. And *she* was lucky to have the both of them.

But before she and Jerry had even reached the elevator, Mira knew there was something weighing on his mind again—and heavily. But like Shelli, she understood the man. Traversing the gradually waking corridors of Walter Reed as they made their way to the exit was not the place to get into it.

Nor was the hospital complex's south garage where Jerry had parked his MPD cruiser.

By the time they'd cleared the sprawling cluster of medical buildings and hit the DC Beltway, Mira was officially worried. Her old partner was lost so deep within whatever was bothering him that all pretense of small talk had ceased.

Hell, Jerry hadn't offered up so much as a syllable during the latter half of the drive to her sublet. Worse, she doubted he was aware of his silence.

The Beltway's congestion behind them, she waited until he'd steered the cruiser onto her side street to park it in the empty slot behind her Blazer.

The slot that was only open because everyone else who worked out of their home in her neighborhood had already left for the day.

"All right, what's wrong?"

Jerry finally glanced her way as he killed the engine, but he still appeared deep in his thoughts, hashing through that unknown issue. "Hmm?"

Did his preoccupation have to do with the high-profile senate-staffer case he'd been working for almost a week now? Two days ago, Jerry had arrested the staffer for strangling his once on-again, now permanently off-again mistress. Had the staffer appealed to his boss?

After all, involved or not, the senator himself would likely be tainted by his employee's arrest come Election Day.

"Did the senator get some big shot lawyer to help out his staffer? Has the arrest gone south?"

"No. We got the SOB. Confession's rock solid. So's the forensic evidence."

Then what was it?

She leaned down to hook her tote off the floorboard at her feet as suspicion niggled in. "Does your rotten mood have to do with the Corrigan case?" The one that was still officially open. Or worse, did it have to do with the man who appeared to have knocked everyone else off the case so he could assume the lead? "Please tell me this isn't about the illustrious Agent Riyad. That jerk's been hounding me since I woke up in the ICU. A few days ago, he even admitted he took a run at you."

Something she hadn't yet discussed with Jerry because Shelli had been with him during his last visit. And while Shelli knew Jerry could handle himself, why worry the woman?

Riyad hadn't gone even further, had he? Had the agent decided to stop by MPD to bitch to Jerry's new boss about him?

That was all the detective needed. To appear to his fellow civilian capital police as though NCIS and other feds had it out for him.

"Nah, Mir. It's not that. Yeah, Riyad stopped by. I didn't

mention it, because it didn't matter. That garbage he tried to feed me about you deliberately deciding to not tell me you'd be boarding the Wildcat, 'cause you were up to something? That's bullshit, and Riyad knows it. Hell, it's not like the information wouldn't have been passed along the standard channels, anyway —and I told him that. Those two SAS officers knew you were on that flight. Clearwater Transport knew, too. Hell, Clearwater *asked* for you to be there. That said, Riyad does have a serious bug up his ass about you. And, uh...I might have an inkling as to why."

What?

She dumped the tote back on the floorboard. "*Spill.*"

Jerry smiled to a young mother pushing a stroller down the sidewalk. He waited until mom and baby were well past the cruiser, and then, "I'll be honest; that man's been on my shit list ever since that crack about us outside the autopsy suite. I was already digging into the guy while you were headed overseas. But once I heard about the crash and your rescue, I dropped it. Had other things to worry about. But when he tracked me down last week and tried to interrogate me in my own fucking precinct?"

Oh, Lord. Riyad really had cornered the man there?

Not smart at all.

Jerry nodded. "Yup, that just pissed me off all over again. So I redoubled my efforts. I contacted someone I probably shouldn't have. But the man owed me. And he's pretty high up at NCIS too, so he's got serious connections of his own. He got back to me late last night. Mir, there's a lot of serious shit swirling around Riyad, and some of it's putting off enough stink to repel a corpse fly. That's another reason why I wanted to pick you up from the hospital. I know you said you were gonna take a couple of weeks' leave at your place in Annapolis to finish recuperating, but I thought you should hear what I learned before you left. And, yeah, I didn't want to get into this on the phone."

If that last hadn't given her pause, the tension and wariness in that muddy gaze of Jerry's would have. It also shot her curiosity up over the edge. Especially in light of the accusation that Riyad had made about her own father.

Not to mention that Riyad had to be leveraging that vile accusation to keep her locked out of the official scrabble for Frank and the stolen radioactive material.

Well, it was time to forge her own key. "What did you find out?"

"Did you know the guy was a SEAL?"

"Riyad?"

"Yeah." Jerry glanced at the postal worker who normally delivered to this street. The thirty-something, though surprisingly already silver-haired woman was still a good quarter of a block away. "The guy's prior enlisted. Went to college compliments of the Enlisted Commissioning Program. Made it to Commander. According to my source, Riyad did eighteen years total—all of them with the Teams. Then he got out."

With eighteen years under his belt?

No one lasted that long and punted. Not anywhere in the Fleet, not even if their designator had them constantly clinging to the drier pilings of shore duty. If making a career of the Navy wasn't the goal, both officers and enlisted tended to get out before the ten year mark, often well before. They certainly didn't wait until they needed just two more to make the minimum twenty required for retirement, and the pension and benefits that went with it. And Riyad had been a SEAL?

Then again, that part kinda figured.

She hadn't had the smoothest of relationships with the sailors in that warfare community, professionally or personally, and for pretty much the same reason. And there was the additional, harsher fact that along with too many of her fellow NCIS agents, she'd been forced to investigate an unfortunate number of SEALs gone shamefully wild.

Though having experienced the FCI agent's stiff, almost puritanical demeanor and that near constant, accompanying scowl, she doubted that cutting loose—legally or illegally—was the case with Riyad.

"Was he injured?"

"Can't be certain, but I don't think that's why the guy resigned his commission, let alone why he joined NCIS before the ink had even dried." Jerry flicked his gaze to the nearing postal worker as he shook his head.

And that new glint as he turned back?

He definitely had Mira's attention now. "What went wrong?"

"A mission went south. Critical one. It involved a team insertion via a SEAL delivery vehicle off the coast of Iran two years ago. Riyad was in charge. He and his men were supposed to slip in and pick up a VIP package who wanted to defect. Not sure how they were supposed to get out of the country. Mostly because they never got in. All my source knows is that when the submarine launched the SDV, there were six SEALs inside. Four bodies turned up days later, all off the coast of Oman."

"So, there were two survivors. Riyad and another man?"

"Not exactly." Jerry shot another glance at the postal worker, then fell silent as the woman slid what appeared to be a pizza flyer into the slot for Mira's sublet.

The air thrummed with what the detective was clearly waiting to add as the postal worker took a few moments to sort through her bag before she added several letters to the other slots. Finished, the woman descended the steps to continue down the sidewalk. Both Mira and Jerry waved as the postal worker passed the cruiser.

The second the woman hit the set of steps behind them,

Jerry leaned closer, his voice downshifting to a bare murmur. "The SDV from the mission—and *it* never washed up, mind you —was a prototype. It had new capabilities that the Fleet does not want floating around out there. And yet, there's an excellent chance the submersible's doing just that...for someone other than us."

"Holy *shit*."

Jerry nodded as he straightened. "I know, right?"

Oh, yeah. Look at what had happened when one of the CIA's RQ-170 Sentinel drones had crashed a hundred and forty miles *inside* Iran back in 2011. The surveillance craft's resulting wreckage and stealth technology had been a bonanza for the Ayatollah and his Islamic Revolutionary Guard Corps' ever-zealous Quds Force—the IRGC's version of the CIA and US Special Operations Command rolled into one.

Not surprisingly, Iran's engineers and robotic scientists had been hard at work, exploiting every discernible shred of the wreckage since.

And if the IRGC and the Quds Force had gotten their hands on a next-gen SDV? One that was in excellent condition—and *working*?

This was freaking huge. And seriously classified.

No wonder the detective hadn't been up for chitchat during the drive from Walter Reed. She didn't know what Jerry had done for his source in the past to get this now, but it must've hit career-saver level.

She was now wondering why, old partner or not, Jerry was risking not only his NCIS pension and his current career with MPD but the right to live his life outside the walls of the federal prison at Leavenworth, just to pass it on to her.

"Mir?"

She was almost afraid to respond. "Yeah?"

"There's something else. The SEAL that survived with Riyad?

The one the Navy thinks took the SDV? According to my source, it's Senior Chief Zakaria Webber."

"*What?*"

Zak had stolen it? Oh, shit. The implications were beyond earth-shattering.

At least to her.

Those same implications explained so much of her interactions with Sam Riyad. Hell, they pretty much covered all of them, including those endless scowls and especially that acidic snark the agent had dripped outside the autopsy suite.

This was why Jerry had risked it all to pass the intel on to her.

Jerry nodded, his heavy sigh filling the front of the cruiser. "Yeah, I thought that name sounded familiar. That is the guy you almost married, isn't it? Right around the time your career with the Fleet ran aground at the nuke school?"

"Yep." Only Zak's timing and ability to fuck up her life had reached an all-time high, hadn't it? One she might not be able to crawl back down from. Not without spending the next forty-years-to-life at Leavenworth herself.

Not if Agent Riyad had anything to say about it.

No wonder he'd wanted her off the case. She couldn't even blame him. She had connections to Frank Nasser and Zak Webber.

Even more damning, Frank and Zak had *met* because of her.

So why had Riyad led with all that suggestive crap about her so-called epic friendship with Frank, only to follow it up with that filthy accusation that her father sympathized with terrorists? Because he'd wanted to get a bead on her baseline before he'd introduced the subject of Zak—and the very real possibility that her ex-fiancé had turned traitor and *was* a terrorist?

Or had that been the agent's second assault? Had he been

about to throw her past with Zak into her face when she'd fainted on him?

If so, he wouldn't have gotten far.

She might've known Zak a lot better than Frank, but he was in her past too. She hadn't seen Zak since she'd returned his engagement ring the same day she'd resigned her commission with the Navy. Nor could Riyad imply that they'd been friendly since. She'd rejected the call Zak had made the night after she'd called off the wedding.

He'd never placed another. And there was all the malicious shit Zak had dripped into his fellow SEALs' ears afterward.

"Mir...there's more."

Damn it, she didn't want there to be more.

This was bad enough.

But Jerry refused to let her off the hook. "You remember telling me about that weird neon green substance you saw beneath the nose and coming from the mouth of that constable on the *Pacific Tern*?

Oh, Lord. "Jerry, please don't say—"

But he was already nodding. "Those SEALs that washed up? My source says they had neon green shit in their lungs. Now, that could be a coincidence."

But it wasn't. And they both knew it.

This time, Jerry's harsh sigh filled the entire cruiser. "What the fuck's going on?"

She pressed the back of her suddenly aching skull into her headrest. "I do not know."

Right now, it was all she could do to pray that what Frank and Zak had already done was not tied to her father.

But when had she ever been that lucky?

Christ.

The silence stretched out, and this time, she was the cause.

She desperately wanted to share the accusation Riyad had

made against her dad with Jerry. But if Jerry had been pissed because Riyad had tried to corner him at the precinct, learning that the agent had labeled her father a traitor would have her old partner truly seeking blood—Riyad's.

Jerry would go right back to that nose-bleed NCIS source of his and he would not be backing off until he had answers.

Something told her Riyad wouldn't take well to a friend of hers stepping into what the agent clearly believed...and evidently was...his case.

At least now she understood why such a junior agent had been able to smack Bill Ramsey back and live.

Whoever Riyad was reporting to was *very* high up the NCIS food chain. Higher than Ramsay and Jerry's source put together. Quite possibly the great white shark at the top of *both* NCIS and the Fleet's joint chain: the Secretary of the Navy, himself.

"Mir?"

She dragged her focus from her Blazer's license plate and nudged it across the front seat of the cruiser to the simmering concern that awaited her.

"There's something you're not telling me."

Guilt sloshed in.

She'd forgotten that this man knew her as well as she knew him. Before she could open her mouth, Jerry's hand came up.

"It's okay. I'm not a bishop on the great salted chessboard anymore. Got a bunch of new pieces and a new board to concern myself with. And I'm fine with that, or I wouldn't have voluntarily retired from the first one. But this is your board, Mir. And with the level of players that appear to be involved, you're gonna need all the information you can get if you hope to make it to the other side intact."

All the information? He had more?

Of course he did. This was Jerry.

She waited for it.

"My source coughed up one last detail. It seemed minor late last night. But now I'm thinking it's got the potential to pay off in a major way. Riyad's first assignment as an agent was in January of this year. He was flown out to the *USS Griffith*. The ship was deployed to the Indian Ocean at the time. She was scheduled to return to San Diego before Riyad stepped aboard, but didn't. Something kept the *Griffith* at sea for over a month longer than she should've been...and no one seems to know why."

The *Griffith*? She hadn't heard anything about an incident aboard the amphibious warship back in January. No Marines attached to the vessel had been sent up for court-martials. No Navy officers from the wardroom had been relieved for cause. "And your source has no idea why Riyad was there, let alone what the *Griffith* was doing?"

"Above his pay grade."

"Wow." Make that a double. Especially given the cesspool of information this particular faucet of Jerry's had already leaked.

"Yeah. Anyway, I did some additional snooping early this morning. Got a hold of the *Griffith*'s crew roster. You remember a master-at-arms named Michelle Yrle?"

"The junior petty officer who brought us that tip about the sex-trafficking group in Groton?"

"That's her. She's a chief now. And, yep, she's currently assigned to the *Griffith*. Yrle remembers how we kept her name out of it back then when the case soured and her old commanding officer was sharpening his blade and looking for heads to whack off in revenge for his buddy's tarnished rep. Yrle was...eager to return the favor."

"Was Yrle aboard the *Griffith* when Riyad was there?" Because if the woman had been, as a chief master-at-arms, she'd have had to have at least met the NCIS agent, however short his stay had been.

Jerry nodded. "Not only was Yrle there, the chief worked the same investigation. Her impression of the man? Riyad was hiding something. She couldn't get a bead on what that some- thing was, but she did not like him. At all."

Join the club.

"Did Yrle give a hint as to what the investigation entailed?"

This time, Jerry's head moved from side to side. "I tried, but she wouldn't. Couldn't. But she did let on that it was serious. Got the feeling it had SECNAV-level interest. Which dovetails into my source's impression of the whole thing."

The Secretary of the Navy? It seemed her instincts about Riyad reporting to the great white shark himself were correct.

But as intriguing as all this was, it was also a dead end. "That's it; we're back to square one."

Instead of nodding, Jerry's head shook again. "Maybe not. There might be a way to cheat your way through an entire row. According to Yrle, there was someone else aboard the *Griffith* the same time that Riyad was there. That Army MP sergeant we worked with during the security detail for General Kessler."

"Regan Chase?" Finally—something positive.

"Yep. And I hear the woman's with CID now."

"She is." Not only was Regan an Army special agent and NCIS' counterpart in camouflage, she was an outstanding detec- tive. Regan had recently solidified her bloodhound reputation this past December too, when she'd worked the psycho-toxin case that had involved an entire team of Special Forces soldiers recently back from Afghanistan. Some of whom who'd gone on to murder their loved ones and/or commit suicide—on Christmas Day, no less.

But dogged rep aside, "Why would an Army investigator have been sent to a Navy warship operating in the middle of the Indian Ocean on a hush-hush tasking?"

"Dunno. But I take it from the gleam lighting up those baby

blues of yours that the two of you just might be friendly enough for a call to find out."

Mira didn't know what was going on in her eyes, but she could feel her grin and her burgeoning hope splitting in. "Jerry, we're *extremely* friendly."

Especially since she'd been the one to tip Regan off to an explosives' case in Hohenfels that had eventually led to Regan's recent marriage to the same major who'd been in charge of that Special Forces team in Afghanistan.

Jerry's grin split that much wider. "So, what the hell are you doing sitting out here with me?"

Mira reached down to the floorboard to hook her left hand through the straps of her leather tote once more. Her right was already on the inner handle of the cruiser's passenger door. "Thanks, Jerry. For the info—" She tipped her chin toward the rear of her Blazer. "—and getting that back here. Shelli was right; I need it."

"No, problem. Now, go get 'em, Mir. And text me from Annapolis, or wherever you're really headed. Let me know you're okay."

"Will do."

A moment later, she'd abandoned the cruiser and was heading for the steps of her sublet. As soon as she finished phoning Regan, she'd be packing for her very real drive to Annapolis. She had no intention of stopping by the realty office while she was there, however. She had another meeting in mind. One that just might lead her to the man who Agent Riyad had somehow forgotten was the key to tracking down the radioactive fuel from those stolen assemblies—*before* it could be used.

Frank Nasser.

God help either of the men if they got in her way again.

10

She was being followed.

The odd, prickling sensation at the back of her neck had Mira executing a swift turn to her right, pointing her scuffed tennis shoes across the red-bricked street she'd spent the better part of the last hour walking up, down and around.

Upon reaching the curb, she stepped onto a matching sidewalk and executed a second, swifter right.

As her U-turn took her up the opposite side of the thoroughfare she'd just traversed, she appeared to allow her gaze to drift lazily along the dusk-laden shops and pedestrians for someone who appeared even slightly out of place.

No one did.

The tension was getting to her. That was all this was.

Because the sensation had disappeared.

She refused to worry. Even before she'd escaped the confines of the DC Beltway, her brain had been whirling with everything she'd learned from Jerry and everything she'd yet to learn from Regan Chase, but—God willing—would be, as soon as her friend had a chance to return her voicemail.

By the time Mira had arrived in Annapolis two hours ago,

she'd dumped her hastily repacked leather tote onto the hard-wood foyer of her grandmother's stifling, too-proper McMansion and walked right back out the front door.

She'd thought about heading to the marina, but there'd been no point in showing up there yet. Both the yacht and the man she was waiting on were at sea.

Besides, after spending seventeen days trapped with her own thoughts at Walter Reed, she'd needed to be around people. Lots of them. Young, old; male, female; tourist and longtime resident. Even the current sprinkling of US Naval Academy staff and the occasional raucous cluster of midshipmen.

The more varied and chattier the mix, the more she should've been able to enjoy her impromptu bout of people watching as she consumed her shrimp scampi before she'd bailed on her favorite childhood restaurant to lose herself in the crowds that were milling and shifting through the streets of historic, downtown Annapolis.

Walking had been her and her brother's go-to de-stressor in their teens. The rich red bricks, colorful storefronts and canvas awnings of Main Street had been one of their favorite jaunts, and one that had always worked for both of them in the past.

It should've worked even better for Mira tonight.

Save for the odd day here and there to attend her grandmother's funeral and take care of business with the Ellis family mausoleum, she hadn't been back since she'd headed to Boston University for freshman orientation. The added anonymity she'd acquired over the eleven years since should've made this particular jaunt perfect. Very few people in Annapolis knew her anymore, let alone well. And none of them would be aware of what had happened to her aboard the *Pacific Tern*.

More importantly, not a single soul in town knew of her past connections to not one or two, but now *three* former sailors of questionable national loyalty.

And yet...someone had recognized her.

The prickling sensation.

It was back.

She swore she could feel that someone's gaze searing in between her shoulder blades as she and her nondescript gray sweatshirt and faded jeans continued to casually slip in and around her fellow strolling pedestrians.

She should've taken the time to swap out her sweatshirt for a hoodie. The bone-straight, ash-blond hair she'd inherited from her father made her stand out like a one-oared rowboat amid one of the infamous sailboat regattas her grandmother had loved to sponsor, but had lacked the talent and drive to actually compete in. Unlike her daughter-in-law—at least until her mom had been confined to that rolling chair.

Shoving the bulk of her thick ponytail beneath her collar, Mira quickly retreated onto a less-populated, cobbled side street.

Eight turns through portions of five more streets had her two blocks from her house. The sensation of being watched had faded with her first pivot.

Caution forced yet another unnecessary turn. She followed it up with several more until she'd looped back to her street, this time within doors of the three-story, pillar-and-brick monster she and Nate had been trying to unload for years.

Maybe this summer they'd hit the market just right.

All she knew was that she would not be talked into another renter and the contract that would ensue—no matter his or her military rank and accompanying level of desperation.

Mira scanned the street a final time as she withdrew her key to the front door. Satisfied that no one was watching, she finally ascended the slate steps. Unless her imagination had been spinning tales for her instincts again, she'd lost her shadow.

Relief swept in as she closed the front door.

Before she could hook her tote off the dusty hardwood, her phone rang—and she recognized the number.

Regan.

Mira retrieved her tote, hitching the straps over her shoulder as she crossed the foyer. "Hey, Rae. Thanks for returning my call."

"No problem. Sorry it took so long. It's been a rough few days with a rougher investigation. But we pushed through. I just got home."

"Excellent on the solve. And no worries. You've got great timing, in fact. I just walked in myself. So, how's life with King Kong?"

Her friend's husky laugh filled the line. "Well, he's currently out of the country, and I don't even know where. But you should probably stop calling him that."

"Why? You do it."

"True...but I married the man, remember?"

Mira grinned as she threaded her way through the drop cloth-covered furniture that filled the formal living room on her way to the kitchen.

It had been four months since she'd gotten that text and the trio of attached photos, and she still couldn't wrap her head around it. Regan really had married a gorilla. In her Army camouflaged utilities, no less, and still reeking of fumes from a C-130 flight from an overseas mission with that same gorilla. A mission that had taken Regan and Major Garrison to Pakistan in mid-January of this year...and quite possibly aboard the amphibious warship that Jerry had mentioned.

Either way, the matching smiles in those photos had shone brighter than the Milky Way at sea, a thousand miles from shore and the inevitable light pollution that came with civilization. Mira had known then that the couple's relationship, despite its disastrous beginning, was going to last. It was nice to know someone's could.

"In your voicemail, you said that Colonel Hartwig released you from the hospital this morning. How are you feeling?"

Mira dumped the tote atop the butcher-block work station in the center of the kitchen. "Outstanding." It wasn't even a lie. "I'm in Annapolis for a day or so. I just took a walk around the historic district and—" Other than that pesky shadow she'd kept sensing. "—it went great. I wasn't even winded."

"That's fantastic. I still can't believe you survived that fall."

Neither could she. Especially since so many sailors hadn't.

"Anything more on the investigation that sent you over the side of that ship?"

Other than the fact that she'd been yanked from it—by the FCI agent she desperately wanted to cut to the chase and ask her friend about?

Mira swung around to the refrigerator instead. She'd been about to seek out a towering caramel latte to fuel her night's coming research when that weird sensation had prickled in and knocked her off mission. Her previous tenants had left the fridge plugged in and running. Maybe they'd left a can or two of soda within.

Nope. Other than a carton of expired milk, two equally outdated tubs of yogurt and half a jar of green olives, the fridge was empty.

She shut the door. "There's nothing new to report. Clearwater's still piecing the evidence and chain of events together."

Not surprisingly, the nuclear transport company had closed ranks with the assistance and blessings of the UK, French and US governments, with just enough of the truth woven into the official statements and responses from all to support the lie: the potable water aboard the *Pacific Tern* had somehow been poisoned. No, Clearwater and the UK's forensic scientists still didn't know by what, nor could they confirm if the substance had been manmade. All Clearwater knew for certain was that the unfortunate illness and sudden death of every single member of the *Tern*'s crew had caused the incident that led to a breach in her hull.

The massive tarps that had been draped over the bow of the *Pacific Kittiwake* and the starboard beam of the *Tern* as the sister ships had limped back into port had not only implied collision but supported the rest. Namely that the transport casks and radioactive, mixed-oxide assemblies within that had been stowed in the *Kittiwake*'s cargo hold—there'd been no mention of the *Tern*'s hold where the casks had actually been, of course—had sustained zero damage during the incident.

Naturally, not a soul aboard the *Kittiwake* had come forward to dispute the company's statements, much less the false picture they painted.

As much as Mira hated letting those lies stand now with one of her best friends, like the sailors and nuclear constables aboard the *Kittiwake*, she had her own non-disclosure-bound hide to consider. Just as Special Agent Regan Chase did with her cases. Which was why this call was so difficult—and even more dicey.

Damn it, just broach it.

"Mira?"

"Yeah?"

Her friend sighed. "What's wrong? Because I'm getting the feeling from your gloomy silence that something is."

With a cream-and-sugared caffeine boost off the menu, Mira headed for the walnut cupboard that should've contained her mother's glassware, but didn't. "I need to ask you a...sensitive question. It's about someone you've worked with."

The soft thump of another cupboard door closing reverber-ated through the line, giving her the impression that Regan was standing in her own kitchen at the moment, somewhere off Fort Campbell, in Clarksville, Tennessee. "Yeah, I had a feeling this wasn't just a catch-up chat. Mostly since we did that a few days ago."

Mira located her mother's glasses and snagged one. She moved to the sink, letting the water run for a moment before she filled the tumbler to the brim. "Guilty. And I wouldn't ask...but I really do need any insight you can offer."

"What's the name?"

"Sam Riyad. He's with NCIS. Well, our foreign counterintelligence division. He's new, but I understand you were aboard the *Griffith* while he was there."

Silence greeted the name and qualifying remarks. It was so sharp she could hear Regan carefully setting a glass or cup down on her own counter half the nation away.

Shit. She should've left the *Griffith* out of it. "Rae, it's obvious I stepped into something I shouldn't have. I'm sorry. I'll drop—"

"Mira?"

She set her own glass on the counter, water untouched. "Yes?"

"Sam Riyad's a SEAL."

"Yeah, I know. I also know—though I'm not supposed to— that his last mission went bad. According to my source, Riyad lost four men and a specialized piece of gear on that mission. That's why he got out." Given his focus, he'd joined NCIS to gain the authority to track down that SDV and Zak along with it. "Agent Riyad's—"

"—*not* NCIS. Hell, the guy's not even FCI. Not according to *my* source."

Mira's hand hit the rim of her mother's glass, sending it bouncing off the upper lip of the porcelain sink and crashing to the floor.

She ignored the shards of crystal and water that splattered and puddled around her feet. "Are you certain?"

"I am. I was stunned, too. But in retrospect, it makes sense. You're right; I was on the *Griffith*. I investigated two deaths while I was there...and I admit, I shouldn't have been working the first. Conflict of interest. Riyad argued against my assignment at the time for that same reason—and harshly. When I wasn't pulled from the case or even shunted to the number two slot, I assumed someone in the joint chain above both of us had told Riyad to sit down and shut up. Hell, maybe there was some ego in there too on my end, because I chalked up the approval to my solve record on past cases. And, well, because as a spook, Riyad wouldn't have known the first thing about working a homicide. Which he immediately proved he did not. Upshot though? Turns out the case was mine because I was the *only* investigator aboard—and the situation surrounding it was classified. Sam Riyad was just my shadow to ensure I didn't screw with anything."

The Kleenex the man had used in lieu of those missing gloves in Commander Corrigan's condo office flashed through Mira's mind. Along with that awkward moment during the autopsy when Riyad hadn't seemed to know why the denier had tried to pass him a simple jar of Vicks.

Riyad's reaction to those dislocated metacarpals pulsed in as well.

For a split second, the strength of the odd niggle that came with the latter memory confused her—and then it didn't, as the explanation behind it snapped into place.

Oh, *fuck*.

Zak.

Was it even possible? Hell, she already knew it was. Frank Nasser might not have had the skills or the stomach to execute the level of carnage in that condo...but Zak would. And Zak had come to hate the JAG with a passion.

The soles of her tennis shoes crunched through the galaxy of glistening shards as she paced her way across the terracotta tiles.

"Mira? Are you okay?"

No.

"Yeah. Just...dealing with a mess on my end of things." Now there was an understatement. "Are you certain your info's correct?" She'd corroborate it herself, if necessary. But given the tail that likely *had* been attached to her during her walk tonight, and who was most likely behind its attachment, this might not be the best moment to pump her own NCIS sources about Riyad.

"I'm certain. Do you remember Agent Jelling from when you flew over to Germany to assist with the attempt on General Ertonç's life?"

Mira spun around and crunched her way back across the kitchen. "Yes."

"Well, I had reason to suspect that Riyad was there too, listening in on that fight that John and I had in the CID parking lot the night we wrapped up the Ertonç case. Specific statements that John and I made cropped up during the investigation that I was sent to the *Griffith* to pursue. And the way they cropped up suggested that someone had leaked the existence of that argument to a terrorist."

Mira ignored the implication that Riyad might have spoken out of turn to the enemy—for the moment—and focused on the rest. "Riyad was in Hohenfels?" More than eighteen months ago? "Why?"

"At the time, the guy believed that John was connected to another SEAL on that failed mission you mentioned. Riyad was tailing John. Now, I can't prove that Riyad was near the parking lot that night. But in January, John asked the guy point blank if he heard our fight. Riyad denied it. His supposed alibi? He claimed he was stateside that night. So I texted Agent Jelling and asked him to verify the man's location."

"And?"

"At the very least, the stateside part's a lie. Riyad took an off-the-books hop from Langley to Germany the day before the argument. Where he went after he landed, Agent Jelling never found out. Jelly was shut down in mid-search—by Admiral Kettering. Kettering called Jelly personally and ordered him to keep his mouth shut about anything he might have learned about Riyad and his movements up to and including, or rather *excluding*, General Palisade."

Oh, Jesus. This went deeper than she'd feared.

Though with that stolen nuclear material out there, most likely already converted from the ceramic pellets in those assemblies, and a former Navy nuke and two SEALs—one still evidently active duty—involved in the entire mess, perhaps she shouldn't have been surprised. But that the very admiral in charge of the overall US Special Operations Command at McDill had ordered the withholding of information from his own direct subordinate, the three-star general in charge of the Army's Special Operations Command at Fort Bragg? It was flat-out unfathomable.

Except it *was* happening.

"Anyway—" Mira caught the whir of a microwave kicking in on the opposite side of the line. "—you got a feel for Jelly's tenacity when you joined us in Hohenfels."

That she had. Mira spun around and took another trek through the broken glass. "Let me guess, the man kept pushing."

"He did. He had intended to back off. Concerns about his wife and kid. But then he remembered a buddy who graduated from your criminal investigator and special agent courses at Glynco the same time as Riyad. Jelly was pissed over being shut down, so he gave his buddy a call. Riyad wasn't at Glynco. If you check the paperwork, the dates add up, but Riyad was never physically in class. Not even under a different name. Jelly's buddy says there were no ethnic Saudi students in the course at all—not even hanging out with the staff and ghosting the classes. Jelly's friend was polishing his Arabic then, so he was actively hunting down native speakers."

So, why the subterfuge and outright lies?

And if Riyad was still with the Teams, why had he been able to go toe-to-toe as he had with Bill Ramsey on an internal NCIS matter and not get kicked into the dirt?

Granted, Admiral Kettering clearly had Riyad's back. But given everything she'd seen and survived these past two months, not to mention everything that Jerry and Regan had been able to put on the table today—

Zak.

Those dislocated metacarpals snapped into focus again, along with everything that had happened before and after. The blood splattered over the bedroom of that condo. The level of hate it would've taken to shove that wine bottle between Corrigan's legs. The pros who'd broken into Frank's grandfather's home and stolen his water wings. The fact that a surface-to-air missile had even been aboard one of those offshore fishing boats. The near simultaneous deaths of those nuclear constables and the precision shooting that'd taken out the remainder of the *Pacific Tern*'s crew. And finally, that yawning hole in the *Tern*'s steel skin and those stolen assemblies.

It was all tied together. It had to be.

And the man who possessed the knowledge, planning, skills —and experience—to be able to knot up the various strings so meticulously?

She turned to slump back against the upper door of the stacked ovens. "Rae? Do you remember that SEAL I dated my freshman year of college, then a few years later?"

A soft snort split through the line. "The one who turned you off buff, pretty guys for good? How could I forget?"

A pause followed, one pregnant with the confession Mira had offered at the beginning of their call: namely, that she knew about the failed nature of that Navy SEAL mission off the coast of Iran, the missing SDV...and who had stolen it.

Because of that pause, she now knew that, Army counterpart or not, Regan had learned of those details, too.

"Mira...you never told me the guy's name."

That was true. When she'd shared her confession all those years ago, she'd still been raw about the entire affair. She was even more so now, but she coughed it up.

"Zakaria Webber."

Flat-out silence greeted the confirmation.

It stretched out, the tension within tightening so much, the phone line was vibrating with it—along with everything they'd just covered. Mira could actually feel Regan connecting Zak's name and that failed mission to what had—and had not been—in those official releases from Clearwater. And all the implications therein.

They weighed down her friend's breathing, and the agonizingly slow exhalation that followed. "*Wow*."

"*Yup*."

"Mira, I have to ask...Riyad and Webber...they're both SEALs. They supposedly hate each other, but in light of the critical lies that Riyad's been telling—"

"Is it a front? Are they working together?"

"Yes. I have to be honest. Given what I've learned about the man since the *Griffith*—and things I discovered before I met him—I can't rule the possibility out."

"I know." With everything she'd also learned and experienced firsthand since she'd walked into that blood splattered condo, neither could she.

Worse, Riyad's personality seemed to mesh with Zak's, and not in a good way.

"Crap. Mira, I've got another call coming in, and I need to take it."

"It's okay. You go ahead. I appreciate your information and especially your candor. I have a lot of thinking to do."

Not to mention, several serious decisions to make. Starting with whether or not she should phone Ramsey now and leave an ugly, detailed message about every blessed thing she'd learned today—including what she'd finally figured out about his silence.

"Call me later if you need an ear."

"Will do." But she wouldn't, and they both knew it.

As it was, the two of them had skirted perilously close to the edge of things that should not have been shared, if they hadn't plunged right over that edge. It was best to let this topic lie unless the situation became even more critical that it already was.

Mira hung up, the shock of it all ricocheting through her.

Zak had not only embraced terrorism, he was guilty of torture and first degree murder. The worst part was that, deep down, the idea that Zak might be capable of violence that wasn't Navy or SEAL sanctioned wasn't a complete surprise.

Not even this level of it.

At first, it had been the little things. The depth of Zak's possessiveness.

Even when she'd been a naïve eighteen-year-old college freshman visiting her brother at Camp Lejeune over spring break, it had felt too intense to her.

She'd gone to a party with Nate, one thrown by a buddy of his. Since several SEALs that Nate and his fellow Marine Raiders had worked with were in town, they'd been invited too. Zak had stood out. With those dark and exotic Yemeni features, she'd been seriously attracted to the man, and yeah, that honed body of his hadn't hurt.

Nor had the fact that Zak had just made chief. He'd been feeling invincible that night, and the innate confidence that he'd exuded had sucked her in deeper.

They'd gone out every evening of her break.

With Zak's solid, twenty-six years to her not-quite-nineteen, her brother had felt that Zak was too old for her, especially given his SEAL career and combat experiences.

She hadn't listened.

Not at first. But by the time she'd returned to class at BU, the reality of the ten hour drive from Boston to Virginia Beach had begun to kick in, as had Zak's primitive take on relationships and especially women. Fed up during an argument, she'd hung up on him. When he'd shown up unexpectedly the following weekend, he'd been livid to find her studying with a male friend, and she'd been forced to accept that Zak was more of a Neanderthal than her brother. While that didn't matter with Nate, since that problem belonged to the women her brother dated, it had mattered with Zak.

And it had hurt.

She'd not only slept with the man, he'd been her first.

But after Zak had lit into her study partner and come close to striking him, she'd held firm. She told Zak she was done with dating; she needed to focus on her classes. To her shock, Zak returned on graduation day. He apologized for his behavior the first time around. He claimed he'd grown and asked for a chance to prove it. But while he'd managed to suck her in again to where she'd accepted an engagement ring, he hadn't changed.

Oh, he'd faked it well enough during OCS. The beginning of nuke school too. And then that laptop had disappeared.

While she'd been fighting the charges so she could keep her reputation and her career, Zak had let his real feelings slip. The incident had done them a favor. The laptop would turn up, but it didn't really matter. Once Mira got pregnant, he expected her to get out and stay home. So turn in her resignation now and be done with it.

She'd ceded to half of his decree. She'd resigned her commission, and then broken up with him. She'd gotten another taste of the depth of the man's temper when she'd returned his ring, and he'd finally realized she was serious.

There would be no more reconciliations.

But she wasn't the only one who'd been clued in to Zak's true nature.

Riyad had been too.

Those dislocated, and then relocated, digits of Corrigan's?

She might not have known that Zak was capable of that specific technique, but Riyad had. He'd recognized it. That was why he'd abandoned the autopsy suite without a word. She'd stake her freshly healed body and brain on it.

Mira stared down at the glistening shards that she'd managed to track around the terracotta tiles while she'd been pacing. Fortunately, like the furniture she and Nate had inherited, the house's cleaning closet was fully outfitted too.

But first, she'd need to soak up the water.

She headed for the garage. A search through the drawers of the workbench along the far wall revealed a few old rags she could use. But on her return to the kitchen, she caught the subdued glow of a white light through the window of the exterior door that led out to the driveway.

A moment later, the light disappeared...only to be replaced by footfalls.

Her shadow?

Despite her efforts, had someone tracked her to her home?

She wasn't waiting around to ask. Not politely.

Dropping the rags on the cement floor of the garage, she

headed for the kitchen—and the replacement SIG Sauer she'd retrieved from the Field Office. As she slipped inside the house, she could hear the front door opening—then closing.

And then, more footfalls.

She'd reached the middle counter and had her tote opened when a dark, sinewy form with barely an inch on her five-seven swung around the corner. Despite that scruffy facial hair, not to mention the seriously shaggy mop that hit the tops of his shoulders, she knew that face.

"*Nate?*"

Relief burned in, and for so many reasons, as she let go of the tote, glass spitting out from her soles as she sprinted across the kitchen to throw herself into her brother's open arms.

He scooped her up, swinging her around, the strength of his own relief crushing the air from her lungs even as he growled into her ear. "*Jesus*, Mir! You left the goddamned door unlocked. I could've been *anyone*."

She swiped at the joy streaming down her cheeks as Nate finally stopped spinning them long enough to lower her back down to her feet. "I know; I know. It was stupid. I took a call when I walked in and forgot—"

"You *forgot*?" He reached around before she could stop him and swept his fingers over the small of her back, meeting sweatshirt and skin...and that was it. "And you're *naked*? Christ, Mira, didn't I teach you anything? With all that's been going on—"

"I'm not unarmed, okay?"

He tugged the front of her sweatshirt up far enough to expose her navel and one of the souvenir scars she'd received free of charge during that Wildcat crash.

And that was it.

"Then where the hell is your SIG?"

She tipped her head toward the butcher-block workstation. "Over there. In the tote you bought me for my graduation."

Along with the spanking new NCIS credentials she'd also picked up on her way out of DC. "Wanna check?"

"What I want is that weapon fused to your body twenty-four-seven. One or two backup pieces wouldn't hurt, either. Like the souped-up .38 I also gave you for Christmas a few years ago. Fat lot of good *that* present did. I know what you're working on—because I've been working the opposite end. Home or not, this is no time to get complacent."

"Yeah? Well, I'm not—working on it, that is. Not officially."

Tension ratcheted through that gorgeous mixture of Filipino and Caucasian features. "That's not what my agency contact said, not more than three hours ago."

So that's who he was reporting to this time.

Well, the CIA weren't as in the know as they believed, were they? If they were, the director would've taken the time to consult the Almighty Riyad.

"Things change. I'll explain in a minute. Right now, I want answers." She reached up to smooth her palm over the crop of facial growth that covered the lower half of her brother's face. Was it her imagination, or had it thickened since she'd seen him last?

Who knew? Three years was a long time to judge.

Too long.

But still, "What are you doing here? Ramsey said you were in so deep that they couldn't pull you."

Her brother's dark stare turned so cold, so fast, she could feel the frost spreading out into her. "They damned well should have. I had to find out for myself about the Wildcat crash and your *coma*. I can't believe you were on that fucking ship."

"Trust me; I wasn't there for long."

"Mira, this is no time to joke. It's a miracle you survived that fall." Nate pulled her back into his arms, forcing the air from her lungs a second time as he hugged her again.

She didn't care. He felt so good. Every warm, beautiful, still relatively uninjured and, for the moment at least, *safe* inch of him.

Glass crunched beneath her soles of her tennis shoes as he set her down, then the soles of his boots as he released her and stepped back.

"What the—" He took in the glittering splinters and spattered puddles of water still littering the terracotta. "Are you okay?"

"I'm fine. I dropped one of Mom's tumblers." The cleanup she'd been so intent on a few minutes ago could wait. "I'll get it later. Let's go in the other room."

Nate headed for her tote. Retrieving her holstered SIG, he walked it over to her and pointedly waited for her to tuck the polished leather into the waistband of her jeans at her back.

"Satisfied?"

He snorted. "Nope. But it'll have to do."

His frown deepened as he reached out to trace a finger along the scar that had hitched a permanent ride along her left temple. She thought he was going to start in on that helo crash and swan dive, and the miracle of it all again, but he didn't.

Instead, he hooked his left arm around her shoulders and guided her across the shard-covered tiles. Reaching out with his right hand, he hit the wall switch to turn on the overhead chandelier in the living room's vaulted ceiling as they entered.

They stopped in front of the drop cloth-covered couch, both of them staring at the portion of stairs that were visible in the foyer beyond. Their mom's flip-down mobility chair was still attached to the metal risers that traveled along the rich, mahogany paneled wall all the way up to the second floor.

She should probably have had the lift removed after their mom had passed. Except their grandmother had hated its *ugly, marring* sight so much, she'd left it out of spite.

Her grandmother had known why, too.

Payback for all the nasty comments and in-their-faces snipes to her *trailer-park-trash* mom and *that bastard, mongrel* brother of hers over the years. Imagine—a lady of superior breeding like herself having to live with *them*. Mira could still see those pinched, judgmental lips. Feel the shudders that had accompanied them.

The irony had never failed to escape her. That the grandfather that she and Nate had never met had willed this monstrosity of a house directly to their dad, who'd then signed it over to their mother when Daddy dearest had swapped them all for his new business and guilt-free life in Saudi Arabia. Of course, they all knew that Dad had only signed the house over because if he hadn't, *his* mother would've kicked her daughter-in-law and grandkids out on their asses the next day.

Hence, since their mother had known her days were numbered from the moment Benjamin Ellis' greatest sin had succeeded in incarcerating her in that wheelchair, the woman had taken pains to draw up her own will to leave the house and the few remaining nickels in the Ellis coffers directly to Mira and Nate.

"You think anyone's ever going to buy this place?"

With her luck impinging on any potential deals? Hell, no.

But she shrugged. "Maybe some dreamer with more money than brains will want to turn it into a bed and breakfast."

This was Annapolis. There was that built-in need to house the endless stream of tourists and all those visiting families of Naval Academy midshipmen. Of course, that same dreamer would need a lot of drive and more than a few handyman skills.

The house might look great on the surface, but there were issues beneath.

Just like with their father and grandmother.

Nate picked up on her mood and sighed as he turned to tug the cloth off the hand-carved, camel-back sofa.

A cloud of dust motes stirred up to dance amid the light shining down from the fixtures, drawing Mira's eye toward the air vent a good twelve feet above the floor on the far wall of the room. It was spotless. Turning around, she noted the dust that coated the significantly lower vent at the baseboard behind them. If the previous tenants had been such clean freaks that they'd sanitized the vent cover twelve feet up the opposite wall, wouldn't they have wiped down the one they simply had to bend over for?

She turned back to the twelve footer—this time, noting the darker shadow blocking a tiny section of the spacing between the lower vanes.

From *inside* the vent.

Looping the fingers of her left hand over the cuff of the long-sleeved tee shoved up to Nate's elbow, she gave his scarred forearm a squeeze. "You didn't happen to take a stroll down our favorite street before you made your way here, did you?"

His hands froze in mid, drop-cloth fold. "No. Why?"

She shot a pointed glance up at the vent, shifting her head awkwardly to get a second, confirming glimpse of the shadowy blur that was definitely there before she answered. "Because I did. I came back too soon, though. I was hoping you'd made your usual stop for caffeine at the place on the corner and left it in your car."

Nate's dark brown stare sharpened as he, too, studied the vent.

His swift shake let her know that he hadn't noted anything out of place, but his swifter nod let her know that he believed that she did.

As did the callused index finger that came up to press lightly into his lips.

Shhh.

She nodded her agreement as her brother set the drop cloth on the mahogany coffee table before heading for the foyer. She could see him bending down to rummage through a dark, canvas duffle twice as big as the tote she'd left in the kitchen.

Less than a minute later, Nate had returned, a small, field-grade, multi-function radio frequency detector in his right hand. He switched the RF detector on and pointed it up toward the vent. A split second later, her eyes had electronic confirmation.

The house was bugged.

11

N ate switched off the RF detector. "No, I didn't stop. But that's a great idea, Mir. If I remember correctly, the Mud Hen doesn't close 'til ten. Coffee's on me."

They headed for the foyer together.

Her brother bent low to hook his free hand through the straps of his duffle, swinging it up from the hardwood to drop the RF receiver inside the canvas and close the zip. Though it was obviously too late for precautions, Mira locked the front door from the inside before executing an about face and heading for the rear of the kitchen along with Nate.

Leaving the lights on, they slipped out into the dark through the French doors, which were completely obscured by the overgrown thicket of trees that the realtor had been nagging her to have thinned since last spring.

She was grateful for her recalcitrance as they slipped across the flagstone patio, then the pitch-black backyard to turn into the property catty-cornered to theirs. Nate waved her to the tree-covered sidewalk as they neared the street.

The companionable silence of their childhood settled in, albeit tautly, enhancing the deceptively cloistered feel of the cooling night as they continued to turn this way and that, cutting down the sides and across the backyards of additional homes in their old neighborhood until her brother finally stopped beside a beat-up Land Rover that was more rusted-out-red than its original midnight blue.

The SUV was slotted in amid a line of more upscale cars that appeared to be waiting on owners enjoying a dinner party down the street.

Mira got in the passenger side as Nate stowed his duffle in the back seat.

He'd probably swept this vehicle for listening devices the moment he'd acquired it, while she hadn't even realized there was a need to check hers.

A bug. Possibly several.

In her *house.*

The implications of the discovery continued to ping-pong through her ire-infused brain as Nate started the SUV. He drove out of the neighborhood, once again heading in and around the streets of the nearby business district for several minutes, putting additional distance between them and the audio receiver in the house, and the very real possibility that her tail might have returned and was now skulking about the shadows —or even waiting in another beat-up car—with a high-end parabolic microphone in tow.

The latter was more than possible. Because if Zak was behind the violation of her home, he wouldn't have drawn the line at a single stationary audio bug.

Nate finally backed the Land Rover into a dead-end street near Annapolis' bar district. He parked in front of the only other car on the lane, a blue VW Beetle, so they could retain full view of the cross street in front of them and any other cars or pedestrians that might attempt to follow them in.

As the engine died, he reached over to pop the glove box in front of her and retrieved an empty, signal-blocking pouch.

Mira nodded as she leaned forward to tug the replacement phone Ramsey had brought to Walter Reed from the back pocket of her jeans. She tucked the phone inside the pouch and secured the flap, effectively cloaking it from the planet, along with the potential that the device could be used to listen in on her pending conversation with Nate via its internal mic or track them with GPS.

Nate scowled as she dumped the pouch atop the Land Rover's dusty dash. "Should've given you that sooner, but I forgot I had the spare. All right, Miranda, who the fuck is bugging you?"

Lord she hated that name, and Nate knew it. Just as he knew why.

Which underscored how serious this was.

She matched his frown within the dark of the SUV. "I don't know." There were just so many possibilities. She could even play *what if* and pretend the bug had been installed to creep on her previous tenants, but— "I think I was followed earlier tonight. I ate dinner at Lulu's, and then I took that walk around the historic district. I got back about an hour ago. I never actually saw a tail...but I felt it."

Twice.

"Who knew you were coming to Annapolis?"

"A few people. Jerry's known the longest. Most of the day."

Her brother shook his decidedly shaggy head of hair. "Nah, he wouldn't have tipped anyone off, let alone sent someone to plant something in your place."

True.

"Who else?"

She shrugged. "Another agent. Not NCIS. But I told her less

than an hour ago on that call I mentioned." Even if she'd had the time, Regan would never have sold her out.

Of course, there was the returning and—in light of those dislocated metacarpals of the JAG's—distinctly vengeful specter of Zak Webber to consider.

Hell, even Sam Riyad could've had it planted. Given how deep his tentacles appeared to be in all this, the not-so-former SEAL could've asked another NCIS agent, or even an office worker, to keep him informed as to her whereabouts. If so, he'd have gotten a call when she'd stopped by the Field Office to retrieve her replacement gear and sign out on recuperative leave as she'd left DC.

But she wasn't ready to broach the topic of Riyad or Zak with her brother just yet. She had a much more pressing issue to discuss: that stolen radioactive fuel that had yet to surface.

"Nate, what are you even doing here? Has something happened on your end? Did you get a lead on the assemblies? Is that why you're stateside?"

"I wish. I haven't gotten that tight with my target—yet. But I know there hasn't been any chatter about the goods on the known terror channels. At least, not according to the agency guy I spoke with after my flight touched down at Dulles International this morning. But I am getting close. I gained enough trust for today's trial."

Trial? "Those assholes tested you?"

Logically, she knew that was a positive step. But this was Nate on the other end of it, potentially facing repercussions she didn't even want to think about.

Not after the blood-splattered walls of that condo.

Once again, Nate had picked up on her mood. "Relax. If all goes well, I should have standing when I get back. Possibly enough to leverage a few key answers."

Get back where? She desperately wanted to ask.

But she knew better.

Nate surprised her with a stunted sigh. "Shit, given how long ago you started on this—and where it took you—you probably know more than me. Look, I've been off the grid for about six months this time, studying in another madrassa. I can't reveal its location, but I've been posing as a disillusioned Filipino-American ex-Marine turned Servant of Allah. There were rumors that this particular madrassa was feeding into a terror pipeline that's hooked the agency's interest, and that, I have been able to confirm. Then about two months ago, the woman who cleans the rooms slipped me a note. Once I broke the code, I knew about the assemblies that were stolen from the *Tern* and what to look and listen for. But that was all I knew. There are no TV or other electronics allowed to students in the place, so I hadn't heard anything from a news source, until—"

They both stiffened as a group of five men ambled up to the corner off their left, playfully shoving and joking with each other as they made their way through the muted glow of the single streetlight shining down across the way. She'd have guessed tourists, save for the fact that Nate had parked well off the out-of-towner trail. Must be locals, heading for a crawl through the bars.

At least the men wouldn't be driving home afterward.

She waited until the group had passed. "So what's the test?"

Nate flicked his attention behind the Land Rover, then up and around the now empty crossway before he sat back in the driver's seat to relax.

Or at least, he appeared to.

Because that frown was still tense. "Money. Three weeks ago, I was called to the imam's quarters. There was another man there—one I hadn't spotted at the madrassa before. He didn't introduce himself, just told me that my US passport and I were needed to deliver 'religious supplies' to a mosque in the States.

Unlike the students, the higher ups have access to electronics and satellite TV. At first, I was so pumped that the Al Jazeera interview about a ships' collision playing in the background barely registered. Until I realized the ships they were discussing were the *Kittiwake* and the *Tern*. Then I heard the new guy tell the imam that the collision was all a cover-up. He didn't get into the specifics of the stolen assemblies, but he did tell the imam that our government was up their lying ass in it, along with the French, Japanese and Brits. His proof to the imam: that a British helicopter had taken off with an American agent aboard and that *she* and the Brits had gotten a nasty surprise when the helo finally reached the ship."

Nasty? Mira actually smiled at that, albeit grimly. That was not the word she would've used to describe that missile. Though it was accurate.

"Sis?"

"I'm fine. Go on."

Her brother raked his hand through hair that would've died beneath the blades of a barber's scissors months ago, had he not been holed up in that madrassa. Then again, those dark, shaggy strands and the scruffed, mustache-and-beard combination did support his disillusioned Marine cover story, and beautifully. "Right. Well, I admit, the pronoun *she* did give me pause. But even the big brother in me knew the odds were seriously slim that the American agent was you, so I pushed it aside at the time. But the other info? That these assholes knew the collision was a cover-up, but hadn't leaked that fact to Al Jazeera or anyone else themselves? That meant one thing."

"The terror group that the madrassa's feeding into is involved in this."

Somehow.

Nate nodded. "Yup. When some of us newer guys were sent to town to retrieve food stores a few days later, I slipped away for a minute. I stole a phone off a local and called my contact at the agency. I told him about the money drop I was scheduled to make in the States, then I told him what I'd overheard about the *Tern*. I asked about the woman on the helo, too. And when he went silent, I knew. I was livid. His excuse? You were in coma so there wasn't a damned thing I could've done. Well, he was wrong. I told him that when I showed up with the money, I *would* be visiting you—conscious or not. But by the time I arrived this morning and was able to phone him again, I was told that you'd woken up and stunned everyone with the speed of your recovery. He said you were doing so well, the docs agreed to let you come here to finish recuperating on your own." Her brother's shuddering exhale reverberated through her. "*Thank God*."

"Oh, Nate."

He reached out, the fingers of his right hand threading into those of her left, locking down hard as his voice turned hoarse. "Mir...I should've been there. I—" His jaw continued to work as he broke off, but that was it.

He couldn't get the rest of the words out.

"It's okay. I knew then that you'd have come, if you could have. But, Nate, your mission is *vital*. I know that, too, and better than most. And, hey, I experienced some seriously vivid dreams while my brain was healing. You featured in those often enough. So, in a way, you were with me." And he was here now.

When she needed him even more.

Especially his advice.

"I don't deserve that, but thank you." He dragged the cooling night air in and nodded. "All right, now fill me in on the part you skipped over in the kitchen—'cause, yeah, I noticed. You said you weren't on the case anymore, not officially. Why? Do you have lingering neuro issues or other injuries from that crash and the fall overboard that I wasn't told about?"

Great. Leave it to Nate's instincts to circle back to that dangling item—and to worry. "I told you the truth; I'm doing great, considering. Yes, I need a lot more sleep than I used to, and the scars on my shins itch like crazy—worse, if there's fabric covering them." Like right now. "I also tend to get lightheaded if I stand too fast, which is frustrating as hell. But my doc seems confident my brain will fix the lightheadedness on its own. If not, there are meds I can try. But we both want to wait and see, especially since my fuzzy peripheral vision has already straightened itself out."

"Then why are you glowering?"

"I'm not—"

"You are. Now spit it out."

Damn. She hadn't repeated that vile charge of Riyad's to Jerry Dahl or Regan Chase, but this was Nate. As much as she wanted to shield her brother from the repercussions of the mere accusation, let alone if Riyad had proof, she couldn't. This concerned Nate's father too, even if the bastard had refused to acknowledge their biological bond. And there was the other, professional reason that Nate needed to know. He'd be returning to the very front of the line of the war on terrorism.

And soon.

"Mir?"

"Dad might be a traitor."

"*What?*" Her brother gaped at her for the first time in their lives. And then he shook his head. Firmly. "No. I don't believe it. Look, I know as well as you that the man's an absolute asshole— and, hell, he's guilty of murdering Mom. But...a traitor? No fucking way." His hand slammed onto the driver's side of the dashboard, kicking up a decade of dust as the denial and the glare that came with it seared in deeper. "Where the hell did you hear that?"

"A man named Riyad. I thought he was FCI, but he's not. He's—"

"*Sam* Riyad? Commander of SEAL Team Twelve?"

She nodded. It wasn't as though the Teams published a public roster, so she hadn't known which team, let alone that the jerk still *was* a SEAL, until she'd spoken with Regan, but yeah, "That would be him. I met *Agent* Riyad the night I was assigned to the Corrigan case, shortly before I flew to Lakenheath and boarded the Wildcat. Riyad dropped that bombshell about Dad on me three days ago while I was at Walter Reed—and he thinks he's got proof. I take it you know the guy?"

"Some. Not well. We've passed each other in country over the years. Syria, Iraq, a couple of spots in Africa, but the teams I worked with never included him in the moment. I did overhear once that he's a card-carrying member of the crappy childhood club too, but I wasn't nosey enough to ask why. Now I wish I'd gotten to know him. Why the hell is he running around, shooting his mouth off about Dad to you of all people—" Just like that, the fire in her brother's eyes snuffed out. Ice replaced it. "Oh, *Christ.* Mira, please tell me he's not saying Dad's mixed up in that shit that's missing."

"I don't know. Riyad and I never got that far. I...blacked out." She held up a hand before Nate could latch onto that. "Before you start in with the worry—I'm fine." Three solid days of additional brain scans and other tests had proved that. "It didn't even have to do with that lightheadedness. It was just plain, old-fashioned shock."

A monstrous one.

As for the older bastard who'd spawned the both of them, during those three days, she had given the idea of their dad and the stolen assemblies some thought.

Okay, a lot of thought.

While the company their father had set up in Saudi Arabia

did center around chemicals, it didn't deal with the nitric acid that would've been needed to convert the plutonium and uranium in the ceramic pellets from those stolen assemblies.

But that didn't mean her father hadn't purchased a significant quantity of nitric acid and a few other key items that might've drawn Riyad's attention, had the SEAL been looking. Say, protective gloveboxes for the actual handling of the material and enough raw cement to create the six-foot-thick barriers that would also be necessary to shield whoever was assisting and overseeing the conversion...if those same people wanted a shot at growing old after the job was finished.

From his own, deepening glower, her brother had just made the same connection. "Did you ever tell Dad about Frank Nasser and what happened at NPS?"

And with that pointed question, Mira knew that Nate's latest call with his agency contact had provided pretty much all the information she'd been able to ascertain about the Corrigan murder and the MOX theft before Riyad had kicked her off the case.

"No." She hadn't even told Nate. Not then. He'd been in Iraq when everything around that laptop had crashed in. She hadn't wanted him distracted. Not with his life on the line on a daily, sometimes minute-by-minute, basis. She'd saved the entire fiasco, including her broken engagement and career change for her brother's homecoming.

The latter tidbit regarding her switch to NCIS had been easy to share, since by the time she and Nate had linked back up for a visit, she'd already graduated from the special agent course at Glynco that Sam Riyad had *not* attended.

"Sis?"

"He called me."

"Who? Benjamin Ellis, the Spineless?"

She nodded.

"When?"

"Over two months ago. At the time, I was...distracted by something that had happened. I didn't even check the number —not 'til afterward. I just picked up."

"What did he want?"

She watched as a sleek orange tabby padded through the glow glistening down from the streetlight in front of them. "I have no idea." She turned then, venting the part that had succeeded in rattling her to the only other person left on the planet who'd get it. "Nate, he didn't even ask how I was doing. He just started in on his amazing *other* wife. Said her *love* had made him realize a few things."

"Shit." Disgust rolled off her brother as he leaned against his headrest. "All right, I'll bite. What supposedly profound realizations has he experienced?"

"I don't know. I was so pissed, I hung up before he could finish. But I called the number back...a few days ago." The morning after Riyad had dropped by her room to grill her about Frank and lay those remaining tainted cards of his on the table.

Well, most of them. The SEAL had kept his tawdry knave from her view, along with that jeering joker. Or Riyad thought he had. Because she'd gotten enough of a glimpse throughout the day to extrapolate the rest of the man's hand.

"Mir, are you sure dialing that number was wise, especially now?"

Hell, no. Particularly because that call, and the fact that *she'd* initiated it, could be traced right back to her, more easily than her father's outgoing conversations had been.

But, "What would you have done?"

Nate finally sighed. "Same thing." He joined her in watching as a second slinking animal—this one a dog with shaggy gray fur—made its way through the glow of the streetlamp. "Okay, so what happened when you called him?"

"It went straight to voicemail. There's something else, too. That call I hung up on? Dad phoned back and left a message while I was in the shower. I deleted it without listening to it." The original and the backup. She'd been that furious. The data would've been overwritten while she was still in her coma. "If I hadn't—"

"*No.* Stop right there. You cannot beat yourself up about that, let alone about him. Hell, if that man had phoned me—for the first fucking time in my life, mind you—I would've hung up on him and deleted any voicemails too. As for the bigger picture? If that bastard has waded into something that's going to get him the life sentence he deserves, that's on him. Frankly, he'll be getting off easy. After what he's done, someone should've hacked off the man's dick and shoved it down his throat a long time ago. If Riyad can bring the asshole down, I say more power to him. I'll even help."

Silence followed that pronouncement, and it was pulsing with all the resentment and rejection that her brother had been forced to shoulder since he was two years old.

But then, Nate just let it go. Probably for her sake. He shoved a hand through his unshorn hair as a heavier sigh filled the Land Rover. "What did Ramsey say?"

"Nothing." Only it hadn't been nothing, had it?

More like that supermassive black hole she'd been experiencing with her boss of late—where information and a steady stream of texts and voicemails from her went in, and once again, not so much as a peep from him appeared able to make it out. Once she'd been able to connect that weird standoff in her hospital room between her boss and Riyad with everything that Jerry, and then Regan, had passed on about the very much *active*-duty SEAL, she'd realized what had really been going on.

Ramsey wasn't out of communications range or tied up with a critical case. At least not one so critical that he couldn't manage a one-word return text. No, her boss had been ordered to call her that night and send her to Commander Corrigan's condo, and then Ramsey had been ordered to stand down —from her.

At least his fury toward Riyad in the hospital had let her know that her boss had gone to bat for her with their entire chain of command.

Not that it had mattered. It was shades of that not-missing laptop all over again. Given everything she'd come across in her career with NCIS, not to mention the terror cases she'd assisted with and the arrests she'd made, she did understand the precaution.

But it still hurt.

And when she added on the shadow that she'd felt when she'd been walking through town earlier and the bug in her house, she knew why. Sam Riyad had deliberately pulled her NCIS authority and her support system—and then he'd *left her in play*. Alone. Cut off and adrift. He believed that eventually she'd get desperate enough to lead him to Frank and Zak... because she was involved in this mess.

But Nate did not need to know that. He had enough on his plate.

"Sis? You do know who's behind all this, don't you?"

Oh, God. So much for shielding the man. Nate already knew the worst of it. He'd just been waiting to see if she did, because brother or not, with his current tasking, Gunnery Sergeant Nathaniel Ellis shouldn't be offering up that name.

So she did. "Zak."

"I knew that fucker was bad news when you were dating him —the first time."

That he had.

And Nate had said so, too. "But I wouldn't listen."

He reached out, absolving her with that indulgent smile of

his as he tucked a strand of hair that had escaped her ponytail behind her ear. "You were just a kid. My eighteen-year-old baby sister. And even though I didn't want to face it, I knew he was your first." His smile bled off as those old ghosts and the memories that went with them churned through her brother's eyes. "I know; I'd barely hit twenty-one myself then. But I'd already been to Iraq once and I was getting ready to deploy again. So it kinda felt like I had a decade of life experiences on you at the time."

That might well be. But she'd managed to accumulate her own shit-store of questionable exploits since. And she definitely wasn't a kid anymore.

"You want me to talk to my agency guy? We're supposed to have a face to face at oh-dark-hundred this coming morning. He's bound to have some pull above Commander Riyad. I can—"

"No."

"Miranda—"

"I said, *no*. Nate, you do not screw with my career. Do you understand me?" She refused to let her actions, let along her fuckups, blow back onto him. "I can handle *Commander* Riyad, and I will be—starting tomorrow morning, as a matter of fact. I have a lead. I can't get into the specifics. But if it pans out, I may be able to zero in on Frank." And *he* would take them to Zak and the radioactive fuel from those assemblies.

God willing.

"But if this lead of mine doesn't pan out, I need you, Gunny Ellis, back in that madrassa, wherever it is. Hell, the world needs you there. Because you are the only one who's even met another person who might be connected to these bastards."

"*If* he shows up again."

True. There were no guarantees in either of their jobs, let alone easy successes. "If he doesn't, a subtle grilling of the imam may be able to point you in the right direction."

"That's the plan, Agent Ellis."

"Then stick to it. And don't worry about me." She tapped the scar riding her left temple. "Baby sister or not, I've proven I can take care of myself."

"That, you have." A new respect shone in those dark eyes of his, one born of an acknowledged, equal footing.

It warmed her from the inside out.

His focus shifted to his watch, then returned to her. "I should've told you earlier, but I'm under the gun. I fed the imam a story about needing to visit family outside DC, bearing gifts and tales of my fictitious job in Manila to keep them from sending Homeland Security after me. I was granted twenty-four hours. I used up half grabbing the Land Rover so I could drop the goods off at the agreed spot and drive here. I've got a couple of hours left, but then I have to be back in DC for that face to face with my agency contact. I can push the meet by an hour or two. But by noon, I'll have already dumped this piece of crap and be belted into a coach seat for a flight out of the States. Is there anything—and I mean *anything*—I can do for you before I go? I'll squeeze it in somehow."

There was. "Three things actually." Well, one really. But the others would make what she had to accomplish tomorrow go a lot more quickly and smoothly.

She hoped.

"Name 'em."

Mira pointed to the signal-blocking pouch on the dash. "Do you need that?"

Nate shook his head. "Like I said; it's a spare." He snagged the pouch and dropped it in her lap. "Keep it."

"Thanks. It'll save me a stop." But if they could swing this, Nate would be taking the pouch and the phone Ramsey had purchased for her back to DC with him—at least to the airport parking lot.

"What's the second item?"

"It's more of an action." Though this was the critical part, and it was tied to the first. She tapped the device hidden in the pouch. "Can you call me at this number before you leave Annapolis? Just tell me goodbye. I'll tell you that I forgot a few things, so I'm headed to DC to pick them up."

"I can do that. But you do realize that, if you've got bugs in the McMansion, you've probably got a GPS tracker stuck to your vehicle."

She nodded. "I know."

The moment he caught on to her third, as yet unspoken request, that gorgeous, gleaming grin of his lit up the driver's side of the SUV. "You want my wheels."

"Yup." He'd already told her he'd planned on dumping them. "You take my Blazer." The tinted windows and the dark that would still be blanketing this part of the country would help with the deception as her very male, not blond sibling pulled out of the garage. "Bring my phone and the pouch along for the ride, separately. Once you hit the Beltway, pull into a busy gas station and move the tracker to a local's car, then tuck my phone in the pouch." Yeah, the phone would disappear from the grid immediately, but with the GPS still spinning out data, there was an excellent chance the former's silence might not raise an alarm until it was too late. "When you get to Dulles, park the Blazer in the airport's short term parking with the key and my bagged phone in the glove box. I'll find it all."

Eventually.

As for her shadow and the delay she was hoping for, she hadn't noticed her tail on the drive here—and she had been scanning for one. That meant that whoever had been assigned the job was either paranoid or lazy enough to stay out of sight and let the GPS tag spit out her current locale. In either of those cases, it could take hours for that same paranoid or lazy whoever to get suspicious enough to move in close enough to those tinted windows for a confirming visual.

Hours were all she needed, and not many at that.

By eight a.m., her morning errands would be complete, and she'd be down at the harbor, waiting impatiently for her ship to come in. Well, make that a motor yacht.

But it would do.

It had to.

HER YACHT HAD COME in early.

So early that according to the harbor master, if she'd stopped by around nine last night instead of six, she'd have been able to greet her old "friend" then. But since the white lie Mira had told the harbor master wouldn't have held up to the feeble light of dusk, she'd been better off stress-walking around Annapolis, and then evading her tail before returning to the house to take Regan's call.

Heck, even if she had met Walid Rahmani before, walking up the pier the moment the *Huriya II*'s crew had looped their first mooring line around a dock cleat wouldn't have been prudent. Odds were that everyone aboard would still have been coming down off the adrenaline-driven dregs of channel fever, if they hadn't already crashed completely due to the sleep deprivation that also tended to ensue as an ocean-going vessel, no matter how large or small, drew close to port.

Better to wait until this morning to give everyone aboard, especially the man whose favor she desperately needed to court, a decent night's sleep.

Unfortunately, it was not quite eight a.m. Mira had yet to see anyone stir on Rahmani's eighty-eight-foot behemoth of a motor yacht. Those aboard the smaller white, luxury sailboats berthed to port and starboard of the glistening, graphite-gray *Huriya II* appeared to be tucked firmly in their bunks, snoring away as well.

It was going to be a long wait.

Resigned, Mira continued to sip at her rapidly cooling break-fast latte as she settled into the driver's seat of Nate's rusted-out gift, blessing her brother for the Land Rover—and so much more.

There'd been no need to run any of her remaining errands this morning, save this critical one. Nate had taken care of the others late last night.

Once he'd parked the Land Rover close enough to the house, yet far enough away so that she could return to it unimpeded and undetected, they'd hoofed it home. There, she and her brother had slipped back through the overgrown thicket that obscured the doors to the kitchen and into the pink-brick alba-tross they couldn't seem to sell. With Nate inside the house, she'd headed out the conspicuous front door to pull her Chevy Blazer into the garage. Once that door had dropped, Nate had joined her.

With his RF detector switched to magnetic mode, her brother had immediately zeroed in on the GPS tracker inside the Blazer's right rear wheel well.

Whoever had attached the gem was definitely lazy. Wheel wells were one of the first places a federal agent would look if he or she needed to inspect their vehicle by sight alone. But then, what agent would've anticipated that someone in their own blessed agency would be tracking and listening to their every move?

And they *were* listening to hers.

Nate's slow, systematic search of the house had revealed three additional audio bugs. A bit of an over-precaution given the range on any one of the four. Of course, finding that quartet of audio bugs and the GPS tag had confirmed the rest.

The phone Ramsey had given her was definitely tainted.

Fortunately, that issue now had a workaround as well. While she'd taken a power nap, Nate had snuck through the covered French doors yet again to execute a swift, round-trip visit to a twenty-four-hour superstore. She'd woken the proud, if still seething owner of not one, but three burner phones she could actually use.

Surprisingly, there'd been no video camera in the house.

Riyad and/or Zak had probably saved that particular device for the bedroom of her sublet. After all, both men were creeps, as well as assholes.

Even more alarming: those audio bugs and the GPS tracker were all high-end, *government* issue. Yes, with his skills, Zak could've gotten ahold of them—but it was much more likely that the devices had been placed by the *un*-Agent Riyad.

Like Regan, she was becoming more suspicious of the active-duty SEAL by the second. The more Mira thought about that failed mission off the coast of Iran, the more she was forced to wonder why Riyad was even alive. The green shit that had been found in his fellow SEALs' lungs had also killed every single nuclear constable aboard the *Pacific Tern*—and most of the nuclear transport ship's crew. According to Ramsey, those who'd survived, only to get shot in the head, didn't have it inside them.

All told, over four dozen men and women, plus the entire family of the *Kittiwake*'s captain, had died from that poison.

So *how* had Riyad lived?

The most likely explanation was also the most chilling.

What if Riyad hadn't ingested the poison along with his supposed nemesis, Zak...because the men *were* working together?

While that rapidly increasing possibility was frightening

enough, with the active-duty SEAL having invaded nearly every aspect of this investigation, including those that were predominately Army, where the devil was she supposed to turn for help?

Save for Regan, Jerry and Nate, there was no one she could trust. But with the trio's respective careers, she shouldn't be involving any one of them unless the situation was critical. Hell, with Ramsey's behavior of late and who might well be surveilling him too, she couldn't even turn to her boss. Not until she had a solid lead on Frank—or proof that Riyad was up to his own rotten, radioactive flippers in this mess.

In short, she was on her own. At least for now.

Fortunately, she had a place to start. Just as soon as those aboard the *Huriya II* began to wake. Though the delay in that waking was a boon.

She'd already made her first call of the day. Shortly before Nate had left Annapolis, she'd used that tainted phone from Ramsey to make her morning call to Walter Reed's ICU, only to get the same depressing response she'd been getting since Caleb had been admitted. Worse, that particular *I'm sorry, Agent Ellis, there's still no change* had been more demoralizing than usual knowing that someone was listening in on and recording her pain. For that reason alone, she'd chosen to phone the nurses' station again, instead of Caleb's hospital room.

There was no way she'd willingly subject Malcolm McCabe to the same mental and emotional violation, whether the Marine would ever be aware of it or not.

Polishing off the remains of her caramel latte, Mira tucked the paper cup into the Land Rover's grimy drink holder. Resisting the temptation to scratch the barely healed scars that covered her shins, she leaned over to open the SUV's glovebox instead. The three burners her brother had purchased were stowed within.

It was time to expend, then dump, the first.

While she refused to involve her friends in this any deeper than she already had, she did need to alert Regan and Jerry to the likelihood that when Ramsey had handed her that replacement phone at Walter Reed, it had already been cloned. Though with Riyad and/or Zak involved, she doubted either friend would be surprised.

First Regan, then Jerry.

With Fort Campbell's clocks set an hour earlier than those along the Eastern Seaboard, it was 0703 in Kentucky. If she was lucky, she'd catch her Army counterpart in between her morning physical training regime and leaving for her office on post. This was one message that should not go to voicemail.

The line began to ring, but there was no immediate pick up. Not surprising. Regan had that weird photographic memory when it came to digits, and the final seven connected to this throwaway device wouldn't have been a phone number that Regan had seen before. Though the Maryland area code should help.

"Hello?"

Mira kept it cool. Casual. "Hi, I just wanted to call and let you know the borax trick you suggested for my house worked. I'm ant-free...now."

A slight pause filled the line, and then, "No problem. And you're welcome. Hey, I'm in the middle of something. Can I call you back? It should just take a sec."

"Sure thing."

Mira hung up. Less than three minutes later, the burner in her hand rang. The number on the screen was not the one assigned to Regan's CID phone, but it was headed up by a Tennessee area code.

Tension filled the line as Mira picked up. The sort that came with her and Regan knowing they were now both using throwaway phones.

This time, her friend cut right to the chase. "What the hell is going on?"

She filled Regan in on the previous night's developments—and the fact that, although her Army counterpart hadn't offered anything incriminating during their call, what they had discussed had very likely been recorded via Ramsey's gifted replacement and/or the audio bugs in her home.

"Your *boss* gave you an infected phone?"

Mira stared at the luxury yachts gently bobbing against the maze of wooden docks in the distance, feeling anything but calm, balmy and relaxed. Fortunately, she couldn't see the *Natty Mir* from where she was parked. There were too many other sail-boats and motor yachts in the way. "Yeah, it looks that way. I think Sam Riyad was behind it."

A soft curse slipped into the Land Rover from the opposite side of the line as Mira described the weird standoff between the men in her hospital room.

That curse might not have been hers, but it matched the one that had been reverberating through her gut all morning.

Her fellow agent's dark sigh added to it all. "Mir, there's some stuff I didn't offer up last night, and for good reason. But I did a bit of thinking after we got off the phone. Given the vessel that I don't think you accidentally *fell off*—and if what I think's missing from that transport ship *is* truly missing—you need to know a few things about what I've been working on and how it all connects to Sam Riyad. It may help you track down what's missing before it gets...used."

The curse in her gut pulsed louder as a svelte woman on the yacht to starboard of the *Huriya II* made her way above deck in a barely-there, scarlet wrap.

She could also see movement on the stern weather deck of Walid Rahmani's sleek motor yacht now. "Fire away."

"Do you remember the news about what happened at Fort Campbell this past December—on Christmas Day?"

"If you're referring to the soldiers from your husband's Special Forces team who killed their loved ones and began committing suicide, yes."

"I am. The story was correct. Our soldiers were infected with a psycho-toxin. It was obtained from someone with connections to the Russian biological warfare agency, *Biopreparat*. I'm not sure, but there may be more of that neurological agent out there. Hell, from what some of us were gassed with in Kabul, I suspect there are a few other nasty concoctions floating around among these bastards, too."

"Does any of it produce a neon green substance in the respiratory system?"

"Not that I know of."

Shit. Odds were, she was dealing with a different warfare agent, then. Though, chemical or biological, she'd now wager it had come from *Biopreparat* as well.

As her Army counterpart began to touch on the highlights of an intricate terror case that linked the deaths of nearly half that SF team and several of their wives to those Pakistani cave murders that had also made the news a few weeks later in January, the caramel latte Mira had finished began to slosh through her stomach.

A US Army Arabic translator, an Afghan doctor employed at the Craig Joint Theatre Hospital at Bagram Airbase who'd had access to coalition troops, not to mention a former US Army CID agent who'd gone on to join the Diplomatic Security Service so that he could infiltrate Embassy Pakistan? And *at least* one dirty Navy SEAL?

"*Christ*, Rae—how deep does this go?"

Given the connection to those poisoned SEALs on that failed mission off the coast of Iran just over two years ago, not to mention Sam Riyad's lies about being in Hohenfels, Germany, months later, how long had this all been going on?

Who the hell was behind it all?

Zak? Or that active-duty SEAL sporting a faux, NCIS suit?

Or *both*?

"Rae—"

"I know. It's bad. And...there's something else. Agent Jelling's not the only one who caught Sam Riyad in a lie. I think Riyad stole a critical piece of evidence, too."

Oh, Jesus.

"I can't prove it, mind you. But while John was in surgery in Pakistan, I got a call from Riyad. He claimed that he was at the airport in Islamabad, pursuing a Webber sighting. He even warned me that he'd likely be out of touch for a while—though he was right about that part, because I haven't heard from him since."

And the other? The inference that Riyad hadn't been where he'd said he'd been when he'd made that call?

The verb her friend had used was rife with it. "Claimed?"

"Yeah. It was another lie. I pieced it together the following day. I was tracking the chain of custody on a pair of wraparound sunglasses that had fallen from the shooter who'd tried to kill John outside the embassy. Naturally, I wanted those sunglasses."

She would've too. Those glasses would've had the shooter's DNA on them.

"What happened to them?"

"The SF soldier who found the glasses bagged them and had a Marine from the embassy lock them up in the regional security officer's safe to preserve the DNA and any other forensic evidence on them. When the soldier went back a couple of hours later, the glasses were missing. The safe had been locked the entire time."

"What about the DSS agent you arrested for treason?"

"Scott Walburn had been temporarily assigned to the embassy then. There was never a need, so Scott wasn't given the combination."

Oh, Lord. She already knew what was coming across the line next.

And it did. "Yeah. Sam Riyad had access to the safe's combination. He got it from his biggest fan, the embassy's deputy chief of mission, Warren Jeffers."

Holy crap. "The DCM confirmed that?"

"Under oath. Jeffers said Riyad came in and asked for the combination...shortly before I received that phone call from Riyad during John's surgery. And a Marine embassy guard confirmed that he saw Riyad coming out of the RSO's office around the same time—with a large, new, oddly stuffed manila envelope under his arm."

"Let me guess. The SF soldier stowed the wraparounds in a fresh manila envelope."

"Yup."

This was so much worse than damning.

There was only one reason for Riyad to steal those wraparounds. The SEAL was protecting whoever had been wearing them.

The caramel latte began to churn through her stomach in earnest.

Mira closed her eyes, pressing back into the SUV's headrest as the terrifying implications continued to spin in. By the time she opened her eyes and caught a glimpse of the dark, looming shadow that was skulking in from her left, its owner had already reached the driver's side of the Land Rover.

And her.

12

"Just a second, Rae."

Mira shifted the phone to her left hand as she slipped her right beneath the hem of her light-weight gray sweater to grip the replacement SIG Sauer P239 tucked in at the back of her slacks. Only then did she turn to fully face the heavy Arab features of the early-twenty-something man now standing opposite of the Land Rover's driver's window. He was dressed in the long-sleeved, ankle-length traditional Arab thobe common to the Middle East and other Muslim countries, the fabric's dark-blue hue matching that of the simple taqiyah covering the crown of his head.

The man smiled broadly, displaying an impressive collection of stark-white, even teeth between his thick mustache and beard.

She hiked a questioning brow in response.

Mr. Gleaming Smile's string of words got muffled and tangled up in the SUV's grimy glass. She could've sworn he'd said something about breakfast...and her.

Surely she was mistaken.

Either way, she relaxed—a bit. Keeping her right hand

between the small of her back and the stained fabric of the driver's seat, she juggled the burner phone so she could depress the correct button to zip the window between them down.

"I'm sorry, sir. I didn't quite catch that."

If possible, that grin widened further as its owner bowed slightly, tipping his blue prayer cap toward her. "Good morning, Agent Ellis. I am Atif. I am here on behalf of my employer, Walid Rahmani. Haji Walid is currently breaking his fast. Once he has finished, he is willing to speak with you. Perhaps in...twenty minutes?"

Okay, the part about breakfast had been correct. But the rest? How had Mr. Smile—or his boss, for that matter—known her name?

The dock master?

Probably. And that sunny smile was waiting. She withdrew her right hand from her SIG and nodded. "Thank you, Atif. I'll be pier side in twenty."

She tucked the phone back against her ear, raising the driver's window as the man turned away to depart for the docks. And then, "Rae? Something's come up. I need to hang up and meet with a man who may be able to get me closer to locating that...missing stuff we touched on."

"*Go*—and good hunting. Don't worry about me; I need to get on post myself. But call me if you need me. Any time, and from any number."

"Will do."

She hung up and pulled the battery and SIM card out of the phone she'd just used, swapping the temporarily decapitated device for one of the virgin burners in the glovebox. Mira retrieved the swath of silvery gray silk that she'd tossed into her leather tote after Jerry had dropped her off at her sublet yesterday morning, then bailed out of the Land Rover. Tugging the stretch band from her ponytail, she wrapped its length into a low bun and used the band to hold it in place before topping everything off with the scarf. The crossed ends of the silk went over her shoulders; the virgin phone into the right rear pocket of her slacks. She took the time to ensure that her credentials were still seated firmly in the left, then smoothed her sweatshirt down over both pockets and the holstered SIG hooked inside the waistband above.

She was ready to meet with Rahmani. The one person Frank Nasser might've actually turned to for advice or help these past few months. Especially since the massively successful software engineer's current yacht bore the name of his much more humble first: *Huriya*. She'd looked up the Arabic term; its English translation: *Liberty*.

Unfortunately, Abdul Nasser's old friend wasn't ready to meet with her.

She had eighteen minutes to kill. Worse, in light of where she was currently standing, there was really only one logical place to kill them.

Hell, why not?

The confrontation was going to have to happen one of these days.

She followed Atif's path toward the docks, stepping up onto the sun-bleached wooden slats. But instead of turning to the right as Atif had, she paused in front of the security shack and nodded to a man whose lined and weathered face attested to a life spent on the open ocean. Happy ones too, based on the tales Grady Scala had regaled her and her brother with when their walks had taken them this far as kids.

"Hey, Grady."

"Hey, yourself, Mira. Long time, no see. The dock master said you'd be by this morning, so I went ahead and let Mr. Rahmani's man know that you wanted to speak with his boss when Atif split for groceries at dawn." He tipped his shock of shoulder-length snowy hair toward the subdued scarf covering hers. "I'm guessing that was okay."

"Absolutely." It also explained how Atif had known to stop beside the Land Rover. Grady must've told him what she looked like. "And thanks. I'll be headed over to the *Huriya II* in a few."

"Ah, you can't resist a peek at your own floating treasure, can you?"

Oh, she could. But she had seventeen minutes left to kill. With the lingering adrenaline piggybacking onto her morning hit of caffeinated sugar, she was wound up. Sitting in that Land Rover and watching the endless seconds tick by would not cut it. Nor would openly pacing beside it in view of the *Huriya II*'s expansive windows.

Not if she hoped to pull off this interview smoothly enough to walk away with an answer to one of the most pressing questions that had been searing through her brain since she'd woken in that intensive care unit at Walter Reed.

Where the hell was Frank?

By this time tomorrow, Nate would be burrowed back inside some jihadi-fronted madrassa redoubling his efforts to blend in —and quadrupling the risk to his life. Knowing that made her more determined than ever to locate the fuel from those assemblies.

The first step to it all was Frank.

She was certain of it. Why else had he been trying to strangle Captain Whitby on the bridge of the *Tern* when she found them?

Impervious to her darkening mood, Grady fell into step beside her as she hung a left. Not only did she not deter him, she adjusted her stride to accommodate the man's slower gait. Grady was one of two in this town who could still recognize her in a crowd of tourists. And her memories of him were equally precious...to a point.

Together, they turned again, heading for the thirty-two-foot sturdy Westsail sandwiched between a pair of significantly sleeker cabin cruisers that were also forty years younger and twice the length.

Grady whistled as they came to a halt off the *Natty Mir*'s bow, genuine appreciation shining within his faded blue gaze as it touched on the mast and furled sails, before sliding down the heft of the double ender that had once been her mother's pride and joy. According to her mom, this very sailboat and the *Natty Mir*'s plethora of nearly identical sisters had succeeded in bringing the cruising life out of the fringes and into the main-stream for America back in the seventies.

That faded blue turned to her. "Your momma's prized water baby still looks great."

That she did.

The blue strengthened, along with the grin beneath. "She can hold her own with most of the other gals here too, no matter how much they cost. I appreciate you and Nate letting me take her out to put her through her paces one more time."

How could she have asked anyone else?

"You're welcome, Grady."

Though the man was definitely biased. Not to mention, the *Natty Mir* had been up on the blocks, existing in nautical suspended animation in a covered dry dock for the last eighteen years of her life. Ever since the day her mom had accepted that she'd never board the boat alone again, much less take her out onto open water.

Her mom had been convinced that Mira or Nate would want the cruiser, so she'd stubbornly hung on to it. They'd even talked about hiring someone to take them out after their mom had passed. But in the end, they hadn't. There were just too many memories associated with the *Natty Mir*. And after learning what they had about their father years earlier, most had become too damned painful.

Their mom had finally convinced their dad to join his family for a sail down the coast when Mira was ten and Nate was months shy of hitting his teens. At first, it had been amazing. Especially since their folks had been getting along for a change. And then the night after they'd pulled into a slip in Miami, the bastard who'd spawned them had dropped his bombshell. Their trip was nothing more than a drawn-out goodbye. Within the month, he'd be leaving for his new life in Saudi Arabia—without them.

The news had put a bit of damper on the sail home.

And when they'd finally reached Annapolis and their mom had collapsed on the dock right where Mira and Grady were currently standing? Well, that had killed any love of sailing that might've remained in both her and Nate.

The ambulance had taken them all straight to the hospital.

A slew of tests had followed. One hell of an incriminating answer later, their guilt-ridden father had left for Al Jubail a few weeks early, and their mother had been fitted for her wheel-chair. There she'd stayed, until her heart and her hope had finally given out the day after Mira turned eighteen...and she'd laid her mom in her coffin.

"Mira?"

"I'm okay, Grady." She forced a stronger smile for his benefit. "Just a lot of memories attached to this old boat...and the dock."

His hand came up to cup her shoulder and squeeze gently. "I know."

Of course he did. He'd been here, working on his own twenty-eight footer several slips over the day they'd all returned. He'd called the ambulance.

"You're really gonna sell her, huh?

"That's the idea." In a roundabout sort of way.

Ironically, the *Natty Mir* had been pulled out of dry dock, thoroughly overhauled and tucked into her enviable private slip to help sell the McMansion. The realtor was convinced that the addition of the boat and the slip would pique interest. After all, quite a few folks looking to buy in Annapolis were interested in sailing, too. And if the new owners weren't? Well, the *Natty Mir* and her slip would be sold off separately.

Either way, her mother had been dead for eleven years now. It was past time to let her sailboat go. Maybe the *Natty Mir* would get renamed and create more memories for some other family—good ones this time.

Mira retrieved the burner she'd tucked into her back pocket, using it to check the time. "I need to meet with Mr. Rahmani soon. But first, I've got a new contact number to give you. Just in case a potential buyer stops by with a question that you can't answer." Though there wouldn't be one, and they both knew it.

With her mom gone, Grady knew more about the *Natty Mir* and her slip than anyone on the planet.

She waited as he withdrew his own phone, then rattled off the number to the throwaway that she'd decided to use as her current phone—at least until she could trust her own chain of command again. She slipped the burner into her pocket.

He tipped his forehead toward the scar that was now a permanent feature of hers. "So, you gonna tell me what happened there?"

Why not?

This was Grady. Though she kept it light. Vague. "I was on a helo that crashed into a ship, then I got knocked into the drink for good measure."

That faded blue flew wide. "*Jesus.*" He shook his head. "Don't take this the wrong way, but there's a pretty good chance someone up there doesn't like you."

Yeah. She knew who. But he wasn't up there. He was very

much down here, on earth. At least, she prayed so. Unfortunately, she didn't have so much as an inkling as to where to find him. But that was why she was in Annapolis.

"I should go."

Grady nodded and tipped that shock of pure snow her way once more. "Don't be a stranger."

"I won't."

But by the time she'd turned to walk back to the head of the dock, she already felt like one.

Reversing her path all the way to the security shack, Mira pushed past it, clipping along the wooden boards of the docks until she reached the final turn. Atif and his flowing blue thobe and gleaming smile were waiting for her at the base of the short gangway that bridged the watery gap between the weathered slats and the buffed teak platform at the stern of the *Huriya II*.

The young man gestured her aboard first, then followed her onto the yacht. "Good morning, Agent Ellis. Allah has granted us a beautiful day, has he not?"

"Hello again, Atif. And, yes, he has."

Atif motioned her toward the glass sliding wall that had been pushed to the left to offer open access to the motor yacht's spacious dining/lounging cabin. "Please, make yourself at home. Haji Walid will join you shortly. Would you like coffee, tea or perhaps juice, while you wait? We have pomegranate and orange today."

The breakfast latte she'd polished off had contained more than enough caffeine and sugar to jumpstart her day, thank you. Another hit of either and she risked the jitters. But to refuse Walid Rahmani's hospitality before they'd even met would be rude.

And potentially unrewarding...for her.

"Pomegranate would be lovely. Thanks."

The young man nodded and turned to descend a set of steps discreetly hidden at the rear port corner of the main cabin.

No doubt they led to the galley and crew quarters below.

Mira took in the oblong glass dining table, and black and steel chairs that commandeered the forward port corner of the space. The table sat eight, six more than the scuffed laminated number in her tiny sublet kitchen. And the gorgeous L-shaped sectional beside her? She was terrified to approach it, let alone sit.

How the heck did that supple ivory leather manage to stay supple and ivory in port, let alone at sea?

Something told her Atif earned every penny of his salary.

The glass coffee table centered over the blood-red area rug intrigued her more. Or rather, the copy of the Qur'an sitting on the table at the far end. Like the sectional, the book was covered in leather, but a smooth, saddle brown. The intricate scrollwork and detail in the flourishes that appeared to have been painstakingly hand stamped around the edges were even more impressive than the couch.

They whispered, *open me and look inside.*

"It was meant to be a gift."

She spun around to find Atif hovering near the glass slider and holding her pomegranate juice. Standing in front of the darker Atif was another, older male whose hair, mustache and beard had long since mellowed into a steely gray.

The illustrious Walid Rahmani. He had to be.

Eighty years of age, if memory from her chat with Frank served, and heavy set. Rahmani had roughly two inches, three tops, on her five-seven. Like Atif, his employer was also dressed in a traditional thobe, capped off with a simple taqiyah, though the fabric of these was tinted a warm flaxen. While Rahmani's initial smile was not as white and gleaming as his employee's had been, it was wider and even more welcoming.

"Agent Mira Ellis, this is an honor."

Honor?

Her bemusement increased upon spotting the accompanying twinkle in Rahmani's dark eyes as he placed his right hand over his heart. "*As-salamu alaikum.*"

Mirroring the gesture, she offered him peace in return. "*Wa alaikum assalaam.*"

As they lowered their hands, Atif set the glass of juice on the coffee table and withdrew to the concealed steps to disappear below deck.

The twinkle in those remaining eyes mellowed into an equally curious, friendly respect. "I am Walid Rahmani. But you know this, yes?"

"I do. Mr. Rahmani—"

"Walid, please." He waved his hand toward the shorter portion of the L-shaped ivory leather. The seat he was offering was next to the Qur'an that she'd been admiring and the glass of pomegranate juice that Atif had left behind. "Sit."

Rahmani smiled again as she complied, but this one was directed at the scarf that she'd taken the time to drape over her hair.

The thobe, the honorific that Atif had used twice in her presence. Haji was reserved for Muslims who'd been to Mecca and completed the personal spiritual journey of the hajj. Frank had been spot on about his father's old friend. Walid Rahmani was still walking the Islamic walk, and quite seriously.

The modesty of the scarf and the lack of her more comfortable jeans and sweatshirt had been a good call.

"Thank you, Haji Walid."

He inclined his silvery head as he joined her, sitting catty-corner to her on the sectional. He waved his hand toward the leather-bound book between them. "Of course, I was not able to gift this to him, or it would not be aboard the *Huriya* with me."

Him?

Frank.

She was certain. She was also certain Rahmani intended for her to know that.

But why?

While she and Frank had discussed his grandfather's friend at length, especially after Corrigan had shown them the signed statement claiming that they'd been spotted searching through the drawers of the instructor's desk at NPS, looking for the missing laptop, she hadn't been certain until this moment that Frank had met Rahmani.

"He was here, then? Frank Nasser?"

"Yes, the grandson of my friend Abdul was here. He visited for a time. Stayed aboard the *Huriya* with me for nearly two weeks. It was almost a year ago now and shortly after he left the Navy. Farid—Frank—was seeking direction in his life and wondered if he might find it with Allah."

"If you don't mind me asking, how was his mood then?"

"He was troubled. He felt he would never be accepted among his fellow officers; that he had wasted years of his life attempting to be. That angered him. I cautioned against this. I had hoped he would find peace while he was here, but he did not. If anything, he became more unsettled."

"Do you know why?"

"Not precisely. But a few days after he arrived, Frank renewed his acquaintance with a man he had met years ago. From when you and Frank knew each other, I think. This is how I know your face. I have seen your photo. The one taken of your class at the officer candidate school you attended together in Newport. On the last day."

Rahmani had seen that photo of their OCS graduation? The one snapped during the celebratory dinner that had followed?

Perhaps not so surprising, since Frank was in it, too.

Ironically, that photo was one of the few she still had of Zak, and only because it contained most of her friends from OCS. She'd transferred the same photo to her tainted phone before she'd left her sublet yesterday. She'd transferred it again, before dawn this morning, to the burner phone currently tucked in her back pocket.

Mira retrieved the burner, located the photo within and used two fingertips to enlarge the shot and move it around until Zak's face nearly filled the screen. How could she have missed the stiff look he'd given the guy on her other side back then?

Easy.

Seven years ago, before that missing laptop had blown up her and Frank's lives, she'd still had her head in the sand regarding Zak.

Well, no longer.

She passed the phone to Rahmani so he could get a good look at Zak's face.

Nodding, he handed the burner back. "Yes. That was him. They met several times the first week and every day during the second. At first, I accepted what this man said, that he and Frank were studying the word of Allah together."

"But something made you suspect that they weren't?"

Those slightly gnarled hands spread. "How could they have been? Frank was still so angry, and growing more so with every passing day. If they were studying the Qur'an, this would not have been so."

Yeah, she wasn't so sure about that.

Surely Rahmani knew how the contents of Islam's holy book could be, and often were, twisted to fan the flames of anger and hate.

Just as the texts of other religions were.

But that particular anger; its source? While Rahmani had already alluded to it, she needed it spelled out. "Haji Walid, was

Frank still upset about the accusation of theft that was made against the two of us at nuke school?"

"Very much so. He believed that the accusation was responsible for his lack of progress in his Navy career. He told me that you got out of the Navy because of it. That you became a special agent in their criminal service so that you could prevent false charges to others. He wondered if you had suffered the same suspicions from others as he had, or if you had been allowed to rise above it with your new job."

Now there was a dicey query. If someone had asked her that months, or even days ago, she'd had offered up an unequivocal *yes*.

But this morning, after she'd been stripped of her case? Bugged and tapped with a *government* GPS transmitter? Forced to purchase burner phones and to deliberately set out to evade her fellow agents so she could continue to work that case?

The man next to her was waiting for an answer.

Did she dare?

Mira purged her frustration with a soft sigh and gave Rahmani what she needed from him in return. The truth. "I have good days and not so good ones. And lately? Haji Walid, I have to admit, there have been more than a few of the not so good ones. But I do have faith that it'll all work out in the end. I have to."

He seemed pleased with her response as that dark gaze of his drifted down to the Qur'an between them. And then it rose again to find hers. Resolution filled it.

"He came back."

Hope lurched within. Mira forced herself to hold it at bay. "Frank?"

A nod met her query. That was it.

Shouldn't there be...more?

"When?"

"In March. The morning of the twentieth to be precise. I remember the date. Atif and I were readying the *Huriya II* for the very voyage from which we have just returned. I was forced to contemplate delaying our departure so that I could arrange a flight to fulfill a decade's old debt to a brother in Allah. And I would have."

The hope escaped her heart and invaded her entire body. Adrenaline crashed in with it, hitting her so hard and so fast that she nearly stood up in the middle of their conversation, so she could pace the cabin as she tried to contain it.

But she didn't.

Mira reached for the glass of pomegranate juice, forcing herself to concentrate on the more sour than sweet taste as she ordered her nerves to *calm down*.

It wasn't easy.

Commander Corrigan had been murdered on March the nineteenth. That Frank had come to see Rahmani the following morning was huge—and even more revealing.

Years ago, Rahmani and Frank's grandfather had immigrated to America together...in the forward storage hold of a vessel twelve times the size of the one she was currently aboard, and in much shittier shape. Rahmani shouldn't have made the trip though. Too many men had shown up to board the vessel at Muscat. And since all but Rahmani were Omani, he would be the one to remain behind.

It was Abdul who'd convinced the vessel's owner to let Rahmani aboard. Abdul offered to split his water and food ration with Rahmani for the month-long journey. Trapped in the hold with little air and less light, both men had almost died along with several others. Upon their arrival in the States, Rahmani had sworn an oath before Allah. He owed Abdul Nasser his life. All Abdul or one of his relatives had to do was show up and ask, and the favor they wished would be granted.

At their lowest point during that laptop fiasco, Frank had offered to extend the favor to her. While running was not his first choice, he'd told her that if they showed up on Rahmani's doorstep, the man would get them out of the country. His grandfather's friend would even set them up financially in their new life, no questions asked.

Frank had not been joking.

But neither did she believe that Frank had wanted to take that escape this time either. Nor had Frank asked Rahmani for it. The proof had been in Frank's hands that morning on the bridge of the *Pacific Tern*. She now knew exactly what had been going through Frank's head when he'd had his fingers wrapped around Captain Whitby's throat. Just as she knew where he'd asked Rahmani to send him.

"Cherbourg."

"Yes."

As profound as that tiny, three-letter response was, she needed more. She had to know everything this man knew or merely suspected for her to have a hope in hell of assisting Frank with his goal. But the only way she was going to get the truth from the man seated on the ivory sectional catty-corner to her would be if, once again, she gave the truth herself. As much as she could.

"Haji Walid, I'm sure you've seen the news. Heard the... explanation...of what happened between those two ships that limped back to port."

A light flared within those dark eyes. It wasn't driven by surprise. It was more of an acknowledgment that Rahmani's own growing suspicions were correct.

She hadn't mentioned the radioactive fuel in those MOX assemblies.

She hadn't needed to.

She was sitting on a supple leather couch in the main cabin

of a ten million dollar yacht. A man didn't claw his way from starving stowaway to becoming a software engineer and creator of his own Fortune 500 company by wallowing in ignorance and denial. Given what Rahmani knew of Frank, and Frank's former profession, along with the name of the city that Frank had requested a flight to, and what had and had *not* been on the news, Walid Rahmani had been more than able to fill in the holes all by himself.

And he had.

The glint in those dark eyes confirmed it.

"Please. Sir, I need to know what happened when Frank came here the second time. *Everything* that happened. It's critical. There may be countless lives on the line."

And this man knew that, too.

The glint flared, then faded as those eyes grew solemn. "As I said, he showed up on the twentieth of March. He was shaken. Something had happened. Frank would not tell me what. He said he could not go home to Abdul, because my old friend had already suffered severely for misdeeds that were not his. Nor could Frank go to the police—that like before, assumptions would be made, and this time, there would be no changing of minds. Frank told me he needed time to think, that he had a decision to make. Late that evening, he came to me and requested the flight to Cherbourg. As he was so exhausted he could barely stand, I sent him to bed while I began the arrangements. He slept in one of the cabins below where you and I sit now. By morning, I was ready to give him the details for his flight, hotel room and a rental car—but when I rose for prayer, he was already gone."

"Do you know where he went?"

"No. As I said, he was simply gone. The small bag he had brought with him was missing as well. Atif did not see him leave either, for he was also abed when Frank left. But then...a friend of his showed up a week later. This friend said he was concerned about Frank. He said he knew Frank had come to see me. He wanted to know what Frank said to me while he was here, and if he left anything in my care."

"A friend? The one from the year before?" She pulled up the OCS group photo and zeroed it in on Zak, then turned the phone toward Rahmani. "This man?"

"No."

Okay. "Did this new friend give his name?"

"Yes, but it was a lie."

Shit. That was it then. She didn't have photos of any of Zak's cohorts in this. She didn't even know who they were. All she knew was that Frank was not one of them. Not willingly. Unless Rahmani could describe Frank's new "friend" down to the freckles on his nose—if they existed—this was another dead end, and one she could ill afford.

Unless...it was a long shot, but—

"You said this new man lied about his name. How did you know he wasn't telling the truth?"

"Because, while he did not know me, I knew him. Correction. I knew *of* him."

"How? You recognized him from somewhere?"

"Of a sort. He is Saudi, as I am. Or, as I was born. I am American now. But I knew the prince's family years ago, before I made my way to Oman. His grandfather and his father, most especially. Despite the grandfather's status in the kingdom, he was not a good Muslim. And the father? He became a favorite of the crown prince's and a diplomat. But the path his father walked was more shameful than his grandfather's, because his father claimed that his first wife and their son died in Kuwait some thirty years ago. And yet, there the son was, the very image of his grandfather and his father, standing on this vessel almost two months ago on the twenty-ninth of March: Samman bin Ahmad Al Saud. Though that morning, he called himself—"

"Sam Riyad." She wasn't sure why she'd blurted out the SEAL's name. Much less how she knew that Riyad had come here *while* she'd been boarding that Wildcat to fly out to the *Pacific Tern*, but she did.

Rahmani's nod proved it. "I see you have met him, too."

Oh, she and Riyad had met, all right.

Though that was one man who'd better hope he never crossed paths with her again, because there was an excellent chance he might not survive.

And a *prince*? What the hell was that about? How many faux identities did the bastard have?

She shoved that question aside in favor of her newest, even more critical query. At least with Rahmani.

She might actually be tempted to pray on the book lying on the table, if it would produce the answer she wanted. "And did Frank...leave something in your care?"

The glint returned to those dark eyes, and this one was driven by satisfaction. "Not precisely. The leaving of it was more a careless accident. Atif found the item when he was cleaning the cabin after Frank left. He brought it to me. Once I realized what it was, I was...hesitant to throw it away."

"But you didn't give it to Sam Riyad?"

Or whoever the hell Riyad really was.

"No. Samman lied to me—about his name, but more importantly that he and Frank were friends. I could tell from the anger in his eyes and the way he spoke of Frank that what Samman felt was not friendship, but hate. So I did not trust him with what was left behind." Those slightly gnarled fingers reached out, pressed down along the spine of the Qur'an.

Rahmani slid the book the rest of the way down the coffee

table until it was near the edge of the sparkling glass, inches from her.

Evidently, he wanted her to take it.

But this couldn't be what Frank had left. Because while Rahmani stated that the Qur'an had been intended as a gift, he'd also said it had gone unreceived.

"Please, it is yours now. You must care for it, until it can be passed to him. You may even find solace within the pages yourself, during your search for him. Try surah eight, verse seventy, seventy-one. I believe you may find the wisdom within helpful in your other...quest, as well."

It wasn't until Rahmani rose from his seat that she realized that Atif had returned to the main cabin from below decks.

A moment later, she heard several male voices down on the dock.

They were growing closer.

"I hope I have been of assistance, Agent Ellis. But now, I must turn my attention to my other guests who are about to come aboard."

She had no problem getting the heave-ho, especially when it was offered as politely as that one had been. But Rahmani hadn't given her whatever Frank had left behind, much less told her what it was.

Unfortunately, the voices had moved up onto the teak platform at the stern of the boat, and Atif was waving two western-suited gentlemen inside the cabin.

Damn. She definitely couldn't continue this conversation, no matter how euphemistically couched. Not with witnesses. Worse, if she pushed Rahmani in front of his other guests, she'd lose any chance at obtaining what she desperately hoped would be a clue to solving this mess—and finding the fuel from those stolen assemblies.

She'd have to make another attempt.

She'd give it a few hours. Spend the morning walking around town, then swing back by the docks to check on the *Natty Mir*...and drop by the *Huriya II* to say hello.

Resigned to yet another inescapable delay, she retrieved the leather-bound Qur'an and stood. "Thank you very much for your time, Haji Walid. If you don't mind, I'll exchange phone numbers with Atif before I leave. In case one of us has a need to add anything to our conversation at some point in the future."

"Of course."

She nodded to the suited men as she passed, then paused out on the landing to offer her number to Atif and type his into the burner. Returning the man's renewed smile, she disembarked the yacht and made her way to the security shack at the head of the marina. There, she paused to ask Grady if he'd mind giving her a heads up should he learn that the *Huriya II* planned on getting underway in the near future.

Upon receiving Grady's ready thumbs up, she walked into the parking lot to where she'd left the beat-up Land Rover.

Once inside the driver's seat, she tugged the scarf from her hair and stowed it inside her tote, then propped the Qur'an up against the steering wheel to satisfy her curiously regarding the pages within. They were as smooth as the hand-tooled leather of the cover and just as gorgeous. Bright blues, greens, golds and reds tinted the scrollwork and flourishes that formed the two horizontal boxes of text on each page. One in English, the other in Arabic.

Moving backward to her, but forward in the Arabic-formatted book, Mira searched for surah eight, verses seventy and seventy-one as Rahmani had suggested, only to find the spot already marked with a slip of torn paper. And the chapter heading?

The Spoils of War.

A bit on the nose, but okay.

Mira moved the shred of paper further down the Qur'an's inner seam so she could read the English translation that waited for her, unimpeded:

O Prophet! Say to the captives in your hands: 'If Allah finds any goodness in your hearts He will give you that which is better than what has been taken away from you, and He will forgive you.

But if they seek to betray you, know that they had already betrayed Allah. Therefore He made you prevail over them.

...WHAT HAS BEEN TAKEN AWAY...

Her suspicion had been spot on. Once the "collision" between the *Tern* and the *Kittiwake* had made the news, Rahmani had added his knowledge of Frank's distress to the former Navy nuke's burning need to fly to Cherbourg and had figured out that at least some of the radioactive assemblies that had been bound for Ishida had been stolen.

And while she did appreciate the confirmation and the moral support in her search for the missing fuel, especially in that final verse, she wanted whatever the hell Frank had accidentally left behind on the yacht the day he'd disappeared even more.

Frustrated, Mira flipped the makeshift bookmark over.

And froze.

There was a Washington, DC, address penciled on the reverse. In Frank's distinctive, near indecipherable scrawl.

This was what Frank had left.

It had to be.

She leaned forward and tugged the burner phone from her pocket and opened its internet app. Was that *six three four five*? Or *six three four six*?

She opted for the latter—and hit pay dirt on the first try.

Her heart began pounding harder than it had during all those physical training sessions that her therapist had subjected her to back at Walter Reed as she realized the implications of the gift that Walid Rahmani—and Frank's carelessness—had given her.

The address was for an Islamic mosque inside the Beltway.

But not just any mosque.

Sheik Ibrahim's masjid might be small and tucked away in an unassuming part of town, but it came with a rather notable reputation, as did its imam. Not only did the mosque cater to immigrants who adhered to the strict orthodox views of the Wahhabi sect, Sheik Ibrahim was a reputed jihadi sympathizer. One who law enforcement, federal or civilian, had been unable to solidly link to terrorism—as yet.

Her curiosity had definitely been piqued, along with her impatience and hope. It would take roughly an hour by rusted-out Land Rover to get to that address to satisfy all three. And when she added on the fact that it was just past nine-fifteen on a Friday morning? The Friday after Ramadan, no less?

She had nearly four hours until *Jum'ah* prayers commenced.

Christian congregations weren't the only ones known to experience a spike in attendance following their holy days. Muslims did too.

Welcome to human nature.

If she made it in time for this *Jum'ah*'s spike, she and her about-to-be veiled face just might be able to get lost in the crowd...while she searched for a target.

Shoving her main burner into her pocket, Mira reached across the Land Rover to retrieve the final virgin phone from the glovebox.

Seconds later, she was punching in Jerry Dahl's number.

Yes, she still needed to give her old partner a heads-up

regarding that tainted gift from Ramsey. But she had a few requests to make of the MPD detective and his new department's resources, as well. With Jerry's logistical help and a quick peek at the Metropolitan Police's prior research, she might be able to make it through the side door of Sheik Ibrahim's mosque...and skulk around long enough to locate her next lead.

One that just might take her all the way to that stolen nuclear fuel.

13

J erry and his department had come through.

The traditional black, triple-layered, Saudi-style niqab and abaya that her former mentor had purchased at an Islamic clothing store currently covered Mira from head to toe, allowing her to blend in from the moment she'd parked across the street from the modest, two-story building that housed the mosque. The MPD intel that Jerry had been able to bring along for her to review before coming here had taken care of the rest.

The Metropolitan Police's ongoing research had produced a list of several potential sources, all of whom were connected in one way or another to a dozen known radical Islamic jihadists who had frequented Sheikh Ibrahim's masjid through the years.

Within seconds of removing her shoes and entering the moldering cleaning closet of a room that served as the women's section of the mosque, Mira's gut had whittled that list down to one.

The imam's daughter.

From the snatches of whispered conversation that Mira had been able to overhear between Jalilah Ibrahim and her identically veiled and defiantly *not*-prostrated-in-prayer friend, the imam's daughter had turned eighteen the week before. That same morning Jalilah had informed her father that she was now legally an adult in their new country. As such, she would be dating a boy she'd met through school who was not Muslim, because religious affiliation did not matter to her.

Furthermore, she would no longer cover for her father should he lose his temper with others as he so often did and take it out on her. Why?

Because she deserved *more*.

If he could not deal with that, she would be moving out.

While brave, the impromptu gauntlet the girl had thrown hadn't been particularly prudent. Given the way Jalilah kept gently pressing her fingers beneath her right cheek and the edge of her jaw through her veils, not to mention the blow-by-blow description she'd offered her friend, Sheikh Ibrahim had not only picked that gauntlet back up, he'd wrapped his fist around it as he'd slammed both into his only daughter's face...several times.

Mira shifted the gorgeous Qur'an that Walid Rahmani had entrusted into her care, pretending to read the opening passages through her own veils as she strained to hear more of the conversation taking place to her left.

According to the audio being piped into this stifling space, the masjid's congregational prayer was about to commence.

Jalilah and her friend, Lizet, couldn't care less. The former desperately wanted to call her boyfriend to let him know that her father was threatening to pull her out of college and send her to a cousin in Saudi Arabia. Both girls seemed to believe that should that happen, a forced marriage—to that cousin or another—would quickly follow.

Hence, Jalilah was desperate to use her friend's phone.

Unfortunately, Lizet's father had forced her to leave it at

home so she'd concentrate on the coming congregational prayers and sermon.

"I'll go to his office. He has a drawer *full* of phones. I'll use one to call Paul from the bathroom and have it back before *Jum'ah*'s over. He'll never know."

Her friend leaned closer. "Oh, that's *perfect*."

Lizet was right; it was perfect.

For Mira.

She closed the Qur'an and stood, bringing the leather-bound book with her as she wove her way through several devout women and the infants, toddlers and older children filling the prayer carpets that were crammed into the room.

Slipping into the hall, Mira made her way to the bathroom she'd noted near the "women's" entrance to the mosque—an unadorned emergency exit that led to the back alley and a trio of ripe commercial dumpsters.

Given that charming afterthought of an entrance, not to mention the musty closet where women had been relegated to pray while their male counterparts gathered in the main, airy hall at the center of the mosque, that bathroom was probably the only one for her gender in the building.

Mira pushed through its door, frowning as she cased the layout.

Figured. Like the women's prayer room, the restroom was little more than a faintly lit closet with a pair of stalls at one end and a single scuffed porcelain sink, plus a small wooden cupboard, at the other. Beneath the sink and its exposed piping sat a green, ten gallon plastic bucket, presumably for washing feet before prayer.

A small clouded mirror with black splotches encroaching from around the edges hung above it all, summing up the female experience in this place.

At least the stalls had doors.

Sheikh Ibrahim should be ashamed of himself. For striking his daughter and for subjecting the women of his masjid to this. Mira had seen better facilities for Muslim women in three different developing countries—and it was one-eighty out from the inviting mosque across town where a fellow female NCIS agent worshipped.

Mira tugged the niqab Jerry had provided from her head. She laid the suffocating layers of black nylon on top of the cupboard, along with Walid Rahmani's Qur'an. Using her finger-tips, she rubbed at her eyes, then smacked her cheeks to redden the skin and encourage a bit of swelling.

It didn't take long. While ash-blond hair might be a hindrance when attempting to shadow someone or evade a stubborn tail herself, the sensitive and easily marked skin that came with it would only enhance her coming ruse.

Turning on the tap, she used several drops from the trickle of water to layer tear tracks over the streaks and blotches. Smudged mascara would've enhanced the effect, but she didn't bother with makeup on the best of days, which this was not.

It would have to do...because the door was opening.

From the coral-painted toes peeking out from beneath the entering shroud of black—along with the plainer fingers clutching a bargain-basement phone—Jalilah had managed to steal a burner from her father's stash.

Not that Mira was sitting in judgment on the girl, especially since she was brandishing her own fourth throwaway of the day, this one thoughtfully provided by Jerry when he'd passed off her niqab, abaya and the other items she'd requested.

The best part?

Her former partner had preloaded the phone with the photos she'd requested.

The girl turned to face her as the bathroom door closed, inhaling softly as she spotted the faux tears.

Mira spun away, facing the cinderblock wall as she nudged a quaver into her voice. "I'm sorry. I sh-shouldn't have—" She broke off, filling the gap with several sniffles and a noisier hiccup. "—come today."

"Are you okay?" She could hear Jalilah Ibrahim's bare feet padding across the cement floor. They came to a halt behind her own sock-covered heels. Moments later, the girl's fingers pressed into the shoulder of Mira's matching abaya. "Ma'am, can I help? The sermon has just started. I can send someone in for your husband—"

"*No.* Please. I'm afraid that's... It's impossible." Mira pulled her breath in audibly as she shuffled around to find Jalilah unveiled now as well—and nearly cursed.

Beneath the light of the naked bulb overhead, it was obvious that Jalilah hadn't been exaggerating to her friend in the prayer room. If anything, the girl had underplayed the extent of her father's latest round of abuse.

A week on from that thrown gauntlet, and half of the right edge of Jalilah's heart-shaped jaw was still purple and swollen, along with the crest of the delicate cheek above. The girl's bottom lip was still a bit swollen too, with a half-healed split marring the center. Given that level of rage, Mira would wager the girl was sporting additional bruises to her torso and limbs, if not more serious injuries. With the high collar and the rest of Jalilah's abaya cloaking the girl from her wrists to ankles, there was no way to tell without prying.

Despite the reason that Mira was here, in this bathroom, targeting this girl for assistance, she very much wanted to pry. Jalilah Ibrahim needed assistance of her own. Desperately. The girl might've turned eighteen a mere week ago, but those dark, soulful eyes amid that battered face?

They were wise beyond their years.

Mira reached out with her free hand. "Are you—"

"Okay?" The girl nodded as she leaned back just far enough to keep those woeful bruises out of reach. "I'm fine. I'm mostly healed up now."

Yeah, she wasn't.

Nor did those visible marks account for the battered heart beneath.

Jalilah wadded up her niqab and tossed the head covering onto the cupboard next to the Qur'an Mira had set down, then stepped closer. This time, Jalilah was the one who reached out, her fingertips touching the faux tracks that Mira had created. "Don't worry about me. My tears have had time to dry. Your pain is fresh." That dark, too-mature gaze lowered to the simple gold band Jerry had also provided for this makeshift undercover operation. "Are you sure I can't get someone to find your husband?"

The guilt that had been roiling through her gut since she'd spotted the girl's bruises doubled. Yes, Jalilah was legally an adult. From the intel that MPD provided, which Jerry had then passed on to her an hour ago, the girl also did computer and admin work for her father. Which meant Jalilah had the right to be in his office. Hence, successful or not, what Mira was about to ask would hold up in a court of law.

But it still felt wrong.

And those bruises and that split lip?

If it hadn't been for the fuel from those missing, mixed-oxide assemblies, she might've been tempted to call this off here and now. But the plutonium and uranium *were* missing. Hundreds of thousands of lives were at stake—secular, Christian, Jewish and Muslim, too. As wrong as it felt to capitalize on the physical and emotional pain of this single girl's situation, it was more than necessary.

It was vital.

Mira sucked up the guilt and pushed forward. "My husband

—" She lowered her own gaze to the ring, spreading her fingers as she raised her hand. "I'm afraid, that's the problem. My h-husband—" She drew her breath in as she appeared to gather the courage to finish. "Akram divorced me just over two weeks ago. I had no idea anything was wrong in our marriage. But I could've handled the divorce. Mostly because—" She cursed herself even as she let the grief enter her own blue eyes as they focused on those very real bruises. "—he h-hits, too, when he's upset. But when he left, he took my son. It's been sixteen days, and I have no idea where my b-baby is."

"Your husband divorced you and stole your son—during *Ramadan*?"

Mira wiped the remaining water from her cheeks with the back of her left hand as she nodded.

"What a bastard."

Mira let that pronouncement lie unacknowledged, staring silently at her unadorned right hand, deliberately drawing attention to the throwaway phone that Jerry had provided an hour earlier and miles away from the mosque.

"May I?"

Mira nodded, refreshing the phone's screen before she held it out.

Jalilah set the burner she'd brought with her onto the cupboard as she accepted Jerry's. Queued up were the photos Mira had asked him to retrieve while she'd been on the road from Annapolis. The first was of a friend of theirs, Heba, and Heba's then eighteen-month-old son, Eman. Of course, you couldn't tell that the woman in the photo was Heba, let alone that the mass within that blotting-out black *was* a woman, since Heba had been visiting her husband's very traditional family in Bahrain when it was taken.

But that just made the boy's unruly, inky curls and sweetly dimpled cheeks stand out all the more.

As the girl swiped right, Jalilah moved into the trio of photos that Heba had taken of Mira holding the baby shortly after his birth in San Diego, and again the following year. Unfortunately, Heba hadn't been at home when Jerry had called with the photo SOS, so those three pictures plus the first one with Eman and his real, very loving mother were all that Mira had to support her subterfuge.

Fortunately, it was all she needed.

"What's his name?"

"Eman."

Jalilah passed the phone back with a soft smile. "He's beautiful."

"Thank you." Mira pressed the phone to her chest as if she was reluctant to let Heba's little guy go. "I came here earlier this morning. I thought if I could speak to the imam, he would tell me where my husband's friends live. Their phone numbers and addresses have to be on the mosque's membership roster, right? They know where he took Eman. But one of the men stopped me before I could knock on the imam's door."

"Sadiq?" Jalilah shook her head. "Yeah, he's a jerk. He'll never let you pass."

"But surely the imam—"

Another shake, and this one was firmer. "He won't help you either. He always sides with the Muslim *man*. Trust me, I know. But I can get the addresses for you."

"Are you sure? How would you even know where to look?"

Pink tinged the smoother skin that surrounded the healing purple. "My father. He's the imam. My name is Jalilah. I work in his office after classes and on weekends. I can get into his computer, print the membership roster and be back here with it before *Jum'ah* ends."

"I'm Maryam. Jalilah, I would so grateful for your help, but I don't want to get you into trouble."

"I'm already in trouble—because I wanted out of his family."
She tapped the bruise on her cheek, the split in her lip. "The
imam did this to me, and it was not the first time." Jalilah held up
her burner. "That's why I came in here. I went to his office to get
this, so I could call my boyfriend. We're going to—" She stopped
short and shook her head. "It doesn't matter. We have at least ten
minutes before the sermon's over. That's plenty of time to get the
roster." The girl snatched up her niqab and pulled it down over
her battered face before Mira could stop her. "Wait in here for
me. I'll be back."

Moments later, Jalilah was gone.

But the burner the girl had brought into the bathroom was
still there, sitting on the cupboard next the Qur'an that Rahmani
had entrusted into Mira's care.

Sign from the Great Above or not, Mira grabbed the
forgotten phone.

She located the number attached to the sheikh's burner
within its settings and typed the digits into hers, then slipped
her burner into the pocket of her abaya. The sheikh's went back
on top of the cupboard in the same position it had been in
before.

Mira was settling in for the wait when she heard them.

Male voices.

Terror surged—and it wasn't for her.

That muted conversation was following the path she'd taken
from the women's prayer room and up the hall. She could make
out two distinct voices now. One was still low; the other was
slightly louder, deeper. Their owners passed the bathroom and
continued on toward the imam's office...where Jalilah was
currently breaking into her jihadist father's files. And that
deeper voice? The dark, heavy chuckle that accompanied it?

She'd know it anywhere.

Zakaria Webber was in the corridor.

Holy shit.

Mira grabbed the remaining niqab from the cupboard and tugged it over her head and neck. As she pulled the more translucent veil and the heavier so-called "privacy" layer down next, she freely admitted that she'd scorned that descriptor the first time she'd heard it offered as a selling point. But God, Allah —or whoever—as her witness, she prayed that final layer of translucent black nylon would provide her with exactly that now.

Privacy.

And even more stealth.

She launched another frantic prayer heavenward as she tugged her latest burner from the left side pocket of her abaya. This entreaty was twice as intense and entirely for Jalilah. At the moment, Mira didn't care if the girl returned to the restroom with or without that roster. So long as the girl returned—and in one piece.

Mira's next prayer went up on behalf of Bill Ramsey.

She punched in her boss' number, knowing full well that her call would show up attached to digits that the man would not recognize.

So, if he was in an important meeting, why pick up?

Ramsey's phone rang.

For Jalilah's sake, she hoped Zak and his cohort had stopped shy of entering the imam's office. And for her own sake? If Zak *had* paused outside the office and he heard her speaking to her boss? Well, the bastard was bound to remember what she sounded like too. And Zak knew she was NCIS.

Ramsey's line continued to ring...*unanswered.*

Mira was tempted to draw the SIG at the small of her back, but she didn't. She couldn't risk Jalilah spotting it on her return. The girl might sound the alarm.

Yet another excruciating ring, and Mira's call finally went to

Ramsey's voicemail. She didn't have time for an exchange of texts to explain where she was and what she was doing here, so she hung up and punched in Jerry's number.

That call, too, went to voicemail—instantly.

Christ.

If her old partner wasn't on the verge of executing a critical, no-knock—*silent*—warrant, she'd flay him alive.

She was about to text Jerry when the door to bathroom swung open.

A wave of relief swept in along with Jalilah's cloaked form.

The abaya swirled in around the girl's ankles, framing those dainty, coral-tipped toes as she slumped against the door with a shudder. "I can't believe it. He cut the sermon short today. He *never* does that. The man is too in love with the sound of his own voice, preaching to the reverent masses." The girl's right hand slipped up inside her generous left sleeve. "But I got it."

She brandished the sheaf of rolled-up papers between them.

Despite the fact that the names and addresses within were no longer critical, Mira took the roster. Any potential leads were now moot—at least to her.

As was following Frank's trail.

Her main target was *inside* the mosque.

"Thank you so much." She scraped her voice down to a bare whisper. "Jalilah, one of those men that passed in the hall? I know his laugh. He's a friend of Akram's."

"The Saudi or the Yemeni? I'm sorry, I don't know their names."

Saudi?

Was it possible that the other, lower, voice had belonged to Riyad and she'd been so stunned on hearing Zak's again that it hadn't registered with her?

Shit.

"Maryam?"

Mira shook her head. "Sorry. He's Yemeni."

"Oh, him." The girl shrugged. "He left. Well, they both did. They're leaving the city too, and soon, I think. But not until after they dine with my father. They're both off to wait for him at the restaurant. I heard them talking as they left. Strangely, both of them had American accents."

Well, that didn't bode well for Riyad, did it?

"Do you know where they're eating?"

"I'm not positive, but they went out the women's door. There's a Syrian café nearby and that's the shortcut. Go to the end of the alley and take a right at the street. It's midway up the block, also on the right. I think they overcook everything, but my father likes it, so that's probably where they'll eat. But you won't see them up front. They always eat in a special room in the back."

Well, that precaution made sense, didn't it? Half the blessed world was searching for one of those men, and the other half should be.

But Zak had already left the mosque and was on the verge of leaving DC.

She had to get out of here.

Now.

The girl must've read the impatience in her face. Despite her efforts, Mira knew it was there. Because it was searing through her soul.

Mira grabbed the sheikh's burner from the cupboard and tossed it to Jalilah as she shoved hers into the pocket of her abaya. "Let me give you a number." She rattled off Jerry's private number and waited as the girl typed it in. "Do not return that phone to the office. Hide it. Because you're right; you don't have to put up with the abuse. Jalilah, if you really want out, call that number I gave you. Tell the man who answers that Maryam said to call him. He'll arrange everything."

"I don't understand—"

"You don't need to." Mira folded up the roster and pulled the hem of her abaya up to her waist so she could shove the papers into the front pocket of the slacks she'd donned to meet Walid Rahmani too many hours and miles ago. Somehow, it felt like years. "All you have to do is call. The man who answers will get you out."

Apprehension and confusion continued to swirl though those dark eyes peeking through the veiled layers of Jalilah's niqab. It was so intense, Mira could almost hear the girl's thoughts churning within.

Minutes ago, Mira had been in tears and needing Jalilah's help. Yet now, here this strange woman was, offering hers.

And so much more.

"I'm sorry; I need to go." She closed her hand over the girl's, squeezed. "Don't wait to call. The danger to you is closer than you think. And it is *very* real."

With that, Mira grabbed the Qur'an from the cupboard and slipped past the imam's daughter, all but bolting from the bathroom. She turned away from the men milling about the front of the hall and headed for the door that opened to the alley as quickly as she could, and without drawing attention to herself.

Screw her shoes. She'd never locate them in time to find Zak.

If she hadn't lost him already.

The bastard wasn't in this section of the alley. Nor was anyone or anything else, save for the trio of commercial dumpsters and their rotting contents.

She pulled up the abaya's overly long hem and then her sweater so she could wedge the Qur'an between her holster and the small of her back. The book secure, she drew her SIG, keeping the 10mm buried between the resulting voluminous folds of her shroud as she cleared the space beyond the final dumpster of potential threats.

Still no Zak—or anyone else.

Damn.

She gathered up her hem again with her free hand, this time so she could jog along the cracked blacktop of the alleyway without tripping, wincing as something cut through her right sock and into the pad of her foot. But she didn't stop. Not until she reached the line where the blacktop met the equally fractured and weathered concrete of the street beyond. Mira paused to sweep a frantic glance to her left, then her right.

There.

She could see the sign for the Syrian café, its scrolling Arabic lettering already lit up and pulsing in neon red above the sidewalk, despite the fact that it wouldn't be dark for hours. But while there were at least two dozen pedestrians within shouting distance of the café, none appeared to be heading in or out. And the only pair of men who were headed toward it were wearing dark tee shirts and jeans.

Not thobes.

No, she hadn't taken the time to confirm their garb with the imam's daughter. She hadn't needed to. Not only would Zak and his Saudi cohort have worn their traditional, long-sleeved floor-length thobes to attend *Jum'ah,* they'd have donned the traditional white tee and linen pants beneath—*not* jeans. What better way to conceal their faces and blend in at a mosque frequented by newer, conservative immigrants than with an accompanying pair of ghutras?

They must be inside.

Mira retreated into the alley, just far enough to conceal her actions. Dropping the hem of her abaya, she worked Jerry's burner free from the left pocket.

She needed backup and she needed it now, and unfortunately, it had to be male.

Her right hand and her SIG still concealed within the nylon

folds of her abaya, she used her left to thumb Jerry's number into the phone.

The moment it began to ring, she stepped onto the sidewalk and turned right, heading for the café. She might not be able to get into that backroom, but she could station her niqab-concealed face in a corner of the main eating area, hopefully within view of Zak's, until Jerry and his fellow officers with the MPD had a chance to arrive.

Adrenaline surged as the line picked up. "Mira? Is that y—"

An iron hand clamped over her mouth before she could answer.

A split second later, the attached arm jerked her into the left side of an equally rigid thobe-covered torso and locked her there —pinning her gun arm to her side in the process—as another distinctly familiar voice penetrated the fabric of the niqab at her right ear. Though this one was more of a growl and seriously pissed.

"Don't do anything stupid."

Riyad.

14

W here the hell had the bastard come from?

On second thought, Mira knew. Riyad had been lying in wait just inside the recessed doorway of the electronics store on her right. With her vision partially obscured to the front and completely blotted out on her periphery, Riyad had managed to slip up next to her without her realizing he was there, despite that white thobe of his.

Easy enough for a SEAL with over a decade and a half of combat-honed instincts. Not to mention one determined to stay concealed...because he was dirty.

The iron palm released her mouth and descended to clamp itself over the back of her right hand. "Now, let go of the SIG, nice and easy."

"Or?"

"I'll take it from you. And it won't be nice."

She let go of the SIG.

She could feel the jerk slipping her 10mm into his thobe. His left hand shifted from her shoulder, retreating along her back to wrap around her upper right arm, even as his right reached around her front to pluck the burner from her fingers.

Her former partner's voice bellowed up from the speaker as Riyad's thumb headed for the phone's off switch. "Riyad? You fucking bastard. You let me speak to Mira now, or I'll have every cop in this city crawling up your ass within seconds—and that includes the federal ones."

The thumb paused.

She turned her head, but all she could see was that red-and-white checkered ghutra and the twin black, roping loops of the agal that held the headscarf in place. "Jerry will do it." And once that happened, SEAL or not, Riyad would not like the odds. Especially if the bastard still really *was* a SEAL and attempting to remain in stealth mode...and not a traitor like Zak. "That's his burner you've got. I'm sure it's tagged."

After all, the phone that *this* asshole had ordered Ramsey to pass to her while she was still recovering in the ICU at Walter Reed had been.

Those oddly scarred, dusky fingers passed the burner to her.

She raised it to her left ear to afford her and her former partner what little privacy she could. "It's me."

Jerry's shuddering sigh filled the line. And then, "You okay?"

Did a massive thump to her pride count?

"Yeah. I'm fine." She glared at Riyad through the niqab's veil as he finally turned his head enough to make viewing his face possible. "I can't see shit in this thing though."

She couldn't even see Riyad looking at her. Not completely. Despite the day's overcast sky, dark, wraparound sunglasses covered the upper half of his face.

She focused her attention on the call. Now that the adrenaline had begun to ebb from her blood, she could hear voices in the background on Jerry's end. A bit more focusing, and she caught enough to realize he was inside the MPD.

"So, what do you want me to do? I can and will have a shitload of patrol cars there in less than a minute—and I'll be right behind 'em. Just give the word."

"Hmm?"

"Mir?" Jerry had taken the hint and lowered his voice. If she was lucky, he'd make the switch to their old "yes/no answers" tactic as well. "You need me to call Ramsey; give him a heads up on what's happened and everything we've discussed?"

"Yes."

"Will do. I take it you also want me to track you 'til NCIS can take over...maybe even after they do?"

"Of course."

"Okay. What about the mic in your phone? Should I engage it and listen to what that bastard has to say to you? Record it?"

"Sure."

"Got it, but I gotta ask. Are you sure this is wise?"

Why not? What was the worst Riyad could do to her?

Make her walk the damned plank?

She'd already done that—and survived. "Not a problem. I'll call you when I can."

"Roger. And—" His gruff sigh grated through the line. "—I am so sorry I missed your call. Had a meeting with my paranoid asshole of a boss. Man's so petrified of leaks, he installed a fucking cell phone jammer in his inner office this morning and didn't bother to tell anyone. I'll be staying out of there 'til you tell me you're home free—personally."

"S'okay." But she'd make him pay for the lousy backup later.

In droves.

She caught the soft chuckle that followed. "Yeah, I know you will. Now keep the battery inside that phone or we're screwed. Bye."

She hung up, that filthy scowl of Riyad's still fused to her face. No, she couldn't see it though those wraparounds. But she could feel it, blistering her skin.

The man held up that iron palm.

She dropped the phone within it and waited as that, too, went into one of the pockets of his thobe.

He pulled her deeper into the alcove of the electronic store, but instead of laying into her as she'd expected, he reached up as if reseating an earpiece beneath the opposite side of the flowing red-and-white fabric of his ghutra. "It was her."

A pause.

"Yeah, I've got her secured. We're leaving now."

Secured?

Who the hell was he talking to? And where did this bastard think he was taking her? Because she wasn't about to go anywhere with him.

"I am not—"

The fingers around her upper arm bit in.

"Damn it, you—"

They bit in harder.

She got the message.

She stood there beside him for more than a minute. Silent. Fuming. Wondering what the devil Riyad was waiting for. Seconds later, she knew.

A black Ford Explorer with tinted windows pulled up to the curb, stopping directly in front of the alcove. Riyad hustled her straight to the right rear passenger door. Opening it with his free hand, he all but dumped her inside and prodded her across the vehicle until she was seated behind the driver.

By the time Riyad wedged his frame inside and snapped the door shut, she was seething more than she had been out on the street. Nor was this latest round of fury and discontent a result of the SEAL's most recent actions—but, rather, the shameless, studied *in*action of the two men who occupied the front seats of the Explorer.

Rafe Valdez and Ishaan Bhatti. Both fellow, stalwart NCIS

agents. Neither one deigned to so much as turn around and look her in the eye as they betrayed her. Yeah, she was still suffocating beneath the veil, but neither man even tried.

Valdez simply pulled the SUV away from the curb and merged into the early afternoon traffic.

Assholes. All three of them. The man beside her, most of all.

The reason behind all that pointed avoidance from her fellow agents had thickened the air: *traitor.* Riyad had put that vile suspicion about her loyalties into their heads, too. Just as he'd tried to do with Ramsey.

Ironic considering the SEAL was the one who'd produced the more questionable actions of late.

With traffic filling both lanes, the Explorer was forced to pass the Syrian café slowly enough for her to casually case the main seating area. She adjusted the niqab's veils until only the translucent one covered her face, but she still couldn't locate Zak. If Jalilah's instincts were right, he was in a backroom somewhere.

Hell, for all the cover and concealment that *wasn't* needed, Zak could've been seated at the whitewashed metal bistro set on the sidewalk out front, studying the vehicles as they drove by. With the SUV's smoked glass, and Valdez and Bhatti up front and wearing western suits, the two agents looked like run-of-the-mill security for the wealthy Saudi and his dutifully cowed female charge in the back.

She did spot a junior NCIS agent seated inside with another man she didn't recognize near the café's bay window.

The interior of the restaurant was covered, so any rear exits would be too.

As much as Mira wanted to relax into her seat, she couldn't. Zak might appear to be cornered. But those ex-SEAL instincts, skills and experience of his would be hell to outguess. And there was the still-current SEAL seated beside her.

Was this all just a faux front to Riyad? Because she hadn't seen another Saudi seated at any of those visible tables either. So if the Saudi Jalilah had spotted in the mosque's hallway wasn't in the backroom with Zak...was he seated next to her?

Granted, the timing was tight. But until Riyad provided an alibi for every second of the past hour, she'd remain as suspicious of him as he was of her.

How had Riyad even known that she was in play at the mosque today? Because from that comment he'd made into his body mic, he had. Except she'd donned the niqab and abaya miles away as she'd wrapped up her meet with Jerry.

She could feel the tension thrumming across the backseat, ratcheting tighter as Valdez continued to guide the Explorer through downtown.

Several minutes passed with nothing breaking the silence save the sounds of DC city traffic and life. As the SUV turned onto one of the capital's more historic streets she realized their destination. A hotel. But not just any hotel. An older one on par with the excessively moneyed Mayflower across the city.

Now wasn't this interesting?

As interrogation venues went, the Mount Laurel wouldn't have been her first guess. And that was what Riyad had in mind: interrogation. She hadn't known the man long, but she was learning how to read his moods and surmise what was most likely behind them. Though it wasn't difficult, since the SEAL's entire emotional spectrum appeared to fluctuate between Pissed Off and Livid.

Valdez brought the Explorer to a halt beneath the Mount Laurel's stone awning. Within seconds, both agents had opened their respective doors and vaulted from their seats, adding to the wealthy Saudi illusion as Valdez immediately moved to open her door while Bhatti handled Riyad's.

Valdez passed off the SUV's keys to a blond, crimson-vested

valet and finally met her gaze, only to flick his toward the rear of the vehicle.

Yeah, she knew the drill.

Fortunately for these men, she was just curious enough to hear what new accusation Riyad was eager to level on her that she complied. Besides, Jerry might not be physically present, but he was serving as her very vigilant, auditory backup. She allowed Valdez to appear to respectfully herd her around the rear of the SUV—from a noticeable, non-touching distance. The distance remained as Riyad entered the hotel and led the way through the lobby with her and her cloud of veiled black trailing the obligatory two steps behind and their "security" further back.

The charade held as they made their way into an elevator along with a pair of quietly conversing and subtly curious businessmen.

Upon reaching the third floor, Riyad—still wearing those concealing wraparounds—exited first and resumed the lead as their silent procession headed down a wide hall with a line of cherry doors accenting both sides. Midway from the next turn, Mira spotted yet another agent she recognized standing guard, presumably to prevent someone from entering the cleaned room and planting a listening device inside.

Imagine that.

Riyad paused beside the guard, his clipped nod encompassing all three of her fellow agents.

Valdez and Bhatti continued on with Agent Davenport in tow, the trio disappearing around the corner as Riyad withdrew a keycard from his thobe.

He unlocked the door and stood back to motion her inside an overly generous suite outfitted with a couch in gray linen, a set of matching plush armchairs, a cherry coffee and accent tables, and an executive desk setup in front of a wide window beyond it all. She passed a set of French doors that led to a slightly smaller room with a king-sized bed, swinging around and coming to a halt beside the second armchair.

Riyad had already closed the suite's outer door and followed her deeper inside, stopping a mere foot from the arm of the opposite chair.

A black, long-sleeved Henley and a pair of cargo pants nearly identical to the getup he'd worn when he'd last visited her at Walter Reed were draped over the arm. His jump boots and a fresh pair of dark socks waited at the base.

Still silent, and still staring at her shrouded form, the man removed the agal from his headpiece and tossed the weighted loops onto the chair's cushion.

The red-and-white checkered cloth of his ghutra followed, along with the simple white prayer cap beneath—and then the wraparounds.

The moment Mira spotted what looked to be the beginnings of a blackening left eye, she realized why he'd worn the sunglasses for so long.

She refused to comment on the eye, or the reddened area beneath that darker cultured growth at the edge of his jaw.

Riyad continued to watch her as he removed her SIG and a 9mm from the pocket of his thobe, balancing both weapons next to the clothes on the shoulders of the chair. A loop of thirty-three wooden Muslim prayer beads followed, along with his and her phones. When the man doffed his heavy leather sandals and started in on the top button at the collar of his thobe, she decided the time for speech had come.

She tipped her head toward the French doors and the bedroom beyond. "You paid for that space, too. You might as well use it."

The man's only response? A slight tic had begun to flag at the square of his jaw, just beyond the reddened area. The fact that she could see it pulse despite the dark growth that surrounded it was a testimony to just how furious he was.

Along with something else.

He didn't trust her not to bolt.

She was certain when he remained in place, palpably alert as he kept his entire body between her and the outer door to the suite—and the only exit.

Given that she'd evaded the tail he'd assigned to follow her the night before and for at least most of today, perhaps she shouldn't have been surprised.

She was, however, bemused when he finished with the buttons and raised the hem of his thobe to his waist, then tugged it and the white tee beneath over his torso and head. He laid the thobe and tee over the empty arm of the chair and moved on to the waistband of the matching white sarawil that ended above his knees. Seconds later, the Saudi-style shorts were following the path of the thobe, leaving him naked save for white briefs and a flesh-toned wrap that no doubt secured a spare handgun and a knife or two to the small of his back.

The man didn't bat an eye as he stood there, nearly naked.

Neither did she.

Why should she? He'd gawked at the barely healed burns on her lower legs in her hospital room. And, okay, this man had been marked by life too. But the majority of the scars were old. They were also *everywhere*. Even through the first, translucent veil of her niqab, they seemed to glow stark white against that bronze skin and the serious collection of honed muscle that rippled beneath. Hell, the man's entire torso, and arms and legs were covered with two, three inch slashes, along with the rounder marks of what appeared to be cigarette burns—except, the mottled circles were larger.

Cigar?

The rumor her brother had shared about Riyad being a

member of the crappy childhood club filtered in. Except that rumor didn't mesh with the evidence standing in front of her, unabashed and almost...defiant. Those rounded cicatrices and countless thinner scars were not the product of a sadistic parent. They were the unmistakable work product of a professional. One versed in the art of creating pain with the intent of extracting information...or simply for torture's sadistic sake.

During her years with NCIS, she'd come across her share of those types of scars, too. But this many? They'd been on corpses.

What the hell had happened to him? How had he survived?

Don't. The confrontation that had been brewing long before Riyad had used her fellow agents to herd her into the relative privacy of this room wasn't about him. Even if the agent in *her* was forced to wonder if the horror he'd endured while gaining those marks had eventually led to a division in the SEAL's loyalties...away from his country.

At least, the country they shared.

Or had Riyad always been loyal to the land of his birth? And others of nefarious intent who might, or might not, call it home?

That pressing query went unasked as well—for now—as the man apparently decided she'd seen enough. He reached for the cargo pants hooked over the arm of the couch. The black cloth slid up those powerful thighs, the white at the top disappearing completely as the edges zipped into place. The waiting matching Henley followed the opposite path down over those scarred arms and torso.

He leaned against the chair to don his socks and boots, then straightened as he flicked that congenital glower of his over the shroud that covered her from head to toe—and finally spoke. "You plan on ditching that costume, too?"

Costume? Well, that descriptor suggested a distinct ideological position in all this, didn't it?

Or was it part of his act?

She pulled the niqab off her head, then removed the abaya. She laid both over the back of the chair next to her, giving the man a full frontal of the gray summer sweater and black slacks she'd donned that morning—and nothing else.

Leaving Rahmani's Qur'an concealed in its makeshift home at the small of her back, she smoothed the wisps that the niqab had pulled from her low bun, then tipped her head toward the prayer beads on the back of the chair beside him.

"The tasbih's a nice touch—for an atheist."

Those broad shoulders shrugged, the ones that complemented an admittedly attractive face above. Though the horrific sea of scars hidden beneath was anything but. "I'm more of an agnostic. But, yeah—" The shrug made another appearance. "—the beads give folks something else to focus on besides the real me."

Right.

"You don't believe me."

She almost laughed at that. "Why would I?" There were so damned many lies surrounding this man.

"Oh, I'm not the one spinning tales, lady."

"Excuse me?"

That blackened scowl turned molten. "Your entire fucking story stinks. It has from day one. You don't know your father's a terrorist, even though he calls you for help. Then he leaves you a forty-second message whining about the shit he regrets in life and then tells you about the coming drop—in open code, no less —and you still don't have a goddamned idea what he said."

"Because I *deleted* it." She shook her head in disgust—and not all of it was directed the man who stalked forward to better focus that ire on her. "Okay. In retrospect, I might've hit play and let the message run, and then deleted it. To be honest, I can't remember. My head was a bit screwed up that morning, since I'd shot someone the afternoon before. A rather singular experience, at least for me. So excuse me if I'm just a lowly NCIS agent —a *real* one mind you—and not some active-duty SEAL so inured to killing that one more death at my hands doesn't set me back a pace, *Commander*."

The glare narrowed. "You know."

"Yeah, I do. After all, honest-to-God investigators do tend to....what's that strategy called? Oh, right—*investigate*."

If she'd earned a point with that one, his smoldering disbelief refused to honor it. "What about Nasser? You claim to have no lasting connection to the man, and yet you ID'd that bastard while we were all at the scene, standing over the JAG's body. And let's not forget Webber. You supposedly haven't seen your former fiancé for seven years, and somehow you show up *precisely* where he's been holed up. Let me guess: I'm supposed to believe you two being in the same building today was a coincidence."

"It *was*."

"Try again."

"Why? You may not have made it to Glynco, but you know exactly what I've been doing. You bugged my house, tagged my Blazer and cloned my phone."

He did honor those points with a nod, but it was downright curt. "Yet none of it managed to slow you down. So tell me, why did you leave the house for your reunion with your brother last night, and why the stunt with your phone this morning?"

"Because you *bugged* me. Would you have stuck around? And I didn't show up at the mosque today to meet with Zak. I was there tracking down a lead on Frank."

That revelation didn't rate a nod, curt or otherwise. But Riyad did take another step forward. He was so close she had to crane her neck to meet the suspicion that continued to radiate down on her. "Okay, I'll bite. Where'd you get your lead? Hell, for that matter, what have you been doing since you gave my guy the slip in Annapolis? And I do mean *after* you swapped vehicles with your brother."

"I met with a source."

"Bullshit. There's no one left in that town who's connected to Frank, but—"

She nodded as she watched that same source's identity click into this man's dark, doubting mind.

"—Walid Rahmani. Are you saying he's back?"

"Yep. The *Huriya II* docked late last night."

Riyad crossed his arms. "I'm still not buying it. I spoke to the man months ago. He doesn't know anything."

"Oh, he does. Rahmani also knows exactly what happened on the *Tern*, and not because he was involved in any way—so kick that idea out of that suspicious little brain of yours right now. Frank visited his grandfather's friend *after* Commander Corrigan was murdered and *before* Frank and Zak left for Cherbourg."

That earned her another nod. "I know that. But Nasser didn't say anything about his coming plans to Rahmani, let alone admit to murder."

Mira refused to offer everything that Rahmani had managed to piece together. Mainly because she didn't trust this man enough to not swing around and take a crack at Rahmani out of spite. But, "Rahmani had something of Frank's. Something Frank left behind when he slipped off the *Huriya II* after the murder and before the hijacking."

"Try again. I covered that possibility with the old guy when I was there."

"So?"

His responding scoff drilled down through the remaining distance between them. "That's your new story? You do realize they're getting worse? You honestly expect me to believe Walid Rahmani's been holding on to a critical piece to all this shit for months, and he just gave it to you out of the goodness of his heart?"

"Could be." She nudged a shrug up into that blistering disbelief. "Or it could be that I'm the better investigator. On the other hand, if you hadn't lied to the man about the nature of your relationship with Frank—or hell, if you'd simply deigned to give Rahmani your real name—he might've given it to you, *Your Highness*."

He didn't flinch.

Then again, she hadn't expected him to. But those faint streaks of pink darkening his cheekbones? The whole weird-ass prince thing was true.

Who'd have imagined it?

Definitely not her. Though she had been curious, not to mention suspicious, so she'd googled the name Rahmani had given her on the yacht while she'd been waiting for Jerry to show with the abaya and the rest of her gear.

Nothing had popped. Not even that Samman bin Ahmad Al Saud was supposedly dead. But that hadn't been surprising. According to conservative estimates, the Saudi kingdom had some eight thousand princes.

This one finally shook his head—and that glower was back in place. "Don't be impressed."

"Oh, trust me. I'm not."

She wasn't just referring to that title, either. She was referring to the asshole nature of the very common man looming over her, doing his best to intimidate her.

And he knew it.

"You are aware, *Agent* Ellis, that your good buddy Rahmani got a kick out of smuggling Muslim immigrants into the country on those fancy yachts of his."

She nodded. "Yeah, I am."

Frank had told her that, too. But it hadn't been so much of a

kick as payback for those Rahmani had felt were truly in need—
as he'd once been.

Besides, "The man stopped on 9/11. Hasn't done it since. He
felt the risk was too great. Not to himself, mind you—but to his
chosen country."

Evidently even Riyad knew there was no comeback to negate
that very real, exculpatory fact, because he didn't even try.

And good Lord, how many of his SEAL sources were lily
white?

He crossed his arms. "All right. Let's have it. What critical
clue did the magnanimous Rahmani supposedly entrust to *you*?"

Wow. Was that a case of royal snark? Or just plain old
everyman jealousy?

Either way, she tucked her right hand behind her and
reached beneath the hem of her sweater to tug the Qur'an from
its temporary home.

She held it out.

"That's what Nasser left?"

"No. This is a gift that Rahmani had intended for Frank, to
help the man find his way in life. Peacefully. Rahmani asked me
to give it to Frank. He suggested that I might also find solace
within. Specifically in surah eight, verses seventy, seventy-one."

She nudged the Qur'an closer, but Riyad refused to so much
as touch the cover.

In fact, the SEAL's hands were all but nailed into the crooks
of those opposite elbows.

This close to the man, she could make out that odd collection of fine white scars that marred most of Riyad's fingers. They
began at the tips, cutting up through the darker skin. The
pattern suggested that he'd once had to claw his way out of
something...or had tried.

And his posture? It was beyond stiff. She'd almost swear the
man felt...trapped. By a simple book. So much so, she was loath

to push this. But she had to. This was too important. Nor would any amount of curiosity, or pity, negate the utter shit this man had subjected her to. She pressed the Qur'an in above those crossed forearms, until the edge met that black Henley and the muscular wall of resistance beneath.

"Take the book. Read the passage."

"Don't need to. I know it."

"And given what we're desperately seeking, you don't find the suggestion of that particular verse in that particular chapter concerning *The Spoils of War*...intriguing?"

"Nope."

"Hmm." She nudged the Qur'an into that stubborn chest once more. "Give it a whirl, anyway. You never know what other enlightenment you might find inside."

A sharp, heavy sigh pummeled down into the hand-tooled leather, but he finally unlocked his arms and accepted the book. Opened it.

One of those dark, doubting brows hiked as he spotted the torn slip of paper that Rahmani had tucked inside the pages.

Of course that slip was now also tucked inside a plastic evidence baggie that had been properly sealed and annotated in the parking lot when she'd met with Jerry before she'd driven to the mosque, because, well, it was evidence. The forensic precaution hadn't escaped even Riyad's attention.

Nor what was written on the slip within.

"This is the address for the mosque."

She nodded. "It's written in Frank's handwriting. And before you malign me for recognizing it, remember: Frank and I attended OCS together. We also sat in the same classroom at NPS. And sure, that was all seven years ago. But try to remember something else. Things like the recalling and comparing of handwriting samples is also in the skill set of say...a properly-trained investigator." Mira reached out and flipped the evidence bag over to expose the sole fingerprint that she'd been able to raise on the reverse with the supplies Jerry had brought to their meeting. "That's another skill of investigators: recovering finger-prints and running them through the system."

"I take it this print belongs to Nasser."

It did indeed. The man's right index finger, in fact.

She settled for a nod in lieu of a gloat—but proceeded with the nudge. "Now, I've shown you mine, Commander. It's time to cough up yours. Just what the devil do you have on my father—and how is he tied into all this?"

"I didn't say your father was—"

"You didn't have to. *Investigator*, remember?" She retrieved the Qur'an and the evidence bag from Riyad's grasp and balanced them on the arm of the chair beside her, then deliberately mimicked that earlier, *I'm out of patience*, crossed-armed pose of his. She capped hers off with an even more mulish frown. "Now spill it."

He shook his head. "It's classified."

"Fine." She truly had expended the last of her patience. Fortunately, she was also technically still on leave.

She gathered up the niqab and abaya, since it looked as though she'd be needing both again, and soon, then retrieved the Qur'an and the evidence bag containing the mosque's address.

"What do you think you're doing with that?"

She held up the bag. "This? Why, I'm turning it into evidence. It's called chain of custody." She shook her head. "You really should've shown up for those procedural classes, Commander. See, I can't leave this here with you, because you're not really a special agent—and I can't take it on the plane with me, because I'm about to leave the country. So, I'll stop by the Field Office and sign it into evidence before I go."

"And where are you flitting off to now?"

"Saudi Arabia."

"Are you *serious*? Woman, you need to let Colonel Hartwig take another look inside that head of yours. If you think I'm letting you—"

"Yeah, that's just it. I don't give a crap what you think. And for your information, you can't stop me. I don't care if Admiral Kettering put you on this case. *It's not really your case.* Long-lost Saudi prince or not, you don't have the authority to pull my father into an interrogation room at the local Al Jubail precinct and question him. Not if you expect those answers to stand up to the scrutiny of a court of law. But I do. If that means I need to grab a fellow agent to fly over with me to appease everyone's sense of conflict of interest—and, hell, the Saudi male's need to keep the little *woman* in her place—then that's what I'll do. Either way, I'm flying to Al Jubail today. As soon as I land, I'll be asking my father the questions that you've refused to answer. And then I'll—

"Damn it, you can't."

"Oh, but I *can*." The relationship between their government and the Saudi one hadn't deteriorated that much. "And you, Commander Riyad, cannot stop me."

Especially if this asshole managed to abuse his Joint Special Operations Command connections to get her NCIS credentials pulled. Because then, why she'd just be a doting, civilian daughter chatting with her long-lost daddy.

And if Riyad tried to carve her name onto the top of the nation's latest no-fly list?

Well, that was fine with her, too.

She had a feeling Walid Rahmani would be happy to help her out of a bind that the *prince* had caused. And with that money and snazzy yacht of his, Rahmani could.

Mira tucked the evidence baggie into the Qur'an to protect it as she swung around that unyielding stack of pissed-off muscle to stalk out of the room.

Or she tried.

Riyad's right hand snapped out as she passed, locking around her upper arm much as it had out on the street today and in the alcove.

And, yet, this was different.

As was that odd look that had entered the SEAL's eyes. The one that wasn't threaded with impatience but...reluctance.

"Goddamn it, will you just hang on for a moment? Please." On the heels of that last word, a whole host of bizarre new emotions joined the open war inside that murky stare. Within seconds, the persistent scowl that she'd have sworn had been tattooed into this man's face at birth evaporated. In its place—a palpably tense frown whose edges were crimped in with the inexplicable tinge of...regret?

"Okay, what's wrong?"

No response.

"Damn it, Riyad. I don't have time for this. Whatever this is, you need to spit it out now. Otherwise, I have evidence to sign over to someone else so it can be locked up in a safe, and then I need to pack. I have a plane to catch."

"He's dead."

"What are you talking about? Who's dead?"

The only people they'd been arguing about were Frank, Walid Rahmani and—

No.

Goddamn it, no!

But even as the denial pierced her mind, causing that light-headed cloud of nothingness to threaten, she knew it was true. Just as she knew *who.*

What made it all worse was the man in front of her. The one who for some reason looked as though he'd just had the rug pulled out from under his narrow, unshakable worldview and was scrabbling around for another. Because that same man was also nodding. Slowly. Steadily. A moment later, his iron grip softened all the way down to something that felt suspiciously like comfort.

And then came the clincher. The one emotion she never would've expected to see bleeding into this man's eyes. Not for her.

Compassion.

"Mira, your father's dead, okay? Ben Ellis was murdered...in the middle of that message you deleted."

15

M ira evaded the pity radiating down on her. She focused on those scarred fingers that were wrapped around her right arm instead. They were loose now, almost gentle. Supportive. That didn't matter. She wanted them *gone*.

So she could do the same.

The moment Riyad realized what she was looking at, he released her.

She was grateful. Loose or not, she wouldn't have been able to pull away from his grip on her own.

"Agent Ellis? Are you...okay?"

She couldn't open her mouth, either. Not even long enough to form a simple *no*. It was all she could do to let her lower body take over, to put one foot in front of the other. She edged a careful path around the SEAL, then deliberately bypassed the doors that led into the attached bedroom. Those panels were made of glass.

She needed privacy.

The inexplicable tears clogging up her throat had overtaken the countless questions screaming through her mind and heart.

In another second, perhaps two, they would begin to fall. And that man, strangely rooted into place behind her, was *not* going to bear witness to her weakness.

Pushing through the door to the bathroom, she turned and managed to close it behind her. It wasn't until she went to flip on the lights and throw the lock that she realized she was holding her niqab, her abaya and the Qur'an.

She dropped the fabric at her feet and fumbled with the switches in the dark, accidentally engaging the lights and fan together. She left both on and toggled the lock to the door. The book and the bagged evidence ended up beside the sink. She sank down to the floor where she stood, her ass settling on the icy, marble tiles, her socked feet on top of that Saudi shroud of black as she pulled her knees to her chest and clung to the remaining shreds of sanity for all she was worth.

Her father was dead. *Murdered.*

While he'd been leaving the voicemail that she'd not only intentionally ignored but deleted.

Yes, she'd hated the man. Yes, he'd absolutely deserved that hatred. But she wouldn't have ignored the plea of a total stranger. Estranged or not, the man was *still* her father...or had been. He'd reached out to her with his dying breath.

And she'd done *nothing.*

What kind of a human being did that make her?

Oh, God. Dropping her forehead to her knees, she let the white noise of the fan overtake the shame and the guilt that blistered in, until the only thing left was the steady roar of the blower and the numbness that had come with it.

She welcomed the latter; it succeeded in obliterating the entire world. She had no idea how long she sat there. Seconds? Minutes?

Hours?

That last might be the most accurate guess, because the next sound that managed to cut through the fan and the fog it had nurtured was knocking.

And then a voice. "Mir? You okay in there?"

Ramsey.

"Hey, kiddo. Can you unlock the door for me?"

She still couldn't seem to speak, so she tried standing. She swayed as that infernal lightheadedness closed in, but she pushed through and got there. Reversing the toggle on the lock went more smoothly. She left the opening of the door to Ramsey.

Those soft amber eyes and warm, gentle smile filled the space. "You ready to come out?"

No. But it was time. She nodded and waited as he gathered up the fabric from the floor, then the Qur'an and the evidence from the counter.

"Where's Nate?"

The worry in those eyes increased. "He flew out this morning. He's headed overseas to resume his undercover mission at the madrassa, remember?"

Oh, right. "Yeah." She scrubbed her cheeks as everything else filtered in. Frank. Zak. The deadly fuel from those stolen assemblies.

Riyad.

She scanned the sitting area of the suite as she followed Ramsey out of the bathroom. The SEAL wasn't there. Riyad didn't appear to be in the bedroom as they passed the French doors on their way to the couch, either.

"I asked him to leave."

She nodded as she sank onto the gray cushions. She didn't want to know where Riyad was headed; she did not care. She just wanted the bastard to stay wherever he was—because that meant he'd remain out of her sight.

Unfortunately, Riyad's last words to her were still ricocheting around her brain. "Is it true? Was Dad murdered...while he was leaving me that voicemail?"

"Yes." Ramsey tossed the shroud on the armchair still holding the ghutra and agal that Riyad had placed there earlier. The Qur'an ended up on the coffee table. "For what it's worth, he didn't mean for it to come out like that. He feels like shit."

Good.

"He should." She hoped to hell Riyad was a top performer for the Teams, because the man had zero future as an investigator. Death notifications came with the job.

And he sucked at it.

Worse, she had the distinct feeling that Riyad had known since before they'd even met in the JAG's condo that her father had been murdered in the midst of reaching out to her. From the guilt that was eating through the amber as Ramsey unbuttoned the jacket to his navy suit, he had too.

He sank onto the couch beside her. "I am so sorry. I wanted so badly to tell you. And I admit, I came damned close a few times, especially the last time we spoke at Walter Reed. But in the end..." His raw sigh filled in the reality of the rest.

She nodded, and voiced it for him. "You were under orders."

She had a good idea who was behind those orders, pushing his conviction that she was somehow involved in her own father's murder. Which was ridiculous. If only because she'd been in DC, half the world away, when her dad had been killed in Al Jubail.

Not that Riyad had offered even that basic detail. She'd had to glean the location of his murder from the area code on the calls her dad had made.

Well, she wanted the rest, and she wanted it now.

"What was his evidence?" Not only was she loath to speak the bastard's name, there was no need. Ramsey knew. "I want to see it."

Apprehension and regret sifted through the amber as it settled on the coffee table. Until that moment, she hadn't realized that he'd brought a crisp manila folder into the suite with him. He'd set it down beside the Qur'an.

She reached for the file.

Dark, mocha fingers closed over hers. "Mir—"

"Damn it, I *deserve* to see what's in there." Ramsey might be trying to protect her, but he obviously agreed. Why else had he brought it along?

He released her hand—reluctantly.

Snagging the folder, she brought it to her lap and opened it. Half a dozen 8x10 inch color crime scene photographs and a coroner's report lay within. The first picture showed her father dressed as Riyad had been when he'd jerked her into that alcove. Except her dad's ghutra and prayer cap were missing, and he was lying prone on the tiled floor, his arms flung wide from his body. The back of his thobe was torn and bloody. And the bruises to the right side of his face and neck?

Her stomach lurched.

She flipped through the remaining photos quickly, just to get through them. To absorb the horror of what had been happening in Al Jubail while she'd been deleting that voicemail and cursing this man to hell and back for even possessing the nerve to call.

Once the brutal shock of it all had begun to ebb, she started over. During this second pass, she forced herself to take her time. To study each crime scene still as though she was working a case with some stranger she'd never met.

Yet, in some ways, this was like looking at a stranger.

The man depicted in the close-ups was significantly older than the one in her memories. A solid two decades older. His short hair was no longer flaxen. It was the lightest of silvers, and it had thinned considerably. The fine lines from her child's mind had changed too; they were carved in deeply around this man's eyes and mouth.

And the *blood*.

Like the bedroom in the JAG's condo, it was everywhere— staining the low, yellow lounging pillows that lined the tiles at the baseboard of the wall where her father's body lay. There were swaths of rust smeared along the wall above, too. Hell, she could even make out a single, dense spurt of arterial blood.

Nor did the similarities end there.

Her father's fingers. From the way the knuckles were swollen, she could tell each one had been dislocated...and then shoved back into place.

Zak.

Riyad was wrong. Ramsey, too.

Technically, at least.

Zak might've gotten the drop on her father during the voice-mail that he'd been leaving for her—but he hadn't been killed at that moment. The information in the interviews of her father's co-workers, friends and neighbors would need to be whittled down to clarify the timeline and know precisely how long Zak had kept the man alive. But from the amount of swelling that she could see, the bastard had spent hours torturing her father.

The depth of the bruises roping the sides of her father's throat and the dark, twin thumb prints pressed into the front in the autopsy close-up that had been included added more to the story. As did the coroner's assessment of the excessive damage to the hyoid bone beneath those dark thumb prints.

Like the JAG, Mira didn't think her father had coughed up the answers to Zak's questions. Not to the ex-SEAL's satisfaction.

In the end, after all that torture—not to mention the slash to the neck that would've caused her dad to bleed out anyway— Zak had changed his twisted mind and opted to choke the remaining seconds of life out of the man.

Viciously.

"What was in the voicemail? What did my father say?"

Ramsey reached out, carefully retrieving the folder from her lap. He took the time to tuck the photos and the report neatly within, then closed the file and set it on the coffee table. His hands returned to cover over hers, drawing them closer to settle them on the knees of his trousers. "Your dad apologized for bringing up Noura during his first call. He thought if he hadn't, you might not have hung up on him, and he'd have gotten out the rest. But he'd gotten so nervous when you actually picked up that he just started talking. He said he should've begun where it mattered: that he was ashamed of himself for not being there for you and Nate while you two were growing up. He'd wished he'd stood up to your grand-mother's rants and pleas, and acknowledged Nate as his biological son from the moment he learned of Nate's exis-tence. And that...that he was *so very sorry* his lust and his cowardice killed your mother."

That last admission caused her chest to burn.

Mira tried to draw in a breath to cool the latter, but it was useless. Because the pain wasn't in her lungs, it was in her heart.

She tugged one of her hands free so she could scrub the heel of her palm through the tears that had begun to flow.

That was a heck of a lot of sorry. So much, it might've been relationship changing. Though it would've taken years of work —from all of them. But especially her dad. And *only* if the man had truly hardened his spine enough to do it.

But Riyad wouldn't have given a crap that her father had supposedly seen the light and was living with the regrets they'd exposed. She might despise the SEAL, but even she knew Riyad was smart enough to have needed more to base his suspicions on.

Something concrete.

"And the rest? The part that made that asshole so certain my father and I were dirty?"

"Ben said he was sending you something. That you'd know what to do with it when you got it."

She shook her head. "I didn't get anything from him. Not at home, or the office." The only anonymous delivery she'd received had been that horrifying letter from Caleb McCabe, and that had arrived at the Field Office the morning before her father's voicemail. Which meant her dad had died before he'd had the chance to mail whatever it was.

What had he wanted to send her? And had the package had something do with Zak? Was that why the torture had lasted so long and been so sadistic?

They'd probably never know.

Unless... Letters and parcels got held up in customs, on both ends of the international post. At times, the wait could surpass the month mark, or longer. "What about—"

"During your coma?"

She nodded.

Her boss shook his head. "We thought about a customs' delay. But nothing showed up while you were in the ICU, either. At the Field Office or your townhouse."

"Let me guess. Riyad took the watch on my sublet." And if the jerk had been inside, she had at least four more bugs to locate and exterminate before she could relax in her own home.

"Yeah, he did. Look, kiddo, I know you two don't mesh, but you gotta understand. The guy's been after Webber for two solid years now."

"I'm aware of his obsession." Just as she was certain that her boss knew precisely *how* she'd gained that awareness. "I'm sure you've seen a transcript of my call with my friend and CID colleague, Regan Chase."

The man's leathery skin was dark enough that she shouldn't

have been able to tell that he'd flushed, yet she could. "Yeah. I read it...along with the write-ups of a few others."

Nothing like having your private phone conversions recorded and a personal printout sent to your boss to read at his leisure.

At least she and Ramsey were on the same page regarding what she knew about this case and the asshole of a seemingly prime player who had his nose buried in every aspect of it... whether it needed to be there, or not.

And then there were the lies.

To Regan, Rahmani—and herself.

It had to be asked. "Can you account for Riyad's movements earlier today? *All* day? When I was inside the restroom at the mosque, I heard Zak and another man pass by in the hall. And the imam's daughter? When she came back in, she didn't know their names, but she referred to the two men as the Yemeni... and the Saudi."

Her boss stiffened. But then he relaxed.

Nodded.

"I can see why you might suspect Riyad. But you're off base there. The man's just gone about this in a way that's rubbed folks wrong—and raised more than a few hackles. Hell, I've had my own issues with the guy. But he's not dirty. If you won't take my word for it, take Agent Bhatti's. Riyad was partnered up with Bhatti when they entered the mosque earlier today. They cased the place together, then had to pull back and send in a replacement team once Riyad spotted Webber—and you. Before and after the mosque, Riyad was in full view of Agents Valdez and Bhatti, as well. Whoever that Saudi was—and we're bound to have a few surveillance photos—it wasn't Riyad."

Fine. That alibi might account for today. But what about the most important mystery regarding the man? "Why is Sam Riyad even alive?"

She didn't have to offer more than that. Ramsey had read the transcript of her calls with Regan and undoubtedly Jerry, too. He was aware that she knew about the missing SDV and the four SEALs who'd washed up off Oman with that same green shit in their lungs that had killed the constables and crew of the *Pacific Tern*, along with the family of the *Kittiwake*'s captain.

"Riyad was ill."

"Excuse me?"

Ramsey nodded. "The day before the mission went down, Webber wanted a meet. He'd cleared the chief's mess aboard the submarine for a few hours so the six of them could eat while they worked out a few details that supposedly bothered him. Webber poisoned the men during the meal, knowing that what he gave them would hit critical mass while they were under the ocean. What Webber didn't know was that Riyad had been feeling off. There was a twenty-four hour stomach bug moving through the sub's crew at the time. Riyad must've caught it, because after he'd eaten, he stopped by the head to vomit. He felt fine afterward, so he hit his rack, logged the necessary sleep and got up to execute the mission. But there was enough stuff left inside him that if he hadn't made it to the surface when he did, he'd have died too."

"Did they test his blood and bodily fluids afterward?"

"Yes. And it was tainted. Mira, he was in the ICU for a week afterward. It wasn't until some doc decided to transfuse him that they got a handle on it."

All right then. Not a terrorist. Just a class A bastard.

All things considered, she was relieved. "Was there anything else on the voicemail from my dad? Any background noises to enhance and exploit?"

The shift in subjects had let Ramsey know that her fears regarding the active-duty SEAL's loyalties had been negated—because he too relaxed. Her boss ran the fingers of his right hand through the tight, silvery curls of his afro as he shook his head. "There was nothing else on the voicemail. Just the distinct sounds of an ambush, and then the message cuts off. The phone went off the grid around the same time."

"Zak destroyed it." Which would be why the call she'd made a few days ago had gone straight to voicemail.

"That's the prevailing assumption."

That wasn't the only assumption whirling around the edges of her life.

Dirty or not, "And that's it? That's *all* Riyad had? Some promised package that was never delivered?"

The jerk had tried to ruin her career and her life over that?

The hell with being a lousy investigator. This was worse than incompetent. It was unconscionable, and it was—

Not all they had. There was a strange mix of shadows shifting through that soft amber now. One that smacked of wariness and hesitation. With everything that she'd learned today, did she really want to know what was behind it?

Unfortunately, yes.

"Boss?"

"Your dad didn't just marry his partner's daughter. He fell in love with the woman. Noura says that she and Ben had been trying for a decade to have kids. Three years ago, they did. Fraternal twins, a girl and a boy. Noura and the kids arrived in the States a few days ago...and they're staying in my guest room."

Mira inhaled the shock as she tried to process it. As sucker punches went, this one struck lower and deeper than she could've imagined. She wasn't blown away that her father had produced more children, but that he'd wanted them.

Why? He hadn't wanted her.

And he definitely hadn't wanted Nate.

Her brother had been the daily reminder of the maid their dad had raped after he'd come home drunk one night when he'd been stationed in the Philippines. The maid—who'd been married—had disappeared afterward, never to be seen again... until weeks before Mira's parents rotated back to the States. Nate had gotten ill and his biological mother's husband had realized from the boy's blood type that Nate wasn't his. He'd kicked the woman and her *bastard* son out of their house and marriage that same night. Lagaya's deeply religious parents had sided with her husband and refused to help.

With no husband and no money, she knew the boy would starve.

Ironically, Lagaya had already swallowed her pride and visited her rapist to plead her case—and he'd ignored her. So she'd gone to Mira's mother, then barely pregnant with her. It was Mira's mother who'd taken Nate in, and immediately. She was also the one who'd set the adoption into motion, and she was the one who adored her new son and raised him as her own, never once letting him feel as though he was unwelcomed.

That role had fallen to their grandmother.

As for their mutual father? He'd simply avoided Nate and then the rest of his family—and eventually, his entire country.

And the man had decided in his waning years that he wanted some grand do-over? That he'd been trying for it with a second set of kids?

What a crock.

Apologies left as voicemail—sincere or not—were one thing. But had Benjamin the Spineless really believed he wouldn't just fuck it all up again?

"Mira?"

She stopped, blinked. It was then that she realized she'd stood up without swaying for a change. That she'd paced her way across the hotel suite. She was standing in front of the executive desk; Ramsey was still seated on the couch.

The wariness and hesitation within her boss' features had been replaced by concern.

"I'm...fine."

Liar.

He nodded anyway. And then, both the wariness and the hesitation returned. She could see them clearly, even from across the room.

"There's more, isn't there?"

Of course there was. There was no way the presence of additional kids and a wife who was so close to her husband's older daughter in age that they could've shared birthday candles would push a SEAL's instincts toward terrorism. And, like her, Riyad would also want proof of whatever her father had really been up to in Al Jubail.

Mira wasn't sure how many more surprises she could handle. She desperately wanted to lean back into the slab of dark cherry that served as the top of the desk behind her, grip the edge and hold on for all she was worth.

But she didn't.

She walked back to the sitting area, slipped in between the coffee table and the couch and resumed her place next to her boss.

"Just say it."

"Your dad's partner and their company have been on the CIA's radar for nearly two decades. Almost since it was founded. As you know, Habib provided the money and the requisite Saudi Muslim status. While your dad provided—"

"The technical knowledge." After all, he'd received his chemistry degree upon his graduation at the Academy.

Ramsey nodded. "Yeah." He scrubbed his fingertips through shadow that was beginning to make an appearance on his jaw. "Ben converted immediately, of course, but that was to please Habib and help the business look more Muslim. One of the officers your dad and I served with in the Fleet got out around the same time, and he joined the CIA. When he found out about your dad's company—and where it was located—he tried to run your dad as an asset. To get Ben to pass on, well, anything. Saudi industry information for sure. But what the guy really wanted was a toe in with someone who might be able to dig into the money that seemed to flow from his partner's coffers to certain questionable madrassas in the Middle East, Northern Africa and Southeast Asia."

Post 9/11? What agent wouldn't have wanted that?

As for the CIA's interest in the men and their company, that was a no-brainer, too. Her father had met Habib ibn Ibrahim Al Shammari the same day he'd met her mother and at the same sailing regatta, back in 1986. Her mom and Habib had been competitors on the water. And ashore? While her father had been sniffing after his future American wife, his future Saudi business partner had been pursuing him. Though Benjamin Ellis had been a midshipman at the time, he'd managed to impress the older Saudi with his post-Academy and Fleet business plans. Habib proved willing to play the long game.

Especially when it came with perceived American military ties.

As for the CIA's game?

"Did this agent get it? Did my dad pass on anything of value?"

"No. In fact, Ben refused the whole package. He told his old buddy that when he met the five year minimum as a Saudi resident, he'd be applying for citizenship."

Well, that last part wasn't a surprise. Only because her grandmother had hit the roof after she'd discovered that very intention to emigrate and had proceeded to blame her mom—at the top of the older woman's lungs—for being such a lousy wife that poor, darling Ben had moved to the other side of the world to escape her.

The irony of it.

Even before she'd hit her teens, Mira knew that her father had really been trying to escape himself.

Instead, he'd gotten in over his head. And with that rubber spine of his, he hadn't had the strength to pull himself out. "He knew what was going on with the funds, didn't he? And he was not only okay with it, he was actively part of it."

What a way to embrace a new country and a new religion.

"Probably. His old buddy continued to hit him up over the years, but as you know, Ben never deviated from his plan for citizenship—and he never gave up his partner."

That's what Riyad had latched on to.

Hell, if she'd known the rest of it, she'd have been suspicious of her father and that voicemail about a mysterious package, too.

Thanks, Dad.

But that didn't explain her father's other family. "Why is Noura in the States? For questioning?"

"Yes...and no. The morning before your dad left that voicemail, Habib had a heart attack. The two had a pending presentation for the crown prince's business office, so your dad accessed his partner's computer to continue working on it. He found something on Habib's hard drive. What? We don't know. But it finally lit a fire under Ben, because he went home and called his old friend-turned-CIA operative shortly after 1500, local Al Jubail time. Your father refused to even hint at what he'd seen on Habib's computer. Instead, he told the operative that he'd just returned from putting his wife and kids on a flight to Bahrain for an impromptu "shopping trip." The second they landed, he wanted the three picked up and put on the next flight to the States and protected once they got there. After he received confirmation that Noura and kids were on US soil, he promised to have something delivered that would—and I quote—rock the man's world."

"But he never got the chance." Because her father had called her roughly an hour later, close to 0900 her time—and 1600 in Al Jubail. Her dad had been in the middle of leaving that voicemail for her when Zak had ambushed him and severed the call.

Was she supposed to have received what her father had stumbled across on his partner's hard drive?

Like Riyad, she suspected so.

But her father's intentions were moot now. Because the man was dead. And her mailbox was still empty.

But thirteen days after that call, the *Pacific Tern* had been hijacked. Four of those mixed oxide assemblies had been stolen. Her father must've known it was coming. Had he found proof of the hijacking—or at least the suggestion of it—in the form of purchase orders for the chemicals and other supplies that would have been needed for the conversion of those ceramic pellets?

Possibly. Hell, probably.

But had her father stumbled across more? Had he known where and when the recovered plutonium and uranium were to be used—and by whom?

There was an excellent chance he had.

It would explain why Zak had taken his time with the torture. He'd needed to know precisely how much information her father had given up. And when Zak hadn't gotten his answer, he'd choked her father to death out of fury.

The guilt burned in again.

It deepened as she was forced to accept that Zak wouldn't have even known of her father's existence, but for Zak's relationship with her.

Ramsey was patient. He waited silently. And when she'd finally drawn her breath in deep and let it all out in a rush, he did the same.

Only then did he break the silence. "Are you okay? This is a hell of a lot to process."

And she'd done such a shitty job of it at the start, hadn't she?

When she'd walked away from Riyad, locked the door to the bathroom and crawled into the corner to escape the whole blessed world. She should've been nailing Riyad's ass to the wall in this very room instead. Getting her answers directly from him, so she could get back out on the hunt that much sooner. But she'd been weak.

Maybe the bastard was right. Maybe she couldn't handle him.

Or this.

She kept coming back to the inescapable fact that her father had reached out to her in what had turned out to be his hour of deepest need—and she'd hung up on him. Whether or not he'd earned that hang up through twenty-nine years of shitty, and then nonexistent parenting, was immaterial. If she'd taken the time to listen, she might've gotten him to offer more than that infuriatingly vague statement about intending to send something to her. And if *that* had happened, there was a chance the *Pacific Tern* wouldn't have been boarded at all. The lives of the ship's crew and all those nuclear constables might've been saved, along with the loved ones of the *Kittiwake*'s captain...and Captain Styles and Major Hunt.

So many deaths that might've been prevented. If she'd just picked up that second goddamned call.

"Mira? It's not your fault." Ramsey reached out to tip her chin. "And before you tell me you're not sitting there blaming yourself for all this, don't. I can see the guilt in your face. And, hell, maybe if your dad and I had stayed close, he mighta turned to me. So, see? We've both been excoriating our backs with that cat o' nine tails, when in reality, if the selfish bastard had just forked over the information off the bat—or at least alluded to what it was about—we might've been able to stop it all from the start. But as usual, Ben was thinking of himself. Though I suppose this last time, that selfishness extended to Noura and the kids. But it was still damned selfish when you add in all the folks that may end up incinerated from this. And that man had more than enough technical knowledge to have known that too."

Ramsey was right. About all of it.

But the guilt was still there, thrumming through her gut.

Though now she had several questions pulsing along another, internal path; this one higher up. "What about Noura? Did Dad tell her anything?"

"As far as we know, not a damned bit. Homeland had been going at her with two of our own female agents out of the Field Office in Bahrain. But all Homeland would let anyone tell Noura was that her husband had been murdered. Though in light of the questions, I'm sure she's figured out there's more to it. That's where I've been, on and off, for the past two months—Bahrain. Apparently my name featured a lot in your dad's stories from his Academy and Navy days—and she took the friendship to be solid and still current. I've been using that to try and connect with the woman, but I wasn't getting anywhere. Homeland decided to switch things up, so they brought her here. The call I took when I last saw you at Walter Reed? I'd just gotten the word that her flight had landed at Andrews. I had to leave to pick her up. She's been staying at the house with the wife and me under the guise of that old friendship I shared with your dad. Keisha's been serving as the female chaperone that Noura seems to crave. But the connecting part still isn't working. If anything, Noura's withdrawn further into herself since she and the kids arrived. That's where you come in. Homeland finally agrees."

Oh, Jesus. This time, she could feel the urge to stand crawling up her calves and thighs. Nor was she proud of the anxiety—and, yes, the panic—causing it.

She forced herself to resist. To remain seated.

To just *say* it.

Because she already knew she had no choice but to agree. "You want me to meet her. See if I can get a step-mommy connection of my own going."

"Well, you are the spitting image of your dad. Maybe the shock of seeing that white-blond hair, the dip in your cheek and those big blue eyes will get to her. Her kids are dark like Nate; they all took after their mommas. Plus, Noura wants to meet you. She's asked over a dozen times now, so it just might work. Frankly, there's not much else to try. We're going on eight weeks since that shit was stolen. There's still no chatter on the usual channels. Hell, on *any* channel. Your brother's gotten the closest. But as I'm sure you know, he hasn't made it to the inner circle. Those bastards may not let him in at all, let alone in time to prevent any of the bombs from detonating. They may be willing to use Nate and his US passport—but he's not Arab. And, hell, those fuckheads he's been hanging out with have their own issues with Filipino blood. As for Webber, that bastard's been leading the team of agents who've been shadowing him in circles around DC all afternoon. For all we know, distraction and that merry chase may have been Webber's reason for showing up at the mosque all along. If so, we're screwed. You might be Homeland's last hope, and they're actually admitting it."

Now there was a scary thought.

But...it just might work.

First, last or seemingly no hope, she was willing to try. While her dad might not have said anything to his wife, Habib had been her dad's father-in-law. There was always the chance that *Habib* let something slip in front of his daughter.

"I'll do it."

Though it would've been easier to break the ice with her

brother along. Nate had always been better with kids than her, and these were his siblings, too.

Nate would've—

Oh, Lord. "*Nate.*" He didn't know about their father's murder. About how Zak had accomplished it. He might've despised the man as much as she had, possibly more given that he was product of rape, but he deserved to know.

"I can't even call him to tell him."

Except, even if she could, did she really want this knowledge —those photos—in Nate's head and in his heart right now? Doing what he was doing?

"Your brother knows."

"But—who told him?"

When?

She wasn't sure why that budding black eye and reddened skin beneath Riyad's mosque-ready beard had nudged into her brain, but the timing made sense.

"Riyad told Nate, didn't he?" Judging by the level of bruising that had already set in, "Early this morning."

"Yeah. The commander and I were at the meet your brother had with his agency contact. Seems the agency guy didn't want your brother laying into him again for not keeping him abreast of critical family issues while he was undercover, so he told him."

"And then Riyad added his two cents about Dad and what he's been up to all these years. And what he failed to come through on at the end."

"Yup. But that's not what set Nate off. Hell, it wasn't the bugs, the GPS tracker, the cloned phone or even the tail that Riyad attached to you. Though I suspect knowing about all of that might've helped egg Nate on. It was—"

"The implication that I was dirty, too."

"Got it in one." The man's leathery features warmed on a

chuckle. "I don't think Riyad realized he'd even been hit until he was peeling himself up off the deck."

She probably shouldn't feel as good as she did at hearing that, but frankly, she'd needed it. It had been a shit of a day all around, and it wasn't over yet.

"How did you even know to come here?" Not the hotel per se, but that she'd so desperately needed a friendly face?

Her boss grinned. "Ah, now there's an easy one. The infamous Jerry Dahl. Seems he was listening in on your phone like you asked. He'd be here himself, but he's locked inside an interview room. He got a call shortly after you left the mosque—from someone inside it. The imam's daughter."

Oh, thank God. "Then she's—"

"Safe? Yeah. Jerry drove over and snagged Jalilah from the alley. He managed to get her to her house, stuff her things in a suitcase and drive her to the station to begin the debrief before her father realized she was missing. MPD will take care of protecting the girl and getting her a new identity once they've finished. Though I suspect the FBI and Homeland are gonna want a crack at her brain, too."

"Did she know anything?"

"Not really. Just small stuff. Least nothing big's come to light yet. But we both know the small stuff can add up, so there's hope. Her dad deliberately tried to keep her in the dark, even as he had her working in his office. If you hadn't shown up, we wouldn't even have the membership list she said she gave you."

The roster.

She'd been so rattled, at first because of her suspicions about Riyad and then the news about her father, that she'd forgotten about the papers she'd folded up back in the bathroom at the mosque to tuck inside her pocket.

Mira shifted on the couch so she could pull them out now.

She went to pass the papers to Ramsey, only to realize he wanted to make a trade.

"Wow. A new phone...again."

That invisible, but palpable flush returned. "This one's clean."

"That's what I assumed before. Shame on me."

She swore she could feel the heat from that flush as it deepened.

What the hell. She swapped the roster for the phone, effectively letting the man off the hook. Truth was, she needed his offering too. She had no idea where Nate had parked her Blazer within Dulles' short term lot, nor was she looking forward to heading to the airport tonight of all nights to search for it.

Even if she had been in the mood, she'd still need to clean the infected device of every conceivable piece of spyware that had entered Riyad's smarmy brain.

She tucked her newest official phone in her back pocket and reached for the Qur'an to retrieve the other gift she'd picked up for NCIS and her country today.

"That the address Riyad mentioned when I arrived?"

"Yeah. The print on the reverse belongs to Frank. Right index finger."

"I'll get it logged in." Ramsey held up the folded roster. "This is a major get. One that Homeland's been after for quite a while now."

"The opportunity presented itself."

The man's smile split those leathery features wider as he chuckled. "Yeah, with you, it usually does. Damned fine work, Agent."

Agent. "Does that mean I still have a job?"

"You've always had one. I just needed Riyad to realize that. And now he has. That man took one look at your face when he told you about your father and finally realized you couldn't fake not knowing what had happened to him. He said he knew then that if you didn't know about the murder, you weren't involved in any of it."

"Yay, me." At least her shock and subsequent fade-out from reality had served a purpose. Only now she'd have to work with the SEAL—for the time being, anyway. One more reason to find the fuel from those assemblies, and as swiftly as possible.

At least they'd found Zak.

Now *he* was a major get.

Unfortunately, they had no choice but to deal with the runaround that Zak was currently conducting. If they brought him in early, then what?

Traitor or not, Zak had spent a decade and a half with the Teams, the majority of it in combat. He'd never reveal the location of that radioactive material, much less the plans that he and his cohorts had for it. The only viable strategy was the one Riyad had tried with her. They had to leave Zak in play and track every breath that went in and out of his body, while they waited for the bastard to kick up a clue.

And if that failed—and if she couldn't get anything useful out of her father's widow? Well, then there'd be only one option left.

Wait for the bombs to start exploding.

16

S he was stalling, and she knew it.

Mira sighed as she removed the key from the Land Rover's hinky starter switch. She thought she'd have time to sketch out in her head what she was going to say to the woman who'd usurped the role her mother had desperately wanted with the man who'd not only married her first but had never bothered to legally divorce her.

Unfortunately, it was barely three in the afternoon. Rush hour hadn't kicked in.

So here she was, parked on the street in front of her boss' brick townhouse. Roughly thirty, forty feet from the so-called love of her father's life and the two kids he'd actually wanted. Yes, all three were innocent in the endless drama that had gone down in her own household while she and Nate had been growing up.

But that didn't make this meeting any easier.

According to her boss, while she'd been in the midst of her guilt-fueled meltdown, Riyad had sent Agent Bhatti back to the mosque to hot-wire the battered Land Rover and drive it to the hotel. The SEAL had also sent Bhatti inside the mosque for the shoes she'd left, robbing her of a delaying trip to her sublet and the time she'd needed to wrap her head around what she was about to do: question a total stranger about someone else who never should have been a stranger at all.

Her own father.

But first, she'd have to chitchat with the man's widow and meet the kids.

Siblings.

She still couldn't quite wrap her head around the fact that there was additional Benjamin Ellis spawn in the world. Like a lot of women raised with only brothers, she'd craved a sister while growing up. Younger, older, it hadn't mattered.

But as she and Nate matured, the desire had faded. By then, she couldn't conceive of anyone replacing her big brother.

Though with a twenty-six-year age difference to her alone, these kids were closer to offspring or niece and nephew than siblings, weren't they?

Mira sighed as she reached into the leather tote on the passenger floorboard. She'd placed the bag there in Annapolis just after seven that morning. With everything she'd learned since, it felt like a lifetime. Locating the brush within, she unraveled her tired bun and refreshed the length into a low ponytail.

There was nothing left to do but reach into the Land Rover's back seat to retrieve the pair of modest presents that she'd been able to snag from the Mount Laurel's gift shop on her way out of the hotel.

The gifts tucked firmly inside the tote, and the leather straps to that hooked over her left shoulder, she abandoned the SUV. Less than a minute later, she was ascending the slate steps of the townhouse and entering the communal foyer.

Turning to the right, she drew her breath and her nerves in deep, holding both hostage as she rapped her knuckles lightly against the Ramseys' door.

No response.

Her breath eased out. Perhaps Keisha had taken her house-guests somewhere? She hadn't seen the woman's white Volvo parked on the street.

Was it further up?

Surely Keisha would've informed her husband if she'd made plans, even spur of the moment ones, with a very recent former Saudi national and two kids who'd captured Homeland's interest? And, hell, Ramsey had sent her here to meet with Noura.

Plus, there was that nondescript van slotted in several vehicles down the street. The casually dressed man supposedly dozing in the passenger's seat had managed to check her out at least twice since she'd parked the Land Rover in front of the townhouse.

Mira knocked again.

Not only was there still no answer, she couldn't make out the telltale sounds of young kids playing within.

Nap time?

One more rap against the wood, this one loud enough to rouse a sleeping kid or two—not to mention the agent in the van —but there was still no response.

It appeared no one was home.

Perhaps van-man had a clue as to where everyone had gone?

Mira was about to turn around, when she heard soft footfalls on the opposite side of the door. Moments later, it eased open. A pair of dark, luminous eyes framed by the slit of a Saudi niqab peered out between the door and the jamb.

"Hello, I'm—"

"*Miranda!*" The door flew wide open. "Please, please, come in. *Welcome.*"

Well, that answered her dilemma as to whether or not she should've provided her credentials for proof as to who she was and why she was here. Then again, as much as she'd hated it growing up, her boss was right; she really was the female mirror to dear ol' dad. As for the detestable name that her father's widow had used?

Under the circumstances, she let it slide.

The door closed behind her, but before Mira could get out a word, the reserved woman Ramsey had led her to expect had peeled off her niqab and tossed it onto an accent chair so that Noura could cup her palms over Mira's shoulders, pulling her into an almost desperate hug as she kissed her cheeks so many times that Mira lost count—and outright laughed. This was so not the greeting she'd counted on.

Okay, dreaded.

Noura stepped back, offering up the slimmest of breathing space as she continued to beam her own wide smile of genuine warmth wreathed with relief into Mira's face. "Elder daughter of my husband, you are *truly* welcome. The wife of your father's dear friend is shopping for groceries. But she speaks so highly of you, I know she would welcome you into her home again, too."

That solved the question of Keisha's missing Volvo. "I'm sorry I missed her. And I'm very sorry that I haven't been by to meet you sooner, Noura. I just found out that you and the kids were here, in the States."

Hell, she'd just found out the kids *existed*.

Mira reached into her tote to retrieve the boxes the clerk at the hotel's gift shop had wrapped, one in pastel pink, the other in blue. "A pony with a mane and tail to brush for Zaynah, and a train engine with two cars that attach for Ja'far." The labels claimed the chunky toys were age appropriate for smaller hands and the budding curiosity of younger minds, but what did she know? "I hope they're okay."

From the deepening of that smile and the shimmer of tears within those gorgeous eyes, it was. "Thank you. I know they will treasure them." Noura clasped the presents close with one arm, waving her deeper into the townhouse with the other. "Please, come sit. The children are napping, but I have made tea. Do you like mint?"

Not particularly.

She smiled anyway. "I'd love some. Thank you."

Mira was about to head down the hall to the Ramseys' living room, when she spotted a pair of tiny feet descending the stairs to her left. Gray kitten-covered leggings and a lilac stretch top followed. A pair of sleepy, thickly lashed eyes, cherubic cheeks and a miniature pink bow of a mouth joined them—along with a riot of dark, silky curls that skimmed the tops of those petite shoulders.

"*Your sister.*" Noura had whispered the confirmation, almost as if she'd been afraid to offer it. There was no need.

Mira was already in love. Hunkering down at the bottom step, she waited for the girl to finish descending. From the way Noura chattered happily above her head in Arabic—inserting the name Miranda several times—she was fairly certain that her father's widow was telling Zaynah that this woman was her big sister.

The little girl smiled shyly as she arrived at the bottom step, reaching up to touch Mira's left cheek, the tip of her tiny index finger dipping into the pinpoint dimple that Mira was fairly certain was on full display along with her own smile.

"Hi, Zaynah."

The shy smile deepened as the little girl's fingertips shifted to graze the top, and then down the left side of the blond hair that Mira had pulled into a ponytail.

And then those tiny fingers were grasping hers, and silently tugging her up and toward the living room.

Mira followed as Zaynah led her to the carved camel back sofa that Ramsey's wife had found in an antique store shortly before Mira had climbed aboard the doomed Wildcat. Keisha had since had the sofa recovered in crushed blue. It looked great opposite the pair of cream, high back armchairs flanking the coffee table, but Mira was more enthralled with the tiny hand in hers and the little girl attached to it.

She hadn't expected to be this captivated, this quickly.

But she was.

As Noura busied herself with pouring their tea, Mira sank onto the sofa, her sister standing beside her. But instead of opening the gift that her mother had left on the table, Zaynah lifted the cover of the thick, six-by-eight-inch photo album next to the box. Like the Qur'an, its contents advanced from right to left.

Mira recognized the man and woman in the opening pages. They were wedding pictures of Noura and her new husband—Mira's father.

Since Noura had come to the door wearing the niqab and an abaya that she had also recently abandoned, these photos must have been taken in private, after their guests had departed. Possibly by the other now-deceased man that Mira was here to discuss: Noura's father, Habib ibn Ibrahim Al Shammari.

Unfortunately, that conversation would have to wait.

Noura might have welcomed her warmly, if a bit desperately, but Mira doubted the mother would be up for even careful probing about her husband's and father's dealings with terrorists right off the bat—especially in front of her daughter.

The same daughter who was pointing to her father's eyes. "*Azraq.*" The word was followed by several others, all unintelligible to Mira.

"I'm sorry—" She glanced up at the child's mother. "—I'm afraid your English is vastly superior to my Arabic." Though that wasn't surprising, since English was taught in Saudi schools from the elementary level onward—and had been for decades now. Nearly ninety-eight percent of the country's citizens were fluent.

Noura smiled. "Blue. Your sister says your eyes are blue, like the father you both share. Also, the dimple he had, she says you have it too."

"Ah."

Mira's heart tightened as Zaynah reached up to fit her tiny index finger into the deep dip that Mira had indeed inherited, just as the little girl had done at the stairs. How many times had Zaynah touched their father's cheek the same way...and now, never would again? Mira's heart went out to the girl.

She doubted Zaynah even understood her loss, because the child returned to the album with another one of those shy smiles. As Zaynah flipped through more of the pages, stopping now and then to finger several pictures through the clear film that protected them, she succeeded in flipping Mira's already exposed heart over as well.

The bulk of the book was filled with baby photos of Zaynah and her brother—and their smiling, doting father.

Yes, the photos were lovely, along with the story they told. But this tale was nothing like the one that she and Nate had shared with the same man.

The mint tea arrived and Mira was grateful for the distraction. She left the open album where it lay on the coffee table and sipped at the sweetened contents of the cup, relieved when Noura drew her daughter's attention to the pink present.

The gift was quickly unwrapped and clearly a hit. Girl and flowing, magenta mane-and-tailed pony disappeared deeper into the house.

The moment they were alone, Noura set her cup down. "My husband—your father—he spoke of you often."

"Really?" Why?

And shouldn't he have spoken to *her*?

Though if the man had truly wanted to do that, he'd have had to apologize to Nate first—and sincerely. Ben Ellis had damned well known that.

She'd been lying when she'd told herself that the childhood in that album wasn't hers. It had been. For a time she, too, had been Daddy's little girl—though she'd always felt guilty about it. Nate could've hated her for it too, but he hadn't. Her brother had told her once during one of their walks around town that he wouldn't have had a relationship with their father at all, if it hadn't been for her.

As young as she'd been, she wasn't sure how she'd been able to pick up on the undercurrents between her father and his elder child, but she had. So, without fail, she'd insisted "Natty" tag along wherever she and her father were headed.

When she was six, everything had changed.

She'd overheard her parents talking in their room and had learned far more about DNA and rape than any child should—especially when it concerned a parent. But what had confused and then angered her was when she'd heard her mother insisting that Ben needed to publicly recognize Nate as his biological son.

That's when she finally understood what that word *bastard* and that nasty pinched expression that Nana Miranda always made when she used it really meant.

And her father's response? Their mother had blackmailed him into adopting Nate, so the boy was hers, not his.

That's when Mira had lost it. She'd stormed into her parents' bedroom and announced that if Nate wasn't her father's child, then *she* wasn't either.

And she'd meant it.

Daddy's little girl had disappeared for both of them that night. And, yeah, it hurt to see another girl, no matter how sweet —and especially another boy—in her place.

"Miranda?"

Christ, she hated that name. Almost as much as the old holier-than-thou witch she'd been named after.

She forced a smile as she glanced up from the album. "It's Mira, *please*. Especially for close friends and family."

That last placated her father's widow.

Thank God.

"Mira...your father came to regret many things—most especially that he was not the man that you and your brother needed while you were growing up."

Now there was an understatement.

Not that she had any intention of pointing that out to an actively grieving widow. Somehow, Mira didn't think honesty on that score would be conducive to making the connection she, too, desperately needed to make.

To her surprise, Noura smiled sadly and sighed. "I know it is difficult to sit with me and speak of him. In part, because I also now know what some of your countrymen believe about your father. But *you* must believe me when I tell you that your father was proud of you and your success with your career, and yes, his eldest child, too. Though he very much regretted the affair with Nathaniel's mother and the pain it caused your own, he did not regret his son."

Affair?

That was the story their dad had created to cover his crime?

It was a damned good thing she hadn't been holding her tea, let alone sipping at it. She'd have spewed the contents everywhere.

As it was, she bit her tongue. Hard. She had to. But she was just pissed enough to push it. "If my father was so proud of Nate and me, and how we've chosen to serve our country, why would he support those who wish to attack it—and do?"

"Because he changed—though it took time. For many years,

Benjamin believed as my own father did and as our imam taught. That the madrassas must be supported, no matter the personal sacrifice. But since Ja'far and Zaynah were born, Benjamin had come to accept that not all of what was being shared in some of the schools was as Muhammad, peace be upon him, wanted. Nor did your father wish for his new son and daughter to believe these things."

"So why didn't he stop the flow of money?"

"Your father...I loved him deeply, but Benjamin was not...a strong man."

As massive understatements went, this woman was two for two.

Mira knew better than most that her dad could rationalize anything, so long as it kept him from taking a stand.

And his widow? Noura Ellis was a hell of a lot shrewder than Ramsey had given her credit for.

Had she played the shy, grieving fish out of water for her fellow NCIS agents? Or was Noura now just coming out of her shock—and being honest with the only other adult family member she had left who still seemed to want something to do with her?

The woman did have two young kids to consider.

Knowing that Nate was half-Filipino, and that Mira adored him, Noura was probably hoping like hell that she'd welcome two more siblings who were half-Saudi.

The pinch of desperation that Mira had felt in that welcome hug in the foyer suggested *yes*. Granted, the warmth surrounding it had appeared to be genuine. But Mira had no illusions that at least part of this instant friendship was steeped in Noura's belief that Mira wouldn't abandon the twins now that she'd come to meet them.

Nor could she blame the woman.

Especially given the background information that Ramsey had provided before they'd left the hotel room at the Mount Laurel. A second heart attack had felled Noura's own father the same night that she'd been put on the plane to Bahrain. Once the Saudi crown prince had found out about Ben Ellis' murder and the monetary pipeline to the madrassas—and that the US government knew about that pipeline and wanted answers—Noura's father's and husband's company had been shut down, the entirety of both men's surviving assets immediately absorbed into the king's.

Noura and her children were not only destitute, the Saudi government had also decided that she and her children should remain outside the country...for good.

What better way to deal with any potential geopolitical and religious fallout than to sweep it under an American rug and pretend it never existed?

"Why did my father send you to Bahrain?"

"I do not know. When we left, I believed it was as Benjamin had said; I was to shop for the children. He told me he would join us the day after we arrived. But he did not. Instead, someone from your embassy came to inform me of his...death. And then my father's. This man and others also asked me questions for many weeks, while I remained with the children in Bahrain. But neither my father nor yours ever discussed their work or money within my hearing. My father felt it was not seemly, and Benjamin agreed. Nor do I know what it was that your father intended to send to you. I very much wish I did have this information to offer, for then perhaps I would be allowed to take my children home. But I do not."

Disappointment and more than a bit of panic cut in as Mira reached down and closed the album on that happy father and his adoring toddlers.

She could feel Noura's distress. The woman truly wanted to

provide the answers that she knew Mira was here to obtain—but she simply didn't have them.

Which mean yet another potential lead to those stolen assemblies had just evaporated.

Please God, let the team trailing Zak come up with *something*.

That hope was the only thing that kept Mira on the sofa as she masked her own roiling emotions to focus on those still emanating from the widow seated across from her. "You have my deepest condolences, Noura. For the death of the husband you obviously adored, and your father's passing, too. I'm also sorry you weren't allowed to attend the funerals."

Not that Noura would've been able to be present at the actual burials. Not with the strict Wahhabi views of her father's and husband's sect.

"I thank you. And I offer you my condolences, as well, for the passing of your father."

Mira nodded, accepting the solace more for what might've been than the reality of what had. She'd never really known the man in those photos.

And now, she never would.

Noura retrieved the album from the coffee table, those dark eyes of hers glistening with tears as she gently caressed the cover. "I brought this with me when your father took me to visit my friend, Fatimah, shortly before he died. I shall be forever grateful that I forgot to remove it from my bag when we returned home. One of the agents who questioned me in Bahrain asked to see it. I do not know why he kept it for so long. I had begun to fear it would not be returned to me. But, praise Allah, it was."

Yeah, Mira knew why the album had been confiscated. Given the voicemail her father had left for her, she'd have snagged the album, as well—so she could scour every photo within, along with the covers and spine, for clues as to whatever her father had intended to pass to her. Hell, she'd have probably x-rayed the damned thing, too.

Just as Homeland or NCIS undoubtedly had.

But the devastated widow now clutching that album to her heart didn't need to know that.

The woman glanced up, a tear slipping free as she smiled sadly. "But I have the children to remind me of your father. You do not." To Mira's surprise, Noura pushed the album into her hands. "Please. A gift for my son and my daughter's sister."

Oh, no. Those happy pictures should stay where they'd be appreciated. "I can't accept this. Other than the twins, these photos are all you have left of him." She returned the album to the table. "Zaynah and Ja'far will need them too."

"Take it for a time then, for the comfort, and return it later?"

An ironic and humbling offer, considering the woman extending it didn't know where she and her kids would be a month from now—though *that* reality could well be part of the reason. To strengthen this bond between elder and younger siblings.

Either way, Mira shook her head. Firmly. "But, thank you."

Noura opened her mouth, only to be distracted by several piercing shrieks and a solid thump, followed by a series of increasingly loud wails. It appeared that both Mira's siblings were awake now—and fighting.

Over the pony?

Great.

Noura clearly feared the same source of strife, because she retrieved the pastel blue box as she stood. "Please, excuse me. I shall return shortly."

Against her will, Mira's gaze returned to the album as the woman swiftly abandoned the living room. She could sneak a peek at the rest of those photos, and no one would know. She reached out, then pulled her hand back to her lap.

Furious at the weakness, she welcomed the distraction provided by the ping that came from the latest phone that Ramsey had attached to her old line.

She stood. Turning her back on that painfully seductive album, she slipped her hand beneath her sweater to retrieve the phone her boss had given her at the hotel.

The incoming text was from an FBI agent she knew. He'd be in DC in a few days.

RU up for dinner & a movie?

Unfortunately, her interest in the man had waned well before the last of the handful of dates they'd already shared. But why be rude? Especially since they might have to work together at some point in the future.

She hoped her *thanks, but I'm on a case & it's pretty complicated* would soften the *no.*

From the sad emoji, followed by a cheerier flower, it did.

She could still hear wailing from somewhere on the second floor above, so she busied herself with skimming the remaining texts she'd missed since she'd passed the previous phone attached to this line off to her brother that morning.

Three alerts in, she paused.

The text in question was from another fellow agent, though this one was also a good friend who worked for NCIS like her... in Bahrain. And the information within was a solid attention grabber.

Having a shit day. My latest victim is your doppelgänger.

With everything that was going on with Zak—not to mention those bugs the bastard had placed into the McMansion and her sublet—her curiosity was piqued.

Bahrain was seven hours ahead; it was barely 1530 in DC.

Leo Kealani was likely awake. Especially since he'd caught a new, if decidedly un-fresh murder that morning.

She texted her fellow agent and asked him to send a photo.

Leo was definitely awake and with his brain still firing on all thrusters. Not more than thirty seconds later, her app pinged, and the text was from him.

Check it out. Weird, huh?

Attached was a photo of the victim's face and shoulders, along with Leo's subsequent comments noting that although they'd just found the woman, she appeared to have been murdered several weeks earlier. The body was in excellent condition though, mainly because it had been stashed in a walk-in refrigerator.

Upon enlarging the photo, Mira could tell the victim's throat had been slashed—just like Commander Corrigan's. Leo had exaggerated a bit with his *doppelgänger* comment, but with that bone-straight, long blond hair and the hint of blue beneath those clouded corneas and sunken eyes, his victim was a heck of a lot closer to the features Mira saw in the mirror than the sweet cherub upstairs currently howling like a banshee at her brother.

When Mira realized the shape of the victim's face, chin and jawline were eerily similar to hers, too, her curiosity strengthened into suspicion.

Zak. Had violating and murdering the JAG churned up all the old hate and resentment that his feelings had morphed into following their breakup years earlier? Had Zak decided to take out that renewed fury on someone else? Someone who looked like her...because he couldn't get to her?

It was possible. Because if Leo's timeline was right, she would've still been in her coma and under twenty-four/seven observation by nearly every nurse in the ICU when her near *doppelgänger* had been killed, and thus inaccessible even to

Zak...*especially* if the bastard had been skulking around Bahrain at the time.

Even more chilling, with over seven thousand US military personnel spread out over three US Naval bases and air facilities in Bahrain—including the headquarters for US Naval Forces Central Command/5th Fleet—that part of the globe would also make one hell of a target for a bomb constructed with some of that converted radioactive fuel that was floating around out there...somewhere.

Yeah, it might all be a long shot, but she was getting pretty damned desperate.

She texted her fellow agent once more and asked for a copy of the initial report.

She was about to dip into her email box to clean that up as well, when a knock resounded on the outer side of the Ramseys' front door. Though these raps were heavier than hers had been, she doubted Noura had heard them above those wails.

Visions of Keisha juggling too many grocery bags danced through Mira's mind as she pocketed her phone and headed for the door to pull it open.

Great. Not the woman she'd hoped to see.

Hell, not even a woman—but a man. The last man she wanted to see for the remainder of her days.

Sam Riyad.

17

"Hello, Commander."

The SEAL's scowl cut in with Mira's greeting.

Figured. Though she'd have thought the shitty ending to the scene in Riyad's hotel room hours earlier would've earned her a reprieve from that perpetual distain for, gee, a day at least, that was evidently not the case.

"May I come in?"

"Now, see, this isn't my house. Besides, if you're here to see Ramsey—"

"I'm not." The scowl darkened. "But I did speak with the man at the Field Office twenty minutes ago. The temporary benefits card for your father's widow came through. Ramsey mentioned that you were here visiting, so I told him I'd drop it off since he's headed overseas again, and well...I wanted to speak with you."

Yeah, that's not what that glower was muttering.

Its bearer would rather be anywhere, doing anything, than chitchatting here with her. And who would've thought the jerk was capable of flushing, let alone so deeply?

"And this burning need to speak with me. Is it my boss' idea —or yours?" He had admittedly just met with Ramsey.

A terse sigh darkened the foyer. "Woman, can you just—"

"The name is Mira. To my friends, anyway. To you, Commander Riyad, I am Agent Ellis. Not *woman*."

That tic the man possessed at the left square of his jaw began flagging so strongly it was easily visible within the neatly sculpted beard that surrounded it. He did, however, manage to keep a retort from searing past those lips.

A deep breath and a second, heavier sigh followed the first. "May I come in...please?"

"As I stated, this is not my house. But if you must barge in, feel free to wait in the foyer. Noura's with the kids. You can hand the card over when she's finished. And you can skip the chat with me; I'm not interested." She left the man standing in the open door as she turned to head down the hall and back into the living room.

She heard the door close, then the SEAL's dogging bootfalls.

His fingers snagged her elbow as she reached the couch, turning her around before she could shake them off. "Noura won't take it from me. Hell, the woman won't even look directly at me when I speak, let alone respond to anything I say."

"Imagine that." The *woman* was smarter and shrewder than Mira had already given her credit for. "It's good to know my instincts regarding my dad's widow are sound. Too bad you can't say the same about your own instincts with women, eh?"

The tic started up again.

Oh, hell. As much as she enjoyed irritating the jerk, Noura had two young kids to care for. And though it rankled Mira, her siblings' remaining, now destitute parent would need the food and medical benefits that were attached to that card, at least for a while. She should accept the thing, and quickly, before she pissed off its bearer so much that he stormed off with the card still in his cargo pocket.

She held out her right hand.

Those fine white scars on Riyad's fingertips brushed her palm as he tucked it within.

She ground her teeth against the contact, but remained silent as she stepped sideways to bend down and set the card on the table next to the photo album. She offered a pointed brow as she straightened. "Mission accomplished, Commander." What was it the ass had said to Ramsey in her room at Walter Reed? "You can leave now."

Those presumptuous fingers found her elbow again. This time, their owner nudged her entire body toward the French doors that led out of the living room and into the three-season lounge that doubled as Keisha's overflowing orchid nursery.

"I meant what I said; I'd also like to speak with you—in private."

Yeah, that scowl still pegged the statement as a lie.

Unfortunately, the strength behind it warned her that its owner wouldn't be leaving until he'd vented whatever it was that he felt driven to say. She had a pretty good idea of what that was, too. And she did not want to hear it.

Much less accept it.

But neither did she want Noura and the kids disturbed by another bout of audible fury—on this floor.

"Fine." She led the way through the doors, clamping down on her temper as Riyad not only closed both but positioned that admittedly intimidating form of his in front of the glass panels, trapping her inside the room with him.

He glanced at the rattan loveseat beside the purple, yellow and creamy white sprays of all those blooming orchids. "Would you like to sit?"

"Nope."

An honest-to-God curve nudged onto that pretty-boy mouth as he shook his head. "You have no intention of making this easier, do you?"

She folded one arm over the other and clamped both down. "Nope."

"Mira—"

Her brow hiked as she focused on the slight bruising around the SEAL's left eye. Too bad it hadn't darkened any further in the intervening hours. Even more disappointing, the reddened area beneath that cultivated beard at the edge of his jaw had already faded.

Nate should've punched harder.

"*Agent Ellis.*" Riyad held up his hands, spreading his fingers wide. "I'm sorry, okay? I was wrong about you and your loyalties. I'm also sorry for what I said about your father, especially the way I said it. Two seconds after the words came out in that hotel suite, I knew I was out of line, but I couldn't apologize then. You walked away from me and refused to respond to my knock, much less open the bathroom door."

That would be because he'd hammered her so low with that filthy blow of his, that she hadn't heard his knock.

Hell, until Ramsey had arrived, she hadn't heard anything at all. She'd been lost to the noise of that fan and the numbing knowledge that her father had been murdered while she'd been deleting his voicemail.

As for the way Riyad had revealed that murder? The SEAL was definitely tone deaf.

But her father *was* involved in this.

Nor could she really blame Riyad for suspecting her of treason. Once he'd started digging into Zak's past, he'd have come across mention of her. Looking into her would've led Riyad to her father in Saudi Arabia. This might've all been the epitome of guilt by association, but it had admittedly been one hell of an association.

Though she wasn't about to admit any of that to this jerk. She still just wanted him to *go*.

But that rigid stance? Riyad was here for the count.

She might as well use the man's unyielding presence, along with any lingering guilt that *he* might possess. Because there was something she wanted more than the SEAL's absence. Answers. If Riyad had truly turned his opinion about her and her so-called traitorous motives around, she just might be able to get those answers.

And there was the potential lead attached to that *doppelgänger* to consider.

So she let the rest go, at least for now. "Okay."

"Okay? That's...it?"

She nodded. "You've apologized. It's over. Now—" She loosened the clamp on her arms...a bit. "—what's the latest on Zak?"

Riyad blinked down at her, as if he was trying to wrap his head around her acceptance and the sudden shift in topics, and what he was supposed to do about it.

If he should believe her.

Through the outermost edge of the French doors, Mira caught sight of Noura entering the living room with a calmed child hooked to each hip. The woman took one look at the broad shoulders and Henley-clad back of the man speaking to her husband's daughter and spun back around and headed out of the room—quickly.

Mira swallowed her envy. Would that she could've used culture to avoid this jerk. "Well?"

The man ran a hand through his hair and exhaled sharply. "There's nothing yet. At least, nothing we can use. One of the guys checked in half an hour ago. The entire team is still gallivanting around the capital, trailing after the bastard."

Another one of those scowls seared in. But this one wasn't meant for her. It was born of frustration and directed at himself.

She understood the cause.

Just as Riyad could recognize Zak and his tactical tendencies and anticipate his moves, Zak knew Riyad and had a similar bead on his. Hence, Riyad couldn't shadow the ex-SEAL. He had to leave the mission to others. Others who Riyad didn't necessarily know, let alone have worked with before. And *that* wasn't sitting well with the man.

Welcome to the club. The membership fees for this one were the most frustrating and expensive of all: patience and trust.

The tension in the SEAL's stare ratcheted down as he tipped his chin toward her. "What about you? You get anywhere with your father's widow?"

Since the widow in question appeared to have abandoned the outer room for the duration of the man's visit, it was safe to respond. "Noura says her own father kept his business separate —always. My dad continued the tradition as her husband. She has no idea what the man wanted to mail to me."

"You believe her?"

"I do." Noura had those kids to worry about. And Noura *was* worrying.

The woman might be religious and culturally trapped within that veil of hers, but those kids came first. And that was a good thing.

But while Mira had managed to establish the connection she'd been after, the dead end it led to had that panic pinching back in. If the team of agents Riyad had assigned to follow Zak couldn't cull a clue from his movements around town, and soon, they might as well be waiting around for those explosions to begin.

"You know what I still don't get? Why did Zak torture and kill Commander Corrigan?" Yes, her ex had held the JAG partially responsible for the fight they'd had after she'd rejected the Navy's offer of reinstatement and resigned her commission. And Zak had definitely blamed Corrigan after Mira had returned his ring.

And while she was familiar with the psychopathology that went with a killer deciding to clean house, in this case it just didn't mesh.

Seven years had passed. Shouldn't Zak have gotten over it?

Or hunted the JAG down long before now?

"I...may have the answer to that."

The reluctance within the SEAL's dark stare caught her attention, more than the statement itself. She hiked a brow and waited for the details to follow.

Riyad nodded. "I know you spoke to Regan Chase. I assume you recall Agent Chase's comments regarding the murders that took place in that cave on the Afghan-Pak border last December."

"I do."

"I was sent to Afghanistan and tasked with looking into the deaths before Agent Chase arrived, to see if they were connected in any way to Webber. Agent Chase and I didn't cross paths then; I was headed elsewhere before she arrived."

"And were those murders connected to Zak?"

"At the time, I wasn't sure. But events that occurred in Pakistan in January proved that they were. But about Commander Corrigan; she'd made a reputation for herself when it came to prosecuting terrorists within the Navy and Marine Corps."

Lovely. And to think, the JAG had cut those prosecutorial teeth back at the nuclear power school on her and Frank. Or, rather, Corrigan had tried.

But Riyad was already nodding. "I know; she crossed the line with you and Nasser at NPS. If it helps, Corrigan was officially reprimanded for turning a blind eye to that false witness state-ment against you two back then. But the current point is, because of her subsequent reputation and a critical case detail, Corrigan was added to the Army team that was put together to prosecute

Nabil Durrani and Tamir Hachemi—the Afghan physician and Army translator behind the cave murders. The translator initially claimed that he'd recognized a US sailor meeting with the head of his terror cell months earlier. Hachemi was shown a photo lineup that included Webber before Hachemi and Durrani were flown out to the *USS Griffith*, but by then, Hachemi had already recanted. He refused to look at the photos. But that initial, partial ID is probably why Hachemi was also murdered. We think Webber was that sailor. Though how Webber found out Hachemi even considered fingering him, we still don't know."

So Corrigan had likely been tortured in case the translator had let something slip that she'd yet to figure out. That made sense. Plus, killing the JAG who he believed had screwed up his engagement would've been a twisted, personal bonus for Zak.

"You recognized the dislocation technique at the post-mortem, didn't you?"

"The fingers? Yeah, Webber's done shit like that before. It's one of the reasons we never got on. The guy was fucked up in the head, but he was good at masking it. And he had the skills and the experience the Teams desperately needed. He managed to keep the worst of his nature locked up when he wasn't in country...until it was too late."

That made sense too. But the part about Corrigan and the specifics of the dislocation technique? "You do realize that all this would've been helpful to know two months ago, especially when we were inside that autopsy suite."

The man's flush returned, and with an inexplicable vengeance. "Agent Ellis...I know you're not ready to truly accept my apology, and I don't blame you. But I want you on this investigation. Today. It needs you."

It, not he.

She suspected that was as close as she was going to get.

"*Mira*." He might as well use it. She still couldn't stand the man, but he was coughing up answers now. And she did want the authority to track down the missing fuel from those radioactive assemblies. Desperately. "You want me to accept your apology? Fine; it's accepted—but it's conditional. I want a few things in return."

"Such as?"

"Bring Jerry Dahl back on board."

"He's already here. He's still hung up with Jalilah Ibrahim, discussing anything and everything she did in her father's office at the mosque."

"I know that part. But I want Jerry *completely* aboard. Full access. Send the both of us everything you have from the moment Zak and that SDV went missing. Hell, everything from earlier too, if you even suspect it's applicable. And I do mean *everything*. But honestly? Jerry'll probably get through it all first. He usually does. And that's good—because he knows my brain intimately, so he'll know what he should pass on to me ASAP. And since you know that I've spoken to Regan Chase, you should also know that I'll be calling her again if I feel the case warrants it. Agent Chase has a unique insight on this and, frankly, we need all the trusted eyes we can get."

The man's scarred fingers hooked around his backside and returned holding a phone. He opened his text app and typed in several sentences. Enough to cover Jerry's assignment and the transfer of the entire case file.

A ping followed.

He checked the response. "Done. Next concession?"

"I want the freedom to pursue any case leads that I believe warrant pursuing, wherever they take me. If you can't accept that? Well, given that I was texting a fellow NCIS agent in Bahrain about a long shot while you were walking up to the townhouse earlier—and, yeah, I wasn't even officially back aboard—that one's a dealbreaker."

That earned her a nod, and she swore this one came with a tinge of respect. "Any other conditions?"

"Not at the moment. But I do have a personal promise to impart."

Those dark brows rose.

"If you call me *woman* again with that charming Your Highness tone of voice you've got, you'll be living out the rest of your days as a eunuch."

Silence met that statement, along with an odd look she couldn't quite place.

It took a few beats, but he followed up his silence with another nod, this one cool and clipped. The shadow of that all-too-familiar scowl accompanied it.

She matched the man's motion and raised him a smile. "Congratulations, Sam. We're in business."

"Good." He pocketed his phone. "Now, tell me about this long shot."

"It's still more gut instinct at the moment. There was a murder in Bahrain a few weeks back. The woman looks—"

"Remarkably like you. I saw her photo this morning. But as you said, she's been dead for a while. Why do you think it's connected?"

"I'm not sure it is." Heck, it probably wasn't. "But given the similar looks, the fact that she was most likely murdered while I was under constant surveillance in the ICU and inaccessible to Zak, and that her throat was cut—" The same method of execution as Corrigan *and* her father. "—not to mention, Bahrain would make one hell of a tempting target to Zak and those new munitions of his. It's all just—making me want to dig deeper." If only to make sure it *wasn't* connected.

"That slash to the throat. You think Webber might've killed

her because he was pissed that you didn't die from that crash or the fall from the *Tern*?"

"Who knows?" She'd long since given up trying to figure out how Zak Webber's mind worked. Even years ago, when they'd been dating. "There's something else, too. It's about Frank. I told Ramsey, but I don't know if he passed it on to you."

"Are you referring to Nasser's hands? That he was strangling Captain Whitby—who was ideologically aligned with Webber? I admit, it's a nice exculpatory thought—especially about someone who was once your friend. And I agree that the fact that those water wings were stolen puts a certain light on their presence in Corrigan's throat. But Nasser pushed you off that fucking ship. That's a pretty big indicator, too."

That it was.

But an indicator of what?

"That's just it. I don't know who pushed me. But I do know that before I was pushed, Whitby shoved me into Frank. I think Frank pulled the lanyard to my preserver. If he did, he saved my life, because I'm not sure I would've been able to inflate it after I surfaced. The water was deathly cold and my head was messed up from the concussion." Not to mention the pain from her freshly broken leg on top of the injuries she'd sustained during the helo crash. "The more I think about it, the more certain I am that Frank was trying to kill Whitby *because* Whitby was dirty. If Frank had succeeded, the lack of communication with the *Tern*'s captain would've automatically sounded the alarm in the UK, mobilizing the emergency response team sooner." It would explain why Frank had been on the bridge and not assisting with the theft. Had he slipped away while Zak was distracted with retrieving the assemblies? "But I also know that Frank *was* actively involved in the plot. At least initially. I could read his shame and his regret on that bridge wing. But if I'm right, and

Frank is having second thoughts, we can use that change of heart...somehow."

Unfortunately, to do that, they'd have to find Frank. If he was still alive. So many others who Zak had used to steal the fuel had already been executed.

If Frank had finished converting all of the uranium and plutonium from those mixed-oxide pellets, he was most likely dead now too.

"I hope you're right about the guy's loyalty shift."

She could hear the doubt. "But?"

"Like you said, the concussion screwed up your head. You could've read the situation wrong. Hell, with the injuries you sustained, anyone could have—me included. Plus, it's going on eight weeks since the *Tern*'s takedown. That's plenty of time for Nasser to have broken off from the group—*if* that had been his intention."

As much as she hated to admit it, if Frank was alive, Riyad was probably right.

Her phone pinged. She retrieved it.

The text was from Leo. Adrenaline thundered through her blood, heating her from within, as she caught the opening lines.

Report attached. Autopsy pending. The vic was tortured too. Check out the dislocated fingers.

Mira stiffened. *Zak.*

She was about to share the information with Riyad when his phone rang. She waited as he, too, tugged it from his pocket. Within seconds her adrenaline had begun to bleed off, pooling into a cold, biting dread as she caught the SEAL's latest scowl.

A soft "*Fuck*" escaped his lips.

Riyad continued to listen to whomever was on the other end of the line for several moments, then offered a terse, "I'll call you in a few," and hung up.

"What's wrong?"

Those scarred fingers came up to dig into the crook of his neck as he expelled a harsh breath. "That was the head of the team assigned to tail Webber. I hope to hell that long shot of yours pans out, because they just found two of our agents in an alley a stone's throw from Sixteenth Street. Both are dead. Their throats were slit."

Fuck was right.

The deaths were bad enough. But Sixteenth Street? A certain large White House anchored the southernmost end of that road. Yet another tempting locale for Zak to send one of those deadly new munitions of his.

She was afraid to ask for confirmation of what she suspected. But she did. "And Zak?"

"He's in the wind. And, no, we don't have a goddamned clue as to where the bastard's headed next."

She clamped her fingers around the text still glowing up from the screen of her phone. "I might have a way to find out."

Though it was the slimmest of mights. Worse, the narrow thread of hope she was clinging to was knotted to the end of a lengthier long shot than that *doppelgänger* had been. Because even if Zak had killed a woman in Bahrain, they'd only know for certain where Zak had been several weeks earlier.

Yes, if they were lucky—damned lucky—Zak might've left something on the body or at the scene that would suggest where he was going.

But would it be enough to locate him in time?

18

T he moment Mira exited the terminal at Muharraq Airfield, the late Saturday afternoon's one-hundred-four-degree heat slammed in like a thick, invisible wall.

Fortunately, her next source of air-conditioning wasn't far off.

She'd already caught sight of her fellow NCIS agent. It wasn't difficult. Though he too was dark, Leo Kealani's six-foot-four-inch, black-suited Hawaiian bulk was easy to spot among the shorter, white thobe and ghutra-attired Arabs around him—along with the agent's beaming grin and gigantic, waving right hand.

"*Aloha*, Mir. Long time, no see." He reached her, scooping her up for a brief, hard hug before he set her gently back down onto her feet. "Lani and I were so goddamned grateful to hear you survived that crash and fall."

She laughed. "No more than me."

"I'll bet." Leo snagged her stainless-steel crime scene kit and back-up suit bag before she could argue, leaving her to shoulder her overstuffed leather tote. "Welcome to the Kingdom of

Bahrain—emphasis on *king*dom." He tipped his head toward the silver, four-door Toyota Land Cruiser parked yards away. "Your royal chariot awaits, Agent Ellis."

Shit.

The man's tone might be lighthearted, but they'd worked side by side for two years in Japan. Long enough for her to know this second smile was forced.

"What happened?"

Leo shook his head slightly, the glance he shot over her right shoulder letting her know he didn't want to get into whatever it was within earshot of the approaching, equally well-built, charcoal-gray-suited Saudi.

Neither did she. But it seemed she was stuck with the SEAL, at least for the duration of this trip to Bahrain.

"He's with me." She swept her right hand between the men as Riyad hung up with whomever he'd lagged behind to call before stepping up to her side. "Commander Riyad, meet Agent Kealani, NCIS. Leo, Sam's a current SEAL who's been tracking the ex-SEAL we think may have murdered your victim."

Mira paused long enough for the men to exchange silent nods of greeting over the duffle, crime kit and suit bags that they now both bore, then trained her tightening nerves on her fellow investigator. "Now that the niceties are out of the way—what's wrong?"

Leo tipped his head toward the Land Cruiser. "In the car."

Oh, boy.

She waited as the men stowed the bags in the trunk. Riyad surprised her by stepping ahead and opening the SUV's front passenger door, his slight nod indicating that she should take the preferred seat. Upon closing the door, he commandeered the one behind her—an act that also left his facial expressions and body language frustratingly out of her view.

Perhaps that had been the intent behind the seeming politeness, all along.

Mira waited as Leo fired up the engine and steered the car toward Manama proper—only to turn south on the road that would take them to the Al Juffair district in lieu of continuing across the main island's narrow, ten-mile width before heading south to chew through most of its remaining forty-mile length to reach the crime scene walk through they were scheduled to commence in half an hour.

The moment the Land Cruiser slotted into 27's crazy traffic, she caved into the impatience the agent seated beside her tended to accuse her of. "Well?"

Leo shot her a frown as he kept the bulk of his attention on several local drivers determined to play bumper cars on both sides and behind them. "We're headed to the branch clinic on base, not the villa where I think she was killed."

"Why?"

"There's no crime scene to visit. Not anymore." He shook his head, disgust strengthening his frown. "Shit, Mir, I should've figured this would happen. Our victim's HM1 Sandra Lance. The petty officer worked out of the same clinic I had her body sent to. She's been stationed in Bahrain for three years, so she had to have known that all of Malkiya Beach is a no-go zone for our military personnel, especially the ritzier section that contained the villa where her body was found."

No-go?

Damn. "Let me guess. The villa's owner is a Shi'ite and a vocal member of one of the opposition groups to the king." And, of course, the king was a member of the Sunni *minority* in Bahrain. "His Majesty doesn't want to make waves for fear of sparking another violent, sectarian uprising." Though the likelihood of that risk was getting slimmer given that the crackdown against dissidents in Bahrain over the last decade had been so severe that many who'd become emboldened by the Arab

Spring of 2011 had already been silenced...often via lifelong imprisonment, torture and execution.

But if it looked to the citizens of Bahrain as though their Sunni king was deferring to the US Navy over a prominent member of the Shia Muslim majority?

"Yeah, it's even more delicate than that." Leo slowed to avoid a near collision with a determined, yet seemingly blind, young Arab driver. "The villa's owner is Shi'ite. And while Tariq Al Salman is older and a well-respected member of his religious community, he's also a good friend of the king. Salman says that his Saudi cousin's nineteen-year-old grandson invited a couple of men to stay at the villa without his knowledge. The kid supposedly met these men while visiting the States last year. But when I questioned the little shit, Ahmed Ali suffered a massive brain fart. Ali claims he can't remember which state he was in when he met his buddies, let alone their names or what they looked like. And sometime late last night, Ali took the King Fahd causeway back home. Strangely, he's not picking up his phone today. At least, not for me."

"Great." And since Saudi Arabia didn't extradite, "We're screwed on that end."

Leo nodded. "Yep."

"What about the petty officer? Why wasn't Sandra Lance reported missing?"

"No one knew she was. Lance had excess leave on the books. She decided to use up thirty days before she headed to her new command in the States. Three and a half weeks ago, Lance was supposed to drive across the causeway herself to visit a British friend who's a nurse in Riyadh. They were going to tour the desert sites together."

Crap. This was sounding familiar. "The friend got a call, didn't she? Petty Officer Lance said she was needed at work and would have to reschedule."

"How'd you guess?"

Not a guess. "That's what our suspect forced our JAG officer to do in DC two months ago, only with Commander Corrigan, it was a sister."

"Shit. Sounds like we really are dealing with the same fucker."

Lord, Mira hoped so. God willing, Zak had left evidence behind on Lance's body. Something that would lead them to the location of those assemblies. At least then something good might come of the woman's murder.

Though she doubted the petty officer's family would feel the same way.

"When's the autopsy?"

"It's done. Pathologist showed up this morning, shortly after colors. I was genuflecting over at the damned place, trying to get us back inside the crime scene, so she started without me. I'm not happy about it, but the doc couldn't wait; she needed to boomerang right back out for another autopsy somewhere in Africa. Heck, one of the corpsmen was slated to drop the woman off at the airfield while I was grabbing you. But the doc said she'd leave a preliminary copy of her report at the clinic's quarterdeck, along with her email and a satellite phone number, in case we have any questions."

Like Leo, Mira preferred to observe the postmortems connected to her cases. But since that hadn't been possible, "That'll have to do."

Leo snapped a nod her way before returning his attention to the road and the unruly drivers that continued to jockey in around the Land Cruiser. Traffic signs might be in Arabic and English in Bahrain, but all instruction therein appeared to be little more than suggestions to the locals who even bothered to read them.

Fortunately, they'd arrived at their destination: the parking lot to Naval Support Activity Bahrain. Since NSA Bahrain was a walking-only base, this was as close as they were going to get.

Leo pulled the Land Cruiser into a slot and killed the engine. "You two need time to wash off that fourteen-hour flight?"

Why? The moment she stepped outside, she'd be drenched in sweat again.

Mira twisted around to glance into the rear seat to check Riyad's preferences. The SEAL had been so silent during the ride, she'd nearly forgotten he was there.

Riyad shook his head.

She turned back to Leo. "We're good."

"Excellent. Let's go."

Grabbing her leather tote from the floorboard, she slung it over her shoulder and pushed her door open into the wall of heat, half afraid Riyad would attempt to get it for her again.

For some reason, the polite side of the man's personality, whatever the motivation behind it, reminded her that he was human. Better that he remain in full-asshole mode. There, she knew exactly where she stood with him.

Both men beat her to the trunk. Once again, Leo had snagged her crime kit and shouldered her suit bag before she could stop him.

"You know the docs cleared me to return to full duty, right? And it wasn't a rubber stamp."

The agent grinned. "Blame Lani. She'd have my head if she knew I let you lift something. Like I said, we were...worried. Hell, the whole damned agency was."

Yeah, she'd had a taste of this same, humbling relief when she'd stopped by the Field Office back in DC to pick up her replacement weapon and credentials on her way to Annapolis the day she'd been discharged.

"I appreciate the love, but I'm fine. Really." Damn near

boiling from the heat, mere yards beyond clearing NSA Bahrain's main security gate, but otherwise okay.

Better than okay, in fact. She'd managed to sleep nearly twelve out of the fourteen hours it had taken the C-130 she and Riyad had boarded back at Joint Base Andrews to reach Muharraq. She'd been that exhausted from her second day out of the hospital. She still couldn't believe Riyad hadn't woken her, much less that when she'd finally surfaced on her own, she'd found the man's suit jacket covering her.

Remorse. The man really was capable of experiencing it.

Go figure.

Fortunately, their trek amid the scorching heat didn't last long. The branch medical clinic wasn't too far inside this hundred-and-fifty-two-acre pocket of Americana set within the Middle East.

Within minutes, the men had dumped their bags at the quarterdeck and picked up copies of the pathologist's report that awaited them.

Unwilling to leave her tote behind due to the agency laptop and spare clip of SIG Sauer ammo inside, Mira juggled the bag and skimmed the uppermost page of her report as they all followed the male corpsman past the quarterdeck and through the maze of antiseptic corridors beyond. "Dr. Patrice Barrett?"

Leo nodded as they halted beside a closed door. "Yeah, the doc mentioned you two had worked a few cases before."

"We have." Both she and Jerry, back in San Diego. They'd gotten along so well, they'd taken to having lunch together on occasion. "Patrice is top notch."

Mira accepted a mask and a pair of latex gloves from the sinewy corpsman who'd accompanied them. "Thanks."

She waited for the petty officer to distribute masks and gloves to her companions.

"Okay, let's see what Patrice found." Mira entered the room, setting her tote on the floor before she approached the stainless-steel gurney that commanded center space.

A white sheet covered the body.

Protective gear donned, Mira reached out to draw the sheet down, rolling the fabric in on itself as it came off. To say she was taken aback by the sight that greeted her would be an understatement. Not only had the petty officer's naked corpse held up eerily well in that walk-in refrigerator, there was the rest.

All of the rest.

Leo's heavy tread joined her on Sandra Lance's right. "What did I tell you? *Doppelgänger*, eh?"

Damn...this close up and in person, he was right. The long, straight blond hair, the absence of bangs, the curve to her chin and jaw. Even the slight up tilt to the nose.

"I admit. The resemblance is....uncanny."

"You think your guy knew her?"

With the petty officer stationed these past three years in Bahrain? And with Zak having spent two of those three as a SEAL operating in and around the Middle East? Not to mention that Sandra Lance and Zak could've run into each other in the years prior—before or after Mira had handed the man his ring back?

"It's possible."

Though this would all be that much weirder if Zak had known the woman while he'd been dating her. From a psychological aspect, perhaps even more telling.

And the *guilt*.

Because with those shared features? This woman had definitely been murdered because of her.

Riyad appeared to be affected by the similarities between her face and the one belonging to the body lying on the table between them, as well. Either that, or the man was simply pissed that there *was* a body. Because that murderous scowl had returned.

Mira held the rolled sheet out over the petty officer's battered torso so Riyad could lay it on the counter behind him. She and Leo bent low in unison to study the swollen knuckles of the hand in front of them. The middle joint of the woman's bare ring finger in particular had captured Mira's attention.

The angle was...off.

Straightening, she pointed toward the report tucked into the opening of her tote, smiling her thanks as Leo picked up on the silent request to pass the paperwork to her. Report in hand, Mira flipped through the pages and sections, stopping when she found the write up she'd been searching for.

It confirmed her suspicion.

While the X-rays Patrice had ordered proved that all ten of their latest victim's fingers had been dislocated, bones from three of those fingers appeared to have been fractured while they were being shoved back into place.

Mira moved up to the petty officer's neck. Once again, she saw what she should not see. Not if a combat-honed SEAL was supposed to have murdered this woman.

She pointed out the trio of nearly undetectable, but distinct false starts at the beginning of the slash on the right side of the woman's throat. "You see them?"

Leo leaned closer, a low whistle escaping as he nodded. "Yeah."

"What?" *Riyad.*

Mira left the explanation to her fellow agent as she continued to flip through the report.

Leo wasn't explaining anything, however. Like her, he was busy flipping through his own pages and double checking the comments within against the body.

Mira located Patrice's notes concerning the victim's vaginal orifice and skimmed the significant, yet telling facts within. She turned to Leo as she closed the report. "Zakaria Webber didn't murder this woman. But I know who did."

Given the copycat aspect to this murder added to what had happened aboard the *Tern*, there was only one possibility. Though she doubted the SEAL standing on the opposite side of Sandra Lance's body would agree without harder proof.

"*Who*, damn it?" Riyad again. His gloved index finger swept over the line of gaping flesh across the woman's neck, albeit well above. "And what's wrong here?"

Mira pointed to the tiny tentative slashes closest to her. "You see these three, very small cuts here?"

The man peered closer for several moments, then nodded. "Yes."

"Those are hesitation marks. Tell me, Sam, would a Navy SEAL, especially one with Zak's experience, decide to cut a woman's neck and then have to screw up the nerve while he was actually doing it?"

That dark head shook.

Anticipating her next point, Leo stepped down the body so Mira could lift the petty officer's right hand. She moved her latexed thumb over the top of the middle knuckle of Lance's ring finger. "And would someone as experienced as Zak is at dislocating joints fracture three bones while attempting to shove them back into place?"

"No." Riyad stood there for several moments, visibly absorbing the implications of what she'd said.

The upshot: the man was not happy.

But Riyad hadn't yet heard the clincher, yet, let alone realized the implications.

"Sam—" She caught the man's glower and held it. "—there was a bottle found in this woman's vaginal canal, too. But it didn't contain alcohol and it wasn't nearly as large as the wine bottle that was inserted into Theresa Corrigan. This one was a slender, four-inch bottle of hot sauce. Another object of opportunity, yes, but not one that Zak would've used." Especially since the refrigerator had been so huge, it had fit a body inside on the floor. There had to have been larger bottles in that fridge. Possibly ones containing alcohol. Either way, this hot sauce was a message from—

"Are you telling me *Nasser* killed this woman?"

"I am." She turned to Leo. "You said there was no sign that the petty officer was murdered inside the fridge?"

The agent shook his head. "It was definitely a dump job. A Canadian diplomat and his family found her. They were supposed to be guests of Tariq Al Salman for the month, but they couldn't get inside the walk-in in the pantry room to put their groceries away and the standard-sized fridge in the kitchen was on the fritz. The diplomat broke the lock, figuring he'd buy a new one before they left. He's the one who spotted the US Navy tattoo on her ankle and decided to call us, instead of Salman. Petty Officer Lance might've been murdered elsewhere in the villa, but I was only able to make the one pass. I didn't notice anything out of place. But I'd have given anything to get in that master bath with a bottle of luminol. Unfortunately, I didn't get the chance."

"The owner showed up?"

Leo nodded. "I'd seen photos of Salman buddied up with the king before, so when he started raising holy hell, saying Americans had no right to be on his property, I had a feeling we were going to end up getting screwed. I made a gut call. I had Agent Harrow grab the spare body bag from the back of my SUV while I called an ambulance. Harrow escorted the ambulance to maintain chain-of-custody and make sure the body ended up here, while I stayed behind, snapping as many shots of the refrigerator and the rest of the villa as I could with my phone before I was escorted off the property by one of Salman's bodyguards. I'll forward the photos as soon as we wrap up here."

"Please, do."

As for that gut call of Leo's, it had been a damned sound one.

"This Nasser you two mentioned; is he a former sailor, too?"

"Yes." Mira motioned for Riyad to retrieve the linen sheet from the counter behind him. "Lieutenant Farid Nasser. He's gone by Frank with everyone outside his family since grade school. He's a former surface warfare officer. I'll send his record on, too. We found his water wings inside the throat of our JAG back in DC, but the insignia was stolen from his grandfather's house in Nashua, New Hampshire, shortly before Commander Corrigan was killed. We think—" She took in the hike to Riyad's brow as she accepted the linen from his hands. "—*I* think that Frank was forced to attend the JAG's murder. When you add on that someone turned on the air-conditioning inside Corrigan's condo and that *this* woman's body was left inside a refrigerator..."

Leo nodded as he swung around to Riyad's side of the gurney to assist her in unrolling and draping the sheet back over Petty Officer Lance's corpse, offering the woman what little remaining dignity that they could. "Someone's trying to preserve the victims and any evidence that may be on them."

"Exactly."

Riyad's phone rang. He stepped back, turning away to remove his mask and gloves before he took the call. Several terse, monosyllabic responses formed the SEAL's end of a conversation that was almost as short as his final *no.*

He slipped the phone inside his suit jacket as he swung around. "I need to take off for a few hours. Mira, I'll link back up with you at the Navy Inn. Okay?"

"Fine." Heck, she was bemused the man hadn't simply

turned around and walked out of the room as he had during the JAG's autopsy.

And he was asking permission?

Sure, that ending *okay* of his had been rhetorical, but still. It was truly amazing the level of manners that regret could instill in the guy.

Leo arched a brow as the door closed behind Riyad. "Everything all right?"

"Yeah. That guy just irritates me."

And for so very many reasons.

"Well, hang in there. God willing, this'll be over soon."

"From your lips to his ears." Hooking her leather tote off the floor, she shouldered it as she and Leo tossed their masks and gloves into the trash before following the SEAL out of the room and back to the quarterdeck—and the rest of her bags.

Soon. It was going on eight weeks now. A timeframe that was anything but soon. Worse, she could practically hear the clocks on those bombs that Zak and his cohorts had built, ticking down inside her head...and the ticks were getting louder.

"Are you headed back to the office?"

Leo nodded. "Eventually. I need to head down to Riffa first and see Lani before visiting hours are over. With this case, I haven't been by since the night before last."

"She's in the hospital?"

"Yeah. Her pre-eclampsia's gotten pretty bad. She was admitted to the Royal Hospital for Women and Children this past week to get her blood pressure down. She's okay for now. If she can stay that way for another week or so, they'll induce labor."

That settled it. Leo's wife was nearly eight months pregnant with their first. Mira scooped her crime kit and suitcase bag off the buffed tiles before Leo could. "Go. See Lani. Give her a hug for me. Tell her I'll try to stop by before I head back to the States.

And do not worry about me. I've stayed at the Inn before; I know where it's located."

And she could carry her own blessed gear.

"But—"

"*Go.*"

Leo nodded and headed for the door to the clinic to do just that.

Mira wasn't far behind him. The temperature hadn't cooled. But it was nearing 1700 local time; it should be dropping by a whopping ten degrees...eventually. Her stomach put in a request for food as she headed for the Navy Guest Inn and Suites, but she ignored it. She'd have to hit up the mini mart for something microwavable later; she'd begun to crave the shower Leo had suggested upon their arrival more than sustenance.

An hour later, she was checked into a suite that paled in comparison to the one that had been at Riyad's disposal in DC. But tomorrow's navy-blue suit and ivory blouse were already hanging on a hook in the bathroom, taking advantage of the lingering steam that her embarrassingly lengthy shower had put out.

Since fabric sliding across the scars on her lower legs still bugged her, she donned a pair of shorts and added a gray, *Don't give up the ship!* sweatshirt that a Navy buddy had gifted her a few years ago. She took the time to apply the lotion that Colonel Hartwig had prescribed before she'd left Walter Reed to help with the inevitable itching from those same scars, then combed out her hair and left it to air dry before heading into the suite's sitting room to check her phone for missed texts.

There was just one. It was from Jerry, letting her know that he'd received the files that Riyad had shunted his way. But he'd also caught the cases for the two agents that Zak had murdered in DC. It would be a while before he was up to speed.

Mira sent the detective a thumbs up, then reached inside her tote to retrieve the laptop stowed within.

Her hand surfaced with something softer.

A photo album. The one her three-year-old half-sister had flipped through roughly twenty-four hours earlier at the Ramseys'.

Great.

The last time Mira had seen the book, it had been lying on the coffee table as Riyad departed the townhouse to grab his clothes and gear for the flight he'd arranged while they were still in Keisha's orchid nursery. After the SEAL had left, she'd spent a few minutes meeting her younger brother and admiring his new train before attempting to explain to both siblings and their mom that she had to leave the country for a while.

Her father's widow must've slipped the album into her tote while she was distracted with the kids.

As tempting as the photos within were, especially since she could now view them alone and unobserved, Mira returned the album to her leather bag and retrieved her laptop.

By the time she'd fired up the computer and pushed though the security measures to access her NCIS email account, she was wishing she'd asked Leo to forward the Sandra Lance crime scene photos before he'd left the clinic.

Fortunately, there'd been no need. The pictures her fellow agent had taken inside the Salman villa were waiting for her in her inbox, attached to an otherwise blank email.

Settling in on the couch, she took her time with the photos.

Leo was right. The petty officer's body had been dumped inside the walk-in after she'd been killed. There was barely any blood. Nor was there any visible evidence of biological fluids in any of the photos Leo had managed to take of the villa's rooms.

Like Leo, she was itching to spray down the master bathroom with luminol, though. Her gut was telling her that Frank had murdered Petty Officer Lance inside that vast, sunken tub. If he'd been the only one in the villa at the time, Frank could've easily wiped down the gilded fixtures and scoured the glistening, oval cavity beneath after he'd moved the body to hide what he'd done from Zak and his cohorts.

As for the lock on the refrigerator?

Not only had it been of the combination variety—which Frank's brilliant and determined brain could easily have cracked —the reason for the additional, in-house security undoubtedly lay in the stash of extremely high-end vodka and Almas caviar stored in the pantry's fridge. Between the case of Russo-Baltique and the dozen-odd tins of Iranian Beluga eggs, Tariq Al Salman had close to fifteen million US dollars squirreled away, just in his overflow "entertaining" reefer.

No wonder Salman had been so pissed to find Americans raiding his walk-in—no matter that a dead body had been found inside. And, hell, the corpse belonged to a woman, an American at that. Not worth a tin of counterfeit caviar to many in this part of the world.

But how had Frank found the petty officer?

Had *he* known Sandra Lance?

Or had Frank put in an order for a blond "Navy whore" with one of Zak's cohorts?

The only thing Mira knew for certain was that once Frank had realized that she'd been assigned the case—and that she'd survived her fall from the *Tern*—he'd decided to leave her a trail to follow. Yes, the trail was grisly. But Zak would never have left those hesitation marks, and no one else knew the details of the Corrigan murder but her, Jerry, Sam Riyad and a few, select links in the respective chains of command above them.

And now Leo.

Mira leaned forward to reopen the single, grim photo that her fellow agent had managed to snap of Petty Officer Lance while inside the walk-in.

She studied the position of the woman's body and the surrounding contents of the fridge, looking for anything Frank might've left behind or even positioned oddly that could give her a hint as to how and where to find him.

There was nothing.

Frustration set in.

She was about to click on the next photo when her phone rang.

Laptop in hand, she rose from the couch, crossing the room to balance the open computer at the edge of the suite's desk with her left hand as she used her right to reach for the latest phone Ramsey had given her in DC.

Dread clawed its way down her spine as she caught the name and number that registered with her caller ID. Malcolm McCabe.

Caleb's father.

Oh, Lord.

She'd missed her morning call to the nurses' station. She'd been 30,000 feet above the ground at the time, strapped into a seat in the belly of that C-130, then in the front passenger seat of Leo's Land Cruiser and finally at the clinic, viewing Sandra Lance's body.

She should've called before her shower. It was eleven a.m. back in Caleb's ICU. There were only two reasons that Malcom would phone.

What were the odds that this was the good one?

Answer the phone. Those mesmerizing brown eyes might have finally opened.

But in her heart, she knew they hadn't.

She picked up anyway. "Hello, First Sergeant. How's Caleb?"

The heaviness of the Marine's sigh managed to crush her from nearly seven thousand miles away. "Not good. That's why I'm calling. Caleb spiked a fever during the night, and they can't get it down. They've tried everything. I figured...if you've got a spare prayer that you haven't shot upward...well...this would be the time."

Fuck.

Mira stepped around the corner of the desk so she could press her forehead into the chilly wall. It was the only way she managed to remain upright as she absorbed the pain and disappointment that pummeled in.

She pulled her breath in deep, her fears in deeper. "H-how's his brother holding up? And you? You hanging in there, all right?"

A stunted laugh, utterly devoid of humor, momentarily overtook the line—and the remaining dregs of her hope. "Oh, you know how it is. *Semper Fi.*"

Semper Fidelis. Always Faithful.

The Marine Corps' motto. And the only thread of support the First Sergeant had left to cling to as he, too, sent up his final prayers for his older son.

"Agent Ellis?"

"*Mira.* I'm here, First Sergeant. Just—overwhelmed. I'll be praying nonstop. I'm in Bahrain at the moment on something that's...critical to the country, or I'd be right there beside you and Bobby, I swear...holding C-Caleb's other hand."

"I know you would. Anyway, the nurse is due back with a bag of last-ditch IV meds. I should probably get off before she comes in. I just...wanted you to know."

"*Thank you.* Please...text me updates? Or call."

"Will do."

But he wouldn't. The father in him wouldn't be able to. Not if those updates weren't good. And given that the first sergeant had just made one of the most difficult calls of his life, she knew Caleb was doing worse than he'd let on.

Much worse.

The moment the line cut out, she dropped the phone to the carpet and pressed her hands into the wall as the burning that had overtaken her chest made it into the corners of her eyes, only to spill over and begin the scalding slide down.

She was choking on the agony still pounding in her head and chest, and gulping for air, when she felt a pair of hard palms settle over her shoulders.

Startled, she spun around, glaring up into the face of the one man she just couldn't seem to get rid of.

Sam Riyad.

Why did this jerk always seem to appear right when her life was going to shit?

"What the hell are you doing in my suite?" Uninvited. When she desperately wanted to be alone, so she could wallow in the frantic worry that was still searing throughout her body, even as she was forced to scrub the tattling vestiges from her cheeks with the backs of her hands.

And, damn it, those stark, fathomless eyes did not have the right to hold that much pity. Not for her.

"I didn't mean to intrude. But you didn't answer my knock, and the door was unlocked. You slept so long on that plane, I was...worried."

"There's no need. I'm fine."

He took in the tears she'd missed. "Well, now, that's a lie. Is this about your father?" The stare that saw too much sank down to the floor. Its morose owner stepped back just far enough to hunker low and snag the phone she'd dropped before he straightened. "No. Those tears are for the kid in the ICU, aren't they? First Sergeant McCabe's boy. The one Umber's burning in hell for as we speak."

She nodded. "Caleb. He spiked a fever." As for Umber, "I never should've gone into that classroom. Confronted the chief."

"Horseshit. You absolutely should have, no matter what

happened after. At that moment, that kid had no one on his side but you. Do not regret that you stood up for him. Someday —*when* he comes out of that coma—he'll be telling you that too."

That was just it. Despite the odd fervor in the SEAL's eyes and voice, "I don't think Caleb is coming out of it. That fever? It's bad." So much so that his father had reached out to her, ostensibly for prayers and emotional support.

But she knew what the Marine had really been asking for. Malcolm McCabe needed someone else to sit in that room with him. To help him—hell, to *force* him—to hold it together for his younger boy...when the worst happened.

Another quiet rivulet of terror escaped, dripping down her left cheek before she could staunch it. She saw the SEAL's right hand come up and panicked. Jerking sideways, she slipped out from between the wall of blast-reinforced concrete behind her and the harder wall of human muscle in front.

Sucking up the ache, she scrubbed the remaining tears from her face as she spun around to square off against the man she had *not* invited into her suite.

Unfortunately, as much as she wanted to kick him out, she knew why Riyad was here. "Zak. He's why you left the clinic."

He nodded. "We thought we had a lead on the bastard."

"And?"

He shook his head. "No joy." His left hand reached out to set her phone on the corner of the desk. "You hungry?"

Given that she'd last eaten nearly twenty hours ago? Absolutely.

But dine out somewhere? With him? She'd rather get strapped into a chair on the dental side of the clinic they'd recently visited and undergo a root canal—sans anesthetics.

She was about to beg off from the invite with another of

those lies he'd accused her of when his focus shifted to her open laptop on the desk.

The glower she'd seen leveled on Sandra Lance's corpse in the clinic returned as the SEAL stared at the photo of the woman's naked body on the floor of that walk-in.

Woman.

That single word and the royally crappy tone of voice this man tended to infuse it with pushed into her brain, and suddenly, she understood far more that she'd ever wanted to about Commander Sam Riyad.

"You've got a fundamental problem with my gender, haven't you?" She folded her arms over the *Don't give up the ship!* scripted across her chest. Somehow that rallying cry that a dying Captain James Lawrence had uttered on the deck of the *USS Chesapeake* during the War of 1812 had become so much more significant to her following her experiences on the *Tern*—and with this twenty-first-century, yet still-Neanderthal of a surly sailor. "You don't think women should be in the military, let alone in combat."

He just stood there, that glower darkening to black. And then he too squared off and crossed his arms. "Let me guess. You want the politically correct answer."

"Wrong."

"Good. Because you're not going to get it. Not from me. No, I don't believe women belong in combat. Ninety-nine percent of them can't handle what happens when the shit truly hits the fan. You think you know torture? You don't. Those Army bastards that run SERE training? They don't know it either. Not really."

"And you do? Because you're some badass, elite SEAL?"

To her surprise, he shook his head—grimly. "No, I learned that truth a hell of a lot earlier in life. I hadn't even hit my eighth birthday when I was forced into the light, or rather, the dark.

And trust me, it arrived with a score of lessons that I will *never* forget. And those fuckers who doled them out? They'd honed torture down to an art."

Those scars. The older ones that covered the man's entire body. His fingertips, too. How she could've forgotten about them, even in her fury with their bearer, she'd never know. But she had. Now that she'd remembered, their existence invaded the silence that had fallen between them, pulsing with the need to know.

Pissed with the man or not, she had no right to put him on the spot by asking. And yet, she was driven to. "What happened?"

His entire body had gone rigid. As if he'd had second thoughts about what he'd already offered up and was loath to add more. She didn't think he was going to either, but then his stance relaxed. His arms were still crossed, but he shrugged.

"I was a prisoner of war, or I thought I was."

"*What*?" He'd just said he hadn't even turned eight.

But he followed up that not-quite-nonchalant shrug with a nod. "I was incarcerated less than three hundred miles northwest of here, in fact. Shortly before, and then during, Gulf War I."

"Kuwait?"

Another nod followed the first, though this one was decidedly clipped. "My father was a Saudi diplomat. As you discovered from your conversation with Walid Rahmani, he's related to the king. Like thousands upon thousands of others, mind you. And like my father, all supposedly princely men. He even married a princess—my mother. Who, incidentally, is also my father's cousin. But that's how it worked back then. Hell, that's how it still works. Keeps the money and the power in the family."

Gulf War I.

If Riyad and his father had been in Kuwait thirty years ago, they must've been scooped up by Saddam Hussein's troops during the Iraqi invasion. And since his father was a Saudi diplomat, those who'd captured him would've believed that said diplomat would possess strategic information regarding plans and contingencies relating to the US-led coalition, and passed the diplomat and his son on up the chain.

"So...members of the Republican Guard tortured your father, and when he wouldn't talk, they moved on to you to get him to reveal the intel they wanted?"

"Oh, hell, no. They had no intention of marring that bastard. No, they went straight for me. And those scars you saw? They're nothing. Long-healed, surface marks. The real torture? That goes deeper. It burrows into your head, your heart and your soul...where it anchors in and fucks you up for life."

The man blanched as he realized what he'd let slip—and that she'd figured it out.

Because she *had* figured it out. Just as the vehemence of Riyad's belief that Caleb would eventually understand that she'd been there to help him with Umber, and that the boy would forgive her, finally made sense.

She'd wondered in that hotel room in DC just how far those scars of Riyad's went, and now she knew. They extended all the way down into places that no one, especially an innocent, not-quite eight-year-old boy should ever be touched, let alone tortured. Not to get his father to give up his secrets. Not for *any* reason.

"Sam—"

"I would've done anything to get them to stop, mind you. Anything. And then, when it did, I'd have done anything for them to turn around and start it all up again—so long as they were doing it to *just* me." He shook his head again. This time, she swore the man was trying to shake the brutality of it out of his mind.

The memories.

But they refused to leave.

He pulled a rasping breath into his chest, then let it out. A betraying shudder escaped with it. "*Fuck.*"

She knew then that for whatever reason he'd decided to share this nightmare with her, he had never intended for that part of it to slip out. But he'd already told her they hadn't touched his father.

"Your mom. She was in Kuwait, too. And a prisoner."

The man's arms were still crossed. Every single muscle clenched, as if he'd pulled in on himself, as if that was the only way he could force himself to remain standing in this room and not bolt. Her fingers ached with the need to reach out. To ease the horror that had finally overtaken the glower. But he didn't want anyone touching him, not even the woman he'd chosen to have this conversation with. And no matter what he'd done to her, how he'd treated her, she refused to push it. Him.

So, she just stood there...and waited.

He finally purged his air on a rush, then clipped one of those telling nods. "Yeah. She was there." His throat continued to work for several more moments, but then it calmed. He caught her gaze, looked right into her eyes. It was as though he'd decided that he'd gone so far with this confession, he didn't care anymore. He might as well give her the rest. "They'd put her in the room right next to me. And what they did to me, they turned and did to her. I got to watch it *all*."

"For how long?" How many hours had their shared agony and shame lasted?

That earned her a strangely thin grimace. "Two and a half Qur'ans."

What the—

But then she realized what he meant, and she stiffened. "You're a *hafiz*." A memorizer. Specifically, someone who'd memorized the entire Qur'an.

Suddenly, that comment of his back in DC in the hotel about not needing to read those verses from the chapter on *The Spoils of War* made appalling sense.

Muslims were encouraged to become a *hafiz* before their teens, since many believed there would be fewer distractions then to interfere with the necessary study. But a number of brighter, determined kids managed the feat at much younger ages.

The man that this determined kid had grown into nodded. "Yes. I recited it for our imam within days of turning seven. And before you ask, it took roughly ten hours that first time. But don't be impressed with any of it." He finally unlocked those arms and raised his right hand to rub his palm over the crook of his neck. "My mother pushed it. For almost a year, all I did was read and recite. She thought it would improve her husband's relationship with his eldest son. It didn't. Islam was a prop to him, as was his patriotism." The SEAL's palm came down, and those arms crossed his chest once more, locked in. "That I was a *hafiz* came out during her torture. She thought it would spare me. But those men—" He shook his head. "—they were not religious, either."

No wonder he hadn't wanted to touch the book that Rahmani had entrusted into her safekeeping. "What stopped it? Them?"

The barest glimmer of a genuine smile finally slipped in. "SEAL Team Twelve."

He and his mother had been rescued by SEALs? Oh, wow. That would've made one hell of an impression on a devastated boy of seven, going on eight.

As did the entire, monstrous story—on her.

That decades later, Riyad had taken command of the same team that had saved his and his mother's lives? Yes, the team would've been filled with different men by then. But the symbolism would still have been so very powerful.

And when members of that same team were murdered by another SEAL who Riyad hadn't even suspected as being capable of such betrayal?

The guilt that he hadn't protected his men would've leveled him.

As for the comment that had started this all? She'd worked her way through that too. Commander Riyad might insist differently, but it wasn't that he didn't want women serving beside him because he truly believed they couldn't handle getting hurt.

He couldn't handle it.

Nate was right about those rumors he'd overheard. But the hell with being a member of the crappy childhood club. Riyad commanded that crew, too.

As much as she did not want a connection with this man, much less want to understand him...that connection and that understanding *were* there.

"It's a miracle you lived."

"Trust me; I wasn't meant to. Nor was my mother. That's why she was there. To confess what she knew about my father's so-called patriotism...and then to die."

He'd alluded to his father's less than honorable nature before. "I don't understand. Your father's loyalty toward Saudi Arabia shouldn't have affected your mother's prisoner-of-war status in Kuwait." Hell, it wouldn't have. "Not unless—"

Oh, shit.

The man's brow lifted. Confirmed that ugly, unspoken suspicion. "Precisely. And there were complications. My mother was a Saudi first wife. The one my father had to marry. Not the one he wanted, nor did he want to be forced to keep his two wives and their children in equal, but separate comfort as required by the Qur'an and my mother's very powerful father. But I have to give my own father credit. The solution was simple. Especially since, as you surmised, the bastard knew the Iraqi soldier who was leading our 'interrogation,' and for good reason. The Iraqi was his contact. The man to whom my father provided key information about Kuwait to *help* with Saddam Hussein's invasion of the country. But the interrogator and my father needed to know precisely what my mother knew—and if she'd repeated it to my grandfather. Once they were satisfied, she and I were to be listed as killed during the invasion. Who would ever learn any different?"

Except Riyad knew. Because he'd lived it.

Hell, he was still living with it. How had he put it?

Fucked up for life.

The man's fanatical passion for rooting out traitors made perfect sense now, as did the rest. Zak was Sam Riyad's white whale. And after everything that had happened to the commander and his mother in Kuwait, along with the betrayal and murders of the members of his revered SEAL Team Twelve, he would never give up the hunt.

"Mira?"

"Yeah?"

He reached out, traced a finger along the still livid scar that rode her left temple, then lowered his hand and sighed. "I am truly sorry. That I suspected you in the first place, and that it took me so damned long to see past those suspicions. Even when I came to the hospital while you were in that coma, and after, I still believed you were tied to your father in all this. But Bill Ramsey never did. You need to know that he is *not* at fault. This was all me. Not only was Ramsey a staunch supporter of yours, he demanded that he be the one to tell you about your father's murder, once you were cleared to know. I agreed to that —and then I blew that, too."

She nodded. There wasn't much else she could do. Riyad might honestly regret that she'd gotten tangled up in the line knotted to the harpoon that he'd been sharpening for two years now, but she knew he'd do it again, if he felt he needed to.

Hell, he already was.

"What is it?"

"Frank. You're wrong about him, too. I know you can't see it yet. But even though Zak sucked him in at the beginning, Frank changed his mind. He wants out."

Those scarred fingers stretched out again, this time to extend past her hip to tap the open screen of her laptop. "You honestly think he did *that* to help us?"

"I do."

"You were in a coma, for Christ's sake. If Nasser was trying to get your attention, how the hell were you supposed to pick up on that sick clue of his?"

"Frank might not have known that I was in the ICU." Especially if Zak and his cohorts had kept Frank off the grid and holed up someplace remote so he could convert the radioactive fuel inside those assemblies without alerting the authorities.

The SEAL's mouth opened, only to close as his phone pinged. He reached inside his suit jacket to retrieve the device, frowning at the contents of the text he'd received.

Riyad tapped out a response, then slipped the phone home. "Get dressed; we have somewhere to be."

"What happened?" But she was already closing her laptop and shoving it into her tote. "Did you get another lead on Zak?"

"Maybe. And I hope to hell you're right about Nasser. Because that lead we might have...it's in the form of another body."

19

By the time they'd reached the crime scene, Mira's hopes for a clue that would lead them to Zak and the fuel from those stolen assemblies had begun to dwindle.

For one, there was the nature of the body dump.

Only this body hadn't been so much dumped as washed up onto the edge of Al Masarrat, Bahrain's northern-most, artificially created—and still unfinished—island. They were so far north, in fact, that Bahrain International Airport was several miles behind them, along with the remaining eighty-seven and counting, oversized patches of natural and cultivated sand that made up the kingdom.

And there was the corpse itself.

While it did belong to a woman, she was not blond. Plus, although like Sandra Lance, Mira sported a handful of freckles scattered about her face, the woman lying face down and a frustrating ten feet away possessed a galaxy's worth on her battered and bruised backside alone. Nor did they know if the deceased was even American.

They'd yet to flip the body.

Any attempt at an ID would have to wait until after the official Bahraini state medical examiner finished his initial, mind-numbingly slow, and sole, assessment.

Until then, the frothing edges of those waves would continue to sweep in, saturating the tangle of strawberry curls spread out like a limp crown around the brain-revealing crack at the rear of the woman's skull, before retreating into the glistening expanse of the Persian Gulf, along with any potential—albeit, miraculously clinging—evidence. Worse, that glistening on the water would soon be retreating as well, along with the light that was causing it.

It was 1815. In this part of the world in May, the sun yawned and stretched well before 0500. Within half an hour, that scorching, orange glow would be sinking all the way down to the horizon behind them to curl in for the night.

Which would be why Mira could hear several Bahraini-employed forensic techs setting up floodlights behind her.

She could also hear the soles of Leo's oversized shoes crushing through the sand before coming to a halt at her left.

"Well, what do you think, Mir? Is this Nasser's work?"

"I can't be certain until we get closer." There was always the chance that the redhead had been a victim of opportunity, like the bottle of hot sauce Frank had abused.

Though how many *doppelgängers* could she and Petty Officer Lance have? Especially ones stationed in Bahrain.

Either way, while this new woman might be US Navy and stationed on the kingdom's main island, Mira was all but certain their victim hadn't experienced her final moments on any of them.

She craned her neck to capture Leo's tired stare. "I'll be honest. Even from here there seems to be a lot that doesn't mesh. This woman appears to have been severely beaten. Sandra Lance was not." Granted, with that fair skin, most or even all of those bruises could easily have been obtained postmortem. Standing directly over the body or not, they couldn't be certain which was the case until the autopsy. "Also, there's the most-likely location of the actual dumpsite."

Because this wasn't it.

Mira pointed to the victim's left hand. It was palm up, its severely wrinkled skin an eerie shade of pasty white due to the absorption of water. "Given that the maceration of the skin has extended well past the hallows of the hands, plus that bit of seaweed I spotted in her hair before you and I got shoved into the penalty box? And if we add in the temperature of the water? It's what—roughly eighty, eight-two degrees?"

Leo nodded. "That's about right for this time of year."

"Okay, then. With that level of maceration and the temps, I'm guessing the victim went into the water on this side of the Gulf. Since bodies tend to float backside up and I don't see evidence that birds fed on hers, she probably remained slightly submerged for three to four days, at least, before the currents and tide carried her here."

It could be longer. Though given the warm temperatures, not by much.

Either way, they'd need an ocean current and tide expert to weigh in before they could narrow down their timeline and the geographical starting point of it all. Mira knew just the expert they needed, too. But, first, that victim identification.

She swore the ME was taking his sweet-assed time on purpose.

Why? The man hadn't wanted them here.

Scratch that, Dr. Hassam Al Abbassi hadn't wanted *her* here. Nor had it mattered that, after donning the suit jacket and trousers that had been airing out in her shower, she'd taken the time to wind her hair into a damp bun and cover every strand with the matching black, open-faced hijab she'd packed.

She'd hoped her conservative attire would ease her formal introduction to the ME, in light of the man's thobe and ghutra.

But, no. Not only had the ME refused to glance at her NCIS credentials, much less address her directly, he'd turned away and coldly informed her male companions that a woman had no place at his crime scene.

When Leo and Riyad had insisted that she stay, the doc had ordered all three of them off the barely created islet.

Rather, Abbassi had tried.

Still smarting from his morning's burn, Leo had taken the initiative during the drive from his wife's hospital room. He'd phoned his boss and asked the man to contact the US ambassador. The ambassador in turn had called the palace and politely, but firmly, insisted that while no one yet knew if this victim was American, she was rumored to possess light red hair. And since NCIS had already been kicked out of one crime scene that day, surely letting one or two of its agents stand around to observe one of the kingdom's fine medical examiners wouldn't be beyond the pale, would it?

And, heck, the courtesy might smooth a few ruffled feathers and US Navy gills.

To say that the ME in question had been ticked to find his decree reversed by a palace secretary—and another mere *woman*—would be an understatement.

Dr. Abbassi's payback? He'd taken that "one or two agents" literally.

Which was why Sam Riyad was thirty yards back, marking time beside their vehicles, that scowl of his quite possibly carved into the SEAL's brow for the night.

Leo shifted in the oppressive heat. "You know what really bugs me?"

"Let me guess." Only wasn't a guess; she knew. Because it was bugging her, too. "That erythematic spot above the small of her back?"

"Yeah. What the hell could've caused that amount of localized reddening?"

"I don't know." But if the ME ever deigned to let them move all the way back up to the body, they might be able to figure it out.

If they were lucky, that erythema would lead them to the woman's killer.

On the other hand, "She is a redhead. They tend to have sensitive skin. It could be a simple case of antemortem irritation." Mira flicked her gaze over the vast waters of the Gulf. Despite the fading light, she counted over a dozen sailboats and motor yachts on the horizon. "For all we know, the victim could've been invited onto a party boat and slathered on a sunscreen that she was allergic to."

If she'd been drinking, she might not have even noticed the rash spreading across her back. And, hell, alcohol plus a horny, entitled, boat-owning *sheikh* could explain why the woman had ended up in the water without her clothes.

Though with that crack to the back of the head, their victim had had a bit of help in getting there.

Leo nodded. "You may be right. We had a similar case last summer. A couple of naïve expat workers ended up on one of those yachts. The host demanded more than one of the girls was willing to trade for the pleasure of the jaunt. He got so pissed he smacked her around, then choked her. The bastard dumped her body over the side, thinking sharks would take care of it. And they probably did, because she never turned up. We wouldn't have known what'd happened if her friend hadn't witnessed the murder and kept her mouth shut 'til the boat returned to its slip."

Unfortunately, Mira knew of similar cases. The witness Leo

had mentioned was lucky her friend's killer hadn't tossed her over the side too, as a precaution.

Although, "If our victim suffered a similar fate, she was alive when she went overboard. At least for a few minutes. Check out that finger."

From the angle and ten foot *observing* distance that Abbassi had ordered them to keep, Mira could only make out the one. The torn tip reminded her of the scars on Riyad's. Only the end of their victim's index finger was so shredded, the nail had been ripped away. If the woman had been thrown off a boat, there was an excellent chance she'd done her damnedest to claw her way back aboard. Only to fail.

"Yeah, I—" Leo broke off as the ME stood.

But even as Abbassi turned their way, he continued to ignore them. When the ME stared studiously past her right shoulder to wave a tech forward, she realized he was about to turn the body.

About damned time. The sky had lost more than half its light now.

By the time the ME and tech had the victim lying supine, Mira's patience had been used up. From the set of Leo's jaw, his hang-loose attitude had vanished too.

The agent's towering Hawaiian form joined hers in advancing on the body unbidden and, from the ME's glower, still unwelcomed.

Leo's jaw locked all the way down as they reached the tangle of hair and got a look at the face within. Despite the woman's time in the water, it was relatively easy to see that she'd been pretty in life. But those features were all wrong. The oval shape to the waterlogged forehead and jaw, those almost-too-prominent cheeks, that Roman nose. She looked nothing like Sandra Lance—and, hence, her.

And her throat was intact.

If this woman had been violated, Mira doubted a bottle had been used.

"*Shit.*"

She turned to pull Leo's face into focus. A green tinge had invaded the dusky tone of his skin. "You knew the victim."

"Yeah. Well, not really. I've met her a few times, but only in passing. She was a lieutenant. Christina Kelley. Not one of ours. British Navy. Last time I saw her was a week ago, in a corridor at HMS Jufair."

Mira caught the ME's smirk as he swung away to tell his assistant loudly—and in English, so there'd be no doubt—that the Americans would be departing now.

Leo held his ground, anyway. He pulled off a latex glove, slipping it into his inner jacket pocket to swap the latex for his phone. "I'll let the Brits know."

Mira nodded—then froze as Abbassi moved to the woman's feet, offering up her first clear look the lieutenant's abdomen. Like that erythema on the back, the skin was damaged on this side too. Severely. It wasn't red, though, but blackened with what appeared to be a large ulcerated spot near the center, as if something was in the midst of eating its way out from within. Even more telling, the internal damage extended in a near perfect line all the way up, through the torso and throat, ending—make that, *beginning*—in the woman's mouth. Yes, the body had been in the water a while. But that damage? It was distinct. Mira had seen a photo of nearly identical wounds before.

Back at nuke school.

She reached out, instinctively wrapping her fingers around the left sleeve to the ME's thobe. "Get away from the body. *Now.*"

Leo snagged his first clear look at that abdomen, too, and obeyed.

Abbassi had gone rigid. The man just stood there, glaring at her hand.

Mira ignored that renewed anger and rising indignation as she whirled around to wave Riyad forward.

"Woman, I told you, *he* cannot come here. And you do not—"

"Sir, if you want to wait around for one of your co-workers to show up with a radiation detector, be my guest." She arched a brow at that sanctimonious frown as she swung back. "But while you're waiting, I'd recommend you step away from the body."

She might not have a detector on her either, but she'd only been on the job again for days. Riyad had been hunting those stolen assemblies for eight weeks.

He was bound to have an RDS in his gear.

She faced the island once more, only to discover that the SEAL had reached her side. Riyad had heard what she'd said to the ME too, because he snapped out a nod before jogging over to the white Jeep Grand Cherokee he'd used to drive them here.

Less than a minute later, Riyad returned, his handheld RDS 100 already switched on and moving toward the large, ulcerated portion of the lieutenant's body.

Not only had the ME not taken her advice, Abbassi was visibly seething because she'd dared to usurp his authority. Not to mention she'd actually *touched* him.

Nor did the ME appear to believe her regarding the nature of that wound.

But as the RDS registered a non-gendered and rather specific confirmation that, indeed, this woman's flesh was radioactive, Abbassi moved.

Quickly.

Hell, the ME took off so fast that between the hem of his thobe and the slight rise in the sand, he damned near face planted less than a yard from the corpse.

Seconds later, the irritant recovered and disappeared.

Riyad switched off the RDS and stepped away from the body to retrieve his phone. As his call connected, she could hear the commander offering up a brisk summation of the situation and requesting that they coordinate with the British and get a hazardous materials team out here immediately to set up the quarantine zone.

Ironically, Abbassi had been correct. The lieutenant's body was now someone else's responsibility. Nor would anyone *not* in a hazmat suit be attending the coming autopsy—American, British *or* Bahraini.

She felt more than heard Riyad as he returned to her side.

"It's him."

"*Nasser*?" That dark, incredulous stare met hers as she glanced up. "You honestly think this body is another one of the man's sick breadcrumbs?"

"Who else but Frank would've had access to a substantial quantity of radioactive material in this part of the world and have been desperate enough to feed it to someone?"

"Webber. Maybe the fucker's decided to taunt us—like he just did in DC. Where he left *two* other bodies."

"I disagree." She shook her head. "Yes, Zak's a vindictive bastard. And, no, I don't know why he blew the day leading your men around the capital—and I do think there was a reason. But that was different. He wasn't holed up there. You're a SEAL. So tell me, Commander. If you were in Zak's place, would you risk tipping your hand, not to mention the location of your rogue camp—hell, even a former location—by deliberately feeding that shit to someone and then dumping her body into the Gulf?"

Silence.

It didn't matter. She had her answer. Zak had not murdered this woman, any more than he'd murdered Sandra Lance. Nor had the lieutenant's death been the result of an accidental inhalation of radioactive material. Not with the timeline they were looking at, and not with the amount of endgame ulceration in front of them. The lieutenant had been forced to swallow that tainted poison—and a hell of a lot of it.

That left Frank.

She could tell from that stubborn brow that Riyad still had his doubts.

She didn't. Every instinct she possessed was insisting that this was another one of Frank's horrific clues. But it was also one that had to have been offered up on a wing and a prayer. Because if Frank had dumped the lieutenant's body off the side of a boat, it was a miracle they'd found her before the sharks had consumed the remainder of the evidence.

Speaking of evidence...

Mira focused her attention on the lieutenant's hands—curiosity searing in as she finally got a decent look at all of those fingers.

"Mira?"

"Hmm?"

Riyad grasped the right sleeve of her suit with considerably more finesse than she'd used with the ME. "You need to be standing off from the body, too."

"In a second."

She was already pulling away and bending down directly beside that macerated right hand. Ignoring Riyad's soft, disapproving hiss, she lifted the mutilated fingers with her gloved ones and drew them in closer.

"Commander, can you grab my kit?"

He didn't argue. Probably because he knew it would only keep her beside the body—and the source of radioactivity within—that much longer.

Within seconds, the SEAL had retrieved the stainless-steel case from the spot where she'd stood after she and Leo had been relegated to observer status.

She rattled off the combination to the lock as Riyad knelt on the sand to her right, then heard the lock pop, followed by the kit opening.

"What do you need?"

"Don a set of gloves, and then grab one of the fingernail scrapings collection kits. They're labeled and on top, near the right."

She kept her stare fused to the streaks of black within the shredded red and bits of macerated white flesh that clung here and there. Despite the saltwater in the Gulf, a foreign substance still coated the victim's fingers. It was black and appeared to have been transferred as Christina Kelley had clawed at something, and for her very life. But while the index, middle and ring fingernails had been ripped away like the left one that Mira had noted earlier, there was enough of the substance caught beneath the remaining pinkie nail to send a sample to their lab.

She heard the latex snap on over Riyad's wrists. "Now what?"

She extended her right hand. "Open the kit and pass me the paper bindle and scrapper from within." Both settled into the palm of her own glove. "Thanks."

Using the tip of the scrapper, she worked the viscous substance beneath that remaining pinkie nail into the pocket created by the paper bindle, then passed the envelope back to Riyad. "Seal the edge with the tape."

"Got it."

She held up the tip of the plastic scrapper to the fading light as she heard the SEAL work. Damned if that black, glossy stain didn't resemble—

"Hey, Leo?"

Her fellow agent must've been watching from behind, wondering what she'd found, because he'd moved up to the opposite side of the body before she could lower the scrapper. She held the tip higher as the Hawaiian loomed toward it.

"What you think that is? Oil?"

"That's what it looks like to me. Hot damn, Mir." Leo stared out over the water. "I know you know what this means."

Oh, she did. Despite the horrific state of that body, she smiled. "We've got a lead."

"To whom? Nasser?" *Riyad.*

She glanced up at the SEAL. "At the very least."

Because like Leo, her gut was insisting that this wasn't just any oil. It was unprocessed crude. The kind that came directly out of the ground, even if that ground was located beneath a large body of water that covered nearly ninety-seven thousand square miles of it...say, roughly the area of the Persian Gulf. This woman hadn't tried to claw her way back onto a boat. Lieutenant Kelley had spent the last moments of her life attempting to cling to a seriously slippery stanchion. One that would not only be accessible via a stolen, next-gen SEAL delivery vehicle, and covertly, but also be able to support the nefarious workshop of a seagoing terror cell intent on concealing four MOX assemblies as they converted the uranium and plutonium within.

"Commander—we're looking for an offshore oil platform."

But which one? And was that platform owned by an ally to the north or the south of Bahrain...or the country on the opposite side of the Gulf?

Iran.

"Leo, can you get that sample—"

"Tested? I'm on it." Her fellow agent pulled a fresh pair of gloves from his trouser pocket to replace the ones he'd removed earlier and stretched on the latex.

Mira motioned for Riyad to relinquish the bindle.

The SEAL came to his feet. Only after the commander had retrieved and switched his RDS on to check the reading on the sample within the envelope—and appeared satisfied with the results—did he pass it to Leo.

"Thanks. All right, Mir. I'll call you with the results ASAP.

Also, just so you know, the British are up to speed on the lieutenant's body and that we think her murder's related to that package of theirs that went missing two months ago. They're sending someone to—" Leo glanced at an approaching silver Land Rover. "Scratch that; he's here."

"Excellent." Otherwise she'd have had to stick around and make sure Abbassi didn't order his technicians to do anything stupid with the lieutenant's body—like roll the woman back into the Gulf to get rid of her. "I'll call the tide expert. Get him started."

Riyad leaned over to re-stow her forensic gear and snap her kit shut as Leo departed. Hefting the stainless-steel case in his left hand, he straightened as he held out his right. "Let's go."

She stood a bit too quickly, swaying as the lightheadedness swirled in.

"Whoa, there." Riyad's arm braced her upper back, steadying her. "You okay?"

"Yeah. Just got woozy for a second. It happens when I stand up too fast." Still more often than not, since her coma. But she wasn't about to tell him that.

The man looked concerned enough as it was.

And that annoying scowl had returned. "You haven't eaten since the flight, have you?" He pulled her in closer, anchoring her to his length as he walked her over to his SUV—whether or not she needed or wanted the assistance. "I know you didn't eat while we were in the air, because you were passed out from exhaustion. Christ, wom— *Mira*."

"Good catch." Especially since, between this Neanderthal and the ME who was now cowering inside his vehicle, she was annoyed enough to make good on that eunuch threat. "And I'm fine. I'll grab something from the mini mart and bring it to my room when we get back." She opened front passenger door and slipped inside while Riyad set her kit on the rear seat next to her tote. "I've got a couple of calls to make, but the tide expert's up first. I've dealt with Dr. Brom before. He's a miracle worker."

Only tonight, she needed that miracle to come in at warp speed.

Frank had taken a hell of a risk force-feeding a British lieutenant radioactive material and then kicking her off whatever oil platform he and Zak's cohorts had either kidnapped or lured the woman out to. And that meant one thing.

The clock wasn't just counting down—it was nearing zero.

The SEAL must've agreed with the ominous timeline, because he'd nodded to the oncoming British contingent as if he already knew both men, then climbed into the driver's seat to start the Jeep's engine. Within minutes they were leaving Al Massarat and the desolate portion of Diyar Al-Muharraq's collective sands behind and entering Manama proper.

To her surprise, Riyad didn't turn the Jeep south toward the base.

Instead, he pulled into a parking lot next to a kebab stand and killed the engine. The customer area beside them was crowded with men dressed in white thobes, with nary a woman or tourist in sight.

"What—"

"Keep your hijab on and stay in the car." On that rude note, he got out and shut the door. Though why he'd bothered with the warnings, she had no idea. The jerk had used his remote to lock her into the SUV like a recalcitrant teenager as he and his charcoal, western suit headed off to join the men-only, thobed crowd at the kebab stand.

Granted, they were probably smack in the middle of one of those Shi'ite-dominated, "no-go" areas, but manners still mattered.

Whatever.

She retrieved her phone, blessing her boss for the latest

incarnation as she accessed her contacts and located Mark Brom's number. Fortunately, she knew the tide expert well enough to cut to the chase. She quickly briefed Brom on the specifics of her newest case—sans a few classified details that wouldn't affect his calculations anyway.

The doc was currently away from his lab, but vowed to return ASAP.

It would take a few hours though, before he'd be able to phone her back and let her know where the woman's body had gone into the Persian Gulf. Even then, Brom would be offering up multiple possibilities that he would not be able to narrow down until Mira provided him a more precise time of death.

Unfortunately, she understood.

By the time Riyad returned to stow a heavenly scented carryout bag beside her crime kit in the rear of the SUV, Mira had finished her call.

The SEAL handed her the sole, opaque takeout cup that he'd purchased as he climbed into the driver's seat. "Drink this."

Hello?

"You do know that, while I am NCIS, I'm not actually in the Navy, right? So although I am expected to—and do—follow orders from my superiors...*you* are not one of them." Not to mention, she might not even like what was inside that cup.

That oh-so-familiar scowl cut in. "*Drink.* It'll help stabilize your blood sugar."

She liked this man so much better when he was wrong.

She took a sip from the straw. "Pomegranate juice?"

He nodded as he restarted the Jeep and merged them into the stream of early evening traffic that would take them to the base. "It was that or soda. You don't need the artificial crap that comes with the latter."

"Yeah? Well, maybe I like the artificial crap." Especially when it arrived in the form of a tall, frothy, sugared-up caramel latte.

Riyad ignored her grouse in favor of the phone he'd slipped out of his suit pocket. She had no idea who he called, since the conversation that followed was in Arabic, leaving her to decipher every twentieth word, at best.

She retrieved her own phone from the dash and divided the remainder of the ten-minute drive back to NSA Bahrain between finishing the juice Riyad had forced on her and an impromptu briefing with her boss...who'd actually picked up for a change.

She hung up with Ramsey as the Jeep pulled into the base parking lot.

Riyad killed the engine and bailed out.

She did the same. But when she opened the SUV's rear door to grab her stainless-steel case, her crime kit and the bag of food were already missing.

Pulling off her hijab, she tucked it into her tote, then slung the leather strap to that over her shoulder, counting down the minutes that took them through the pedestrian gate and several more turns until they'd reached the Navy Inn and the door to her suite. Riyad followed her inside and set her crime kit down beside the coffee table. The carryout bag ended up on top.

Instead of pulling out one of the foil-wrapped pitas stuffed with kebab meat, he set out all four, along with two lidded, cardboard bowls, two bottles of water and a pair of forks. And then *he* sat. On the couch. In her suite.

Great.

Unfortunately, while the man hadn't given her the choice, he had paid for the food. It would probably be rude to kick him out before he had a chance to eat what was enough for four normal humans...or perhaps one admittedly very hungry NCIS agent and an even hungrier Navy SEAL.

She set her tote on the carpet next to her side of the couch as she offered up her verbal thanks for the meal he'd provided and sat.

It seemed churlish not to.

She was bracing herself for small talk between rapid, *get the man on his way* bites, when Riyad's phone rang. He apologized for the interruption, then sat back against the sofa to take the call—in Arabic. She ended up consuming the entire, surprisingly tender lamb kebab wrap that she'd selected, followed by a generous shepherd's salad, while listening to yet another one-sided conversation she couldn't understand.

She'd finished with her food, but that call was not over.

It was never going to end.

And her scars. For some reason, the ones that'd been caused by the burns to her shins still itched more than those on her temple and abdomen ever had.

She finally stood and walked into the connecting bedroom, closing the door behind her and slightly louder than she'd needed to. If she was lucky, the man seated on her temporary couch would take the hint and be gone by the time she'd swapped out her suit for her *Don't give up the ship!* sweatshirt and shorts. She even unpacked the rest of her bag, brushed out her hair, then cleaned her teeth before reapplying the lavender-scented lotion to her scars twice, hoping the lengthy delay would send an unmistakable signal.

If it had, Sam Riyad was impervious. He was sitting on her couch when she reopened the door and finally off the phone... waiting for her.

She couldn't even yawn and claim exhaustion to get him to leave. He'd timed her marathon stretch of sleep on that plane.

He'd polished off two of the remaining kebab wraps and his own shepherd's salad, but had made no move on the final wrap.

How the hell did she get rid of a SEAL who was clearly in no mood to leave? "You should take that last pita to your room, Commander. Put it in the mini-fridge before it spoils."

He shook his head. "That's yours. It was a backup kebab. Chicken. Lamb can be an acquired taste."

So was he.

And one she was not inclined to become acclimated with.

"*Commander?*" His brow hiked as he leaned forward to gather up the empty containers and foils, tossing them into the carryout bag before he reclined against the back of the sofa once more. "It was *Sam* when we left the Ramseys' and boarded the plane. Even in that autopsy suite. And now it's commander again. Why?"

Until that moment, she hadn't realized that, but he was right. She wasn't sure how to answer him though. Because she didn't know the answer.

"Does the distancing that comes with the renewed title have to do with...what I told you...about Kuwait?"

The torture and abuse that he'd hinted at? "God, no."

"Then why do I feel as though we've taken a step back?" That pointed brow clearly had not accepted her denial.

She sank down to the edge of the couch, floored by the implication that he thought she felt differently about him because of what had happened to him when he'd been a boy.

Except...she did feel differently. And she couldn't quite put her finger on why.

While she still did not like this man, the connection she'd felt with him in this room earlier? Try as she might to stamp it out, she couldn't.

It refused to leave.

But since they were talking about that confession of his, "Why did you tell me?"

She caught the beginnings of a not-quite-careless shrug, but then he killed it. That fathomless stare captured hers and held it. "You deserved to hear it."

"Because of the way you told me about my father's murder?"

He nodded. "And the rest."

The rest? "I don't understand. What else is there?"

He sat motionless for a good half a minute, as if he was trying to work out how to say whatever it was that he'd yet to offer up. He finally lifted a hand and rubbed it along the cultivated growth on his jaw as he sighed. "What happened to you on the *Tern*... I'm guessing the nurses didn't tell you, but...I came to the ICU and sat with you while you were in your coma...a few times."

One of the nurses had mentioned that she'd seen him in her room, sitting beside her bed. The nurse had even wondered if he was a boyfriend.

It hadn't registered at the time, but he must've stopped by more than just *a few times* for that specific assumption to have taken root in the nurse's mind.

Just how often had he come by to sit with her? How long had he stayed? And why was that hand making a second, slower pass along his jaw?

"How many visits did you make?"

"A dozen or so. Maybe more."

And she'd been unconscious throughout them all?

Yikes.

Still, "Okay. So you know more about my pulse and breathing rates than I'd like," not to mention, her private bodily functions, "but—"

"You got to me."

"Excuse me?" She'd been all but dead to the world and on the verge of remaining in that state—or the worst one —permanently.

But he nodded. "And the fact that you were able to get to

me...pissed me off. I was so sure you were in it with your father. And that made me angrier."

Given his past, and his own father, she wasn't surprised.

It also explained the endless collection of glowers and scowls that the man had directed her way. Many of which were similar to the one she was receiving now.

But if it was confession time again, she had a few items that she'd like addressed. Especially since she had no intention of responding to the personal question that had been threaded within that implication he'd made just now.

He might think he wanted to know if he had also gotten to her, but he was better off keeping that query inside his head.

He wouldn't like her answer.

"How did you know it was me at the mosque?" She'd been wearing the niqab that Jerry had provided over her abaya at the time—with all three of those "privacy" veils firmly down. And yet, this man had been so certain it was her he'd spotted inside that he'd lain in wait for her in the electronics' store alcove off the street.

"Your smell."

"I beg your pardon. I do not—"

"You do. Everyone does. That's why my men don't wear manmade shit on a mission. But it's not a bad smell, and it's more a fluctuating mix." A slight smile quirked in. "Right now, your shampoo, body wash and deodorant are scented with vanilla, but there's lavender in there too. The toothpaste you used when you left the room earlier was fennel. And there's something beneath it all. Something softer, sweeter. It was in that ICU room, and every time we met before and after. So that scent's all you."

Holy crap. How was she supposed to respond to that?

"All right...so you're pretty good at the SEAL stuff." Damned good. "But the rest?" She shook her head. "Why did you even try to pretend to be an NCIS agent—even FCI—when you went aboard the *Griffith*?"

"Admiral Kettering. He made the decision and his aide took care of the paper trail. But there was no time for me to sit in on any of the classes at Glynco. We knew Webber wanted to turn your friend's husband—and the man was headed to that ship. Webber had made overtures to him over a year and a half ago at Ft. Bragg."

"Major Garrison?"

The SEAL nodded. "We needed to know if Webber succeeded, because a few things suggested that he had. And we needed to be certain—since none of us had a goddamned clue that Webber had been turned until four of my men were dead. We also knew Webber had crossed paths with you, though I now realize you weren't aware of that. Senior Chief Webber seemed to be...watching out for you. Otherwise, you'd already be dead. Case in point: I only ordered two bugs to be placed in your Annapolis house, not four, and two others in the townhouse. If you find more in your sublet, they're his, too. Based on that and a few other...discoveries, we figured the senior chief might be trying to turn someone inside NCIS. In retrospect, possibly so he'd know if we were close to catching him once the assemblies were stolen."

"So you set yourself up as bait aboard the *Griffith*. Hoping Major Garrison would try to turn you."

"Exactly."

"It didn't work though, did it?" She shook her head. "How you expected to pull it off, I'll never know. You should stick to your day job, because you make a lousy cop."

"Hey, I read the manual."

Oh, good God. He'd *read*—

"Scratch that, I only skimmed it. During the helicopter flight out to the *Griffith*." The jerk had the audacity to shrug. "That's all I had time to do."

"Well, *hell*, Commander. I fell asleep to a documentary about BUD/S last year. I guess I'm ready for the Teams. Sign me up."

That earned her a flat-out full smile. It transformed the man's face so thoroughly that her breath clogged unexpectedly in the middle of her lungs.

She had to look away to clear it.

"Touché." The smile had faded by the time she'd glanced back. "Now, it's my turn. I have a question, too. Your father. That voicemail he left."

"Why did I delete it?"

The SEAL nodded.

"Honestly? I figured it was just more gushing about his current *wonderful* wife and life. That, and I assumed he finally needed something from me, and whatever it was, he could damned well get it from someone else. Either way, I wasn't in the best frame of mind that morning to deal with any requests, let alone him."

"Because of what had happened in that classroom the afternoon before with Chief Umber?"

"Partly. But there was a lot of old crap mixed in, too. My dad and I? We haven't been close for decades. But that was just fine with me—and I'm serious about that. What your father tried and failed to do? Mine succeeded. My dad...he murdered my mom."

Confusion furrowed though the man's brows. "From the information in the file I read, I understood that you mother died of complications from syphilis."

Wow. He really had done his homework on her. Maybe he had a future as an investigator after all.

"Mira?"

She nodded. "Yeah. She did die because of syphilis. But my

father gave that goddamned disease to her. And he *knew* he'd passed it on—or at the very least, he knew there was a significant risk that he'd given it to my mom when he popped positive and was treated for it while his ship was on deployment. But he never bothered to call her, much less tell her in person when his ship returned to port. So, my mom? She thought she had the flu. By the time he came home—syphilis-free, naturally—her case had already passed into the dormant stage."

Which was a huge part of why Ramsey had remained in their lives. Her boss might've started out as her dad's old Naval Academy roommate and friend—but he'd ended up a lifelong cherished uncle to her and Nate, and a rock to their mother. Unfortunately, Ramsey had also spent these past two decades choking on the guilt that should have drowned their father outright. He'd seen the vial of antibiotics in her father's stateroom back when they'd served together, and he'd known damned well that his buddy—married or not—morphed into an indiscriminate whore the moment their ship hit port. But like most sailors, Ramsey had "minded his own business."

Until it was too late.

"Surely she had symptoms afterward, before she ended up in a wheelchair."

"She did. Because syphilis is like that. But she never told anyone. Hers were all nerve-related. Ironically, my grandmother died of multiple sclerosis before I was born. My mom thought all those neurological symptoms meant that she had MS too."

"I'm so sorry. She must've been in deep denial to not go to a doctor."

"She was. She was also terrified my dad would leave her once he knew. Of course, he abandoned her anyway. And before you ask, he absolutely knew before he left for Saudi Arabia that his wandering dick and shiftless cowardice had put her in that chair and damaged her spinal cord, and especially her heart, so severely that she was marking time until her body gave out completely. He just didn't care. Not enough to stick around and help. Oh, he left money, and that monster of a house. Along with the mother-in-law from hell. He *claimed* he hadn't asked for a divorce because he hadn't wanted her to lose his medical benefits. That was bullshit. He didn't bother divorcing her, because he didn't have to. He just converted to Islam and took a second wife."

"And that second wife? How did your meeting go with her and the kids?"

Hmm. "I guess you could say it was...bittersweet."

Mira leaned forward and reached into her tote, fishing out the photo album that Noura had slipped inside without her knowledge.

She passed the book to Riyad. "Noura thought I'd want to linger over it." And she did. But not for the reason her father's widow believed. "Go ahead. Take a look."

He flipped it right side up, Arabic-reading wise, like her baby half-sister had, and opened it to those initial wedding photos of her father beaming down at a woman who was not her mother. "Huh." He flipped through until he'd reached the photos of Noura pregnant, with that once again beaming father's hand fused to a swollen belly.

Riyad kept flipping through the pages, reaching the daddy-with-newborn-babies shots, then the ones of her father and the twins as toddlers on a gorgeous beach somewhere, splashing in the froth. "Yeah, these have gotta hurt."

She shrugged. "They do, and they don't." Because the man in those photos? She tapped that doting papa. "He's my father...but he's not. Does that make sense?"

The man seated beside her nodded slowly. "It does."

Given everything Riyad had told her in this room before

they'd left to view the body that had washed up on Al Masarrat's beach, she believed him.

He turned to the final page of the album—and she flinched.

"What's wrong?"

"That picture." Hell, that sailboat. "That's my mom's boat—the *Natty Mir*." And that particular photograph of the boat... "It shouldn't be in here."

Confusion threaded back through the man's brows. "Why not?"

Because every other photo in that book featured a slice of her father's life with Noura and/or the twins. Every single one.

But this picture? This last snapshot contained her father, her mother, Nate and herself. They were clearly visible in the sailboat's recessed cockpit.

They were also all smiling in the photo, too. Laughing even.

"I remember this day. We'd just pulled into the slip my mom had rented in Miami. Some woman on the opposite side of the dock snapped that photo with a film camera. She had it developed and gave a copy to my father before we left."

And that second, later, day? None of them had been smiling then. Her dad had let his plan to abandon them all for Saudi Arabia slip out the night before.

She'd never seen the photo again.

"He must've taken it with him when he left for Al Jubail."

Riyad fingered the small envelope that was attached to the inner back cover of the album. "There's something in here." The tip of his scarred index finger slipped inside and surfaced with a memory card.

"That's for the digital files." Her father had done that with a DVD for the sole starter-family album that was stuffed in a box in the attic of the house in Annapolis. "It's a backup in case the photos get wet or otherwise destroyed."

All the photos?

She stiffened. "It's not possible." Surely, it couldn't be that obvious. Because this particular photo of the *Natty Mir* had not been born as a digital file.

They'd never even possessed the negative.

Not to mention that, according to Noura, an agent from Homeland or NCIS had taken possession of the album for a while. The memory card was stored in plain sight at the back. Surely the agent would've combed through the files within?

Unless there'd been a mix-up and the agent had dropped the ball.

"What's not possible?"

"Hmm?"

"You said—"

She realized then that she'd spoken aloud earlier. But it was the other, unspoken thought—the blinding, if irrational hope—that had taken over her brain.

"Hand me the data card."

She turned to wrench her laptop from the leather tote. She set it on the coffee table and used her common access card to clear the computer's security wall, then accepted the data card from Riyad, inserting that into a slot along the side.

Like the album, the data card contained one hundred ninety-nine digital photos of her father's second life...and that single snapshot of his first.

Her father must've created the *Natty Mir*'s digital file by running the original print through a scanner and then added it to the others on the data card—unless that last file did not contain an image of the *Natty Mir* at all...

Despite the fact that the right side of Riyad's torso was now fused to her left as they stared at her laptop's screen, Mira tapped the errant file, opening it.

The same image from her childhood appeared on the computer screen.

So much for that theory.

She took the time to click through each of the other hundred ninety-nine files on the card.

Nothing but happy families in every one. Definitely no text files containing plans for the *Pacific Tern*'s takedown. Nor were there any scanned papers or receipts that pointed to the conversion of the mixed-oxide pellets inside those stolen assemblies. She even checked the data card for hidden files.

And came up dry again.

Had she really expected to find something?

The agent who'd confiscated the album from Noura had done his damned job—just as Mira had known he would. Hell, the mere fact that Riyad hadn't been aware of the album's existence before she'd shared it with him proved it was a dead end.

She slumped against the couch.

"Perhaps your father was simply trying to say that you and your brother were equally important to him when he included that photo."

Her dad? "Not a chance." Plus, she wasn't meant to see this album.

Or was she?

She straightened as a fresh bout of hope sparked. Her father's widow had made a similar comment at the Ramseys' house. "Noura did tell me that my dad was proud of me and Nate. That he'd followed our careers."

And there was the rest.

Had Noura really forgotten to remove the album from her bag as the woman assumed? Or had Ben Ellis had done what his widow had? Had he remembered it from their recent visit and deliberately slipped the album back into his wife's bag?

If so, why?

He couldn't have known he'd be murdered and that Noura would lose everything afterward, including their personal possessions. So this album hadn't been put there to keep his memory alive. Which meant he'd had another reason.

What had Ramsey told her in that DC hotel room? *Your dad said he was sending you something.*

She was beginning to think that he'd done so before he'd called his old Navy-turned-CIA buddy. But he'd never intended for it to arrive via mail or parcel post.

He'd tucked it into this album, hiding it within that digital photo of his first family all those years ago aboard the *Natty Mir.*

She leaned forward and opened the computer's terminal window so she could access a program she'd had cause to use six months earlier. The case had made the cable news too, along with her brief explanation and example of how a pedophile who'd been stationed in Japan had hidden his vile photos within "clean," innocuous photos before uploading the resulting files so that a similarly twisted cohort in the States could download those same files and extract the vile photos from within.

Steganography was popular with hackers and those who dealt in sensitive business information, too...as well as traitors and spies.

And that interview she'd given? If her father had truly been tracking her career, he could've caught the initial video on the news, or even the replay that was archived on the channel's website.

She typed in the command to access the program she'd put forth as an example in the interview.

"What are you doing?"

"Apply that patience SEALs are known for, Commander."

Either her order or the use of his title—or both—earned her a fresh frown.

She ignored it, reaching across the laptop's keys to snag the photo album Riyad had set down on the coffee table in front of him. "But cross your fingers."

She needed more than the same program that her father had used. She also needed the altered, carrier file's name—but *that* she already had, since it would be the name for the digital file on the data card that corresponded to their old family photo: *nattymir*. What she didn't yet possess was the name of the hidden file that she needed to extract and the password to facilitate the extraction.

Pulling the hardcopy of the old family photo from its protective sleeve, she flipped it over to find everything she needed scripted on the reverse.

Miranda in the Natty Mir, 06-28-2002

"Shouldn't that be 'on' the *Natty Mir*?"

She let the comment slide and opted to satisfy the curiosity behind it as she returned to the laptop to type in the information her father had provided just after the terminal's blinking cursor. "No. He's telling me that *Miranda* is the hidden file we're after. It contains the information my father wanted to pass to the CIA through me. It's currently stored *in* the digital *nattymir* jpg file via steganography—a technique hackers and others use to hide data, or a photo, within another photo. And that hyphenated date at the end? That's the password to unlock it."

Which she'd just finished typing in.

"I've heard of steganography, even seen it used a few times."

His line of work? She imagined he had.

"But isn't that—"

"Too easy?" She shook her head. "Nope." It was just easy enough. "He would've wanted the album and data card to look innocuous enough to pass inspection with the agents from the CIA or Homeland who'd be picking up his wife, and then undoubtedly grilling her as they searched her belongings." Which they and NCIS had. "But once Noura and their kids were safe—or if something happened to my father and Noura inevitably showed me the album—he'd want it to be easy enough for me to recognize what he'd done and be able to decipher it pretty much immediately."

Which she also had.

"Clever." The SEAL seemed surprised.

She wasn't. "I never said my father was stupid." Just a spineless bastard who'd walked away from the legal, American wife he'd opted to kill.

Mira created a name for the new file and hit enter so the program she'd loaded could work its magic. Once the new file popped up, she opened it...and for the first time in well over twenty years, she smiled over a gift from her father.

"*Holy fuck*, woman."

She let that comment slide, as well. Mainly because, like the man beside her, she was too busy devouring the purchase orders for nitric acid and an ion exchanger, along with a new photo. Or rather, a screenshot of a map of the Persian Gulf.

And at the center of that map?

An orange flag marking the location of an abandoned oil platform twenty-five miles north of Bahrain and thirty off the eastern Saudi coast. And on that flag? The black, three-bladed trefoil symbol for radioactive material.

With Zak Webber's name beside it.

20

That scowl was back.

With the faint glow of green that barely lit up the belly of the helicopter, Mira could feel the glower more than she could actually see it. Weirdly, it was more intense than the one its owner had been wearing while he'd been accusing her of treason back in the States.

This one hadn't been forged in fury, either, but trepidation.

For the first time in his career, she suspected that the SEAL seated across from her in this stealthed-out Black Hawk was downright reluctant to execute a mission.

Why?

Because she was on it.

Oh, he'd tried to stop her. Less than three hours ago, Riyad had lowered the lid to the laptop in her room at the Navy Inn and stood as he'd calmly informed her that he would be commanding the mission to board the oil platform her father had flagged. That meant he'd be selecting the SEALs who'd be part of it. Emphasis on SEALs. Since she did not possess that Almighty Trident, she would not be joining them.

And that *was* an order.

She'd simply reminded the man again that while he was in the Navy, she was not. Nor was she afraid to go over his head in that Navy chain of command of *his*.

She hadn't been moved by his subsequent "serious concerns" regarding her health either.

Yes, she'd gotten lightheaded at the beach, but she recovered immediately. And thanks to him, she'd been well fed since.

As for their mode of transportation out to the platform, she had indeed endured a violent helo crash. Fortunately, she couldn't remember anything between spotting the fiery trail of that surface-to-air missile and waking up in the wreckage on the *Tern*.

Hence, she had no qualms about boarding another.

When that hadn't changed the commander's mind, she'd rolled out the sixteen-inch guns. Not only was she NCIS, there was a decent chance that her suspect was aboard the platform. A suspect who might not impart everything he knew to Riyad or another SEAL. But given that history and bond of friendship that she'd once shared with Frank? The same history and friendship that Riyad had made such a stink about?

Because of it, she alone stood the best chance of getting the critical information they needed out of the former Navy nuke, and they both knew it.

And Zak?

Yes, he'd last been spotted in DC. But they couldn't rule out the chance that Zak might've headed back to this part of the globe around the same time that she and Riyad had boarded the C-130 that had flown them from Andrews to Muharraq. Hell, Zak could've ultimately murdered the two agents who'd been tailing him around the capital so that he could leave DC and return to his stash of radioactive fuel undetected.

The mere possibility of Zak's presence on that platform—while remote—provided even more reason for her to go.

Riyad had been forced to relent. Though the glower that lingered now assured her that it would be a long time before he'd forgive her for backing him into a corner on this.

Fine with her. At the moment, she was more worried that *neither* Frank nor Zak would be there.

Lieutenant Kelley's body had been in the water for three days at least, possibly four or five. If Zak had learned that Frank had dumped one hell of a clue into the Gulf, every one of those bastards might have already pulled up stakes and moved on.

With that radioactive material.

According to the sensor readings from the reconnaissance drone that was currently circling high above the steel behemoth, the platform was not kicking off radiation. Nor did there appear to be thermal, biological hotspots within, walking around or stationary.

But both could be shielded.

The offshore drill site her father had flagged had been abandoned by Saudi Arabia four years earlier. Zak had been off the Navy's grid for the last two of those four. That was plenty of time for the man to have quietly moved in the concrete and other insulating materials that would assist him and his cohorts in concealing their radioactive and other nefarious activities.

Unfortunately, Riyad was correct about another of his concerns. Given Zak's SEAL skillset, there was a solid chance the structure was booby-trapped in key places or, hell, rigged to explode outright...via remote detonation.

They might never know which, until it was too late.

For that reason, Riyad had decreed that she'd remain aboard this helicopter with its Night Stalker pilots and crew—*in the air* —until he'd given the all-clear for the Black Hawk to return to the platform and actually land.

That was okay by her, too. She had no desire to get in the

way of another violent, saltwater takedown, especially since doing so could get someone still *in* the Navy killed.

From the single index finger the crew chief had just held up, they were sixty seconds out from that takedown's nerve-wracking commencement—at least for her nerves.

Mira glanced at the personal dosimeter strapped to her right wrist.

According to the MBD-2's readings, she was in the clear. God willing, the radiation levels for Riyad and his men would stay that way during the coming assault.

A handful of terse breaths later, the Black Hawk hovered mere inches above the platform's aging helipad.

Riyad gave the signal, and eight armed and camouflaged SEALs disembarked in rapid succession through the yawning, starboard side of the bird.

Thanks to a near full moon and her own acclimated night vision, Mira caught hints of their outlines as the men spread out to begin securing the platform, losing sight of the SEALs and the steel structure altogether as the helo regained altitude, then banked away toward inky, open water.

The rhythmic thumping of the helicopter's blades competed with the stress pounding in her chest. She forced herself to focus on that starboard opening and the starry, watery night beyond, pretending a patience she didn't feel as seconds ticked into minutes...and the minutes began to add up, and then multiply...

An eternity later, the crew chief's wave caught her attention. He sent her a thumbs up, letting her know they'd received the all-clear to return.

The thumping of those blades finally succeeded in edging out the stress as her pulse rate slowed to almost normal.

Another minute passed before she caught her next glimpse of the dormant platform and one of the SEALs they'd left on it. M4 now slung across his back, the stack of shadowy, camouflaged muscle loomed near the edge of the helipad, waiting for them. Even without the moon's assist, she'd have known it was Riyad. It was in that powerful, self-assured stance. That comment he'd made in the suite in DC? He was right. That thobe he'd worn had been a costume. Hell, so were the black Henley and cargo pants he preferred, along with the suit the man had sported earlier today.

But those camouflage utilities he wore now? Riyad hadn't donned a uniform at Muharraq Airfield; he'd pulled on a second skin.

His true one.

The SEAL disappeared from view as the pilot banked the bird again, this time to guide it in for its actual landing.

Within seconds, the Black Hawk's wheels had kissed the pad and settled in for an iron embrace.

The quadruple blades were still powering down as the camouflaged form who'd been waiting leaned in through the starboard side.

Riyad waved her out. "We've got something! Could be someone."

Some*one*?

She released her safety harness and tugged off her hearing protection, passing the rabbit ears to the crew chief as she headed for the door.

The commander gripped her right arm, assisting her and her incongruous navy-blue suit out into the salted, crude-oil-laden moonlight, whether she needed the help or not. "Watch that step; it's deeper than you think." The moment the soles of her leather shoes met the steel of the helipad, Riyad released her. He tipped his helmet toward a set of skeletal metal steps that led down to the narrow walkway that would take them over open water and inside the upper level of the offshore platform. "This way."

"Who'd you find?"

"Not sure yet. But those bastards were definitely here." He briefed her as they crossed the pad. "Based on the state of the galley and the amount of trash lying around, they were burrowed in for months, probably well before Corrigan's murder. As you anticipated, they'd shielded the extraction area with concrete. But other than that shitload of personal garbage, the leftover nuclear waste and gear from the MOX conversion and a shattered laptop that was dumped in a vat of seawater, the place has been cleaned out. Couldn't even find the empty assemblies, but they could've pitched them into the water below. We'll send divers down in the morning to check and look for anything else they might've tossed that we can exploit for intel. As for the rest: we've got a thermal signature inside a compartment two levels down. But it's weak, so don't get your hopes up. Upper level must've masked it. Could be human, could be a trap. My men are cracking the door open as we speak. If—"

He broke off to listen to one of his men on his earpiece, before offering up a terse *affirmative* into his mic.

"Okay, the compartment's open. Definitely human. Let's go."

They reached the bottom of the steps.

That steel grip of his found her upper arm, escorting her across the narrow, open walkway, once more without asking and despite the safety railing on both sides designed to keep anyone, including her, from taking that hundred and fifty-foot plunge into the blackened water below.

Then again, while her pride might be rebelling at this lengthier assist, having experienced a similar enough dive recently—that she *did* remember every terrifying second of— her nerves appreciated the contact. It kept her grounded.

The moment they reached the other side, he released her. They took an immediate right and descended a level. Yet another turn and a short walk down an inner passageway still reeking of oil, they entered an old, dusty office, backlit by portable lights.

One of the SEALs stood near an inner door beyond the desk. The junior man took one look at Riyad, mouthed *Nasser*, then frowned as he shook his head.

Shit.

She moved ahead of Riyad to step inside a tiny storage room lined with empty shelves and another one of those portable lights. Was that really Frank lying on the filthy floor between them, covered with a silver mylar emergency blanket? She almost didn't recognize the man. Every square inch of Frank's face—and what she could see of his neck and upper shoulders —was black and blue, and distorted by over a dozen crusted sores and swelling.

It was miracle he was alive.

Squeezed in between the crown of the man's bloodied head and the far wall was another camouflaged SEAL. This one was hunkered down and doing his damnedest to coax the contents of a field IV bag into Frank's veins. She didn't need that second frown and slow shake to know that the *alive* condition was about to end.

And that shallow, labored breathing?

Frank was minutes from death, possibly less.

She turned to Riyad. "Can you get the book? It's on top of my crime kit, under my seat in the helo."

She'd brought along the Qur'an that Walid Rahmani had entrusted into her care when she'd boarded the Black Hawk. She'd figured that if she'd been wrong about Frank and he hadn't been trying to help them, a religious and possibly guilt-inducing gift from his father's old friend might help to bring him around.

The commander nodded, then turned to pass on her request

to the SEAL standing at the desk just outside the door with a second, pointed nod.

Turning back to Frank, Mira closed the remaining inches of filthy floor to those abused feet. She moved up to his mylar-covered chest and squeezed in catty-corner to the SEAL working quietly but steadily to keep his impromptu patient alive for as long as possible.

She wasn't sure if those red and purple lids were closed on purpose, or if they were permanently swollen shut.

And, *Christ*, where was she supposed to touch the man?

She settled for a sliver of unblemished, if grayish, flesh along his right collarbone. "Frank?"

Eyes moved beneath those swollen lids. And then they lifted... a bit. A soft, but blinding smile curved around the scabbed split in her old classmate's lips as he focused on her, his voice slurring. "M-mira. You f-found the sailors, f-figured it out. I knew you would."

"Sandra Lance and Christina Kelley?" She nodded. "I did." As much as she wanted to rail at him for those horrific murders, she couldn't.

She needed their killer's help. Desperately.

His smile faded. "S-so sorry about the *Tern*. I h-heard Zak c-coming, so I p-pulled your lanyard and p-pushed you. It was the only way to s-save you from Z-Zak. I told him W-Whitby lost his nerve—appealed to you, then p-panicked when he saw me and p-pushed you overboard. Zak sh-shot him on the spot. Still feel like sh-shit—but it was Whitby or m-me, and he'd s-swallowed the whole fucking g-gallon of Kool-Aid. But it gave you the best ch-chance to make it h-home and alert the others."

He might be right about that. But they'd never know now, would they?

"It's okay, Frank."

"Hmm." His lids lowered for a moment, then cracked open

again, his voice still slurring. "I p-prayed you'd made it. Then Zak t-told me you had. Still don't know how."

"The surface-to-air missile. It caught the attention of the *Juan Carlos I*. The ship arrived in time for one of their lookouts to spot my swan dive."

The crusted split began bleeding as another smile cut in. "See? You're a s-survivor—no m-matter what. I knew that at NPS."

She patted the spot of just-grayed flesh. "Hey, you were there, too. You survived. You can do it again. You will."

His smile faded, but the blood continued to seep from his lip as he tried to shake his head. "Only m-made it 'c-cause of you. Then...and now. Had to. I know I'm d-dying. It's okay. Just had to h-hang on to g-give you my p-present."

"Zak?" Please Lord, let it be him. "Do you know where he took the plutonium?"

"S-sorry. He trusted me m-more after the *T-tern*...but he doesn't trust anyone c-completely. It's all f-front. That's how he s-sucked me in. Went on about how the Navy screwed us both. By the t-time I knew the plan, I c-couldn't get out. M-made a mistake. Told him no. Th-that I couldn't kill all those p-people. Sh-should've called NCIS instead. R-regret that."

"Your grandfather?"

That battered head nodded. "He nearly k-killed him. He did kill me. Used his g-goons to do it. He got off on you working Corrigan's m-murder, too. S-said he should've left a bow n-nailed to her h-head. Underneath, he's a c-cold, twisted fuck."

"Yeah." At eighteen she hadn't been able to see the real Zak beneath that pretty face and surface charm either. But during their second go 'round, she'd matured enough—and had decided to get out before it was too late.

"He hates you."

"I know."

"No, Mir. That bastard really h-hates you. He was g-glad when you woke up from your c-coma, 'cause he wants to t-take you out himself. He's got it p-planned."

"How? When?"

He shook his head. "Wouldn't s-say. I j-just know he's waiting for s-something, then he'll g-grab you, so...be c-careful."

"I will."

The SEAL at Frank's head checked his vitals. She caught the frown he shot her and the message behind it: they were losing him.

Step it up.

She hated herself for pushing a dying man, much less one who she'd once considered a friend, but she had to. "So, what's my present?"

God willing she'd like this one. The two this former fellow officer had left for her in Bahrain had turned her stomach and broken her heart.

"Zak's g-goons? Never used real n-names. B-but I f-found a mini iPad on the s-sailor from the v-villa. WiFi only, but I've been m-making notes. Snuck some p-pics. It's h-hidden—" He broke off to cough, then groaned, despite whatever meds the SEAL had slipped inside that IV bag. "S-sorry. Fuckers b-broke my ribs. Leg, too. But whatever's in that bag is k-kicking in. Feels g-good. Cold...but g-good."

Cold? That symptom wasn't from the meds from the IV. That was the chill kicking up from death as it began to circle in on the man in earnest.

When Frank's eyes drifted down, she was certain.

"Nasser?" *Riyad.* His camouflaged form had moved up to fill the door's frame. "Where's the mini hidden?"

Those swollen lids lifted. The dark, bloodshot eyes within tried to focus beyond their owner's naked feet, then searched for her face again when they failed. "F-fire station, outside the g-galley. B-Behind the CO2 c-canister."

Riyad turned and nodded toward the SEAL he'd sent after the Qur'an, sending the man off again. Rahmani's gift was in the commander's hands as he swung back.

He passed the book to her, but she held on to it—for now.

"Frank...we need to know. How much plutonium does Zak have?"

"N-not sure. W-worked as s-slowly as I c-could, but I f-finished. S-some is earmarked for l-later. By them, or s-someone else. D-don't know s-specifics...and it's g-gone. Has b-been for w-weeks."

"We know. The SEALs searched for it—"

"N-no, the b-bulk left. S-some stayed. A S-Saudi c-came with Zak and others—two, th-three days ago. C-can't be sure. L-lost time after they l-left me here to d-die. He picked up the b-bombs Chang—th-the Uyghur—b-built."

"A Saudi picked up the bombs?"

That battered head managed a slight nod, but the swollen lids within sank lower.

"How many?"

"T-two. F-first is simple; remote d-detona-tor. The second is more c-complex. Needed b-barometric fuze to d-detonate...th-three hundred feet. Worked in the g-galley with Chang. He left to take a d-dump. I s-sabotaged the switch. C-closed it b-back up. It sh-should fail. C-can't be s-sure. Not m-my area and h-had to work f-fast."

A barometric fuze? Designed to detonate at three hundred feet?

Zak was looking to create a low air burst, and with a—

"The plane?" Riyad again. "Who's the pilot, Nasser? Where is it? And what's the target?"

"N-not sure on p-pilot, but c-could be the S-Saudi. Don't

know t-target. There's a p-picture of h-him on th-the—" Frank's body went stiff as he broke off, stared sightlessly.

Mira glanced at the SEAL holding the IV. "What's—"

"Seizure. The guy was having one when we breached the door. Be ready to ask your last question, Agent. But you might not even get that."

A soft whoosh of air escaped as those eyes regained what little vision that was left and tracked back to hers. "I-it h-happened ag-gain, d-didn't i-it?"

Shit. His voice was slurred almost beyond deciphering now. Despite everything this man had done, her eyes began to burn—for him. "Yeah."

"S-sorry a-bout th-the s-sailors. T-tell th-the f-families."

"I will." Somehow. Though she was feeling the massive weight of that same remorse. Yes, Frank had killed the women. But Zak would never have known about Frank and sucked him into his vile schemes if she hadn't let the bastard into her life, not once, but twice. "I promise. This is a gift from Walid Rahmani." She laid the book on Frank's chest, and drew his bruised and swollen hands from beneath the silver mylar sheet to gently stack them on top. "It's a beautiful Qur'an. He asked me to give to you."

"Th-thank y-you. A-and...f-for th-the...f-friend...sh-ship."

Oh, God. Her vision was compromised now, too.

From her own tears.

"Take care, Sailor. Fair winds and following seas." She leaned down to kiss that bruised temple, but it was too late.

Her old classmate was already dead.

Regret seared in as she stood and turned to the door. Her tears were streaming freely. She tried to staunch them as she walked forward, blindly smacking into something dense and impenetrable. When a pair of hardened arms came up to wrap around her, anchoring her to more solid muscle, she realized it was a chest. She hoped to hell the camouflaged expanse belonged to Riyad, because she didn't know the other men and she was simply too razed to move.

But how could it be him? She felt too good.

Safe.

Except, this was Riyad holding her. He murmured something she couldn't understand into her ear as he guided her out of the storage room. Leaning back against the edge of the desk, he drew her in closer. She let herself stay there, too. Probably for longer than she should have. She finally pulled herself together and straightened.

Stepped back.

She scrubbed the tears from her cheeks. "Sorry."

He shook his head. "S'okay. You all right?"

Hell, no. Despite all that had happened these past months and the monstrous acts that Frank had committed, she'd just watched a former friend die.

Everything inside her *hurt*.

"I'm fine."

The man tipped her chin up. That intense stare of his probing too deeply, marking the truth within as he dried the tears she'd missed with his thumb. But he didn't call her on it. "You said you'd take me right to him. And you did."

A lot of good it had done. "He couldn't even give us *one* of the targets."

"Sure, he did. It's in here." The scarred fingers brandished the mini tablet she hadn't even realized he'd already received, let alone powered up and skimmed. She'd been that absorbed in what was happening with Frank.

"What's in there?"

"A hell of a lot. Those surreptitious photos he took? One is of the Saudi he mentioned. The good news is, I know the bastard. Or rather, I know of him."

Did she really want to ask?

She did anyway, "And the bad?"

"That would be why I know him. Omar Al-Khalil was recently added to the terrorist watchlist—ours and his own country's. One of my men is on the phone as we speak, getting the full story, but the reason Omar caught our eye is due in part to his cousin, Yusuf Bashar. Bashar's an American citizen and a contractor in charge of security at Ras Tanura. Not sure if you know, but Ras Tanura is the Saudis' largest oil export terminal in the Gulf. They move upwards of six million barrels through there a day, nearly seven percent of the world's demand. That makes for one hell of a tactical *and* strategic target. Houthis out of Yemen—backed by Iran—tried to hit it with a series of missiles and drone strikes a couple of months ago. They failed."

If Ras Tanura was the target, and Zak and this Omar Al-Khalil succeeded?

With a *nuke*?

Short term? It would knock the entire world for an incalculable financial loop. Long term? Depending on the specifics of the bomb that Zak's mystery Uyghur had built, who knew when the area would be habitable again?

"Oh, Lord."

Riyad nodded.

"Sam—"

He held up a scarred finger. "Just a sec."

He paused to listen to someone communicating through that earpiece of his. The information being relayed brought a fierce light into those dark eyes along with a grim smile. "Outstanding, Chief. Leave a fireteam here to set the watch until we can return. Agent Ellis and I will be topside momentarily."

Momentarily?

His focus shifted to her.

"We're leaving—now?" Save for the radioactive areas, she still had this entire, multistoried offshore platform to process for evidence and, God willing, clues that just might tell her where Zak and his remaining cohorts had gone.

"Yusuf Bashar has been out sick for a week, contagious and supposedly unable to have visitors. He was due to return to work this morning at zero seven hundred, in roughly—" Riyad lifted his wrist to check the watch strapped next to his dosimeter. "—four hours. But he's there now. Just arrived, in fact. To catch up on paperwork."

At three in the morning?

Given everything Frank had imparted, "That's rather curious timing."

And even more suspicious.

"Yeah. And since Bashar's one of our expats, we're going to go pick him up. Escort the man to Bahrain and have a little chat with him."

"In the Black Hawk?"

Those camouflaged shoulders kicked up. "We're currently thirty miles east of the man. That bird sitting topside can hit well over two hundred miles per hour, making it the quickest way to get him out of the country. We'll be in and out of Ras Tanura in under an hour, and touching down at Muharraq Airfield well before dawn, which the Saudis want—along with a seat at the table during the chat." He caught her stare. Held it. "But you're staying inside the helo until we reach Bahrain. Understood?"

Okay by her. "So long as I'm part of that chat, too."

"Deal."

TWENTY-FOUR MINUTES LATER, that intense frown had returned.

This time Mira was sitting to the left of its owner inside the belly of the Black Hawk when Riyad received the information that caused it. It arrived via the wireless link that the commander still shared with his men—but, frustratingly, not with her.

She finally reached across her chest to poke that iron biceps, waiting until the scowl shifted down to her before she mouthed, "What's wrong?"

Riyad lifted the hearing protection cup from her right ear as he leaned closer, his deep voice riding the deeper pummeling of the helicopter's blades as both filled her. "My chief just heard from one of our contacts in the kingdom."

"Saudi Arabia?"

He nodded as he shifted his own ear cup so that she could speak directly into his, too. "Omar Al-Khalil bought a plane last week. Cessna Citation Mustang. Roomy enough to toss a bomb in the cabin. It was purchased via a Turkish shell company, so it took a while to trace it. Ran him five million US dollars."

"And?"

Because there was more. Why else had that frown deepened?

"Khalil doesn't know how to fly."

Oh, boy. "Zak does." He'd gotten his private license shortly before he'd shown up at her graduation, asking for that second chance.

Had he kept up those particular skills over last seven years?

Did it really matter? For all his former SEAL experience, not even Zak could open the hinged door of a private plane in mid-flight—while flying it—and kick out a bomb. Not unless he'd figured out how to circumvent the laws of physics.

And if he planned on having someone else in that cockpit while he did the deed? Given the altitude the Mustang would need to maintain to plant a bomb on target, the air pressure outside would be too great to get the door open. Not to mention, both scenarios would require a hell of a lot of practice.

That meant whoever was slated to fly the plane planned on dying when the Mustang descended to three hundred feet, and the bomb detonated from within.

Skills or not, that pilot would not be Zak. Not with at least one more bomb already completed and the rest of that radioactive material out there—and God only knew how many more targets those bastards planned to level with it all.

Riyad must've been thinking along the same lines, because he nodded.

The commander reseated her rabbit ears, then his, as the Black Hawk's crew chief caught his attention, leaving her to wonder—just how many men had Zak been able to turn over the course of this sickening quest of his?

Men like the *Pacific Tern*'s captain and at least one of the vessel's nuclear constables. Men like a former Afghan-born, trusted US Army translator, not to mention the former Army CID-turned-Diplomatic Security Service agent that her friend Regan Chase and John Garrison had rooted out this past winter.

Men like *Frank*.

How had Zak been able to get to all of them?

Then again, the bastard had managed to suck her in for a while, too, hadn't he?

Twice.

Was that why he'd come back around for her old classmate? Had he hunted Frank down because of her? Had her rejection of his marriage plans played some part in all this? Had she irreparably dinged Zak's overly sensitive pride?

Unfortunately, as NCIS, she'd seen sailors turn for less.

Either way, she was more determined than ever to sit in on that chat with Yusuf Bashar to find out exactly what Omar Al-Khalil's cousin knew about Zak's plans—and who else the bastard had been able to get to. Only then could they begin to track down the remainder of the nuclear material that Frank had been able to convert.

Fortunately, they were within sight of their newest Saudi destination.

She could make out the array of white lights illuminating the tiny island that contained Ras Tanura amid the jet black waters of the night. The small port and its crude oil and liquefied petroleum gas terminals were connected at the north to the mainland and its refinery via a slender strip of paved road and sand that jutted up from the Gulf.

Relief simmered in—only to slide into her gut and congeal in a pool of dread as she caught the commander's latest, darkening expression...and the cause.

Like Riyad, she could make out a plane beyond the forward window of the helicopter's cockpit. The light pollution from Ras Tanura's port wasn't glinting off the belly of just any plane, but the sleek white underside of a Cessna Citation Mustang.

As with their helo, the Mustang was still over water. But the plane was coming up from the south and just west of the port, and it was losing altitude—fast.

A noticeable, intermittent shimmy had set in as well, as though something was wrong with the aircraft.

No, the pilot. Whoever was flying the Mustang appeared to be having serious difficulty keeping the plane level.

Why?

Curiosity fled beneath the panic that punched in as the Mustang banked inland toward Saudi Arabia proper—and *down*.

Having missed the oil terminals, the pilot now appeared to be attempting a run at the refinery to the north. Only something had caused the nose to bottom out again, instead sending the craft barreling toward the tiny island just beyond the strip of sand and road that connected Ras Tanura's refinery to the port.

It was too blessed late to scramble a fighter jet—and their medium-lift, utility Black Hawk was currently unarmed.

There was nothing they could do but pray...and wait.

The crew chief held up five fingers, relaying the Mustang's current, estimated altitude from one of their own pilots.

The chief's thumb pulled in, signaling that the plane had descended to four hundred feet now...and the craft was still losing elevation.

God willing, Frank had been able to disable that barometric switch. If not, the Mustang was a radioactive nucleus' width from the entire world finding out.

They, however, would never feel it hit.

Mira held her breath along with every man inside the Black Hawk as the crew chief's smallest finger curled in to join his thumb.

Three hundred feet.

A moment later, two fingers remained—without an explosion.

She released the air from her lungs in a rush, only to suck it right back in, along with a fresh round of prayers, as the plane plummeted all the way down to the earth, its steel belly glancing off the southernmost surface of the mostly level, scrub-brush dotted island before it came to a sand-tunneling halt smack amid the shallow surf at the northern edge.

As before, there was no explosion. Just the smoldering glow of red and orange, and that thin ribbon of smoke twisting up from where Mustang's tail had cracked open.

But those growing, now visibly writhing flames within?

The likelihood that they had a terrorist-created Broken Arrow on their hands had blazed in with them. Thank God that postage stamp of earth was uninhabited, because every grain of sand on it was now in danger of becoming radioactive due to the potentially cracked casing of the bomb below.

"Set us down!" Riyad turned to her as their pilot banked the helo toward the wreckage now smoking up from the water. Leaning down, the commander lifted her right rabbit ear, the determination in his voice cutting through the thunder of the helo's blades. "The copilot's contacting the airfield—scrambling additional birds and the hazmat team, along with NEST. Until they arrive, my men and I'll do what we can to contain the situation and secure the area."

She raised her voice above the pulsing blades. "I'll call NCIS!"

Neither she nor her fellow agents would be able to move in to canvas the site for evidence until the Nuclear Emergency Support Team had removed the device and deemed the area safe, but they could gather their gear and begin the prep.

Riyad nodded. "Do it from the helo."

Even if she'd wanted to argue with the precaution, there was no time.

The Black Hawk had landed on the beach upwind of the smoking Mustang—and the red and orange had become more noticeable.

The flames, and the danger that came with them, were spreading.

A split second later, Riyad and the three SEALs he'd brought aboard with him for this impromptu leg of their mission moved out.

Disobeying the letter of Riyad's directive, she followed the men into the moonlit dark, checking the MBD-2 strapped to her wrist as the shoes of her leather Oxfords sank into the sand.

According to the dosimeter, she was still in the clear.

If they were lucky, the surrounding night air and soil would remain so.

Turning away from the wreckage, she advanced beyond the tail of the helo and up the shadowy beach to put some distance between her and those thumping blades as she retrieved her phone. Not knowing what they'd encounter on the oil platform, she'd switched it off back at Muharraq Airfield when they'd boarded the Black Hawk.

The moment her phone powered up, half a dozen text alerts spanning the last several hours popped up in rapid succession. All were from Jerry.

Automatically scrolling to the earliest note, she read them in order.

The first was a general text letting her know that Jerry and his MPD forensic team had finished processing the alley off Sixteenth Street where Zak had murdered the two agents who'd been tailing him around the capital. Jerry had a few hours to fill before he had to leave for the agents' autopsies, so he was sitting down with the files that she'd had Riyad forward to him when he'd been brought back aboard the case.

But the second note? That one was odd, and in the form of an openly disquieting query. *Do we have all the photos from your dad's crime scene?*

The third text was stranger still, and even more alarming. *Something's off with your father's autopsy, too. Can you call me?*

As was the detective's fourth text. *I'm guessing the shit's hit the fan there & you're up to your neck in it. I see Patrice did the autopsy on your dad. Dialing her now...*

A chill slid down her spine as Mira read her former partner's final two texts together. *Fuck. Mir, you there?* And finally, *Call me ASAP. Riyad's lying to you.*

She flinched as her phone rang, nearly dropping it onto the sand at her feet.

It was Jerry.

"Hello?"

"*Jesus*, Mir. Where the fuck are you? I've been trying to reach you for hours."

She glanced down the shadowy beach. The ribbon of smoke had thickened into a steady, billowing plume that all but obscured the stars of the eastern night sky. The steady, writhing glow of the flames beneath allowed her to discern the faint outlines of three of the SEALs as they worked around the wreckage, however.

"Sorry for the radio silence. We've got a bit of situation here. Some of the stuff that went missing turned up...in another form. But we've located that part of it and we're attempting to secure it now. I'll fill you in on the rest when I can."

"*Christ*. I don't know if I should be relieved to know that, or not. Is Riyad there?"

"Yeah. He's not beside me though; he's tied up with that securement. Why? What's the man lying about now?" And why was she even surprised?

Let alone hurt.

"Mir...I didn't want do it this way...but...well, you *really* need to know."

She spun around, facing the ocean as she braced herself. Whatever this was about, it concerned her father—and it was bad. Those initial texts of Jerry's had already clued her into that. Not to mention that tone in his voice. But after those gut-wrenching moments with Frank, she wasn't sure how much more shit she could absorb.

"Just say it."

"I...that is, your...damn it, I can't. I'm sending you a photo that Patrice forwarded to me. I'm so sorry."

Oh, Lord.

Apprehension surged in. She switched the phone to speaker mode and forced herself to click into her text app as it pinged.

Her father's body appeared on the screen. He was wearing

the blood-soaked thobe that he'd had on in those photos from the folder that Ramsey had shown her back in the DC hotel. But her dad wasn't lying on his front this time, he was on his back.

And the blood...it had soaked across the entire width of the linen of his thobe...directly over his groin.

Her knees gave out as the words that Jerry had been unable to say blistered through her brain and her heart. Hell, every inch of her entire body. Her father hadn't been killed by an old ex of hers turned traitor, let alone a complete stranger.

At least, not to him.

Not to her, either. Not if what she suspected was missing from her father's corpse was actually missing...

"Mir?"

She scrubbed the tears from her cheeks and swallowed hard. Cleared her throat. She wasn't sure how she managed to accomplish any of it. This was so much more difficult than watching Frank die. This time, she was dying too.

And she couldn't seem to stop it. "I'm...here."

Barely.

"You okay?"

"No."

"I am so fucking sorry."

She purged her breath and filled her lungs again. But the agony of it all scorched right back in with that salt and smoke-laden air. "Wh-where was it f-found?"

"Mir—"

"*Where?*"

Her old friend's sigh was so heavy, it knocked her all the way down to her shins.

"In his mouth."

She nodded numbly as she reached out with her free hand, bracing her palm in the sand to keep from falling all the way over. "Okay. I...gotta go. I'll...call you..."

Eventually.

When she could think. Breathe.

Figure out how to contain the scream that was clawing up her throat, along with the soul-shredding horror that she just could not deny. Yes, there was a chance her bastard of an ex had been the one to torture and dislocate her father's fingers.

But Zak had definitely *not* killed the man.

Her brother had.

21

S omehow, she'd managed to pull herself together to call Leo Kealani and brief him on the situation surrounding their makeshift Broken Arrow. Mira still had no idea what exactly had come out of her mouth, but her terse rundown must've contained enough information for NCIS and the Bahrain Field Office to get started, because Leo hadn't phoned back. Or worse, attempted to call the commander.

Riyad.

What the hell was she going to say to him?

She'd better decide, and soon. Nearly an hour had passed since they'd landed upwind of that fractured, and now mostly smoldering, Cessna Mustang.

In that time, two other Black Hawks had joined theirs. The first had carried additional, armed security to the scene. The second, the emergency response team from NEST, which Riyad had evidently pre-staged at Muharraq Airfield some time ago.

Once she'd spotted the response team, she'd known her reprieve was about to expire. It was past time to push through her lingering pain and shock.

Riyad and his SEALs had already turned the crash site over

to NEST. The proof was in the distinctive outline of that fierce stack of camouflaged muscle moving up the beach, headed straight for her.

Damn it, she would not confront the lying bastard. Not here. Nor would she give in to the urge to sink down to the sand and stay there.

Nate.

Don't. She'd succeeded in cauterizing the bulk of the horror that had accompanied the photograph Jerry had forwarded, at least temporarily. Unfortunately, the soul-flaying question that had ridden in on its monstrous back still pulsed within her entire body. The question to which she was certain she did not want the answer.

If Nate had murdered their father...had he turned traitor, as well?

She couldn't afford hearing a *yes* to that out here, in the middle of an active recovery mission. It would destroy her. Once she returned to Bahrain, she'd rip off the scab that had managed to form and deal with the entire toxic mess beneath...along with the brooding commander who'd come to a halt directly in front of her.

"I thought I told you to wait—"

"Who was in the plane?" Because two corpses had been pulled from the wreckage and laid into body bags. And there might've been a third that the SEALs hadn't been able to pull free. Despite the rot festering within, she needed a body count and the names that went with them, and now, lest she go insane. "*Well?*"

Those dark brows hiked at her vehemence. "The Mustang had two men aboard. Neither was Zakaria Webber, if that's what has you worried."

It wasn't.

She forced herself to stand there and wait for the rest, prayed he'd give it without her having to push for it...much less explain why she needed to know.

Desperately.

A dozen more of her heartbeats pounded out.

The SEAL finally rubbed the heel of his right palm through the dirt, sweat and soot at his temple and sighed. "The bastard who poisoned his fellow constables and the crew of the *Tern* was flying. Omar Al-Khalil was in the other seat. From what the constable relayed as he died, Khalil changed his mind at the last minute. The two fought for control of the plane." Riyad tipped his head toward the wreckage down the beach. "That's the result."

God help her; relief seared in.

Nate was still out there somewhere in the world. *Alive*. At least for now, leaving her able to concentrate on what she should be concentrating on.

"And the bomb?"

"The casing is cracked, but otherwise it's secure. We got it out of the plane. NEST is boxing it up now. They'll load it aboard their own bird and take it back to Muharraq, so they can examine it in depth. With a good enough look inside the mind of the Uyghur who built it, we just might have a shot at rendering the next one safe. If we can locate that one in time."

Aided by the green glow spilling out from its side, she could see NEST moving the crate into the furthest Black Hawk now. "When do we leave?"

"That's why I'm here. It's time. The flames are out. The security force from NSA Bahrain will remain until the Saudi contingent arrives. I imagine it'll be joint after. Their government wants a look at the wreckage before it's moved. Since this is their land and the metal husk lying on it belonged to one of their citizens, it's not our call. Agents from the FBI will be joining them. Someone from Homeland has already picked up Yusuf Bashar from Ras Tanura, but we're no longer invited to sit in on the chat. At least, not the initial one. Another team arrived at the offshore platform shortly after we left. They're exploiting its intel now, which means you and I, and my men, are cleared to return to Bahrain."

She nodded and swung around toward their helo. She could feel the commander's surprise as he fell into step beside her. She knew he was waiting for her to offer something in response to his briefing as they walked, but she didn't.

She didn't trust herself to utter one more word to this particular bastard than was absolutely necessary, lest she explode with all the others that were safely dammed up at the back of her throat—for now.

To her relief, the Black Hawk had begun to power up by the time they reached it. The blessed, numbing cacophony of the blades that followed removed the ability for easy conversation, necessary or otherwise.

She gave her mood away, anyway, as she claimed a seat on the opposite side of the vibrating bird and as far down its belly from the commander's as possible.

That dark brow of his kicked up again as she secured her harness and hearing protection.

And again, she ignored it.

Nor did she care that Riyad's men had noticed her determination to sit elsewhere.

She was hanging on by a thread, and it was frayed damned near through. The only way she'd make it to Bahrain without her composure snapping completely would be to stare straight ahead and ignore the entire world.

Which she did.

By the time they reached Muharraq and disembarked the Black Hawk, the sun was already stretching and preparing to scorch through another cloudless day. Gathering up her leather tote and stainless-steel crime kit, she ignored the commander as he handed off his visible weapons and his gear to his chief. She continued to ignore the man as they walked off the concrete apron and made their way to the Jeep Grand Cherokee he'd parked nearby before they'd left for the offshore platform.

She even managed to ignore Riyad as he retrieved her crime kit from her hand to stow it in the rear seat of the SUV.

She took care of her own front passenger door as he slid into the driver's seat. From the lock on that lightly bearded jaw, he'd known better than to reach for it.

Just as the SEAL seemed to understand that conversation was neither required nor desired by her as he maneuvered the Jeep through the mostly white, dawn-blushed traffic to NSA Bahrain. The moment he parked the Jeep in a slot outside the gate and killed the engine, she shouldered her leather tote and bailed out.

This time, he didn't reach for her kit.

Smart man.

He wisely continued their mutual silence as they cleared the pedestrian gate and made their way to the Navy Inn.

Unlocking the door to her suite, she stepped inside, knowing he'd follow her. Which he did. He closed the door behind him and waited for her to set her tote and stainless-steel kit down beside the desk—which was also okay with her.

This was exactly how and where she'd wanted this to go down.

The moment she straightened, he tugged off his camouflaged hat, tucked it beneath his left arm and lit in. "All right, we're alone now and not moving. Which you clearly wanted. Now, what the hell's wrong? You intimated back on the beach that this isn't about Webber. Are you still upset over Nasser, then —or ticked because I asked you to remain in the helo? Or are you pissed because Homeland and the Saudis decided to take a crack at Yusuf Bashar without you? Because that one was out of my control."

"Really? You admit there's *something* you don't control? And you expect me to believe you're okay with that?" Now there was a shock.

Confusion crowded through those soiled, dusky features. His right hand stretched out, but she'd already jerked away, wincing as the back of her thigh slammed into the corner of the desk—which made him reach for her again.

"*Don't.*"

His fingers froze in midair. Retreated. But the realization didn't.

That was all but exploding within the fresh scowl of his, though this one was tempered with surprise—and resignation.

"You know."

Oh, give the man a gold star to paste onto that Trident of his. "I do tend to figure things out, Commander. When I'm given *all* the evidence."

Commander. That single word and the disdain roiling within had drawn the remaining anger from those taut, soot-streaked features, trapping it within the man's pained grimace. As if the SEAL had realized that, once again, he'd lost whatever ground he thought he'd gained with her.

Big fucking deal.

Had he really thought this would turn out any different?

Once this conversation was finished—and she'd gotten the information she needed—she was done with Sam Riyad. For good.

"You saw the missing autopsy photos."

One of them. It was more than enough.

"I did."

"It was Patrice, wasn't it? She cracked." He tossed his singed cap on the desk beside her, but he remained those key, two paces away. "She must have."

"She did. Eventually." Though how, Mira didn't know.

She'd yet to call Jerry back and she hadn't spoken to Patrice at all, at least not tonight. Nor would she be able to think rationally enough to speak to either of them until she'd had a chance to process the remaining facts.

Facts that this bastard had yet to dredge up the courtesy to offer. "Patrice gave you two autopsy reports, didn't she? One for me and one for everyone else you'd deigned to honor with the truth."

"Yes. But you should know, I had to force her."

"And did you also knowingly force a respected forensic pathologist to push through a petty officer's critical autopsy and then leave Bahrain before both the case agent of record and I could arrive to discuss with that pathologist what she found... just to make sure she kept her mouth shut about your charming charade?"

His spine had stiffened during that, but he nodded. "The decision was mutual."

She'd just bet it was. Though why she was even surprised that this man had fucked with her case—again—to keep his secrets, she didn't know. After everything she'd learned about *Commander* Riyad, betrayal was right up his alley.

But Patrice's?

They'd become more than colleagues in San Diego. They were supposed to have been friends. And, damn it, that betrayal stung.

The SEAL shoved his hands through his hair, dislodging grains of sand that had gotten caught up in it while he and his men had been hefting that bomb out of the burning Mustang. "I don't understand. If Patrice didn't tell you, then how—"

"Jerry. I told you he was good." The best. And an even better friend. "He realized straight off that the file you had sent to him was missing several key photos of the body. Granted, Jerry wasn't staring at his own father's corpse at the time and *right after* he'd finally been told that his father had been murdered while leaving a voicemail for him. A rather nerve-rattling situation I'm certain you counted on, but—"

"Mira—" She must've infused her glare with just the right amount of contempt, because he broke off. Sighed. Started again. "Agent Ellis. Look, you have to—

"Does Ramsey know?"

That got him to cut off the remainder of whatever excuse he'd been about to give. Simmering silence replaced it.

Which, of course, gave her the answer to her latest query.

"Wow, you really have been swimming in the deep end, Commander." Because withholding critical case information from the senior special agent in charge of NCIS' Washington, DC, Field Office? Once Ramsey did find out—SEAL or not—this man was going to be persona non grata with pretty much every single agent in NCIS.

And Riyad knew it.

That stony expression became that much stonier. "SECNAV made the final call, but I—"

"Oh, well—" *the Secretary of the Navy* "—that makes it all right then."

"As I was *saying*, Agent. SECNAV made the call, but I agreed with it. One look at those missing photos, and you'd have known—"

"That my brother was the only man on the planet who hated our father enough to chop off his dick and shove it into his mouth?"

"Precisely." But the stone had crumbled. Worse, the rubble that had been left behind was infected with compassion. From *him*.

That just pissed her off even more.

She'd assumed that her boss had brought the folder containing those crime scene photos of her murdered father with him when Ramsey had arrived at the Mount Laurel. He hadn't. That folder had been in lying in wait, pre-staged somewhere in that luxury suite before Riyad brought her there. In fact, they were *why* he'd brought her there.

"You were going to show me that file of omission at the hotel in DC. For the shock value. Watch me as I looked at those photos of my father's battered and slaughtered corpse. See if I was detached enough to notice the discrepancies of what was and wasn't there. And if I did? Why, then you'd know if I was complicit."

Yeah, with the same stakes, and in the SEAL's place, she might've done the same thing. But he was still a bastard.

"Well, Commander, I guess you learned something about investigative procedure, after all, while you were busy faking those credentials on and off the *Griffith* last January." She shook her head as the anger and disgust for this man swung around to sock into herself. "This is my own damned fault. I've known from the moment I met you that something was off. Regan doesn't trust you. Her husband doesn't trust you. Jerry doesn't trust you. And whatever you said to Ramsey to get him to support you when you had him shove that doctored folder in my face instead of yourself in that hotel? *He's* not going to trust you anymore, either."

"I don't—"

"Let me see the *rest* of the photos."

That terse frown bit in at being cut off again. She suspected that didn't happen often with this man. Which was a shame.

He deserved so much worse.

She held out her hand. "The mini iPad?"

Riyad hadn't passed it off to his chief after they landed at the airbase. That meant the device that Frank had used to record his notes and take those surreptitious photos of Zak and his cohorts was still in one of the cargo pockets of those scorched and wilted utilities. The SEAL had probably intended to spend the morning holed up in his own suite here at the Navy Inn, scouring the iPad for every ounce of intel he could glean once he'd dropped her off. He could go right ahead.

But first, she needed to see for herself how bad this really was.

It was the only way her aching heart was going to accept what her brain had long since been bellowing.

The commander drew in his breath, then let it out slowly. From the flattening of the chronic frown that followed, she thought he was going to refuse. But then his hand dipped into the camouflaged pocket at his right thigh, surfacing with a white iPad mini smudged with soot from the fingers he'd yet to have the chance to wash.

He extended the mini, careful to leave room for her to accept the device without her having to touch him.

Which she did.

"What's the password?"

"Wasn't one."

Of course. If it had come password protected into Frank's possession, he'd have long since broken in. Nor would Frank have reset it. He'd have wanted whichever NCIS agent found the iPad to be able to access the data within immediately.

And if Zak had found it first?

Well, Frank had already accepted that he was going to be killed anyway.

She powered up the mini and accessed the stream of thumbnails of recent photos. She didn't have to go back far at all to find the most likely corresponding nail in her family's coffin. That tiny view of Zak in profile, standing beside that shaggy hair, scruffed jaw and equally bronzed features that, despite every-thing, were still so very dear to her.

Even as she clicked the thumbnail open—knowing the full proof was coming—the blood roared through her head and chest, and she swayed on her feet.

Riyad reached out for her.

"*Stop.*"

The man's fingers froze once more as she caught the edge of the desk with the heel of her right palm, leaning back into the laminated wood for support. Those scarred fingers of Riyad's curled in, clenching as he dropped his hand to his side.

"You do not touch me again—*ever*. You got that?"

His nod was tight.

And once again, pained.

She ignored both as she gathered up her flagging courage and studied the screen of the smudged mini. The surreptitious photo appeared to have been shot from across a defunct industrial galley. And, yeah, that was definitely her own brother standing next to the former SEAL. Both men were laughing. Worse, the picture had been thoughtfully timestamped several days prior, just before her release from Walter Reed. When Nate should have been undercover, prostrated on a prayer mat in some third-world, zealot-saturated madrassa. But he'd been here, less than thirty miles away from where she now stood. On that offshore platform.

Yucking it up with an entirely different, and utterly terrify-ing, zealot.

Not for the first time did she wish that Nate hadn't been deployed during her OCS graduation. If he'd been stateside, he'd have met Frank then. And Frank would've recognized her brother aboard the platform and given her a heads up that her world was about to go to shit. A courtesy her current so-called partner had failed to extend.

She clicked the photo away and set the mini on the desk, facedown.

Would that she could do the same.

But that active-duty SEAL maintaining her required minimum of two feet away was only here for one reason. She forced herself to face him—and the truth.

"How long have you known that Nate was dirty?"

"Almost from the beginning. Though it was more a suspicion at first. The proof arrived when I was in Islamabad, this past January. And then again, in Al Jubail at the scene of your father's murder. Aside from the specifics of the organ removal, several hairs that appeared to have been forcibly removed were found near your father's body—the roots attached—and a smear of blood. DNA came back to your brother."

Forcible hair removal and a smear of her brother's blood. Her father had gotten in a lick or two of his own, then. She didn't know whether to feel glad or not.

Hell, she didn't know what to feel. If she even could anymore.

She was numb inside.

She had been since she'd seen that photo of Nate *laughing* with Zak. She closed her eyes, but she could still see it. She suspected she always would.

"And that initial suspicion of yours? What caused that?"

"Your brother was spotted hanging out with Webber a few months before my men were killed. The man who saw them knew both well—and said that Webber and your brother appeared to get on extremely well."

The man who saw them. Another SEAL then. Or one of her brother's fellow Marine Raiders. She didn't bother asking which. Riyad wouldn't cough up that part.

Not to her.

Hell, Riyad hadn't told her a single, goddamned thing that she hadn't been on the verge of figuring out for herself first.

No wonder Regan and her husband despised this man. They—

Oh, *Christ.*

What had Riyad said? That he'd suspected Nate *almost from the beginning.* A waypoint that Riyad had understandably marked with the bodies of his murdered men and the SDV's theft. But that mission to Iran had gone south roughly five months *before* Regan had gone undercover in Germany and had that blowout in the CID parking lot that Regan and John were certain had been overheard by this man.

But neither Regan nor the Special Forces major had known about Nate.

Mira shook her head as the suspicion—hell, the certainty—locked in. She knew why Riyad had lied about being in Germany. "You weren't in Hohenfels checking up on Major Garrison. You were there tailing *me.*"

He nodded.

"Why?"

"Your brother had left the madrassa he'd been assigned to infiltrate. He headed to Manila, supposedly at the imam's request. But he slipped away from his shadow and went off the grid for sixteen days. I was attempting to pick up his trail again."

"And did you find Nate in Hohenfels?"

"No." But that clamp to that lightly bearded jaw revealed even more—along with the tic that had made an appearance at the far right.

"Let me guess; there was another Zak sighting." While she'd been in Germany, too. Which, of course, would've made her look that much more guilty to this man.

He inclined his head.

"So you've suspected for almost two years that my brother

was a traitor—and you've known for certain since this past January. Tell me, Commander, how many people did you share those suspicions with—even as you failed to inform me?" And apparently her boss, as well. "You do realize that, while there are no guarantees, if I or even Ramsey had known about my brother's altered loyalties, we might've figured out the rest and been able to warn my father about the danger from his own son."

She might not have respected or loved the man, but she sure as hell hadn't wanted him dead, let alone viciously tortured and then murdered.

Silence settled in again. This time it teemed with regret.

She did not care. Her compassion for the SEAL had been used up.

"How could you do it? You stood in this very room and shared all that *shit* that you and your mother went through because of your father. You admitted that your dad was a traitor to his country. And the entire time you didn't stop to think that perhaps I had the right to know my own flesh and blood was just as bad?"

Except this was all so much worse than Riyad's father's shifting loyalties or her own father's spinelessness and inability to truly pick a side. Nate didn't just want to kill someone; he was plotting to nuke the entire fucking world—*and he had the means to do it.*

"*Well?*"

The tic at the square of Riyad's jaw picked up its pace, visibly throbbing within that cultured beard. "I told you; I was under orders."

"Ah, the All-Powerful SECNAV again." What a lovely out. "And were you also under orders when you stole those wraparounds from the RSO's safe inside Embassy Islamabad last January and knew for certain then that my brother was in on all this? That Nate had just tried to *kill* the husband of one of my best friends—and nearly did?"

It was a guess. A shot in the dark based on that comment Riyad had made regarding the initial confirmation that her brother was dirty: *The proof arrived when I was in Islamabad, this past January. And then again, in Al Jubail at the scene of your father's murder.* Had DNA been behind that proof both times?

She waited for the SEAL to deny it.

She prayed he would.

But he didn't.

Worse, that second round of stony silence offered up the confirmation that she did *not* want.

Like it or not, she'd gotten what she'd needed from this man.

She was done with this conversation. Most importantly of all, she was done with *him*. She would not get sucked into a faux partnership with Riyad again. She'd tracked down Frank. She could track down Zak Webber—and, yes, her own brother, too —alone. And much more quickly without this asshole lying to her at every turn.

She grabbed the iPad mini off the desk and shoved it at him. "Just go."

Riyad's fingers came up, but they wrapped around her hand and wrist instead. "Mira, please. You have to believe me; things changed these past few weeks. I—"

He broke off. Swallowed hard as that tic started up again. She could feel the regret throbbing in with it.

Damn it, she would not let this man get to her.

Not anymore. "You *what*?"

He nodded stiffly. "You're right. I could've gone back to Admiral Kettering and re-argued the strategy to keep you out of the know regarding your brother's involvement. After I fucked up when I told you about your dad, I almost did."

Like she believed that. "Then what stopped you?"

"I wanted to protect you."

Oh, well then, "You've done a fine job of that."

"I know I haven't. And I am sorry. More than you can know. I told you the truth last night. You got to me in that ICU. I tried to stop it, but I couldn't. I...care about you."

How dare he? After everything he'd withheld—and the so very many ways in which he'd done so? The pain he'd caused.

She did not want or need his kind of caring.

She twisted her wrist from his grasp and slipped out from between the desk and him. "You *care*? That's a crock. I've been nothing but a goddamned flesh-and-blood GPS unit to you. And that's fine with me, because I've got news for you, Commander. I don't even *like* you." She shoved the mini into his hand. "And now? Hell, every time I look at your face, all I see is that filthy photo that you withheld of my father and the one of my brother, *laughing* with Zak. And that is never going to change."

It might be harsh. But it was the truth.

And, frankly, he'd brought this on himself.

The man had gone rigid with anger and hurt. But from the resignation that had also begun to seep into his frame, noticeably dragging it down, he'd already accepted it. "Yeah, I figured that out this evening. Though why it took me so fucking long, I don't know." He shoved the mini into his pocket as a sharp sigh escaped. "It's not like this is the first time."

His mom.

She knew then that his own mother couldn't look him in the face. Not since he'd been a boy of nearly eight and trying to recover from the trauma that his mom had been exposed to right along with him. Because every time that woman had stared at her son, all the shame, pain and anger had come back to her, too.

Just as Mira suspected that it was worse now that the son

had grown up to look just like the husband and father who'd put them through it all.

As much as she truly did not like that same son-turned-man who stood in front of her now, the stark devastation within those eyes got to her.

It seemed she had a bit compassion left for Sam Riyad after all, whether she wanted to or not.

Probably because her own rejection had caused this round.

Despite everything that had happened and everything she'd learned, she reached out, only to lower her hand when his phone rang.

He turned away from her to answer it.

This call wasn't in Arabic, although it might as well have been.

The five-plus minutes of conversation were almost entirely one-sided—on the other end. The SEAL's sole contribution consisted of an occasional, "*Yes, sir.*"

Whatever was being relayed was not good.

Riyad's body language might be as silent as those compressed lips, but it spoke volumes. Though the man stood straight again, every sinew of muscle packed within those singed and wilted camouflaged utilities was taut with tension.

He finally hung up, slipping his phone into the same cargo pocket that held the iPad as he swung around. "That was Admiral Kettering. That second bird that was sent to the offshore platform retrieved the shattered laptop that we found. It's in a clean room now. Technicians have begun to recover information from the solid state drive."

"What did they find?"

"One of the files lists potential military and civilian targets under the operational code name of Chokepoint. Second on the list is Ras Tanura."

"And the first?"

"Hampton Roads."

"They plan on nuking *Norfolk*?" *Jesus*. Not only was it the largest naval station in the world, according to the stats passed during the briefing she'd attended following her transfer to the DC Field Office, there were seventy-five warships parked along those fourteen piers. And *six* were aircraft carriers, each carrying upwards of five to seven thousand sailors. And that didn't account for military personnel filling the ashore billets crowded around the base, plus civilian employees and the dependents who'd be in and around those ships and buildings if and when a bomb went off.

Decimating NS Norfolk with a nuke would make the nineteen ships lost or damaged at Pearl Harbor look like—

"*Oh, God.*"

"Yeah." The SEAL shook his head. "This is not good. Especially with that goddamned SDV still floating around out there —somewhere."

Not to mention a former SEAL who not only knew how to use the SDV but had also had plenty of time to teach his skills to others over the past two years.

Including Nate.

Even if every radiation detector in the Fleet was flown to Virginia, if that bomb was coming via under the sea, the odds were slim to none that they'd be able to find it.

Not until it was too late.

But there was more. "If I remember correctly, the *Eisenhower*'s slated to return to port in five days." The current commander in chief had decided to try and boost his standing among military voters following his announcement that the country would be high-tailing it out of Afghanistan in September...no matter what. "Is the president—"

"Still scheduled to fly out via Marine One, touch down and return to port aboard the carrier? Yep."

"Surely Secret Service will get him to see the light."

"They haven't been able to yet."

Great. Like it or not, she was going to have to work with this man for a while longer. "All right, then. We've got five days to change the man's mind and assist with the search. Let's get moving."

She turned toward the bedroom to repack her bag. She could sleep on the flight home—again.

"Not *we*."

She stopped dead in her tracks. Whirled about. "Excuse me?"

The singed, camouflaged sleeves of that combat pullover crossed and folded in along with the hardened sinew beneath. "As I said; that was Kettering. The admiral wasn't crazy about you coming to Bahrain in the first place, but I convinced him."

"And now?"

"You're going home—to DC. Alone."

The hell she would. The head of the military's Joint Special Operations Command might set this SEAL's orders, but Kettering did not issue hers.

"I'll phone—"

"Ramsey was in Kettering's office during that call. He knows about your brother. Detective Dahl informed your boss when he got off the phone with you."

Fuck. Though she wasn't upset with Jerry.

Ramsey had needed to know. Especially with Patrice out there, feeling like shit about that false autopsy report and no doubt ready to fall on her professional sword to gain a bit of personal absolution, if only in the pathologist's own mind.

And Jerry had also known how difficult it would've been for her to call Ramsey and tell him about Nate's double betrayal herself. So her old partner had done it for her.

But couldn't he have waited a few more hours?

Because the grim expression above those stubborn arms had

not eased. "Your boss agrees with Kettering. Given the photos that Nasser managed to take, you're off the case for good. Your flight leaves Muharraq in an hour. You're to return to the Field Office upon landing. I'm sorry. This one's out of my hands, too."

That might well be.

But it wasn't out of hers. She'd take that military hop home as ordered, but she would not be heading to the Field Office. She wouldn't be returning to her desk at all. Not until she had *two* scalps to mount on the wall behind it.

Zak Webber's—and Nate's.

———

22

Biting down on her frustration, Mira nudged her Chevy Blazer onto the Rowe exit that would take her and the nighttime traffic ahead into Annapolis proper. From there, she alone would be continuing on to the McMansion that she'd unwittingly co-owned with a traitor for at least two years now. Like the rest of NCIS, she had five days or less to find that traitor and his cohorts and zero in on that nuclear bomb.

She'd already chewed through damned near all of the first—with *nothing* to show for it.

Though the day hadn't been entirely worthless. The time zone she'd begun within had proved to be a boon.

With Bahrain's capital seven hours ahead of her own nation's, plus that fourteen-hour return flight that Admiral Kettering and her boss had preemptively arranged for her, the C-130 she'd flown back on had managed to touch down at Andrews at three in the afternoon on the same Sunday she'd departed Muharraq.

As for those fourteen hours aboard the C-130?

Thanks to her still-healing brain, she'd spent the first eleven asleep. But the final three had been devoted to scouring the file that she should've been reading during the flight over... including that sanitized collection of photos from her father's crime scene. Even without those mutilated groin shots, her second look at that incomplete grouping had revealed something significant.

The torture that had been visited upon her father?

Every resulting bruise, slice or outright break in the man's bones had been personal. She might not know if Zak had been present during her father's murder, but she doubted he'd even touched the man. She'd seen the results of her brother's skills firsthand—several times. That viciously extensive bodywork had been all Nate.

Yes, she had the advantage of also having learned many of her self-defense techniques from her brother. But the simple fact that she did know Nate—or had—made her all the more confused about that other horrifying discovery.

Namely, that her brother was working with Zak.

Hell, she was still struggling with the idea that he'd turned traitor at all, especially in light of Gunnery Sergeant Nathaniel Ellis' stellar career with MARSOC as a Raider. Admittedly, the needs of both the Marine Corps and NCIS had taken her and her brother in different directions. But she'd managed to see Nate a few times when she'd worked out of the San Diego Field Office and he'd been stationed at Camp Pendleton.

Yes, those California visits had spanned mere days. And the most recent had taken place nearly three years ago—*before* her brother's first undercover assignment in a Philippine madrassa. And, yes, their recent linkup in Annapolis had lasted a handful of hours. But if Nate had turned against his entire country, its Navy and his Commander in Chief, shouldn't she have detected something?

Could her brother have changed that much?

As for her father's murder—as much as it and the details

surrounding it made her blood run cold—that, she understood. While they'd both grown up despising the man, Nate had possessed so many more valid reasons for his hatred. Deep down, she was surprised it had taken her brother this long to confront the bastard.

Though surely those reasons for that specific and very personal hatred couldn't have been enough to drive a steadfast Marine to the mass murder of the very countrymen he'd once put his life on the line for?

There had to be more to it.

But what?

Had that first, undercover madrassa mission, during which Nate had spent months listening to some fanatical imam's twisted view of religion, finally succeeded in converting—or rather perverting—her brother, when years in the pews in front of their grandmother's favorite, poker-up-his-ass pastor hadn't?

Unfortunately, with her career as an investigator and a continuing student of motive, she knew that if the appropriate, deteriorating conditions had converged while Nate had been in that Philippine madrassa—along with a significant enough stressor—it was more than possible.

Just as she knew that her own love and adoration for the only relative she'd had left on the planet who'd loved her back had most likely made her blind to whatever had twisted Nate into who and what he'd become.

That was something she was going have to live with, no matter how this week and the search for Nate, Zak and the remaining nuclear material turned out.

Swallowing the bile that had been sloshing through her belly since she'd taken Jerry's call on that tiny Saudi island, Mira turned her Blazer into the cul-de-sac that she and her brother had learned to skate and ride their bikes upon. As much as she did not want to set foot in the monstrosity at the far end with its pillars and looming pink stonework already immersed in the gloom of night, she had to.

She had nowhere else to go.

No other leads to follow.

Since she'd been well rested upon her arrival at Joint Base Andrews earlier that afternoon, she and Jerry had spent the intervening hours combing through the Land Rover that Nate had driven to Annapolis, and then her own Blazer, which a Washington DC Airports Authority cop had located in a short-term Dulles lot. She and Jerry had searched the vehicles for anything that Nate might've left behind.

They'd found nothing.

She had one shot left—and it was an excruciatingly long one.

According to Sam Riyad, his team had planted two bugs in her childhood home, not four. Since one of those unclaimed bugs had been found in the attic, near the collection of boxes that her brother had been adding to over the years, she hoped to hell that bug had been planted by Nate. If her brother had been in the attic weeks or even months earlier, maybe he'd left something new with the older memorabilia he'd been squirreling away since basic training. Something she could use to pinpoint his current whereabouts—or at least get her in the general vicinity.

If not, she had no idea where to go next, and too damned many hours and days left to stress about it. She might end up at the Field Office in the morning, after all.

The one place she had no intention of going was Norfolk.

Why?

Because Hampton Roads was *not* the target.

Not if her brother had had a role in deciding where the remaining bomb that Zak's Uyghur had built would detonate.

And Nate *would* have had a role—right along with Zak.

Like the SEALs, Marine Raiders came with a host of deadly skills. Skills at which Gunny Ellis had excelled. There was no way he'd be relegated to simply donning a suicide vest or serving as more conventional cannon fodder, any more than Zak would.

Both men were planners.

And there was motive to consider, too—on both Nate's and Zak's part.

Nate's issues in all this were fixated on their father. Slicing off the man's penis had proven that, not to mention where he'd shoved it.

The more she thought about what Nate had done, the more the targeting of Ras Tanura made sense. Her brother had wanted revenge against their father so badly that his hate had extended to the man's adopted country. No, she did not have access to her father's detailed business records. But from what she did know of her father's company as a whole, he and his partner had done quite a bit of business with the Saudi oil industry in general and, she suspected, Ras Tanura in particular.

And Zak?

Even at eighteen, she'd caught the hints of the man's disdain for all things Saudi. Possibly because of her own lingering issues at the time with her father's escape to that very kingdom. As for Zak, he'd been born in Yemen. A nation that was barely a nation and definitely the bastard step-child to the bigger, badder and significantly wealthier country that dominated nearly all of the Arabian peninsula—and its resources. Not only had the chip that Zak had carried on his preteen shoulders made it intact all the way to the States when he'd emigrated with his folks, he'd taken the time to keep it polished up as he'd matured.

Zak would have reveled in the devastation that nuking Ras Tanura would've caused to the Saudi economy—as well as the kingdom's physical infrastructure and ecosystems.

But Norfolk?

Where was that personal connection for either Zak *or* Nate?

Her brother had never even been stationed there. Other than Pendleton, Nate had spent his time either deployed overseas or at Camp Lejeune. North Carolina was closer to Virginia than California, but Lejeune, too, was well beyond the blast radius of the mystery Uyghur's remaining nuke. And Zak? That bastard had at least been stationed nearby in Little Creek, albeit years earlier. Though Zak could've done another stint at Little Creek more recently. Riyad would know that better than her.

If she was wrong, and Norfolk truly was the target, Zak had selected it.

But what if that shattered laptop had been planted?

Yes, the computer appeared to have been dropped by someone aboard the offshore platform, then dumped in that vat of saltwater where it had been found, as if to suggest that corrosion would've taken care of any remaining data on the hard drive.

But it hadn't.

All they'd had to do was get the drive to a clean room and let a recovery technician take care of the rest. It was a situation that had happened often enough for Riyad's remaining SEALs to have immediately sent it off the platform.

Surely Zak would've anticipated that send off?

Planned for it, even?

The fact that the "damaged" laptop had contained a sturdier SSD drive suggested *yes*.

But if the list of targets that pointed to Norfolk being next had been planted to throw them off...what was the true target of the remaining bomb?

Another naval port, stateside or elsewhere in the world? Possibly one that Zak and/or Nate had spent time in?

Or a civilian harbor? Because that would fit the geographical "chokepoint" qualifier too, perhaps better than a military one.

Those bombs had been in the wind for days before their Black Hawk had touched down on the offshore platform. That was plenty of time for Zak, Nate or someone else in their cell to have stowed the first nuke inside a cargo container that was now aboard a questionably flagged merchant ship bound for God knew where. With more than twenty-four million cargo containers in circulation worldwide—eleven million of which were destined to arrive at a US port—they'd never find it in time.

And if that remote trigger went off while said merchant ship was transiting the Suez or Panama Canal?

And when she added in the flexibility inherently provided by the next-gen SDV that was at Zak's disposal?

Hell, the bomb could end up just about anywhere in the world.

That terrifying thought dogged Mira as she retrieved her restocked leather tote and crime kit from the back of her SUV before trudging up the darkened flagstone walk to unlock the house. Her mood was as murky as the interior upon entering.

She flicked on the switch to the chandelier in the echoing foyer, then did the same as she walked into the kitchen to set her tote and crime kit on the butcher-block workstation at the center, just as she had mere days earlier.

The lights helped—and they didn't.

The ones in the kitchen ceiling had caused the broken glass that she'd yet to clean up from her dropped tumbler to glitter over the terracotta tiles at her feet. The scattered shards seemed to underscore the current state of her life.

Part of her wished she had the nerve to call Regan Chase back and confide about Nate. Of all people, Regan would understand.

But how would her friend feel when she discovered that Nate had tried to murder the man she'd married?

Yeah, she didn't have the hour or more of conversation that

the call was going to require. She had an attic to search first—and a constant stream of prayers to direct heavenward while she searched it.

She did, however, need to phone the ICU at Walter Reed.

She'd checked in with the nurses' station before she'd boarded her return C-130 at Muharraq. The news had not been good. Not only had Caleb McCabe still been fighting his fever, but the duty nurse, like Caleb's father, had intimated that the battle the boy was currently locked within would end up deciding his life.

She'd desperately wanted to stop by on her way out of DC. But she'd been afraid that if she did, nuclear bomb and bastard of a brother and his cohorts to locate or not, she'd have sunk down beside Caleb's bed and stayed there until his fever broke... one way or another.

The shards of glass crunched beneath the soles of her tennis shoes as she returned to the butcher-block counter where she'd set her tote. Rooting past the clothes that she'd be donning in the morning, her fingers hit the harder casing of her phone. She pulled out the device, only to realize it was the throwaway burner that Nate had purchased for her before he'd left Annapolis.

Since the number within was the one she'd given to Walid Rahmani's crewman aboard the *Huriya II*, she'd held onto it. And, oddly, it *had* been used by Atif.

Twice.

Both missed calls were less than thirty seconds apart, and neither came with voicemail.

Had Rahmani remembered something about Frank that he believed might help her locate her old classmate? While she didn't relish the thought of giving the old man a death notification over the phone, if Rahmani had remembered something, she wanted that information—immediately.

She hit redial, but Atif didn't pick up. Which was even more unexpected, since the calls Atif had placed had been made around the time that she'd been taking the Rowe off-ramp into Annapolis, some twenty minutes earlier.

It was nearing midnight. Shouldn't Atif and his boss be aboard the *Huriya* and in bed by now?

Was Rahmani okay? He was older, yes, but the man had appeared to be in excellent health. Had he fallen aboard the yacht and broken a bone—or worse, had a heart attack?

She shoved her hand back into her tote, this time retrieving her actual phone. She located Grady Scala's contact number and dialed it. If Grady wasn't manning the security shack, he'd know who was. The guard currently on duty could head over and check that everything was okay, even board the *Huriya* to assist if something was wrong, until an ambulance could make it out.

Grady picked up on the second ring. "Hey, Mira. I was just thinking about you. I spoke to a possible buyer for that lovely lady down the pier about half an hour ago. There's no rush, though. He's already back at his hotel for the night. But he'll be in town all week with the rest of the whole dang country. I—"

"You're at work then?"

"Sure am. Triple overtime. The other guards don't like to man the shack during commissioning week, what with all the foot traffic due to the view of the harbor. But I like people, and the extra money doesn't hurt."

"That's right." With everything that had happened the past few days, it had escaped her mind. Graduation was at the end of the week. "I didn't mean to cut you off—and we can talk about the buyer in a minute. But could you do me a huge favor first and check on the *Huriya II*? I just drove into town and I have two hang ups in a row from Atif. I'm worried about his boss."

"Mr. Rahmani? Oh, he's fine. I was making the rounds half an hour ago. I saw him on the stern weather deck with a friend, just before they turned off the lights and went inside." Grady's raspy chuckle filled the line. "You're not gonna believe this. For a moment, I thought it was Nate. But the guy's hair is down to his shoulders, and I know your brother's still with the Marines, so—"

"*Nate?*"

He was back in Annapolis? During Commissioning Week?

That didn't make sense. Her brother hated the Academy almost as much as their father and grandmother had loved it. *Because* they'd loved it.

Why the hell would Nate want to—

Oh, fuck.

Chokepoint. Her gut was right. Norfolk *was* a feint. The Naval Academy was the target. It had been all along.

That inexplicable rabbit run Zak had conducted in and around the streets of Washington, DC, made sense, too. It—and the two slaughtered agents that capped it off—had been another vile misdirect, like that supposedly damaged SSD drive.

Look over here, while the real action is over there.

Riyad's best men had been tailing Zak around the capital, just as Zak had known they'd be. That left her brother to lose his own shadow at Dulles International quickly and easily, so Nate could double back here to fine tune the last minute details on the bomb they planned to use to take out the Academy. And not only was this target personal to Nate, it made for one hell of an admittedly brilliant chokepoint in Zak's twisted scheme of things—not so much geographically, but for the manning power of the entire Fleet *and* the Marine Corps.

She worked to keep her voice soft, casual. "Hey, Grady, that is Nate. The hair he's sporting is for something the Corps has him working on. I didn't know he was back in town, though. I'll be right there. If you see him, don't tell him you spoke to me, okay? I want to surprise him. But do call me if he leaves."

"Sounds good. I can tell you about the potential buyer for the *Natty Mir* in person."

"Looking forward to it."

She hung up before Grady could add anything else, digging into her tote to retrieve her SIG Sauer and her backup revolver, the latter ironically being the same .38 Smith & Wesson J-Frame that Nate had yelled at her for leaving behind in DC days earlier. She left the revolver's ankle holster on the counter, because that's exactly where her brother would expect to find the .38 strapped to her body, if she wore it at all.

She might know Nate, but he knew her, too.

Or he thought he did.

Her credentials and extra zip cuffs were already tucked inside her wallet in the rear pocket of the jeans she'd donned for the flight home. Both handguns went into the waistband at her back, beneath her rumpled *Don't give up the ship!* sweatshirt.

Weapons secure, she grabbed the black, open-faced hijab she'd planned to wear during her visit to Rahmani the following day, as well as her keys and the latest phone Ramsey had given her, punching in her boss' number as she raced out of the house.

The call went to voicemail.

Shit.

She keyed the Blazer's ignition, blessing the SUV's hands-free phone feature as it automatically picked up her call and routed it through the Blazer's speakers. By the time she'd cleared her driveway and the turn at the end of the street that pointed her wheels toward the marina, she'd finished briefing Ramsey's voicemail on her brother's current location and her suspicions as to why Nate was in Annapolis.

She dialed Sam Riyad's number next.

That call went to voicemail, as well.

She repeated her spiel, concentrating on weaving in and out of traffic as she hung up. Both men and half the damned agency were bound to be in Norfolk by now. She could call the local Annapolis cops—and warn the Academy—which she would do. Just as soon as she was certain that she'd arrive on scene first.

She didn't need any more deaths at her hands. If Nate spotted armed reinforcements before she had a chance to try and talk him out of this, there would be. Because he did plan on detonating that bomb in Annapolis. Though why he hadn't secreted it aboard the *Natty Mir*, she didn't yet know.

Although she had her suspicions.

Just as she knew why Zak and the others from that twisted "homegrown military" cell would've been behind this target one hundred percent.

Commissioning Day.

Over a thousand senior midshipmen, all graduating in a tidy, compact radius—with another three-thousand-plus junior midshipmen watching on. God only knew how many Navy admirals and captains, not to mention Marine Corps, Air Force and Army generals, plus colonels and more junior officers would be packed in as well to see their sons and daughters receive their diplomas and commissions before spreading out to fill billets around the globe. Four years of Navy surface-ship drivers, submariners and jet jock ensigns, *and* Marine Corps second lieutenants, all incinerated in a single moment. Along with the Academy's enlisted and officer instructors, plus its entire physical infrastructure and remaining, soon-to-be radioactive ground.

Together, it all made for one hell of a *chokepoint*.

To make matters worse, the scarlet herring that Zak Webber had planted in that shattered laptop's SSD drive had sent damned near everyone with the skills needed to thwart her brother's vile scheme to Norfolk, two-hundred-plus miles south.

She needed every bit of that backup and now.

But she wasn't going to get it.

Mira forced herself to slow down before she turned the Blazer into the marina's parking lot. Though it was well into night, if Nate, Zak or some other traitorous bastard looked this way, she'd be visible within the glow shining down from the security fixtures that dotted the parking lot and backlit the maze of wooden docks.

She lowered her SUV's sun visor, obscuring her face as she made her final call to 911 to offer up her NCIS credentials and badge number before informing the Annapolis police of the situation. She spelled out both Zak's and Nate's names and ranks in full, so that their photos and identifying data could be pulled up.

Dispatch would most likely forward her information to the Academy, but she took the time to ask.

The reality of what she was about to do slammed in as she hung up. Her fingers shook as she dropped the phone into the console beside her.

Her heart might still be trying to convince her brain that this was all just a huge mistake. But it wasn't. That photo of Nate laughing with Zak aboard the offshore Saudi oil platform proved it. As did Nate's presence here in this marina right now, when he should be overseas, undercover in some madrassa somewhere.

She didn't know how or why she'd lost her beloved brother, but that loss had already happened. And there was no going back. Only forward.

Damn it, she could do this. She had to.

There was no one else.

If Nate spotted anyone but her closing in on the *Huriya II*, they'd be dead before their feet touched the gangway.

And those other feet were already on their way.

It was time to go. She did the only thing she could. She boxed up her emotions and shoved them all the way down to the bottom of her soul—and drew on the ice-cold logic and training that Bill Ramsey and others had instilled in her, instead.

It was the only way she'd get through this.

Unfortunately, while she was an agent, she wasn't an ex-SEAL or a Marine Raider. Not many would see either one of those moving into position, not unless the ex-SEAL or Raider wanted to be seen. She did the next best thing. Concealing her hair beneath the black hijab, she bailed out of the Blazer, keeping to the shadows as she carefully picked her way toward the security shack at the head of the docks.

Grady was inside.

"Hey. That was quic—"

"Grady, I need you to clear the marina—quietly." She withdrew her SIG from the waistband at back of her jeans, tucking it in at the front beneath her sweatshirt as she leaned close to ensure those older, recalcitrant ears caught her murmur and the urgency within. "We have a potential hostage situation on the *Huriya II*. Nate's involved. No time for more. Just get as many folks as you can *out*. Start on the *Natty Mir*'s side."

She didn't need panicked singletons, parents and even kids running down the port side of the *Huriya* and tipping off Nate and the bastards who were with him before she had a chance to make it aboard undetected.

If she managed to make it aboard.

The initial confusion in those faded blue eyes converged into determination and faith—thank God. "Okay. I got your back, Mira. Good luc—"

She'd already moved out, blessing the rubber soles of her sneakers as she crept along the first set of wooden slats, and then down the second, which led to the *Huriya II*. The motor yacht was so hefty, she was berthed at the end of the dock, her bow facing out toward the Naval Academy directly across the harbor.

If those assholes who'd hijacked the vessel were staring at their target as they plotted their remaining moves, she just might make it aboard without being seen.

Even better, Grady's assessment of the *Huriya*'s darkened ship status from their earlier call held. The yacht's topside lights were extinguished, but her interior lights were not. That gave Mira the tactical advantage as she moved into the shadows surrounding the exterior of the vessel.

Nor did she see a lookout as she inched her way up the gangway.

Now that was odd.

Why wouldn't Zak—

Not Zak. That was Nate on the other side of the glass that formed the rear wall of the *Huriya*'s main cabin.

Atif was seated in one of the black and steel chairs along the glass dining table, bound with military-grade flex cuffs, his bruised and gagged visage facing her. A similarly flex-cuffed Rahmani was slumped onto the short end of the L-shaped leather couch, his swollen, reddened eyes focused on the string of wooden prayer beads clamped between the palms of his weathered hands.

And Nate? Her brother was in front of Atif, leaning over to mutter something in the young man's ear just before wrenching Atif's right middle finger out of its socket, and then back in.

The young man's muffled scream didn't make it through the glass. But that fresh wave of tears did.

They burned straight into Mira as she saw firsthand just what her brother was capable of. Murdering their father was one thing. But torturing an innocent young man?

She pushed the pain and horror aside as she swapped out her 10mm SIG for the .38 Smith & Wesson J-Frame at the small of her back. Leaning to the right, she tucked the snub-nosed revolver in between the stiff back of the wicker sofa and its plush, yellow cushion and continued on, seemingly armed, but woefully so.

Deep down, she knew that .38 was the only chance for her and everyone else in Annapolis to make it out of this alive.

Though how she'd get back out onto the weather deck, she had no idea. She'd worry about that later. As for right now?

Damn it, she *could* do this.

Move.

As she reached the closed glass, Atif caught sight of her and stiffened—which caused her brother to grab the Glock at the back of his black cargo pants, drawing down on her as he spun around.

Like her, Nate wasn't smiling.

His fury at being interrupted morphed into shock and embarrassment as he realized who'd interrupted him. Scarlet streaked through the ridges of his dusky cheeks as he waved her inside the *Huriya*'s main cabin with the muzzle of his 9mm.

Mira sent up a final prayer...and slid the glass partition open.

23

"Close the slider behind you." Nate waited until she complied, then offered up a smile—or tried to—as she swung back around. "Welcome aboard, Miranda. I guess I know who Atif called." He patted the young man's bruised cheek. "Rahmani's brave little bastard flushed the phone down the shitter when he realized I was on to him."

That explained why her return call had gone to voicemail.

As for defying Nate? Atif had been brave—and smart enough to think on his feet. Too bad he hadn't had time to leave a message. She might've been able to get here before those swollen fingers had been dislocated. All *eight* of them.

She shook her head as she worked to hide her lingering disgust for the one man she'd always looked up to. But the disappointment?

There was no concealing that.

"*Christ*, Nate. The entire way here, I was praying this was all a huge mistake. But it's not. You murdered Dad. And you and Zak pulled off that takedown of the *Tern*. And then you helped set up the attempt on Ras Tanura."

Her brother didn't answer. But he did step forward to reach

around to the small of her back, retrieving the SIG she'd slipped in a minute earlier. He tucked the 10mm into one of his cargo pockets, then used his free hand to lift her chin.

"Backup piece?"

She lowered her gaze as if embarrassed, unwilling to risk the speech that would give the lie away. Especially to someone who knew her as well as her brother did.

His sigh bathed her face. "Who's on the pier, Mir?"

"No one." She did glance up then, because the remaining facts, along with the fury that was still searing in, would help her expression remain true on this. "Grady Scala is clearing the marina, but he doesn't know why."

"*Jesus.*" Nate's frown deepened as he tugged the hijab off her head as though the sight of it offended him. He dumped the scrap of black polyester on the deck beside them. "How could you walk in here with one bloody weapon and no goddamned backup—again?"

"Backup? That's what you're upset about? You're worried that I might have forgotten all those tips and tricks of yours? Don't you get it?" She shoved the length of hair he'd disturbed out of her face. "I was pulled from the case—*because of you*. No one would take my call on the way here. Riyad probably still thinks I'm mixed up in this shit. Hell, even if he doesn't, I doubt I have a career left—again, because of you. I saw a photo of you *laughing* with Zak on that offshore platform. And then there's the fact that I barely survived a helo crash only to get thrown off the side of a ship and into a coma that should've killed me. Once more— thanks to you."

All of which paled before the murders this man, along with Zak and those other bastards, had committed—and that goddamned bomb NCIS was still searching for.

Her brother's flush returned. "I didn't know about that."

"About what?" That sickening bromance photo?

"The helo. That you went overboard. The coma. I really was in the madrassa—maintaining my official cover—right up until two weeks ago, so I could make the final preps for this week. As for Zak, you'd be surprised who I've had to buddy up to and laugh with these past few years. I eventually heard about your coma from my CIA handler. Zak kept it from me. The fucker thought I'd pull out if I knew you'd gotten caught up in it all. And, yeah, if you'd died, I would have. 'Cause I wouldn't have cared."

That last made no sense at all.

"I don't understand. Why would that have caused you to back out? Hell, how could you get involved with Zak in the first place? Do what you did? You *murdered* our father —monstrously."

Damn it. Keep it together.

Her brother looked confused again, hurt by the anger, condemnation and disillusionment radiating off her and straight into him. "I'll be honest. When I showed up at the old man's place in Al Jubail, I didn't know if I was going to go through with it. If I even had it in me. Yeah, I've killed before. A shitload of our country's so-called enemies. But they were strangers. I might've hated that asshole to the bottom of my heart, but I also knew him. Had lived with him. Shit, at one point, I'd even loved him. So...I didn't know. Not until he looked at me and spoke. And then it was easy."

Oh, Lord. That desolation within her brother's stare? Despite everything, she was almost afraid to ask. "What did Dad say to you?"

"He told me where the bathrooms were."

Now *she* was confused.

But her brother was already nodding. "Yeah. I might've recognized him, but he didn't know me from Adam. It didn't even occur to him that I might've been the son that he'd kicked to the curb long before I was twelve. He thought I was the goddamned house boy. The new Filipino *flip* to take over for the last *fucking little island person* who'd left mid-job. And that job? Cleaning his piss and his shit off the toilet. That's all I was to him, Mir, so that's all he was to me. Oh, he had the gall to beg once I'd trussed him up and he'd figured out who I really was. He even told me he was *proud* of me. Of what I've become. But it was a lie—and don't you try to tell me it wasn't."

She wouldn't. She couldn't.

It had been a lie.

Their father might have been proud of her—and that was a really big might—but he never would've been proud of Nate, let alone have ever acknowledged her brother. In doing so, the man would've had to admit that he'd raped Nate's biological mother. And the proof that their dad would never have been able to do that was in the tale he'd spun for Noura about Nate having been the child of an illicit affair.

But none of that mattered. Nate had crossed an utterly reprehensible line that their father never had. And that hurt. But not as much as the knowledge of what her brother was willing to do here in Annapolis, this very week.

Now, if that backup she'd lied about arrived, and he felt trapped.

"Where's the bomb, Nate?"

"Under the hull. It was supposed to get strapped to the *Natty Mir*'s keel, but I lost my head and blew the staging of Dad's murder. They were worried you'd figure out it wasn't Zak, then the rest, so they decided to strap it to the bottom of this one."

They?

She let that question wait in favor of the more critical one. "Who has the remote?"

"Me. And, no, you won't talk me out of it. So don't bother trying."

She glanced about the cabin, trying to reassure a quietly sobbing, but muffled Atif and a heart-stricken Rahmani with slight nods. But both men knew as well as she did that the odds of them all making it out of this alive were slim to none.

She couldn't see an antenna anywhere.

And with the bomb beneath the *Huriya II* and most likely slipped into the harbor and moved into position via Zak and that stolen, next-gen SDV, there would be an antenna....somewhere. Otherwise the water and hull would interfere with the signal from the remote. It had probably been disguised as a bit of flexible cable running up the yacht's offset, starboard side, so no one would notice it from the dock come morning. If they lived that long.

"Where's Zak?" Other than the four of them, the cabin was empty.

Was he below deck with the others?

Surely they'd heard her and Nate talking?

Nate shook his head. "That fucker and his crew are long gone. It's just me."

Great. She should've shot him in the back when she'd had the chance. It would've been easier on her heart, if nothing else.

Except she hadn't known where the bomb was then...or had a chance at finding the remote. Not to mention the rest of the plutonium and uranium that Frank had been able to cull from those assemblies; she needed to know where it had all been sent.

As for the remote, *that* she'd located.

It looked like a miniature walkie talkie. The casing was black, with what appeared to be a plastic clip hooked over the lip of the left side pocket of Nate's cargo pants, nearly blending in with the slightly darker fabric surrounding it.

She could make a grab for the remote.

But her reflexes paled next to Nate's. Always had.

And she'd only get one chance.

She would have to find a way to distract him. Get him outside, next to that wicker sofa and the .38 that she'd hidden within, before she made her move.

She glanced around the cabin, searching for something she could use to cause that distraction—and lit upon something utterly chilling.

Her brother's ruck sack; it was shoved up beside the long end of the leather couch, next to the black ball cap and wrap-around sunglasses he must've used when he'd slipped aboard the yacht. She didn't know if Nate had planted the bug in the attic, but he'd definitely been up there, and recently. Nor did she know if he'd added anything to his stuff. But he had taken something.

It was sticking out of the top of the ruck.

That something put a whole new revealing twist on why her brother was still aboard the *Huriya II*...and the fact that he had no plans to leave.

Not alive.

It seemed he'd opted to commit his own brand of hari-kari, after all. And she had a pretty good idea as to why. So he wouldn't have to confront her afterward.

As for that dusty collection of snapshots, "You stopped by the house after you dropped my Blazer off at Dulles last Friday and returned to Annapolis. You went up to the attic and took the album I put up there." The only one their father had made of their family's early years.

There was no way Nate planned on mulling over the handful of photos of their dad that were in there. He wanted to stare at the ones of her and their mom...as he died.

Against her will, some of those emotions she'd boxed up slipped out.

"*Oh, Nate.*"

Both hands jerked up. The right one, containing the Glock. And the left, his stiffened palm. Both were warding her off. "*Don't.*"

"But you don't have to do this." Given that album and the comments he'd made earlier, she now realized he didn't *want* to do this at all. Ready to commit suicide or not, he definitely hadn't swallowed some imam's twisted promise of milk and honey, and seventy-two virgins waiting for him in the Afterlife. He was too calm, too collected. Too deeply and profoundly ashamed to be facing her.

Nate had been forced into this somehow.

Except that didn't make sense.

How could he have even gotten to this point?

"Please, Nate, give me the remote. We'll go to the police together. I'll stand by you as you turn yourself in. And after. You know I will."

She'd figure it all out then.

He shook his head. "This is bigger than what I did to Dad; what I'm about to do here, too. I didn't realize that at the beginning. By the time I did, it was too late."

A chill slid down her spine at that last. That comment was eerily similar to the one Frank had made on the offshore platform.

And as with Frank, the shrug that followed was saturated with equal parts resignation and self-loathing. "But that was the bastard's plan all along. He's good; I'll give him that. Smart. Methodical. He finds your weak spots and uses them to suck you in. Before you realize it, you're trapped—and there's no fucking way out but his."

"*Who?*" Because once again, it did not sound as though Nate was talking about Zak.

That shaggy head shook. "It doesn't matter."

"I think it does." She had the distinct impression it was critical.

"No, it doesn't. All that matters is *you*."

"Me?" She jerked her chin toward Atif's battered and swollen face. To those dislocated fingers. "You did that—and committed to doing so much worse—because of me?"

"Yes."

"Nate, I am not worth this." No matter how or why he'd been dragged into this entire mess. Or what he'd done after.

"Yeah, you are. But it's not just you. He knows everyone I care about. Every single person I ever said more than hello to. He's compiled a list. And you're at the top."

"That—"

"Damn it, Mir. Why are you even here? You're supposed to be in—"

"*Norfolk*?" She waited for him to deny it.

But he didn't.

"Exactly. You would've been safe there. For a while."

"And you wouldn't have had to face me."

The scarlet returned. It wasn't just streaking though those prominent cheeks now. It stained every one of those beloved features, along with the shame. "Turns out I've got more of the old spineless bastard in me than I'd like to admit. I'm weak—just like Dad. But at least I put you first."

She didn't want to be first. Not like this.

Damn it, she *couldn't*. "I don't understand. How did you even get sucked into this? The man I know, the brother I grew up with, would never have hurt innocent people. I'm—"

"—*wrong*. Hell, we both were, so don't take it personally." If anything, the scarlet and the shame deepened. "Because, yeah, that's what I've always believed, too. But then I met a kindred spirit—or I thought I had. But I was set up and too fucking needy to figure it out before it was too late. Just as he'd known I'd be."

That *he* again.

And who the devil was this kindred spirit?

"Nate, please. Tell me who did this to you. If we work together, we can take him down." Before the bastard used the rest of that stolen plutonium.

That shaggy head shook again; this time resignation drove it. "Even if I knew his real name, it wouldn't matter. You can't touch him. No one can. And they sure as hell wouldn't believe you. He's too high up the chain, and his connections go higher. Those of us who he's managed to turn or trap into it? We're every-where. He knows when someone's getting close. And then he just shifts his plan or moves up the schedule. Like he's done tonight. He won't get the secretary of defense and all the extra military brass that would've shown up on Friday. But he will get a huge chunk of the next four years of junior officers—hell, more—as the Fleet and the Corps are forced to regroup."

The resignation that had settled into her brother's eyes during that last, more than the presence of the album, proved he didn't expect or want to live past tonight.

"*Please*, Nate—" Despite everything, "—you're my *brother*." She might hate him right now for what he was about to do, but she loved him too.

She took a chance and let a few more of those emotions out of that box, let them permeate every inch of her.

Maybe, just maybe, the profound love she still felt would help her to get through to him. "I swear I can help you—and I will. But you have to help me first. Just give me the remote."

She'd figure out who *he* and that *kindred spirit* were later.

Her brother took a step, then stopped short, as if he'd realized how close he'd come to weakening. But then he shook his head. Firmly. "I wish you could help, Sis. But you can't. You can do something for me, though. I need you to stick close to Commander Riyad. Crawl into the man's bed if you have to. I've watched him—watching you. Trust me, Riyad wants you. He's a rigid, surly son-of-a-bitch, but he's outstanding at what he does. Zak will break his word after I'm gone. He'll come for you. Riyad can keep you safe."

"I don't care about Zak. I care about *you*. And I can keep myself safe. In case you missed it; I'm damned difficult to kill."

"Kill you? I wish that's all that fucker wanted. Zak doesn't want you dead. He wants to *own* you. That bastard's obsessed with getting you back. And the guy who's been holding his leash? I don't think he's going to honor our agreement, either. So you stick with Riyad. He's your best option—and stay the hell out of Yemen."

Nate finally withdrew the remote from his pocket as he used his Glock to point her toward the slider directly behind her. "It's time you got going. I can give you thirty minutes. I can hold off whoever you've really alerted for at least that long. If you drive like a bat out of hell—and don't stop for anything—you'll clear the outer blast radius."

And just *leave* everyone else in the city to die?

A soft inhalation emanated from the short end of the couch, causing Nate to flick his gaze toward its source—and a split-second decision to solidify within her.

She knew her brother well enough to know that she wasn't going to get anything else out of Nate. And like it or not, he was determined to follow through.

Which meant she had to do the same.

Over forty thousand lives depended on it. At least.

She shoved every single one of her remaining emotions back inside that box and welded the lid shut. It was now or never.

"Damn it, old man. I told you to shut the—"

"*Whoa*." She was already raising shaking fingers to her

temples and swaying on her feet as that dark brown gaze she'd adored so much jerked away from Rahmani.

The moment Nate's left hand instinctively reached out for her, she spun around and grabbed onto his right. He raised it higher, keeping his gun from her—but disarming him hadn't been her goal.

Yet.

She jerked her leg up during the split second that he was distracted, slamming her knee squarely into his groin, stunning her brother just enough to spin him around her own body and knock him off balance.

He went flying through the slider, shattered safety glass raining down as he landed on the teak on his back.

She vaulted out after him, shoving her hand behind the back cushion of the wicker sofa as she straightened.

Nate was on his feet by then, too.

The scarlet light from the Crimson Trace Lasergrip that he'd personally attached to the .38 he'd given her all those years ago was trained between his eyes.

Unfortunately, her brother's 9mm was not pointed at her.

He was aiming over her left shoulder—which meant that the midpoint between Walid Rahmani's brows was now Nate's target.

And the remote? It lay too far away for either of them to make a dive for it—and live.

"Hand me the gun, Mir."

"No." She was committed. "I will use it." If nothing else, that piece-of-shit Umber had given her the confidence to know that with certainty. Whether or not she'd actually hit her mark was open for question. But with the bomb already attached to the bottom of the *Huriya*, and armed, she'd do her damnedest to make the shot.

No matter who was on the other end of it.

"You shoot, so will I. You want the old man to die right now? Because you know as well as I do how this is going to end. Either you give me the gun and you get the hell out of here and live. Or I risk that *one* bullseye you've got under your belt and I make a dive for that remote—and, a nano second later, we all end up in hell together."

"*Ashhadu anna la ilaha ill'Allah, wa ashhadu anna Muhammadan Rasul Allah.*"

She might not have understood ninety-five percent of the Arabic that had come out of Riyad's mouth over the past few days—but she knew that statement.

There is no God but Allah, and Mohammad is His messenger.

The *shahada*. The Muslim profession of faith. The first pillar of Islam—and the words that are meant to be whispered into the ear of every Muslim upon birth and the last words they should say, or that should be said for them if they cannot, as they die.

She gathered her courage, because in saying those words now, Walid Rahmani was telling Allah that he was ready to come home—and in saying them loud enough for her to hear, Rahmani was also telling her that she should *shoot*.

A split second later, a shot rang out.

It wasn't hers.

Horror, confusion and, yes, blinding relief seared in as a scarlet spray with bits of brain and bone exploded from the right of her brother's skull, splattering along the top of the yellow lounge cushion, even as his body crumpled onto the deck beside it. She wouldn't even get the chance to tell him goodbye.

Nate was already dead.

Why? *How*?

Had the Annapolis PD arrived?

She turned toward the pier, from where that impossible shot must've come in order to blow out her brother's brain stem and cause instant, flaccid paralysis, to see a still-armed Sam Riyad clearing the top of the gangway. The .38 fell from her suddenly nerveless fingers, bouncing off the teak slats as the rush of blood she'd become so familiar with these past few weeks roared through her head once more.

This time, her legs threatened to give way for real.

The SEAL grabbed her by her arms and hauled her upright and close before she could fall on top of her gun and her brother's lifeless body. "Any other active threats?"

She shook her head.

"Are you okay?"

She shook her head again, then realized how she'd responded and forced the shake into a nod...mostly. Damn it, now was *not* the time to fall apart. That would come later, once she'd found a private hole to crawl into to grieve.

She drew hard on those seven years of training and NCIS experience once again, and pulled herself together.

"Mira, where's Webber?"

"Gone. Before I arrived." Hauling herself from the commander's arms, she took a step sideways and reached down to scoop up the remote.

She passed it to Riyad.

"This what I think it is?"

"Yeah. The detonator. The bomb's under the yacht, attached to the hull."

The SEAL slung his rifle over his left shoulder. "Excellent work. I'll get down there with NEST as soon as they arrive. They're another ten minutes behind me."

And then, that scowl returned.

Given what had just happened, she'd give him this one.

She had to. She had a horrible feeling the intensity and familiarity of that frown were the only things holding her and her shattered heart together.

"*Christ*, woman. What the fuck were you thinking? Why didn't you wait for backup?"

She let that word slide too. The high-handed tone it tended to ride in on had been replaced with the bite of possession—and personal panic.

As for the accusation that had followed; he hadn't waited for backup either.

The police were arriving only now. She could see half a dozen marked and unmarked cruisers pulling up at the head of the pier. Uniformed cops began streaming onto the wharf. A second wave of vehicles entered the marina's parking lot behind the first, coming to a halt bumper-to-bumper with their brethren.

Riyad took in the swarm. "I'll take care of them."

She nodded stiffly. "Rahmani and Atif—I'll cut off their restraints. We'll need a paramedic for Atif. My brother...dislocated most of his fingers."

The scowl deepened. The nod that accompanied it was just as dark. "I'll send one up."

She turned away from Nate's body, leaving the SEAL to deal with the uniformed cops that were already advancing on the gangway.

Entering the main cabin, she located a carving knife within a drawer beside the dining table that Rahmani directed her to open. She severed both sets of zip cuffs and released the gag from Atif's mouth, all the while assuring the men that everything would be okay—even as they reassured her of the same.

But how would her world ever be *okay* again?

Her brother was lying out on the weather deck, those gorgeous eyes she'd adored still open, but sightless and unmoving; the entire right side of Nate's skull missing. The numbness in her heart spread out, consuming her chest.

The paramedics had arrived.

There was no reason to remain aboard the yacht, mere feet from her brother's corpse. She couldn't leave the marina until she'd given her statement, but she could do that down on the dock. Hell, the parking lot would be that much better.

Mira left Atif and his employer in very capable hands and abandoned the cabin. Edging around Nate's body and the splatter of blood and brain matter that tainted the yellow lounge cushion beyond, she headed down the gangway.

She had no idea where the commander had gone. Hell, she still didn't know what Riyad was even doing in Annapolis. How he'd been close enough to the marina to respond to her voicemail. Nor did she care enough to find out.

Not right now.

She needed to be alone for a minute or two...maybe a year.

She headed for her Blazer and the relative privacy it promised. Someone would locate her there soon enough.

She nodded to an NCIS agent she knew as he bailed out of his Explorer, then kept walking. She even tipped her head toward Grady as he paused his conversation with a pair of uniformed local police to acknowledge her.

That was as far as she got.

Grady must've coughed up her identity to the Annapolis cop during her approach, because the senior uniformed police sergeant peeled off and waved her down to take her statement. Moments later, the NCIS agent she'd spotted joined them.

It was for the best.

With a local and a fed standing there, recording her account and asking for the occasional clarification, it meant she'd have to go through this once, and that would be it. At least for tonight.

She must've sounded coherent enough. Within minutes, both agent and police sergeant appeared satisfied with her account, the contact information she'd provided and especially the fact that she'd be retreating to her childhood home.

Since her brother had been shot by Riyad, not her, she was now mercifully cleared to leave the scene. Someone would return her SIG and backup .38 as soon as possible.

The uniformed sergeant motioned a junior patrol cop forward. "Agent Ellis, would you like a ride?"

She waved off the assist. "I'm fine."

But she wasn't.

She knew that long before she crawled into the Blazer she'd left unlocked and started the engine. It was miracle she made it back to the McMansion in one piece. By the time she parked the SUV in the darkened drive, the numbness inside her chest had spread throughout her limbs, deadening them. She was cold now, too.

Shaking.

She opened the driver's door and managed to bail out. She was about to close the door, when she heard ringing.

Until that moment, she hadn't realized that in the rush to get aboard the *Huriya*, she'd left her phone in the Blazer's center console.

She reached over the seat she'd just vacated to retrieve it— and recognized the number.

Malcolm McCabe.

Please, God, *no*. She couldn't survive another direct punch to her heart.

Not tonight.

She braced herself anyway and accepted the call. "Hello, First Sergeant. H-how's Caleb? Is his fever still—"

"They knocked it out! But the news is even more miraculous —my son's *awake*. Scratch that; he just fell back asleep. But I'm told that's going to happen a lot. And I know it's late. I'm sorry. I wanted you to be the first to know."

She pressed her forehead into the slick glass of the Blazer's rear passenger window for support as the relief blistered in. "Oh,

Malcolm, that's *fantastic*. I'm—" She lifted her head, only to realize she'd assured the Annapolis police sergeant and her fellow NCIS agent that she'd remain in town for the night, at least. Not that she was in any state to crawl back into her Blazer and drive two more hours to DC.

Not until she got her shit together.

"I'm in Annapolis. I need to see something through, but I'll be heading back to DC in the next few days. I'll stop by then for a visit."

"Understood. I'm holding you to it. And, Mira? Caleb asked for you. I think he wants to thank you. I know I do."

Oh, God.

She swallowed the lump in her throat as the tears began to threaten in earnest. "O-okay." She had to hang up before she lost it. Now.

So she did.

She shut the door to the Blazer and turned toward the flag-stone path that led up to the house, forcing one foot in front of the other until she'd reached the steps. She managed to clear those, too, without falling flat on her face.

Fortunately, she'd left the front door to the house unlocked, as well.

And, hell, it wasn't as though Zak would be lying in wait for her when that fucking bomb should've been going off right about now.

She entered the darkened foyer and closed the door, before blindly reaching for the switch to the chandelier—only to miss. That was when she gave up.

Somehow, she managed to jerk around and brace her spine against the back of the door as her legs gave out altogether. She slid all the way down.

The second her ass hit the floor, the box inside her shattered.

Everything inside tumbled free.

24

Ramsey had found her on the floor of the foyer.

She wasn't sure how long she'd been sitting there, but it must've been a while because her legs were so cramped, they'd refused to support her. So the man had scooped her up and carried her into the living room where he'd settled her onto her grandmother's camel back sofa and patiently held her as the tears returned—just as Ramsey had held her when her mother had passed over a decade earlier. After her tears had finally run out, those steady hands had tucked a blanket around her to help combat the shock that had settled in at watching her brother die in front of her, too, and then he'd been forced to station another agent in the house as he'd left to deal with the mess that Nate had caused—for reasons Mira still didn't understand.

Worse, thirteen days had now passed since her return to DC, and she still didn't have a clue as to the identity of her brother's double-dealing kindred spirit, let alone the *he* who'd somehow forced Nate into attempting the unthinkable with a nuclear bomb.

As for how both Sam Riyad and her boss had been able to arrive in Annapolis so quickly, that Mira now understood.

Ramsey had been in DC, at a critical meeting at the US Capitol, when she'd called. He'd had a moment to read the transcript of her voicemail a few minutes after she'd left it, and he'd grabbed it. And then he'd promptly abandoned the late-night, hush-hush session of the Senate Intelligence Committee in mid-briefing.

Ramsey had commandeered a helicopter from the steps of the Capitol and flown straight to Annapolis.

As for Riyad, according to her boss, the SEAL had been two paces behind her all along, or just about, since she'd left Bahrain.

It seemed Riyad had phoned his own boss back after he'd left her room at the Navy Inn, insisting to Admiral Kettering that he still had stock in her ability as a human GPS unit—especially after Frank's claim that Zak would be gunning for her.

With nearly everyone else already converging on Norfolk, Riyad had boarded the next flight out of Muharraq, following her to DC and then to Annapolis.

When she'd pulled into the drive of her childhood house, he'd let the bugs his team had placed pick up the slack while he'd stopped by the home of a fellow naval officer assigned as an instructor at Annapolis. There, Riyad had been in the midst of a video conference with NEST, discussing the initial findings regarding the bomb they'd recovered from the Mustang's crash when one of his men had interrupted to let him know that Mira had taken a chilling call of her own regarding Nate.

The SEAL had promptly located and listened to the voicemail she'd left and had taken off for the marina to back her up.

Which explained the nearly identical voicemails that Ramsey and Riyad had left for her, ordering her to stand down from Rahmani's yacht until they'd arrived.

But by the time their respective messages had been left, she was already aboard the *Huriya*, her forgotten phone still inside the Blazer in the parking lot.

As for Riyad's video conference, he and the stateside scientists with NEST had been able to use what they'd learned from the first bomb to render the second safe, before successfully recovering that explosive as well.

Days later, the Naval Academy's graduation and commissioning ceremony had gone off on schedule and without a hitch —with the secretary of defense and his Navy and Marine Corps brass in attendance.

Even better? Beyond a grateful Atif, Walid Rahmani and the first responders who arrived to assist, no one appeared to have been the wiser about the near miss with that second bomb.

Before she'd driven back to DC to visit Caleb and return to the Field Office to file her official report on the entire mess, she'd stopped by the Annapolis hotel where NCIS had arranged for Atif and his boss to stay while the *Huriya II* was being processed by forensic techs and then sanitized of her brother's blood and brain matter.

Rahmani had already learned of Frank's passing, but she was able to ease his grief somewhat by assuring the older man that Frank had died with the Qur'an in his hands. She'd assumed Rahmani would want the book back and had promised him that she'd ensure that it made the trip safely, so he could keep it or re-gift it to Frank's grandfather. But it seemed that Rahmani and Abdul Nasser had already decided that not only should she have it, but the Qur'an was meant to be hers all along.

What could she do, but offer her thanks?

Especially since Rahmani had also confessed that he and Abdul believed Allah had planned for the two men to meet decades earlier and for their lives to unfold as they had, down to Rahmani becoming successful enough to commission the building of the *Huriya II* and to be the man to whom Abdul's grandson would eventually turn. In short, the old friends were convinced that, despite all that had happened these past few months, this had been their part to play in the stopping of that bomb. And although both grieved Frank, his death, too, was Allah's will.

Mira wasn't so sure, especially about that last.

Particularly as the log Frank had stored on that iPad mini, along with those surreptitious photos he'd been snapping, had been brutally honest. Frank had ordered up both his female victims, just as Mira had suspected. The first had been a spur of the moment decision. It appeared that Zak had kept her coma status from Frank as well as Nate. Hence, when Frank had been left alone with one of the local thugs he'd gotten to know and the thug mentioned the blond sailor Zak called up when he was in Bahrain for a quick screw, Frank suggested the thug retrieve the sailor for their own screw. He'd let the thug have his fun with Petty Officer Lance first, and then he'd killed Lance while his partner in crime was passed out, hoping that Lance's looks and method of death would garner Mira's attention. As the thug feared Zak more than the authorities, he'd helped Frank clean up and shove the body in the walk-in.

Since they'd gotten away with it once, the thug had bowed to Frank's second suggestion weeks later and grabbed another woman when he'd taken the emergency launch they'd kept hidden beneath the offshore platform into Manama for supplies. The thug had finally turned on Frank—and ratted him out to Zak—when Frank had once again claimed that he'd killed the girl out of anger when she'd refused to do what he wanted and dumped the body off the rig before anyone else had had a go at her.

Mira hadn't had the heart to tell Abdul Nasser or Walid Rahmani about the murders. Nor were the older men aware of the bulk of the nuclear material that Frank had been able to cull from the ceramic pellets in those mixed-oxide assemblies. The nuclear material that NCIS had yet to locate. Like Zakaria Webber, the plutonium appeared to have dropped off the globe.

But that plutonium was out there.

As was Zak.

Even if she'd wanted to pretend otherwise, the gifts and the assurance behind them that Sam Riyad had left for her in the foyer of the Annapolis McMansion made that impossible. Not that she'd seen the SEAL when he'd gifted them.

With all that had happened, she hadn't laid eyes on the commander since those final moments beside her brother's body aboard the *Huriya II*.

But Riyad—or someone he trusted—was listening.

How else to explain the vase of pale peach roses that she'd found waiting on the table in the foyer upon her return from visiting Rahmani?

There had been no card. But the McMansion's doors had been locked.

Not even Zak would've picked it to leave roses—let alone the large ivory envelope that had been propped up next to the base of the crystal.

Upon breaking the seal, she'd found four bugs inside. Two from the McMansion and two from her sublet here in DC.

None had been Riyad's.

She'd understood the message straight off. Riyad and those he trusted were the only ones listening now. Ensuring that if Zak returned, backup wouldn't be far behind. And if she didn't want that backup? Simply remove the other bugs.

She'd left them.

Mira had told herself that it was because of Noura and her two new, very young, very vulnerable siblings. She'd had them to worry about after she'd invited Noura and the kids to stay here at the townhouse, and afterward when she'd moved the trio to Annapolis and into the McMansion, so they could begin to settle in and start their new lives in the States. But if she was honest with herself, that was only part of the reason she'd left the bugs in place. She'd slept better knowing someone had the watch at night. Yes, even if that watch was ultimately being maintained by Riyad.

Or, perhaps, because it was him.

She couldn't tell anymore. It was all still too raw and painful, and confusing.

She did know that she shouldn't have laid the blame for her father's murder at Riyad's feet in that room at the Inn in Bahrain. Nate was the one who'd allowed himself to get sucked into the monstrous scheme to take down the *Pacific Tern*. Nate was the one who'd failed to come clean while there was time to help afterward.

And Nate was the one who'd tortured and murdered their father and had then been prepared to detonate that bomb aboard the *Huriya II*.

Not Sam Riyad.

As much as her heart ached, she refused to hold the SEAL responsible.

The doorbell to her sublet chimed, startling her from her spiraling thoughts. Mira rose from the couch and headed for the narrow foyer to open the door.

Ramsey's deeply lined eyes and mouth greeted her. And there was a disturbing amount of pure, shocking white supplanting the silver of his cropped afro.

"Boss, you need sleep."

He nodded sagely. "It's been another in a long damned string of all-nighters." He held up a crisp manila folder as she stepped back to wave him inside the townhouse. "But I'm headed home, just as soon as I show you this."

"Good news?" Lord, she could use some.

They all could.

But those deepening lines said no.

Hell.

She held out her hand. "Hit me."

He passed off the file with obvious reluctance. "You might want to sit down."

Probably wise. The whole lightheaded thing following her coma had yet to ease. She led the way past the galley kitchen and into the living room. Leaving her boss to take the room's sole armchair, she resumed her seat on the couch, nudging aside the oversized gift bags she'd be bringing to Walter Reed, just as soon as Caleb had finished his Saturday lunch.

She set the folder down where the bags had been and opened it.

There were three photos within. The first was of an aging concrete compound set amid lush, seemingly remote, tropical foliage and trees. The photo of the compound was followed by casual mugshots of two men. The younger appeared to be in his mid-thirties, the older in his late fifties, early sixties.

Both were Filipino.

Like Nate.

In fact, the younger one had hauntingly similar eyes to her brother's.

"Oh, God." His *kindred spirit*.

It had to be.

Ramsey nodded. "That's Nate's older half-brother, Michael, and Michael's father—the man who kicked Nate's mom out of the house when he found out Nate wasn't his. The compound is located in an Islamic enclave on Mindanao—and, yeah, that's the first madrassa that Nate was ordered to infiltrate three years ago. We received the go ahead from the Philippine president. A Filipino team linked up with Riyad's men to raid it a few days ago. They found Nate's half-brother and Michael's father, along with a few characters aligned to Abu Sayyaf that have been on the watch list for a while."

"They got in his head, didn't they?" Michael and his father.

"Yeah. Once the brother realized Nate was dead, the bastard started crowing about it. Said it was easy. Seems the mother they shared ended up on the streets, turning tricks for US sailors shortly before we pulled our ships and forces out of Subic Bay in ninety-two and turned the base over to their government."

Kindred spirits. She could guess the rest of the appalling story, but she asked for it anyway. "How did she die?"

"AIDS. Led to sarcoma. As you can imagine, it wasn't pretty. The bastard even had an old photo he kept of her that was taken near the end, which Michael shared with Riyad during their interrogation."

Meaning Michael had shared that photo—and that burning need for vengeance—with Nate too. Deliberately.

It explained so much.

And, yet, not nearly enough.

Ramsey nodded. Because he was thinking the same thing.

Someone had put Nate in that first madrassa and set him up for the emotional meltdown that was bound to follow...and had then sat back to watch it happen.

"How did Nate end up on Mindanao in the first place?"

"A tip. One that, given his time and skills with MARSOC and his partial ancestry and looks, Nate was tailor-made to act on." Her boss rubbed his fingertips along the front line of his hair. "We can't prove it, but Riyad thinks it was—"

"Zak." Riyad was right, too. They still might not yet know who the overall, mysterious *he* was who appeared to be pulling the strings in all this, but at the very least, this part of the bastard's vile schemes had originated with her ex.

Three years ago, at least.

Meaning that time-wise, this hooked back farther than Riyad believed. "Zak's the only one who knew the truth about Nate's conception."

"Are you sure Webber knew?"

"Oh, yeah. I was young and stupid and hurting for my brother one night, so I told him." Back when she was eighteen and had trusted the locked lips of a SEAL who'd already made chief and had made a career out of keeping secrets.

Or so she'd believed.

She'd have never suspected that Zak would tuck the knowledge away until he'd found an ugly use for it one day. But, yeah, Zak had methodically searched for and found her own brother's half-brother—his kindred spirit—and had set Nate up.

Because of her.

"Oh, no, you don't. I can see that guilt sliding in. Mira, this is not your fault."

"Yeah. It is."

"Are you telling me that if you'd been in the exact same situation as Nate has been these past three years, you would've been prepared to nuke Annapolis?"

She shook her head.

"There you go, then. We make our own choices in life, kiddo. And we all suffer the consequences."

"True." But all too often, others suffered because of those choices as well.

Ramsey tipped his head toward the pair of oversized gift bags, pluming with lightly crushed sheets of red and blue tissue at the tops. "Those for the twins?"

She shook her head. "A LEGO robot Transformer set for Caleb's younger brother—" That, of course, converted into a car. "—and a plush, uniformed Chesty Puller for the main guy."

"Outstanding choices. Especially the stuffed bulldog."

"Thanks." After nearly two weeks in her new role of big sister to the twins, she was starting to get the hang of it. She hoped. Hell, she prayed so.

She needed the edge with Caleb.

Ramsey understood that too. Her boss had stopped by Walter Reed with her earlier in the week. There, they'd discovered that just as she had post-coma, Caleb was suffering from incredibly vivid nightmares. Only the boy's involved variations on the torture he'd suffered at Umber's hands—and body.

Worse, since Caleb still couldn't walk, he was trapped in his bed.

She'd planned on presenting the uniformed, Marine Corps bulldog mascot as a protector of sorts, which the boy could hold onto or at least tuck beside his pillow when he inevitably drifted off again. So he'd feel safer.

It was time for her to head to Walter Reed to see if it worked.

Plus, like Caleb, her boss could use some uninterrupted shut-eye. She closed the folder on her brother's past and handed it to Ramsey as they came to their feet.

"One more thing." The reluctance was back.

"Yeah?"

"I took the liberty of seeing to Nate's cremation as he requested in his will."

"The ashes. They're back, aren't they?" That was quick. Her brother's body had been at the morgue at the start of the week. Not that she'd been by to identify it.

Ramsey had taken care of that as well.

"They are. Keisha told me to tell you that we'll just hang onto them for a while. 'Til you figure out what you want to do. No hurry at all."

"Tell Keisha I said thank you."

"You can tell her yourself tomorrow. She's expecting you for Sunday night dinner. Jerry and Shelli have already said they can make it."

She smiled at that—and the coming camaraderie and support—as she followed her boss and friend down the hall.

Ramsey paused at the door. He reached out with his free hand, bringing tears to her eyes as he tipped her chin up like her brother used to do. "Nate did love you, Miranda. More than anyone or anything else in the world. Don't ever doubt that."

"I know he did."

He'd just hated their father even more.

She held on tight to the tears as Ramsey released her chin, then nodded and left. She closed the door behind him, wiping at those that had escaped to streak down her cheeks as she swung back through the living room to retrieve the gifts and her tote.

Within moments, she'd returned to the door, juggling all three bags as she reopened it—only to walk smack into the broad, Henley-clad chest on the other side.

A pair of familiar iron hands came up to clamp about her upper arms and steady her as the bags fell and, once again, her balance was threatened.

"Commander! I'm so sorry, I—"

The scowl that filtered in caused her to swallow the rest of her explanation. Though this frown wasn't so much pissed, as pained.

And, okay, given what had happened out on the *Huriya's* aft weather deck, they'd probably gotten beyond that formal title for good.

"*Sam.*"

The frown faded. Which would've been a good thing, but for the fact that its absence revealed the unease that had been simmering behind it.

His hands fell away from her arms.

She waited for the man to say something. Possibly state the reason for his presence on her stoop before noon on a Saturday. Especially since the SEAL team Riyad commanded was based in

Little Creek, Virginia, roughly two hundred miles south of DC...
and her sublet's stoop.

He reached down to hook those scarred fingers through
the loops of her fallen tote and the gift bags, and held them
all up.

Silence came with them.

"Would you...like to come in?"

He inclined that dark head as she accepted the bags, but that
was it.

Well, this was going to be fun.

She stepped back inside the foyer, leaving Riyad to close the
door behind him as she returned to the living room to set both
gift bags and her tote on the coffee table.

By the time she'd turned around, the SEAL was standing
three feet away. Just far enough for her to retain her equilibrium
as that intense stare of his took in the contents of her living
room. She knew he'd been inside her sublet before, at the very
least when he'd removed those bugs. But even if he hadn't, he'd
have spotted the most flagrant addition right off.

The roses.

They and the crystal vase they'd shown up in at Annapolis
were sitting on the cherry stand beside her modest flatscreen
TV.

Tomorrow would mark nine days and, although the pale
peach blossoms might be a bit overblown, they were still
hanging in there. Possibly because she'd been changing the
water and trimming the stems between feedings to nurse them
along.

But he didn't need to know that.

Fortunately, the man's attention was on the photograph
propped up against the base of the vase. It was the final still
from the album Noura had slipped into her bag. Mira wasn't
even sure why she'd asked her father's widow if she could keep

it. But the sight of her, Nate and their parents caught in that rare, happy moment just...helped.

"It's a good-looking boat."

"Thank you." A soft smile escaped. "I'm not sure if I told you in Bahrain, but it was my mom's baby. My dad? He hated sailing."

His brows rose. "That's surprising, since he's the one who went to the Academy."

"Not really. It was too much work. That's why he was a supply officer. He didn't want to have to stand bridge watches underway, let alone work for his pin."

But even more than that, her father, like his own mother, detested having to get his hands dirty. Especially if he had to sweat while doing it.

Unlike the special warfare officer standing in her living room, unnerving her again with that unrelenting focus of his. Riyad had been downright filthy when he'd come up the beach from pulling that bomb out of the Mustang and putting out the fire alongside his men. And, yet, he'd seemed to revel in the labor and exhaustion of it all.

Must be the SEAL in him.

But, Lord—this awkward, stifling silence that kept crowding back in?

It was taunting her. Reminding her of the last words she'd yelled at him about his mere face dredging up the worst agony of her life—for the rest of her life.

Two weeks later, that threat had already faded, along with the bruises her brother had left on those dusky features. Even the skin surrounding Riyad's eye had healed completely.

Too bad her heart hadn't.

"I didn't tell her."

Confusion pushed into the man's brow. "Who? What?"

"Noura. I didn't tell her that Nate killed our father. And I didn't tell her what my brother did...to his body. I couldn't. I don't...want her to hate him." And since the entire fiasco was classified anyway, she'd let Ramsey's vague explanation that her brother had died on a mission stand and hadn't offered up further details.

Hell, she hadn't even been able to call Regan yet to tell her about Nate. If she did, she'd have to admit the rest, including her brother's attempt on John Garrison's life.

"And you? Do you...hate your brother?"

She did, and she didn't.

That might not make sense, even to her. But it was the truth. Though she had no idea how to explain it.

She settled for a shrug.

The tension that had been radiating from within the SEAL since before he'd stepped into her sublet finally began to ease, so it must've been enough.

She tipped her head toward the vase. "I assumed the roses were from you. Thank you."

"They were. I didn't know if you wanted to see me, so I left them when I knew you'd be out. I probably should have put a card inside the envelope, but I didn't know what to write. *I'm sorry* didn't quite seem to cover it. But I am...so very sorry."

That her brother was dead? Or that he'd been forced to shoot him?

"You didn't think I could do it, did you?"

"Take that headshot you'd set up? No, I knew you could. You've have made it, too."

She actually smiled at that. Shook her head. "You must not have read my record closely enough when you were doing your research on me. I'm a lousy shot."

His shoulders flexed beneath the Henley, stretching the fabric as they pushed up. "At the practice range? Sure. But I know guys who can punch the bullseye out of a paper target every single time, distance be damned. And then, when they come face to face with a human, they lock up. They can't pull the trigger. And most of the time, they end up getting shot themselves, sometimes fatally. You're the opposite."

"Yay, me."

Except that didn't really explain why he'd taken that shot.

And he knew it.

His shoulders bunched, straining the fabric again as he pulled his breath in deep. He shook his head as he let it out. "You already knew your brother had murdered your father. I couldn't let you shoot Nate. I didn't want you to have to live with that, too. And you would have. So while you definitely would have made that shot, you would also have hated yourself for the rest of your life for taking it."

He was right, though that didn't make dealing with all this any easier.

"So you decided I should hate you instead."

The silence returned. There was a wealth of tension brimming within the nod that accompanied it. And even more pain. "If that's what you need, yes."

"I don't know what I need." Let alone what she wanted. That was part of the problem. She drew in her own breath, then let it out along with the truth she'd been hoarding for twelve days now. "I don't hate you for shooting Nate."

"But you don't like me either."

"Most of the time? Not really." But while that was the truth, there was more to it. "And then there are other times..."

The intensity of that stare softened. He shook his head as he laughed beneath his breath.

She lifted a brow. "I amuse you?"

He nodded. "Quite a bit. But at the moment, it's me. I never thought I'd be grateful to hear those particular words from a woman. Especially you. But I am."

Nate's comment about watching this man watching her filtered in.

Despite the peace that the mere presence of those bugs in her homes brought her at night, she still wasn't sure how she felt about the rest of Nate's observation regarding the SEAL, much less the actual watching that Riyad had been doing.

Though she had needed it. Because this wasn't about her anymore. She had two new siblings to keep safe, plus their mother. They were her priority now.

Zak was still out there. The only thing that had kept him in check had been her brother. And now, Nate was dead.

Or was that what this visit was about?

"Sam...what are you doing here?"

The silence settled in again. And this time, there was a hesitant, crackling tension to it. As if the man on the other side was apprehensive about what he had to say and how to say it. And then, he just opened those tense lips and kicked it out there.

"I need a wife."

She couldn't help it; she laughed. Except, even she could tell that the sharp sound that escaped hadn't been driven by amusement.

"I should probably explain."

Uh, yeah. "Excellent idea."

"I have to go Yemen—eventually. But the people I need to speak with aren't going to want to speak with me, much less in my capacity as an officer with the US Navy. They're Houthi. My grandfather has connections with these same Houthis—or ones who can introduce me. But he's in Saudi Arabia. And, naturally, the Saudi government would prefer that my grandfather not have those Houthi connections...because he sympathizes a bit too much with them. But the crown prince puts up with them— and my grandfather—because a backchannel that can be trusted during conflict is often more valuable than seemingly like-minded diplomats who, in the end, can't."

She got that. But, "How does this involve a wife?"

"I need a reason to visit Saudi Arabia first. One their government will swallow without looking at it too closely. My visa application will state that I married recently, and I wish to present my wife to my grandfather—to heal the breach that's existed between my mother and my grandfather for three decades now. Officially, my mother and I are still dead to the rest of the family. But my grandfather knows different, and he's reached out before. My mother has always rebuffed him. For her peace of mind, and because our country never needed it, I did the same. I may tell my grandfather the truth about you and me after we arrive, or I may not. It depends on the facts we find on the ground in Saudi Arabia. We would be staying at his compound while I attempt to gain his trust and access to his Houthi connections."

"I'm assuming this pressing need to make nice with Houthis has something to do with the remainder of the missing material from those stolen assemblies?"

"You assume correctly. At first, we believed the material had been taken to Iran. But certain information has come to light that suggests at least some may be in Yemen."

Oh, boy. She was tempted to accept on that tantalizing tidbit alone, despite the fact that Nate had specifically warned her off that country—or perhaps because of it. She couldn't spend the rest of her life wondering and worrying if and when Zak would appear. That said, the preservation of her nerves aside, she wasn't convinced that she was the best person to fill the role that Riyad was creating for this mission.

Wanting to be up to the task wasn't enough. Not with the missing plutonium on the line.

"You're sure I'm the right woman for this?" Especially since there could be others in and around in that compound, watching closely and waiting for her to screw up. As much as she might wish, she wasn't like her friend Regan Chase. She was good enough undercover, but she couldn't lie believably at the drop of a hat as well as Regan could, much less feign affection for someone she wasn't crazy about in the first place.

She worked best when she was rooted in the truth.

The muscles beneath that Henley bunched as they pushed up again. "I know your strengths, Mira. And your weaknesses. As you know and understand mine."

Yeah, that last part was the understatement of the decade—on the surface.

But underneath?

She suspected that no one really knew this man, let alone understood him.

Her proposed involvement in this potentially critical operation aside, "And you're certain this is the right strategy? Bringing a wife along instead of a male assistant or creating an entirely different role that one of your men can assume?"

"I may bring along one or two assistants, or several of my men may simply be there in the background, pre-staged off-site and standing by. Possibly both. But either way, I still need a wife. My grandfather's compound is extensive. There will be places only you can go. People only you will be able to speak to."

Women.

Other wives, female family members, servants.

He was right. A man—long-lost, prodigal grandson or not—would not have open access to any of them. Not in Saudi Arabia.

But another woman would.

"There's one more thing you need to know. And this part, too, is classified—for now. Your friend, Regan Chase? Her husband has been in Yemen for almost a month. Major Garrison was there to follow up on a tip he hoped might lead him to the

Russian who provided the psycho-toxin to other members of Webber's cell."

"The chimeral virus that killed the men on John's Special Forces team in Afghanistan last December?"

"Yes. But Garrison and his first sergeant missed their last three check-ins. Agent Chase has not been informed. She doesn't even know Garrison went to Yemen. Admiral Kettering would prefer to keep it that way...until we know more."

Until they knew whether or not John and his first sergeant were dead.

The SEAL had hit the trifecta of motivations with that last one. From that glint in those dark eyes, he knew it, too. "So, Agent Ellis, what's your decision?"

There was only one.

She'd pretend to marry the devil himself, if need be. Because in addition to that shot at finding Major Garrison and locating the missing radioactive fuel, Riyad was offering her another crack at the bastard who'd sent Nate to that cauldron of hate in the first place—and then exploited her brother's pain to turn him into a traitor.

"I'm in."

∼

Thanks so much for reading my work. I hope you enjoyed it! As you know, an author's career is built on reviews. Please take a moment to leave a quick comment or an in-depth review for your fellow readers HERE.

∼

Are you ready for the next
Deception Point Military Detective Thriller?

Visit www.candaceirving.com
for more information on
Pitch Black
Book 5 in the Deception Point
Military Thriller Series

MEET THE AUTHOR

CANDACE IRVING is the daughter of a librarian and a retired US Navy chief. Candace grew up in the Philippines, Germany, and all over the United States. Her senior year of high school, she enlisted in the US Army. Following basic training, she transferred to the Navy's ROTC program at the University of Texas-Austin. While at UT, she spent a summer in Washington, DC, as a Congressional Intern. She also worked security for the UT Police.

BA in Political Science in hand, Candace was commissioned as an ensign in the US Navy and sent to Surface Warfare Officer's School to learn to drive warships. From there, she followed her father to sea.

Candace is married to her favorite soldier, a former US Army Combat Engineer. They live in the American Midwest, where the Army/Navy football game is avidly watched and argued over every year.

Go Navy; Beat Army!

Candace also writes military romantic suspense under the name Candace Irvin—without the "g"!

Email Candace at www.CandaceIrving.com

or connect via:

ALSO BY CANDACE IRVING

Deception Point Military Detective Thrillers:

AIMPOINT

Has an elite explosives expert turned terrorist? Army Detective Regan Chase is ordered to use her budding relationship with his housemate —John Garrison—to find out. But John is hiding something too. Has the war-weary Special Forces captain been turned as well? As Regan's investigation deepens, lines are crossed—personal and professional. Even if Regan succeeds in thwarting a horrific bombing on German soil, what will the fallout do to her career?

A DECEPTION POINT MILITARY DETECTIVE THRILLER: A REGAN CHASE NOVELLA & BOOK 1 IN THE SERIES

BLIND EDGE

Army Detective Regan Chase responds to a series of murders and suicides brought on by the violent hallucinations plaguing a Special Forces A-Team—a team led by Regan's ex, John Garrison. Regan quickly clashes with an unforgiving, uncooperative and dangerously secretive John—and an even more secretive US Army. What really happened during that Afghan cave mission? As Regan pushes for answers, the murders and suicides continue to mount. By the time the Army comes clean, it may be too late. Regan's death warrant has already been signed—by John's hands.

A DECEPTION POINT MILITARY DETECTIVE THRILLER: BOOK 2

BACKBLAST

Army Detective Regan Chase just solved the most horrific case of her career. The terrorist responsible refuses to speak to anyone but her. The claim? There's a traitor in the Army. With the stakes critical, Regan heads for the government's newest classified interrogation site: A US Navy warship at sea. There, Regan uncovers a second, deadlier, terror plot that leads all the way to a US embassy—and beyond. Once again, Regan's on the verge of losing her life—and another far more valuable to her than her own...

A DECEPTION POINT MILITARY DETECTIVE THRILLER: BOOK 3

CHOKEPOINT

When a US Navy commander is brutally murdered, NCIS Special Agent Mira Ellis investigates. As Mira follows the killer to a ship hijacked at sea, the ties to her own past multiply. Mira doesn't know who to trust—including her partner. A decorated, former Navy SEAL of Saudi descent, Sam Riyad lied to an Army investigator during a terror case and undermined the mission of a Special Forces major. Whose side is Riyad really on? The fate of the Navy—and the world—depends on the answer.

A DECEPTION POINT MILITARY DETECTIVE THRILLER: BOOK 4

~MORE DECEPTION POINT DETECTIVE THRILLERS COMING SOON~

Hidden Valor Military Veteran Suspense:

THE GARBAGE MAN

Former Army detective Kate Holland spent years hiding from the world—and herself. Now a small-town cop, the past catches up when a fellow vet is left along a backroad...in pieces. Years earlier, Kate spent eleven hours as a POW. Her Silver Star write-up says she killed eleven terrorists to avoid staying longer. But Kate has no memory of the deaths. And now, bizarre clues are cropping up. Is Kate finally losing her grip on reality? As the murders multiply, Kate must confront her demons...even as she finds herself in the killer's crosshairs.

A Hidden Valor Military Veteran Suspense: Book 1

IN THE NAME OF

Kate Holland finally remembers her eleven hours as a POW in Afghanistan. She wishes she didn't. PTSD raging, Kate's ready to turn in her badge with the Braxton PD. But the wife of a Muslim US Army soldier was stabbed and left to burn in a field, and Kate's boss has turned to her. Kate suspects an honor killing...until another soldier's wife is found in the next town, also stabbed and burned. When a third wife is murdered, Kate uncovers a connection to a local doctor. But the doc is not all she appears to be. Worse, Kate's nightmares and her case have begun to clash. The fallout is deadly as Kate's lured back to where it all began.

A Hidden Valor Military Veteran Suspense: Book 2

BENEATH THE BONES

When skeletal remains are unearthed on a sandbar amid the Arkansas River, Deputy Kate Holland's world is rocked again. The bones belong to a soldier once stationed at a nearby National Guard post. The more Kate digs into the murdered soldier's life, the more connections she discovers between the victim, an old family friend...and her own father. Fresh bodies are turning up too. Will the clues her father missed all those years ago lead to the deaths of every officer on the Braxton police force—including Kate's?

A Hidden Valor Military Veteran Suspense: Book 3

~More Hidden Valor Books Coming Soon~

DEDICATION

For BMC Ernest A. Phillips, SR, US Navy-Ret.
I miss you, Dad.

ACKNOWLEDGMENTS

My ideas tend to fall well outside the range of my expertise. I'd like to thank the following folks for loaning me theirs. The cool stuff belongs to them; the mistakes are all mine.

My very special thanks to Don Curtis & Special Agent Mike Keleher, NCIS, Retired. I leaned heavily on their expertise & amazing friendships while writing this one.

My deepest gratitude also goes to the following folks for helping with information & plot threads that are woven throughout the Deception Point series:
Dr. Henry C. Lee, Ph.D.
Lt. Col. J.D. Whitlock, USAF, Retired
Dr. John "Jack" Shroder, Ph.D.
Lt. Cdr. Michael J. Walsh, USN, Retired
Lou Zeleznik, DriveCrash

I'd also like to thank my critique partners Amy McKinley & CJ Chase, as well as the awesome members of the Goat Locker. And, of course, my wonderful husband, David. I appreciate the input, support & sanity more than you can know.

As always, my deepest thanks to my editor, Sue Davison, for her uncanny talent for tracking facts & figures, and of course, her truly brilliant editing. Sue, your brain is phenomenal!

Finally, a huge thanks to Ivan Zanchetta for another gorgeous cover. I envy your talents!

You're all incredible!

COPYRIGHT

Printed in Great Britain
by Amazon